THE LITTLE SAINTS

Evan Tyler

Tom,
Thank you for
supporting the hustle,
Evan Tyler

Epicet Media

Atlanta

This is a work of fiction. Names, characters, places, and incidents are either the product of the author's imagination or are used fictitiously, and any resemblance to actual persons, living or dead, business establishments, events, or locales is entirely coincidental.

The Little Saints

Printing History/June 2019

All rights reserved

Copyright © 2019 by Evan Tyler

Cover design © Evan Tyler

.

Dedications

To every man whose soul is restless until it rests in Thee, oh
LORD

PROLOGUE

Each time the kid boards a plane, he makes a list.

His lists are always adolescently simple. Three resolutions are all the kid needs, really. Anything more would be too much to keep up with in a new city.

Minutes before take-off, the kid reviews the newly-compiled list lying flat on his lap.

Point One is the same as it's always been. Point Two he wrote, scratched out, and re-wrote three times before committing to it. Point Three—well, Point Three he only decided upon two minutes ago. Still, it's a keeper.

The list is as follows:

1. Get started changing the world
2. Try to be celibate
3. Find a way to never return home

The kid neatly folds the list and fits it into the inside pocket of his leather jacket before buckling his seatbelt. He lays his head back against the headrest with a soft breath.

It's time for take-off.

El Invierno

شتاء

Geimhreadh

L' hiver

Majira ya baridi

Winter

1.

December 1979

TRUTH IS NOT exactly extraordinary. Not at first sight. Not to the waitress.

Truth is one of those tall, lean punk boys whose arms hang from his short-sleeved T-shirt like winter branches. The blaring stage lights cast an iridescent halo behind his charcoal hair and fade his skin winter white. The strength of his jaw makes masculine an otherwise soft face. Presently his eyes are concealed behind the black sunglasses he's worn throughout his entire performance. At initial glance, he hasn't one outstanding quality.

Yet, at second glance, the waitress is entirely captivated by what appears to be his one exceptional feature—those pretty-pretty lips, remarkably identical in hue to the pale rose of his cheeks. An exotic arc shapes his top lip, his bottom lip is tangerine-lush. His is a mouth made for lip balm advertisements.

The waitress steals snapshot glimpses of Truth's mouth throughout the set until at last, he slides his hair behind his ear, giving a conclusive strum of his guitar and saying a quiet "thank you." When he and his band leap from the stage into the crowd, he makes a bee-line for the bar where the waitress stands talking to the main bartender.

She hits the tap, holding out the next glass for its fill. Busy nights like these offer little time for smooth talk with patrons. However, for pretty-lipped Truth, she speaks.

"What's your pleasure?" she says, turning to him, her eyes adjusting to his height.

He smiles faintly at her English, then leans in toward her to make his words intelligible over the stuttering guitar riffs of the next band which has taken the stage.

"Hey," he says, those lips lightly grazing her ear. "So, you speak English? Rad. Are you a waitress or a bartender?"

"What?" she shouts over the music.

"I'm saying I've never been to a venue where the bartender makes the drinks and also brings them to you. I was just wondering what your official title was or whatever."

"Don't have one. It's a pity. It took years to earn my certificate in bar-tressing."

He doesn't exactly laugh, just keeps that weak smile. It's not quite evident whether he's shy, stoned, or stupid.

"The owner prefers this kind of service," the waitress continues. "He believes it adds charm. I'll be back." She winds her way around him to the other side of the bar and heads over to the group of punks in the corner.

When she returns to the bar, Truth is leaning casually against the counter.

"Your pleasure?" she tries again.

He peers up at the shelf of liquor above, glitter-eyed, and points to the prettiest bottle. "Whiskey."

"You mean vodka?"

"Yeah, yeah. Vodka. That's what I meant."

She pours him a shot of Polish vodka and heads out to deliver another set of drinks. This time when she returns, Truth is accompanied by his bass player. He jingles his empty glass in front of her.

"Another?" she asks.

"Yes, please," he answers rather politely for a boy who's just downed a shot of the bar's hardest liquor.

She pours him another shot.

And repeat. She draws more liquor as he holds up his glass each time she returns to the bar. By the seventh round, the bass player standing beside him is buckling at the knees.

"Come here," the waitress says, waving her finger at Truth. She stands on her tiptoes and brings her nose to his open mouth. "Seven shots of vodka and you've got spearmint breath? *En serio?*"

A better response couldn't have been scripted as the bass player turns toward the waitress, hurls himself on the bar counter, and vomits at her feet.

She shakes her head and begins to laugh. The vomit soup at her feet is no rarity. This is, in fact, La Buena Vida, one of the best spots in Madrid for the restless to actively seek delirium.

"Shit," the bass player mutters, backing off the counter and wiping the sweat from his forehead with the back of his hand.

"Oh, dude, man, I'm sorry," Truth says to the waitress. "Hey, don't worry about it. I'll buy you some new shoes. You could just give me your number, and we could meet at a shoe store or something. They're called *zapaterias* here, right? I just learned that word today."

From the floor, she glances up at him, clearing the mess with a towel. "Thanks for the offer, but I assure you getting my number won't be that easy."

Grabbing a handful of drinks and giving Truth a side glance—she can't resist seeing those pretty lips once more—the waitress pushes her way through the whistling crowd to the other side of the room. Pink and blue lights glaze the black floor. The walls boast of a gothic painter's obsession with carcasses, bones, and star-lit skies.

Truth follows behind the waitress, one step behind as she works, withdrawing a step only when the tip of his tennis shoe touches the heel of hers. He follows as she serves the jiggling crowd, through the whirls of smoke and the puddles of alcohol, through the maze of long-haired boys in tattered jeans and powder-faced girls in fishnets. He pursues her, offering a second apology with a genteel cough, swearing his bass player puking on her shoes wasn't a ploy to get her number. He names a couple other venues in the city where he's played and marvels at how close the punk scene here rivals the ones in America.

At shift's end, the waitress follows the crowd trickling out onto Calle del Espiritu Santo, lights from passing cars and orange street lanterns illuminating her path. Truth is at her side.

Grinning, he says, "Hey, if you slow down a little, I just want to ask you one thing. It's super important."

At these words, the waitress turns abruptly to face him, her chest meeting his as if initiating a duel.

Wholly entertained, Truth doesn't shrink back. "I just wanted to know, will you marry me?"

"Come again?" she says.

"I mean, the second I saw you, I knew you were the girl for me. So, I figured, why wait?"

She folds in her lips to repress a smile. His approach is benign, his drawl neutral, as though he hails from the middle of Nowhere, America. Hers is clear, only lightly accented, as she responds, "Well, now I'm starting to question something."

"What's that?"

"Whether you require hard alcohol to be completely wired."

"To be what?"

"Wired." She is unsure about the slang but nudges his chin and walks on nonetheless. "You'll want to brush up on your colloquialisms."

He strolls beside her gingerly, turning his collar up and burrowing his hands into his pocket. They pass a row of small brick bars and shops. The businesses are closed for the evening, though their tall windows give a glimpse of object shadows in the darkness. It is a rare street falling asleep in this district.

"Colloquialisms?" he says. "Starting to think I hit the jackpot— takes a pretty special girl to not use the slang word for slang." He taps a cigarette out of the pack he pulled from his coat pocket. He forms a wind cup around the lighter, then holds the lit cigarette between two shaking fingers. "Well, uh, since you won't agree to marry me, can I get a name at least?"

"Peter Taylor. Sounds like a suitable name for you."

He laughs. "You've got a shield for every shot, huh?"

"You haven't told me your name, you know."

"Easy. Bobby Carter."

"I thought it was Truth."

This time, he only grins, glancing down at his black T-shirt on which white letters form the word TRUTH. His smile is soft and quiet, lines curving around his mouth like a pair of parentheses.

"It's just a T-shirt," he says. "My name is Bobby, but my stage name's Jimmy Dean. You know, like the, um, like the sausage."

"Like the *sausage*?"

Bobby grins again and takes a drag, the squareness of his jaw further accented when he blows out the smoke. There is something nearly *pretty* about the way his hair frames his face like a drawn theater curtain. The light of the moon proves less harsh than the stage lights, causing his skin to appear light but healthy, like the flesh of an apple. His eyes remain a mystery behind the dark shades that he continues to wear, even in the dead of evening.

The pair turn onto a dimmer lane which offers only a few streetlights and the occasional glow of headlights. He keeps in step with her, idly wagging his shoulders back and forth as they walk between two columns of apartment buildings. She considers how scenes like these—ones with women walking next to strangers in dark alleys—are the makings of cautionary tales.

This evening, curiosity subdues sense.

"Jimmy Dean is a brand of sausage in The States," he says. "I didn't name myself after the sausage though. Just a coincidence. See, I've never met a Jimmy who didn't make a guitar proud. And Dean's my middle name, so..."

"So you accidentally named yourself after a sausage?"

Abashed, he pinches and pulls his bottom lip, edging on a smile.

"Well, there could be worse names," she says. "Plus, the name of your band is genius. Naïve—it sounds strong and romantic. Maybe Jimmy Young would be a better stage name for you—you know, to have a memorable phrase while simultaneously emphasizing your own *wunderkind-edness*. Or wunderkind-edninity. Or..." She looks around as if literally searching for a word. "...or whatever."

While she had hoped her silly play with English words would elicit a laugh, he is staring at the starless sky, awe-inspired.

"Jimmy Young and Naive—you like that? Young and Naive." He says it slowly, smoothly, as though taste-testing the name. After a reflective *hmmmm*, he continues, "Let's play Truth or Dare or something, okay? But you gotta say truth, so I can, like, *legally* ask you something."

Though she isn't familiar with the game, she plays along, rolling her eyes and smiling lazily. "Truth."

"Your name. What is it?"

"Ana Lucia Vicente," she replies, extending her hand to him. "Ana Lucia, like the proper girl's name, not the sausage."

"Ana Lucia." He grasps her hand, his cold-reddened skin highlighting the ashen quality of her fingers. He holds her hand for just long enough to state lucidly his interest, then looks away, again sheepish like a child affably teased.

"How old are you?" she asks.

"How old am I? I turned nineteen a couple days ago. That means I'll be twenty less than a year from now—you know, in case you're into older men or whatever."

Ana Lucia laughs. He's a month older than her.

"Turns out, I'm old enough to drink in Spain too. I don't normally though. That's why I gave the drinks to Kyle. The puking bass player, I mean."

"I suppose that partially explains this evening's events. So if not to fool the unsuspecting waitress, what brings you here to Madrid?"

"The music scene, I guess." Bobby pushes his hair behind his ear with the same hand that holds his stub of a cigarette. "I mean, I don't know. New York is rad and everything, but it just wasn't—it wasn't *us*. A change was, you know, in order or whatever."

"How has the change been?"

"Righteous so far. We've only been here a month though. It's still got the new car smell." Bobby casts his cigarette to the wind, like one of those cool boys who lean against brick walls in the schoolyard when they should be in math class. "If we're lucky, the smell won't fade before we've found what we're looking for."

"What are you looking for?"

"The rational answer—the one my mom tells everybody—is that I'm here to find myself, like the kid from that movie. You know, the one with the kids from Modesto."

"*American Graffiti?*"

"Wow, yeah, that's the one," he says, apparently surprised by how quickly she pulls out the answer. "Anyway, the real answer is that we're here in Europe looking for a record deal. Then, we fly away from this place as fast as we can." As though he can feel the slight, entirely irrational sinking of her heart, he adds, "But that's not gonna happen. Not any time soon, I mean. Naïve's still got a lot of dues to pay. We're not good enough for a record deal. I'm definitely not the kind of musician I want to be yet."

"What kind of musician is that?"

"The John Lennon kind," he replies instantly, without even a hint of irony.

They stop at her apartment building, a flax and cream-colored edifice reaching five stories. She lets herself inside the building foyer. He follows, looking around at the cluster of mailbox units and the five granite steps that lead up to the first-floor apartments.

"It's warm in here," he says. The strident echo of his voice inside the foyer seems to make him nervous. He fiddles with the sunglasses he still wears. "So we're at your place?"

"Yes, my place. For now."

"For now? Don't tell me you're leaving soon. I just found you."

Ana Lucia casts a shy glance to the ground. "Not soon. I just wouldn't mind to leave at some point."

"Ever thought about America? I mean, your English is ace. Way better than my Spanish." He pauses. "So, hey, back to the game. I choose truth for you again. What do you do outside of working at the bar?"

"Outside of the bar?"

"Yeah. Like, you know, your hobbies."

"Oh, well, I...I act."

"You're an actress?" he says. Once again nervous from the echoing of his voice, his volume falls to an exaggerated whisper. "Why didn't you tell me before?"

"You mean right after the marriage proposal?" she says, dramatically matching his whisper.

"Somewhere around that point would've been decent."

"The next proposal I get, I'll be sure that 'I'm an actress' is the response."

Bobby laughs, and instantly, Ana Lucia feels accomplished for having earned a laugh from such a pretty boy.

"Now, I choose truth for you," she says. "If you could wake up tomorrow in the body of someone else, who would it be and what would you do?"

"I don't know."

Lost at what to do with his answer, she stands quiet.

Bobby relieves the awkwardness. "Favorite color?"

"Purple. Favorite city?"

"New Orleans. Sound you like the most?"

This answer Ana Lucia knows without a doubt. "Children playing at the park. Last lie you told?"

"That I didn't know whose body I'd like to wake up in tomorrow and what I'd like to do there."

Her breath catches, her face grows hot.

Bobby takes a step back. "Ah, shit, I'm embarrassing you, huh? I didn't mean it literally. It's just figurative, you know? Like a metaphor for emotional empathy or something."

No doubt, he knows very well how his mischievous grin belies his words. Ana Lucia knots her arms over her chest—a molten image of skepticism.

"Okay, I meant it kinda literally. But I didn't mean today. I just meant one day. When we're, you know.... whatever." He shrugs. "It's super late. I must be delirious or something."

Ana Lucia walks to the stairs, glancing back at him when she reaches the fourth step. "In case you were wondering, you can't come into my apartment."

"I wasn't wondering."

"Then why were you looking at me like that?"

"Not sure if I should tell you."

She looks him over from top to bottom before turning toward the fifth step.

He steps forward to the base of the stairs—a prince at the foot of her tower. "I was thinking about how you probably don't wear a lot of makeup. I don't know any girls who don't wear makeup."

Ana Lucia gives only a slight show of amusement. "I should go now," she says. "Take care of yourself, Bobby."

"Can I come in to use the bathroom, at least?" He pushes his sunglasses to the top of his head. "*Por fi*, Ana Lucia. *Por fi*."

Gray. His eyes are a gray so undecided, they briefly feign powder-blue.

Without the glasses, he is no longer an image of a punk rocker. He is a painter's subject—Botticelli's *Portrait of a Youth*.

"I can't let you use my bathroom," she says. "I've only just met you."

"Come back down here then."

Ana Lucia shakes her head, coy.

"I dare you to come here. Please."

They have returned to the Truth or Dare game they'd abandoned. Ana Lucia feigns reluctance with hunched shoulders as she makes her way back down to Bobby. They are again chest-to-chest.

From his pocket, he retrieves a napkin and small pencil fragment. "I want to call you. Put your number here, will you?"

She takes the pencil and napkin, stares at them momentarily, then tucks them into her own pocket. She grabs his hand and over his palm, traces the numbers of the first telephone number that comes to mind. They stand in static silence, his hand faintly trembling as she writes with her index finger.

When she finishes, Bobby's eyes are fixed on her waist. His desire to touch her makes the air between them thick as fog.

They stare at her waist in unison until a foreign impulse overtakes Ana Lucia. She unzips her coat, takes hold of his hands, and sets them around her midsection, holding them adamantly in place.

His touch produces an unfamiliar magic, a magic she hasn't discovered in all the Tolkien she's ever read. It is indeed a magic of the elements—her knees are water, her cheeks fire—but more than that, it is a magic of the mind, a crowding out of any doubt that his hands belong on her body. It's the magic of knowing.

Quietly, she measures: the length of his fingers as they circle around her sides; the speed of her breath as her tummy rises and falls beneath his hands; the rate at which his hands warm up as he absorbs the heat of her skin through her shirt.

She looks up at his forehead shining brilliant as a silver coin. He is stunned almost to sleepiness, closing his eyes, relishing.

And then stopping.

He steps back, pushing his hair back from his face. "Thank you," he says quietly.

Ana Lucia looks up to read whether his eyes are as sincere as his tone.

Yet, before she can make eye contact, he settles his glasses back over his eyes. "I'll call you. Soon."

With that, he flies out the door.

Ana Lucia makes her way back up the stairs and climbs to her fifth-floor apartment in a pigeon-toed stupor.

As she lies down to sleep, the image of Bobby's face hangs beneath her eyelids like a banner. There is no place for sleep, though there is plenty time for dreams. She pulls up the memory of each moment of their walk, as though editing a movie reel. She recalls his face, always on the edge of a grin. She imagines how her own face had looked. She re-scripts her words. She invents his thoughts.

Thus, she lives a little for the first time since 1971.

A

Thank you, American Boy
For fine-grained form
Tentative hands
Chicago drawl
And scentless-skin
The fatigued leather of your jacket
A reminder
Of the space between
Worn book jackets
And their pages
A long-lost relic of Childhood

Thank you, American Boy
Thank you for Page One

B

Three-thirty
Hallelujah! morning
Home at last
Sprawled out on dusty vinyl flooring
The vinyl on the record player spinning with my thoughts
"Golden lady, golden lady..."
Did you know how much I wanted to touch you?
How I felt like I would die if I didn't
--didn't touch you right...right there
There, I felt the jig of blood through your veins
Marveling
that you are more than a little alive
That girls like you really exist...

2.

THE MORNING AFTER meeting Bobby Carter, Ana Lucia wakes up sober after one hour of sound sleep.

It is one of those mornings where the past is an erupting volcano. Memories collect like soot in her brain, blacking out all else, even the sweet boy from last night.

Though *Tragedy the First* precedes *Tragedy the Second* by five years, Ana Lucia remembers her life's first calamity with greater animation than the second.

To keep her sanity secure, she must mutate the memories that come charging through her mind this early morning. And still, her false memories hold darling bits of truth, like small jewels fallen into dark crevices.

Today, she remembers *Tragedy the First* this way:

Ten years old, she sits on a horse beside her father, Javier. Her father's face is still rock 'n roll handsome, still assembled the way it should be.

The horses Ana Lucia and her father ride are swan-white, the Rio Dulce river green as a crocodile. The waters dimple and glow beneath the royal morning light.

To make their way from the river to the main dirt road, they must enter the woods. Patches of light filter through the tall trees, plotting a familiar pathway. The lush grass and dense flower beds pad the horses' hooves, dampening the sound of their trot.

Though Javier lets Ana Lucia lead the way at first, he soon tugs the reigns to give his horse speed, cantering down so that their horses move side-by-side. He extends one hand to sweep leisurely through the high-growing brush.

He speaks to Ana Lucia in English to keep her well-practiced.

"Livingston is eternal spring," Javier says. "When I lived in Chicago, there was a proper winter. All the flowers and trees died for the season." He pauses. "I just thought of it—you've never seen a bare tree, have you? I suppose one day you will."

Little Ana Lucia looks at the trees they pass. She can't imagine them naked.

Her father continues. "By May, all nature came back to life in Chicago. Just when you think nature is lost, you find she's only recycled herself."

Ana Lucia nods. Even as a child, she knows her father speaks to her in words of philosophy beyond her reach. He wants to keep her young brain groping for higher concepts.

Accordingly, she doesn't have a good response for what he has said.

"Look what God has done, Lucita," her father presses, his blue eyes wondrously observing the canopy of trees above them.

Ana Lucia stops her horse where a rattle snake passes over its front hooves. She looks around, trying her best to be impressed by this land, the only land she's ever known. She tries to love it anew, knowing that as her father says, what is loveliest is not always most loved.

Still, she is distracted. Her father has mentioned God. She can count the number of times her father has spoken of God.

"Daddy," she says, tapping her horse with her feet to get it moving again. "I don't believe in God."

"When did you make that decision?"

"I never decided to believe."

He looks at her, almost grinning. As always, he is impressed by her. "Then how do you explain it? How do you explain everything around us? Did it come to exist on its own?"

She shrugs. "No one knows."

"No one knows? You say no one knows, Chiquita mia?" Her father breaks out into a smile so wide, Ana Lucia hears phantom laughter in it. He strikes his horse. " *Vamos!*"

The horse takes off. Javier hollers, in imitation of a cowboy charging through the woods. He is challenging her to a race.

She brings her horse to a gleeful gallop, the wind whipping back her hair as she catches up with Javier. Reaching a break in the woods, they slow down, stepping into the teeming sunlight and onto the dusty brown road.

Ana Lucia spots another rattle snake. It mazes through her horse's feet, barely avoiding being stomped. She watches as the snake winds its way to her father's horse. She doesn't see it, but she imagines the snake has bitten her father's horse at the ankle when the animal suddenly shrieks.

The horse's two front legs kick up in the kind of violence only agony produces. Javier topples off the horse, his shoulder audibly cracking when he hits the ground.

Ana Lucia is pained by the sight but not hysterical. Her father is strong. This isn't his first fall.

But his horse—his horse is to be feared. His eyes have turned red. The snake has apparently infected him with *evil*.

Ana Lucia watches as the ivory horse approaches her father, stares down at him with those scarlet eyes, merciless. He begins an angry stomp.

The horse stomps and stomps and stomps!

The animal crushes her father's head at the temple. His steel-heavy hooves move to the center of her father's face, denting it, squashing it until there is no face left, just a hole from which gray sap leaks. His brain matter mixes the dirt to make taupe-colored mud.

From Ana Lucia's dry throat comes a blood-red scream. Over time, the scream has hollowed to black, a slowly corrupting memory in her mind.

A mind that refuses to remember *Tragedy the First* as it truly happened.

In this morning's memory, a horse is her father's murderer. Tomorrow it may well be another animal. This is easier to live with than the truth that the world's most civilized animal murdered her father.

Ana Lucia turns over in her bed, attempting to crowd out flashbacks of *Tragedy the First* with thoughts of Bobby Carter. This way, she won't have room to remember *Tragedy the Second* and her grandfather, Luis Rafael, who she went to live with after her father's death. With steady rumination over Bobby's trembling hands on her waist, Ana Lucia can forge the forgetting of how her grandfather had once been a political prisoner under the Franco Regime. She will consign to oblivion the things which he told her his prison days had taught him—things like how to hold slippery tools in the rain, how to sleep standing up, how to stop believing in God without guilt.

Moreover, Ana Lucia will drown out the fact that her grandfather died as violently as her father, a year-and-a-half after the Franco Regime collapsed. Her grandfather had never really known what fruit his political activism produced. He'd hardly experienced the New Spain, free of its post-Civil War cruelties.

Ana Lucia is just beginning to experience the New Spain.

She resolves that today she will be among Madrid's sonic youth who live for the future.

Steadfast, Ana Lucia rises to dress herself for work. In minutes, she is ready.

She eyes briefly a painting lying in the middle of her bedroom floor. The subject of the painting is so gruesome that she must close her eyes and feel her way out of the room, troubled to nausea by the painter's apparent madness.

Stepping outside of her apartment building, Ana Lucia hears the sound of children playing in the adjacent park. The sound urges her to shrug off every thought except anticipation of the human company that awaits her.

Ana Lucia's human company takes the form of bronze-skinned, copper-eyed Khadijah Piaf, who dons white flowers in her hair as an accessory to her bar maid uniform.

On their trek to work at La Buena Vida, the pair stop inside a cafe for breakfast.

"You look like hell today," Khadijah says, sliding into a booth beside a window.

Ana Lucia drops down across from her. "Nothing like KP Early Morning Insults to start the day off right."

"No better-balanced meal than truth. Eat up."

"I may look like hell today, but last night was heavenly."

As life hasn't offered any interesting stories lately, Ana Lucia feels entitled to this hyperbole, even if only to provoke the wowed expression on Khadijah's face until she finishes the tautened account of last night's events, which sound even more meager spoken out loud.

Khadijah looks up at Ana Lucia with her irises so turned up, she gives the appearance of a zombie. Her sarcasm is always so *physical.*

"So, his name's Bobby Carter, and he put his hands around your waist?" she recounts blandly. "Is that all?"

Ana Lucia glances at the waiters who stop to stare at her and Khadijah, intrigued by their ability to speak English. Ana Lucia leans across the table. "I guess if I went full frontal, I would've earned the Khadijah Seal of Approval, huh?"

She appears momentarily pensive. "Possibly. But please, don't feel any need to compete with me. There can be only one like me."

Khadijah proceeds to give Ana Lucia the story of her evening, which included picking a boy up from the street in front of her Carabanchel apartment and doing their business by the dumpster behind Bar Rosas.

"Beautiful tale," Ana Lucia responds as Khadijah finishes her anecdote with a lick of the pastry icing from her fingertips. "I need a favor. Yesterday, the boy asked me for my number. Since I don't have a phone, I had to delve into my resourcefulness."

"You gave him my number?" Khadijah says. "Well done. You can use that excuse for a couple days until you work up the nerve to confess that you're a pauper with a princess face."

"Why, thank you, Khadijah. Your generosity is rivaled only by your effrontery."

"Too many syllables so early in the morning. Let's go."

Ana Lucia nods, waiting for her friend to put the cash on the table.

Khadijah scrunches her eyebrows. "I hope you're not looking for me to pay. I'm broke as a joke, on a quest for quid. Plus, it was your idea to come here."

"My idea?"

"Yes, *your* idea. You said you were hungry."

"*You* said we should stop for food somewhere."

She says nothing in response. Instead, she gives Ana Lucia The Look.

Khadijah proceeds to order another round of hot chocolates and churros. While the waiter fetches their order, Ana Lucia slips out quietly, making eye contact with no one as she strolls out onto the street. She walks until the restaurant is out of sight.

Soon, she hears Khadijah's boisterous laughter behind her.

They are the Dine-and-Dash Duo. They have been partners in minor thievery for the past year. Ana Lucia can't help but think that if God or karma or any of the forces that institute justice exist, she and Khadijah are storing up loads of misfortune for the future.

"We really should stop doing that," Ana Lucia says.

"What else will we do for fun?"

"We won't be able to eat at any restaurant in Madrid soon."

"Don't worry," she says, as they near La Buena Vida. "That restaurant is owned by The Establishment. The Establishment owes us a free meal every once in a while. They've been making money off our backs since the beginning of time."

Ana Lucia can make no argument to the facts, so instead she loops her arm through Khadijah's the rest of the walk to work.

Upon their arrival, their manager urges Ana Lucia to the main room. Customers have already arrived.

A single customer.

Bobby Carter sits at a flower-embroidered spinet across the room, his back to her. Sunlight bounds from the window he faces onto the crown of his head, revealing something Ana Lucia would have never supposed: he is naturally blonde, the slightest trace of new growth shimmering like gold dust against his velvet black strands. He wears a blue pea coat, star-spangled pajama pants, white high tops, and a bun at the nape of his neck so unintentionally sleek it smacks of a chignon. He is a mod prince.

La Vida serves as a cafe during the day; thus, several wooden tables and chairs stand between the two of them. Ana Lucia stands intrigued as his initial do-re-mi tinkering with the keys transforms into a high-pitched mimicry of a song she vaguely recognizes.

He sings quietly about a woman named Eleanor Rigby.

A single verse in, Bobby abruptly pounds on the keys finale-style and angles his face over his shoulder. Ana Lucia dives to the ground, implementing a flight plan of sorts. Daytime has returned her customary shyness.

From beneath the table where she crouches, she hears him say, "Somebody there?"

"No," she replies.

"That you, Ana Lucia?"

"No."

Bobby rises from the spinet and hunkers down on the steps that lead up to the small stage. He tilts his head, catching Ana Lucia's eyes from beneath the table. "Come out, come out, wherever you are."

Having little other choice, she pulls herself up and approaches him.

"You came. Good girl," he says, ushering her down on the step beside him and patting her head in jest.

She fakes a scowl, tightening her mouth as best she can with an emerging smile.

"Curb your enthusiasm," he says. "I just wanted to see you again, that's all. I figured you wanted to see me too."

"From whence comes such self-deception, Bobby?"

"From *whence* comes such angst, Ana Lucia?"

"You don't enjoy my angst? Curious news coming from a boy who sings about—*existential angst,* was it?"

"Awww, look at you—remembering the name of the first song from last night's set. If I had any idea you were diggin' us that much, I'd have slept outside your doorstep instead."

He intends to reel her in by sidestepping the regular conventions of charm. He has succeeded.

Ana Lucia won't let him relish in his success so quickly. She won't permit a smile. Not yet.

"You know, there's nothing wrong with you wanting to see me," he continues. "It's kinda sweet."

"Is this what it looks like when ignorance and arrogance collide?" Ana Lucia hops up from the steps and heads to the supply closet.

He follows her to the closet. "You've got me all wrong, Lucy. I'm—"

"*Ana Lucia.* Will you hand me those salt containers on the top shelf?"

Bobby takes the command as an opportunity to step inside the supply closet with her and partially shut the door. He Quasimodo-maneuvers inside the small space to keep his forehead from jostling the dusty-burning bulb.

Reaching for the salt shakers, his eyes fall suddenly to her shoes. He kneels, clasping her ankle and bringing her foot up onto his bent knee. He reads the words she has doodled with pink marker on her thrift mart Converses. He switches her one foot for the other, browsing through the lines on the other shoe. He smiles, looking up at her in wonder.

"Why are you wearing pajamas?" she inquires before he can ask about the lines.

"It's still early." He stands, looking down at his pajama pants. He holds his hands in front of the crotch, polite but pink-faced. "I'm not trying to be dirty or anything. I was in a big rush this morning. I had to see you as soon as I could. I just needed to make sure you were real. I haven't been getting a ton of sleep lately—I thought maybe I was hallucinating or something. But you're here and better than what I remembered. I just want to get to know you. Nothing so bad about that right?"

"I don't know. Maybe."

"Maybe?"

She pauses briefly to deliberate. "Your hair might be a problem."

"My hair?" From his over-articulated incredulity, she knows he hasn't been insulted over his hair one time in his whole life.

"Your hair is longer than mine," she says. "Should I add hair envy to my many troubles, Bob?"

"*Bobby.* And look, we can work this out," he says, moving her wavy bangs from her eyes with a turn of his index finger. "I've got this Beatles wig back at the apartment. You know, the mop top one?"

"You're serious?"

"Not even a little."

This time, she can't squelch her laughter. It comes out much louder than she intends.

Her slackness affords him the opportunity to take a step closer to her, touching lightly with two fingers the place on her waist he clutched last night.

Ana Lucia's body betrays her. There can be no disguising the quiver in her bottom lip. She stands enveloped by the smell of his hair.

Peaches. It smells like peaches.

"I want to show you something before I go." He pauses. "But first, let me say thank you for letting me walk you home yesterday. I mean, I never really get the chance to be around girls like you. It's..."

He trails off, oblivious to how seductive his loss of words is, how it makes her fixate on what he *could* say rather than what he has said.

"You said you have something for me, didn't you?" she manages.

"Oh, yeah, yeah—that." From the interior pocket of his pea coat, he produces a flyer.

She receives it from him, reading the headline. "Jimmee Young and Naïve. Tomorrow. Eight PM."

"I got up super early to print the flyers, so you could have one. I don't think I can afford to print anymore." He looks long at her, clearly measuring her reaction. "You were right—this name works better than Jimmy Dean. There's this one problem though. The flyer's for a different venue. Yesterday was our last night here at La Buena Vida. My cousin Kyle—well, he books Naïve's shows or whatever, and he said that enough word's gotten out about the band that we'll have to do bigger venues."

"That doesn't sound like a problem. It sounds like success."

"Yeah, but how am I gonna see you if we won't be performing at your bar?"

She looks down at the flyer once more. "With this luck, you must believe in magic, right? Use your magic."

"Song line," he replies straightaway.

"What?"

He leans down to kiss her cheek, afterward opening the closet door. "That line's going in a song. I'll see you there tomorrow."

3.

BOBBY CARTER, NOT so much "Jimmee Young," makes the line into a song. He christens it "Your Magic," and it becomes Naive's biggest crowd pleaser yet. At least, this is what he hopes his future documentary will say.

The narrator of the future documentary—God-willing, Orson Welles—will continue: *Having taken Jimmee Young all of one hour to write on acoustic guitar, "Your Magic" was the song that ultimately moved Naive from crowds of one hundred to crowds of one thousand. After eleven months of playing it at every show, CBS Records finally got word of Naive and was ready to give them the opportunity of a lifetime.*

Bobby is not sure what Orson Welles will say after this, but maybe he's gotten ahead of himself with the details of the documentary. These future events matter very little in the present: New Year's Eve, 1979.

It is thirty minutes before the turn of the decade. Five-and-a-half hours away for his mother and father back home in Connecticut

In America, time has various strides, Bobby has discovered. In his hometown Avon, it takes the steady march of a soldier. In Atlanta, it saunters with the easiness of a Southern drawl. In New York, it runs immortal loops around you.

Vertigo. New York could give a Connecticut kid vertigo.

Here in Spain, time doesn't have a discernible gait. Bobby's ambition rises with the sun some days, with the moon on others. Dinner begins at nine, perhaps midnight for the kids in Malasaña. Naïve's show starts at nine-thirty, though the flyer says eight. The manager of the venue assures them this is normal. The audience is always right. The artist has no say. Not until artist becomes icon anyway.

Bobby can dig it. Because despite their lateness, the audience digs him. Their ants-in-pants dancing makes him smile. These kids require no massaging, no cheer-leading. Evidently, they have determined that they will enjoy the show before it even begins. It is nearly 1980; they haven't come this far not to enjoy the show.

English isn't their thing. Go figure. Aside from Ana Lucia, Bobby hasn't met a Spaniard who speaks English beyond parading the one phrase they all seem to know: "Don't worry, be happy."

However, the crowd does manage to sing along with the band in spurts. They are fascinated by a tongue-in-cheek chorus that simply chants, "Ashes, ashes, we all fall down." Though they've nailed the line by the end of the song, it is hardly lost on Bobby that they have no idea what it means.

Doesn't matter. Everything here means revolution.

At set's end, the crowd disperses to find more stimulation on the streets of Malasaña.

La Movida Madrileña—The Madrid Scene—belongs to the Malasaña district.

Here it is impossible not to be rapt by every lane's levitating libido—breasts made visible through netted blouses and male intentions made known beneath skin-tight jeans. Both the boys and girls wear neon makeup intended not to enhance but to completely make them over.

British and American punk music drifts—even gushes—down the lanes, as psychedelic as *Sgt Pepper's Lonely Hearts Club Band* was twelve years ago. The road is paved with black brick on Calle del Espiritu Santo. Rows of potbelly pigs hang upside down in front of butcher stores and tipsy girls in high heels loiter outside of small bookstores. It's all gloss and grunge in Malasaña, where the undefined is defining itself and an orphan culture is finally giving itself a name.

Bobby watches it all through blue aviator sunglasses as he passes down the gypsy streets with his drummer and best friend Dominic. Naive's bassist, his cousin Kyle, has run off to see about a girl.

"You want to see if we can find Kyle?" Bobby asks Dominic. "We could grab a bite before midnight."

Dominic stops to peer through the window of a *carniceria* where a pig is hung by its hooves. "Good grief, I can't believe they eat this shit here."

Bobby pushes his hair back from his face, an unlit cigarette between his fingers. "You ever seen them eat it before? They scarf it all—butt, brains, feet, everything."

"Dude, I can't even watch my folks eat ground beef anymore. At least, there's some mystery to that. Here, they gobble the shit down fresh from the wild."

Though both vegans, their words are less judgment than wondrous observation. Spain has kept them in perpetual awe since they arrived five weeks ago.

"So, where's the girl?" Dominic asks, pushing his chestnut ringlets behind his ears. Dom is a cartoonist's version of pretty—Betty Boop lashes, plump, heart-shaped lips, and sapphire eyes.

"What girl?"

"The girl from the bar. The waitress."

Bobby's eyes fall briefly on a green-lit bar where a man takes a quiet piss. "I went to visit her yesterday at La Buena Vida to give her a flyer. Thought maybe she'd come tonight. She didn't."

"Tough," Dominic laments, taking a squint-eyed drag of his joint. "But you know, Bobby C., there's like a shit ton of beautiful girls here. Learn some Spanish, you'll get whoever you want."

"But this girl—she, like, speaks English."

"Is she a real Spaniard?"

Bobby chews his lip, shrugs. Outside of Ana Lucia's acting aspiration, he hasn't gathered a solid detail on which to fixate.

He only knows her skin is the color of gold, her curls onyx. Her lips are bubblegum, eyes licorice.

Her English is stately, though not clean. Her vowels are a little slanted, which is the only real proof that she isn't American. Or British.

Most notable are her white Converses, filled in with quotes scribed in Magic marker. One of the lines read, "It was the best of times, it was the worst of times." Another, "Maybe ever'body in the whole damn world is scared of each other." He couldn't make out one of the lines—it was written in Spanish—but he did see the name Cervantes next to it.

He'd planned to ask her about how she'd learned English after tonight's show. He'd shaven and worn his Stooges T-shirt for the occasion.

"Don't sweat it," says Dom, clamping his hand down on Bobby's shoulder. "We got twenty minutes till 1980, then your new life begins. It's gonna be your year, dude. Year of The Young."

Bobby looks down, smiling softly.

Suddenly a voice from behind beckons their attention. "Jimmee Young, Dom—over here!"

Dom turns first; Bobby isn't yet used to being called by his new stage name.

It is Kyle who has hailed them. He sits with his female companion on the ground beside an open bar, two bottles of beer at their feet.

His accompanying wallflower is a show-stopper—pixie-cut, pearl-blonde hair; burgundy lips; black leather pants and a matching vest tight enough to pump her cleavage up to heights requiring a second glance. She peers up at Bobby.

He and Dom squat beside her, overtaken immediately by the brassiness of perfume.

"This is him? This is Jimmee?" she exclaims. The pronunciation of her h's is wispy. She is Irish. "What good deed have I done today to warrant this kind of luck?"

Bobby leans forward, giving Kyle an inquiring look before the girl steamrolls him back against the brick wall, kissing him, her ravenous hands fishing and fumbling up his Stooges shirt. Kyle bursts out into tipsy laughter.

Bobby reaches for the girl's shoulders, drawing her back from him.

He grabs his sunglasses, which have fallen off in the minor tussle, and pushes them back up the bridge of his nose.

Kyle presses the girl back against the side of the building to look at Bobby. "That's how she greets everybody."

She reaches for one of the beer bottles at Kyle's feet, takes a sip and gargles with it before jutting out her hand to shake Bobby's. "Good to finally meet you up close, Jimmee. I'm Betty Warner, your savior who has yet to die on a cross. By the way, your lips taste as good as they look."

Kyle rolls his eyes. "I met her at La Buena Vida the other night. She caught one of our street shows before. She swears she can get us into any venue in Madrid."

"Screw me if I can't," she says to Bobby, faking indignation. "Shit, screw me if I can. Since I've already accosted you, I can only hope you're planning a similar revenge."

"She just take a hit or something?" Dom asks Kyle, chancing that the girl's too intoxicated to mind his insult.

"Why are ye lads so sensitive?" Betty intercepts. "I'm trying to get to know Jimmee Young here." She turns to Bobby. "So, Young, what are your interests? Obviously, rock and roll. What about other recreational activities? Do you enjoy Lucy in the Sky with Diamonds?"

He shrugs. "It's not my favorite song on the album."

Dom nudges him in the side. "She's talking about LSD, man."

"Oh." He stares at his fingernails; they need clipping. "That's not really my thing."

"How's about other kinds of blow?" Betty asks. "Do you do that? Or what about orgasms? Do those tickle your fancy?"

Kyle snorts. "Little Charlie Brown here? Betty, you obviously don't got a clue."

"What haven't I a clue about?" She gives Bobby a gander, then squeals. "O Di-os mi-o! Please don't tell me you're suffering from a lengthy case of virginitis. Dammit—my radar's defective! Well, I've got a treatment for your ailment. Just let me know when you're ready to be cured."

"Yeah, alright," Bobby replies, rising and lighting the cigarette he's kept lodged between his fingers. "We should split now."

"Where are ye going?"

"To see about a nail clipper. You ready, Dom?"

"Yeah, let's go."

Deaf to the subtle dig, Betty follows them as they start off down the street. Kyle catches up.

Betty gaily bumps hips with Bobby as they walk. He recognizes now that her former show was just that; she's more festive than frisky.

From her coat, she pulls a foil-wrapped sandwich. Slices of pork hang from it.

She takes a bite, then juts it in his direction. "Have some?"

"No thanks. Not hungry."

Bobby and Dominic smirk.

As they walk through the crowd, Dominic is the Aaron to Bobby's Moses, apologizing to the people in Spanish as they part the sea of kids going mad in anticipation of midnight. Betty also speaks the language with ease, cursing at the man who nearly trips her up as he lies in the middle of the street. Kyle makes do with his choppy Spanish. Still too shy to test his own Spanish, Bobby is alone with his English thoughts.

He thinks of Ana Lucia Vicente and how sweet her English sounded even when her words were spicy. He sighs.

"Hey, stop!" Betty exclaims, coming to a halt in front of them and holding up her hand. "Looka there."

She points in the direction of a graffiti artist, kneeling beside a brick wall, putting finishing touches on his human-sized bubble letters.

Todos somos iguales, the graffiti reads.

Betty's eyes go alight watching the artist swirl his paint. "Ye know what that is?"

Dom shakes his head. Bobby shrugs, hands in pockets.

She juts her face forward, making a show of her disbelief. "Why did ye lads come to Madrid?"

There are plenty answers to that, yet no immediate responses from any of them.

"Do ye people have any idea what's going on here? What they're making here with their art is history. It's like...it's like..." She taps her chin in thought. "Where ye lads from originally?"

"Connecticut."

"Connecticut. *Faaancy.*" She pauses to deliberate once more. "I don't know nothing 'bout Connecticut. Ever live in Washington D.C., somewhere more socially literate? Oh, it doesn't matter. Just think March on Washington. Think Vietnam protests. Think Bowie and The Young Americans tour. I was there in Washington for it. Best show I've ever seen."

"What the fuck is your point, Betty?" Kyle interjects.

"Sit on it, will you? I'm narratin' here. Look 'round yourselves. These kids got their freedom four years ago, when that muppet Franco died. All the outcasts living in the shadows under the dictator are free to roam in the light now. It's a glorious time." She looks up at

Bobby, a marvelous glint in her eye. "*This* is the world to come. You've arrived just in time for the *future*, Jimmee Young."

Bobby looks around at the twitching city. Fear and excitement meet in the center of his chest.

Betty shouts and bounces on her heels. "Somebody, tell me the time!"

"Two minutes till midnight," answers Dom.

"Where's your grapes, lads?"

Kyle smirks. "Oh, we got 'em. We just call 'em balls in America, Betty."

"Such a clever boy, this one."

"What do we need grapes for?" Dom asks.

Betty huffs dramatically. "We're on the heels of midnight's, lads. We've gotta get ready."

She reaches into her pocket once more and this time produces a large plastic baggie. It is bloated with grapes. "Spanish tradition, yeah? You'll stuff twelve of them in your mouth as midnight is arrivin'. It'll earn ye the luck of the Irish. The mythical luck, not the historical one."

Betty calls for the countdown from Dom. At T-minus ten seconds, she opens the bag of grapes and they grab handfuls, filling their mouths quickly.

Betty smiles at Bobby as he struggles to put the grapes in his mouth. His jaw, grown a little stiff by his exasperation with Betty's non-stop chattiness, isn't easily unhinged.

"You got a tiny mouth there," she says, her own mouth swollen with fruit.

At T-minus five, she begins helping him stuff three remaining grapes into his mouth. Their juice begins sliding down his chin as Betty pushes the last grape into his mouth, in time with Dom's announcement of midnight. Amidst the silliness, Bobby has his first full-bodied laugh of the evening, of the new year.

Bobby marvels at this unanticipated moment of glee. He looks up as if searching for God to thank. Through the blue lenses of his sunglasses, he watches adumbral clouds roll like fog over the midnight sky.

His heart catches briefly. He is pondering where Ana Lucia Vicente is right now and how she is ringing in 1980.

4.

SUPPOSING ANA LUCIA had been born in Madrid instead of Livingston, Guatemala, she would have likely never ridden an airplane.

Supposing her father had been a fisherman instead of a linguist, she wouldn't have developed a romantic handle of the English language.

Had her father not been the victim of *Tragedy the First* when she was ten years old, Ana Lucia could have been spared the trauma of moving to Spain in a confused flurry. One week's worth of underwear, her father's English books, and a pile of pop records had inflated her buckled brown satchel when she boarded that September Pan Am flight to Frankfurt.

Next stop, Madrid, to her grandparents' home.

If she were still in Livingston making a living from the sea like most of the residents, Ana Lucia would not be here now reading Kurt Vonnegut's gutsy commentary on war and life and death. Perhaps the simplicity of sea life would have kept her ignorant of the way tragedy comes sweeping down like a bird of prey.

Yet, there is a part of her that believes that ignorance is the only real tragedy.

And so it goes...that the New Year's noise outside Ana Lucia's window should accentuate her loneliness; yet, she is mature enough now to appreciate that she's far less lonely this night than she was a year ago.

Her attention sways between purring acknowledgement of Vonnegut's brilliance and engagement with a figmental Bobby Carter lying beside her. She remembers his fingers, long and slender, his knuckles, red-tinged and rugged. Stretching wide the fingers of her own right hand, she fits them between her left, make-believing they are his. Bobbing just beneath the surface of this innocent pining are musings of what he would have done with his hands had she invited him in to use her bathroom that first night.

She sighs. Her fantasies are traveling the distance tonight as she reads and re-reads the faint eroticism in the part of *Slaughterhouse Five* where Billy Pilgrim's spends the first night with his new wife Valencia.

Supposing that Ana Lucia were not kept awake by the sweltering her reverie generates from armpit to inner thigh, she would not have heard the knocking at her front door at a quarter till one.

She throws the covers off of herself and steps lightly over the parquet floor which leads to the front door. Upon opening it, she finds a yellow note tacked to the outside peep hole. She peels it off, peering closely to read the chaotic cursive.

Stepping back inside, Ana Lucia opens the double glass doors to the balcony. She grips the iron railing, peering down at the red-brick streets below, where Bobby stares up at her in the midst of the New Year's crowd. From this distance, his lustrous locks and fair skin amid the city lights give him the appearance of a Chinese porcelain doll.

He offers a quiet smile and a soldier's salute. Then, hands in pocket, he turns on his heels, drifting away.

Beneath the raisin-black sky, Bobby stands docked beside a stone-clad building, his heart stomping in his chest like a colt. A shrewd wind whorls his hair over his face, blinding him briefly, sinking him further into his thoughts.

He reckons that prom night would have gone something like this. He would have waited at the bottom of the stairs as his date scrambled around upstairs like Cinderella with her magic mice. Arriving a standard thirty minutes late, she'd have revealed herself to him in the middle of her parents' living room, shiny as a Rolls Royce Silver Shadow.

Ana Lucia is now thirty-three minutes late.

Bobby scuffs his feet against the pavement salt. The crackle is nearly lost in the rowdy stammer and stagger of the New Year's party-goers. He reaches for a cigarette, shaking his head at his own naïveté. In a flush of romantic whimsy, he'd believed that a near-stranger would meet him in single-digit weather.

His folly reminds him of that one dictum his mother created just for him:

"Not every moment is a now-or-never one, Bobby."

Surely, he could have waited until the next day to see her. Or forgotten about her altogether.

This kind of logical thought was the first language of his mother and her psychologist friends. Bobby could dig it. Mostly. But it seemed to him that his mom and the band of the terrifically-educated remained unimpressed with miracles, too busy dissecting the *why* instead of savoring the *what*.

Lucky for Bobby, he is still fazed by even the slightest prospect of a miracle. As Ana Lucia materializes from the midst of the crowd, his ears grow hot with self-assurance.

Soon, she is idling before him, bundled in a buff shearling coat. Her curls are uncovered, taken up in tiny whirls by the wind.

"You're here," he says.

She looks away, her stone-cold breath sketching Van Gogh swirls in the air. "I'm freezing."

"No, no, don't freeze," he says, rubbing his hands down the sleeves of her coat. He lifts her wrist, towing her toward the heavy wooden door of La Fábrica.

She pushes her weight onto her heels, halting them.

"You're not scared, are you? I swear, I'm harmless," he says. He half-smiles. "Basically harmless."

As Ana Lucia tilts her face, pensive, Bobby notices for the first time the taut line of her jaw and the imprint of a crescent-moon dimple on her right cheek. She's more conspicuously pretty than he'd first believed. Her olive skin shines like a wax statue, all her features exceptional. Broad, dark eyes like Diana Ross. Carly Simon lips, full and moist. Debbie Harry cheekbones.

"Trust me," he says. "Just this once."

A nervous bite of her lip and a nod later, they stand inside the building, a three-story brown construction whose outside gives no hint of what is within.

The inside is Halloween: ashy concrete floors; air thick and moody with a redolence of flavored tobacco; low tunnel ceilings and faces painted upon stone walls. The faces are most provocative. If they are observed long enough, they stare back, sometimes flirtatious, other times repulsed.

Ana Lucia quietly takes it all in before they enter one of the small side rooms.

The pair stand at the entrance, staring straight ahead. They are consciously fastened to each other, holding hands as if at water's edge.

"I wasn't sure you were going to come, you know."

"I wasn't sure either. I didn't know if your note meant two in the morning or in the afternoon."

"Shit, you're right. Well, um, were you surprised?"

"Surprised?"

"By the note, I mean."

"Of course not. This kind of thing happens to me all the time." She slides her hand from his, reaching into her coat pocket to retrieve the sticky note he left on her door. She affixes it to the center of his chest, kittenish.

Closing his puppy dog mouth, Bobby moves to the corner of the room to fetch two swivel bar stools. He sets them in the center of the room and extends his hand, offering her a seat.

When she mounts the stool, he spins her around three good times, generating the motion of a Tilt-a-Whirl.

"Stay tuned," he says, patting her head before heading over to the rack of records beside the turntable.

"What is this place?" she inquires, now turning herself in circles, a hyper child.

"It's our, uh—let's see here..." Bobby fiddles with the needle on the turntable. "It's where we rehearse. Dom talked to this guy and got us put up for super cheap. The kid speaks killer Spanish."

He strolls back to Ana Lucia, his steps in time with the chirping voice of a guitar. Alone, the guitar speaks its lines until the hefty beat of a snare takes over the conversation. Piano, cymbals, and bass merge, beginning their own discourse, preparing the way for Minnie Riperton. Her voice is a bird call in the background, speaking fluently to the music as to the wind.

Bobby sits, tapping Ana Lucia's leg to suspend her hurricane spinning.

Her eyes shyly evade his. "You said Dom. Who's Dom?"

"Dom's our drummer, my best friend. I've known him since, like, junior high."

"And you didn't want to spend New Year's with him? He must be hurting."

"More like he didn't want to spend this time with me. He's on the prowl tonight."

"Searching for love to start the new year off with a bang?"

Funny, Bobby thinks. His best friend really will start the New Year off with a *bang*.

"He's not searching for love," he says. "Just lovers."

Ana Lucia's brows are lifted.

"Oh, hey, I'm not—I didn't invite you here for *that*. And you know, Dom's a good kid. Like, let's see here..." He bites the nail of his index finger, a habit foreign to him until this moment. "He was going out with the same girl from Freshman year until we moved to New York. Rosie was kind of—I don't know—kind of a praying mantis type. Super emotional, a bite-off-your-head angry girl. She let go on him a ton when they were together. I guess now he's rewarding himself for everything she put him through."

"So his girlfriend's name was Rosie?" She smiles a little, a charming note of her apparent disinterest with the Dom-Rosie subject.

The sound of her teeth chattering interferes with his nervousness. He removes his coat, holds it out for her.

"Better?" he inquires when she is snuggled inside.

"Much better."

"Righteous." Bobby slides the gold ring from her middle finger and slips it onto his pinkie, theatrically appraising it. "Now, we gotta talk square biz."

"Square biz?"

"Yeah. Like, you know, the reason why you missed the show tonight."

"Am I in trouble?"

"Seems so."

"And my punishment?"

"You gotta dance with me."

"You dance?"

"You doubt? I'm a regular Fred Astaire. Or Sammy Davis. Your choice tonight, Ana Lu."

Her eyes squint merrily at her new nickname. He returns the smile; she has no way of knowing the number of times he'd played with her name before landing on that one.

Ana Lucia is a lumbering grizzly bear inside the two coats she now wears as he brings her to her feet.

Another thing she has no way of knowing: Bobby is familiar with the feeling of slow-dancing with a bulky figure in his arms; his father, not his mother, taught him a simple two-step for the prom he never attended.

He is neither particularly good nor bad at the two-step—never was—but he's content to keep his feet moving on rhythm as he slip his arms through the double layer of coat so he can hold her.

He breathes deep. The feel of her pinched waist and Indian hips...

Magic. Gold sparkler magic.

Then sudden amnesia. He was going to say something before the magic came. What was it? Lord, what was it?

"You have a deceptive shell, you know," Ana Lucia intercepts.

"What-what do you mean?"

"I didn't expect you'd be interested in music like this. It's really—
" she sighs daintily "—*delicate*. You disguise yourself as a rock 'n roll
boy with the long hair and fast guitars, but you're really a pansy, aren't
you?"

"A pansy? I wouldn't use *that* word, but..."

Pink creeps to her cheeks. "I just meant that I'm surprised you
like this kind of music. Have you ever tried blue-eyed soul?"

"Punk gets the job done faster. Plus, I don't have blue eyes."

He tilts his face downward, offering her a wide-open view of his
gray iris. When her eyes shyly miss his, he takes hold of her balled
hand. Unfurling her index and middle finger, he touches them against
his own.

They stare at the mirror image of their V-shaped fingers, as if
expecting to see white light from the spark they feel at their fingertips.

"So, your name is Robert Dean Carter?" she says.

"Yes. Robert Dean, named after my father's father. I was born
December 28th 1960. There was a tornado in Avon that evening. It
lifted the whole hospital from the ground. Half the patients were
injured. The doctors say I slept the whole way through."

"You're *jo*king?"

"Yes, I'm joking."

Her affected concern dissolves to laughter.

Bobby pushes her baby hairs from her forehead, surveying her
sunshine face. "I'm not super interesting or anything. I've lived in
Avon my whole life. Outside of Hartford, you know."

"Hartford?"

"Hartford. It's, like, the capital of Connecticut. In America, you
know? Rad city."

"Really?"

"No."

Her smile this time is less spontaneous and ironically, sweeter.
She apparently wants him to know what a good boy he's being.

"No, it's not a rad city, but it's the only city in all of the U.S.
where flying a kite in the street is expressly forbidden."

"So, you came here because you wanted to fly your kite?"

Her words. Lord, her words.

Elemental magic. Elemental-argental-transcendental—*yeah, yeah, yeah!*

"Yeah," he says. "I guess I did."

Ana Lucia rests her head on his shoulder as Minnie Riperton soars into her fifth octave.

"What about you?" he asks.

"I'm Ana Lucia."

"And?"

"And the rest is more than a boy from Connecticut could handle."

"What do you mean?"

"I prefer not to talk about me. I know you don't understand, but—"

"I don't need to."

Her nostrils clench, bewildered.

"I don't need to understand. I know princesses have their towers. When you let down your drawbridge, I'll come over. For sure."

Bobby lifts her slig0htly so that they are breast-to-chest, tummy-to-tummy, their breath wheel-and-axle syncopated. He angles his face to graze her cheek with the tip of his nose. She inhales. He smiles—she is smelling his hair.

After some time resting his lips at the corner of her mouth, building the courage to kiss her, he feels her jaws move. "Tell me something," she murmurs.

"Yeah?"

"You don't consider yourself a pansy?"

He smiles faintly, perplexed. "What?"

"Nothing, nothing." She backs away from him, holding her conversation with the floor. "I should go home now."

He fights his desire to fight her on the matter. Like a majestic ballad, this rhapsody has to progress slowly to its final love spell.

It's a wonder. What his mother couldn't impress on him, Ana Lucia does without a psycho-adage.

"I should walk you home," Bobby says when they stand at the exit of the building.

"No. I'm okay. It's safe."

"Yeah, but I should—"

"It's okay. I promise."

She shakes herself out of his coat, reaching up to fold it over his shoulder, before jetting off.

His eyes are fixed upon her as she wafts through the maze of people. In the end, the anxious boy inside has the final say.

Bobby darts through the maze, leaving a trail of Spanish curses along his path. Upon reaching her, he seizes her magic hips, swinging her around to him.

His lips make a full stop on hers, pure Rhett Butler style. He regales her with moist lips, taking her mouth like a summer's dripping vanilla ice cream cone. Her mouth parts for him, her breath a steam cloud, offering a warm welcome to his tongue. The deeper his slippery tongue comes in, the more he forces out of her—breath, moans...control.

He breaks suddenly, parting with a kiss at the corner of her mouth, like a period at the end of a complex sentence. Her cheeks are cushioned between his hands, seemingly pressing out the swirls of smoke that flow from her mouth.

"I was gonna completely lose my shit if I didn't get to do that tonight," he pants. "I'll call you. Tomorrow, I'll call you."

B

Tomorrow.
I.
Will.
Call.
Tomorrow is a promise...

A

I've already completed tomorrow's to-do list:

1. Go to the market this week to browse the shampoo aisle. I will wait until the aisle is empty before I unscrew the tops off the bottles, sniff each until I find the peach-scented one you use and put a dab on my inner wrist for a couple hours' safe-keeping.

2. Figure out a way to get out of working tomorrow. There is no telling when you will call.

3. Listen closer to the English-speaking patrons who visit La Buena Vida. My little notebook is full of their slang. Most times, I can figure it out from context. Other times, I'm less sure.

If only I knew the proper usage of the word pansy...

5.

ANA LUCIA WALKS THROUGH her front door in a balmy
cloud, scarcely aware of how she has made it to her apartment so fast.
Piloted by the rote memory of her feet, she is fueled by endless
permutations of Bobby's tangerine kiss as she enters her bedroom.

Stepping out of her clothes, Ana Lucia presses her lips together,
regaled with thoughts of what they must have felt like to him. Like the
inside of a full grape, maybe. As she stares down at her
undergarments on the bedroom floor, she thinks how simple and
sensual her waist must have felt to hands likely disciplined by years of
guitar.

With the sound of a late New Year's firecracker outside her
bedroom window, the cloud of euphoria around her dissolves in an
instant, sugar to hot-hot water. Ana Lucia's thoughts move with light
speed, as though whizzing through a train tunnel. The darkness of her
room is replaced with a strobe light, giving an unquenchable energy to
her imagination.

A familiar circus commences behind her eyes: white horse
stomping and snarling, black-and-red rattlesnake winding its way
around stubborn hooves, puffs of brown dirt billowing in her lungs.

A happy knife pushing through ornery flesh.

Her own scream, trapped in her throat like stagnant water
beneath the soil.

Divided streams of exquisite-red blood oozing from the woman's
plaster-white forehead.

Soon, sound is added to the visions—the sound of children's
laughter as they play in the park.

Jajajaja! Jajajaja!
Run
Chase

Jump
Fall
Fall
Jump
Run
Chase

Laugh, laugh, laugh—Jajajaja! Jajajaja!

Her imagination rises with the slow drift of a bubble and bursts with a splash, leaving behind only the echo of children's laughter.

Her ears ring with the laughter, haunting her until she is moved to action. She scampers to her closet, scrambling through her belongings until she happens upon her brushes, a canvas, and several twisted tubes of oil paint. She scoops them up by the armful and drops them onto the middle of the floor. She drops to her knees.

The mad artist must begin exorcising the frightful images onto the canvas.

The Little Saints

The apartment Bobby shares with Kyle and Dom is a psychedelic dump: leopard-print wallpaper, viridian velvet sofas, ubiquitous mustard sheet vinyl, even in the two-by-four kitchen.

And piss-colored rayon drapes. Piss-colored drapes for every window!

The newly-renovated bathroom proves a holy reprieve amidst the bedizenment. It is as an altar—monochromatic marble flooring, a caged chandelier, and a marble shower-tub.

Bobby heads straight for the bathroom when he arrives home.

In the comfort of the dense white steam, Bobby closes his eyes and lathers his hair. He recalls how he almost cried every night for the first two weeks after arriving in Madrid. Having fallen upon a terrifying case of insomnia—*Holy Mother, how long can a man live without sleep?*—he spent dawns considering that everything good in the world was happening everywhere but where he was.

And then comes a girl who, despite her bold intelligence, can't place Hartford on the map. In turn, he gets to be the boy known for more than his George Harrison reticence; he gets to be knowledgeable. At times, even a little quick on the draw. More of a Lennon type.

Bobby sighs merrily, turns off the shower. He folds a thin towel around himself.

Good grief, she's pretty. Not eyes-half-open, from-stage-high, in-the-deep-dark pretty. She is good-faith pretty.

She is Ana Lu, whose voice brought to mind chocolate milk the first time she spoke to him.

He has decided that though she is a bit cagey, she isn't crooked. Perhaps it *is* better to avoid flipping over all your cards at the start of the game.

Entering his bedroom, Bobby nearly drops the towel he holds around his waist at the sight of a body coiled beneath his sheets. He creeps toward the bed, tentatively folding back the sky-blue sheet.

Betty Warner's eyes flash open. She slides up to sitting position, her back ironing out the buckling wallpaper.

She is in her undergarments, her former ensemble puddled into a black swamp on the floor beside the bed.

Her threadbare bra makes visible russet nipples. Bobby looks away, binding tighter the towel around himself.

"Greetings," she says.

"What are you doing here?"

"Kyle sent me."

Bobby slips his damp hair behind his ear. "Yeah, but why?"

"I guess because he expected me to jag him when we got here. I told him I wouldn't ride him if he came with pedals. He didn't like that, so he sent me here as my penance. He didn't tell me the room belonged to you though."

"Oh."

"Hey, don't look so craist-folin, eh."

"So *what?*"

"Craist-folin."

"I don't understand."

A theatric huff. "*Craist. Folin.* In other words, *disappointed.* What kind of vocabulary have you, Young?"

Bobby shakes his head, chafed. "So, you're going to sleep in my bed tonight then?"

"Unless you prefer me sleep on the floor."

Bobby glances at the floor. Good grief, this vinyl....

"That's' not what you want, is it?" Her eyes suddenly well up. "Is it?"

Bobby nabs a T-shirt from a pile of newly-washed clothes at the foot of his bed. He holds it out to her tentatively.

"Don't worry. I'll find somewhere else to sleep," he says.

She receives the T-shirt from him, wiping away her tears with it, and at the same time gripping his wrist. "Don't you want to know what's wrong?"

"I—"

"I can't go home."

Her ensuing silence goads him to words. "How come?"

"Because of *him.*"

"Oh. I'm sor—"

"Don't you want to know who *he* is? He's me fella. I should've known better than to go cohabitatin' with the creep. I tried to get into the flat tonight, and the muppet locked me out. Wouldn't let myself in no matter how hard I pounded on the door. He shouted at me, said, 'would you rather come in and get the shit beat out of ya or would you rather stay the night in the streets?'"

"Oh. Man."

"He hates to know I've been out with blokes past midnight. But I ask him, how's that fair? He runs around with every brand of whore day and night, gets pissed, comes home with the wild shits—"

"The what?"

"—vomits like a newborn, passes out on the floor, and expects me to be his maid. His fecking maid! I'm not a slave, Young." Another melodramatic huff. "And you should see this girl he spends all his time with. Has a face on her like a plate of mortal sins. Are ya Catholic?"

"What?"

"He claims she's his cousin, but I don't believe it."

"I'm going to sleep now, okay?"

"You're not like that, are you?" she says.

"Like what?"

"A chauvinist. Filled to the brim with that machismo thing."

He shrugs. "Only on Thursdays."

She grins. "Go to sleep already, ya little dope"

Bobby snags a T-shirt and flannel pants from his drawer. He changes in the bathroom and heads to Dom's room next door.

A neon pink light shines from beneath the closed door. It is Dom's Bat signal; he has a girl tonight.

Bobby sighs, returning to his room. He pulls a blanket from his closet and lays it over Betty quietly before lying down on the floor at the foot of his bed.

Soon, Betty is leaning over the edge, her face a shadow over his. "Are ya still awake?"

"I guess."

"Good. I have spectacular news for you. I'm Naïve's new manager. 'Spose that's the most important news of the night."

"What?"

"Tonight, Kyle made me manager. I'm takin' over for him. That way, ye lads can focus on more artistic endeavors."

Bobby swallows down his urge to rush into Kyle's room and catechize the kid. Chances are, he's not even home yet. Even if he were, there'd be no arguing Kyle's decision. Bobby got Madrid. In return, Kyle gets whatever he wants.

6.

THOUGH THE GUATEMALAN army claimed to have incontestable evidence of it, Ana Lucia didn't know if her father, Javier Vicente, had really been a Communist or not. More to the point, her father was not of Guatemalan origin. He was a Spaniard, an enigmatic foreigner. Besides that, the Guatemalan government had come across evidence that Javier's father was a fire-starter in his own country.

Javier Vicente's father—Ana Lucia's grandfather Luis Rafael Vicente—most certainly was *not* a Communist. He was an Anarchist.

Luis Rafael had grown up in second-world poverty, the fifth of eleven devoutly Catholic children who shared a single bedroom in a forty square meter apartment.

Luis Rafael's father had worked and died in the coal mines of Asturias, only visiting his family in Madrid twice each year. He was one of a thousand nameless souls whose blood cried out from the ground, the so-called collateral damage of Spain's initial failed industrial revolution.

It seemed by Providence that at nineteen, Luis Rafael was recruited into the Confederación Nacional del Trabajo, an anarchist organization focused on taking power from corporations and giving it back to the people through unions. Their wild, *humanitarian* ideas— ideas stressing that those who labored most should benefit most from their work—coalesced seamlessly with his own.

These were the ideals that landed Luis Rafael in Franco's labor camp at the age of forty.

He'd been out of the camp three years when Ana Lucia was sent to live with him and her grandmother after her father's death.

On the plane to Madrid, it occurred to ten-year-old Ana Lucia that she would be an alien to her grandparents.

First, they didn't know she existed until their son was murdered. Second, there was no physical resemblance to bind them.

They, like Ana Lucia's father, were fair-haired, luminescent-eyed. For all of her grandparents' flat and sharp edges, Ana Lucia was curled and round—nose, chin, hair, bottom.

Ana Lucia's hair became The Great Divider. It seemed to embellish their differences, beginning with language disparities. In Guatemala Ana Lucia's hair was *colocho*. In her new house in Madrid, that word was forbidden. Such words weren't *real* Spanish. No, no, no. Curls were referred to as *rizos* in the Mother Country.

Interestingly, Ana Lucia's grandmother could talk about her hair, but she always stopped short of touching it, as though it would bite. Ana Lucia knew it wouldn't bite. She had good curls, soft curls. Big, shiny, *obedient* curls.

Still, they were *snitching* curls.

They gave away the fact that their son hadn't married a *real* Guatemalan. He'd married a Garifuna.

Ana Lucia's first week living with her grandparents, they tried to be kind to her, despite not seeing their son in her. Neither could she see her father in them in any way that mattered. But she tried. And that's all Ana Lucia's father ever required of anybody. For all things, just try.

For her, it began with the reading of advanced English. Her father started her on a *Tale of Two Cities*.

Just try, Lucita. Just try it.

Ironically, reading advanced English became a life-saving skill.

Monday of her second week in Madrid, Ana Lucia's grandmother warned her that Luis Rafael could not be stressed for his bad heart, caused by the labor camps. Unfortunately, she didn't mention a word about his mind.

"Ana Lucia, come," her grandfather said one evening as he sat in front of the television.

"Yes?"

"When is your birthday?"

"January."

"Date, not month."

Her cheek twitched. "January second. Nineteen sixty-one."

"You'll be eleven soon."

She stood quiet, still a couple of yards from him.

"Yes or no?"

"Yes."

"You're an adult. When you lose your father, trust me, you become an adult."

She nodded.

"You learn to take care of yourself. You have to. There's no other choice."

Again, Ana Lucia nodded.

"The first lesson in learning to care for yourself is to care for your mind. You learn this in solitude. *I* learned it in solitude first."

Didn't he already know how acquainted she was with loneliness in that house?

Her grandfather stood, drawing close to her. He pointed and began walking. He was leading her.

To a closet. The coat closet near the front door. He opened it.

"Go inside."

Ana Lucia stared at the black closet.

"Are you afraid of the dark?" he asked. "The dark won't hurt you."

Realizing that he could not coax her, Luis Rafael ushered her inside. Not with ferocity, just a slight push.

She thought it would be a few moments' punishment. After what she measured herself to be an hour, she thought her grandfather had simply forgotten he'd put her in the closet. So, she pounded her hand flat against the door until she couldn't anymore. She tried her fists, at first to get her grandparents' attention, but later, to see if she could break the door down. After some hours, she couldn't tell if she'd broken her own hands—there was no feeling left in them.

Three days, she was there in that closet. Three days in solitary confinement.

There, she learned that while loneliness is a conquerable demon, aloneness decomposes the brain on a chemical level. Hunger can be warded off through sleep. Urine will dry. The eyes adjust, the mind makes its way through the darkness. Numbness of cramped limbs grows inconsequential.

But a world without human touch—without the only light that matters—wounds the soul in ways unparalleled. She learned that one cannot live on memories alone, not even the memories of a beloved mother or father. Hope fails in the face of aloneness.

When Ana Lucia was finally released, she knew that if Jesus Christ had been in the tomb more than three days, He may have never risen.

Jesus Christ is the first to greet Ana Lucia when she arrives at Khadijah's apartment in the early morning. The framed Persian miniature on the foyer wall depicts Him as a fuzzy-haired child sitting upon the lap of his hickory-skinned mother. It is forbidden art but a gift Mr. Piaf received before leaving Morocco.

Ana Lucia eyes shift from the portrait to Khadijah.

Stepping inside the apartment, Ana Lucia shivers, her curls damp and bloated from the snow mist.

"I need you to take my place at work today," she says.

"Come again?"

"I'm sick."

"You're lying."

"Lying? Why would I lie?"

In the background Khadi's mother calls out to her. Arabic, normally punchy and virile to Ana Lucia's ears, is a bird song on the tongue of Mrs. Piaf.

"She says we can go to the kitchen," Khadi says. "Come on."

Ana Lucia removes her beat-up pilot boots, outlined with slush, and places them neatly at the end of the descending line of boy tennis shoes. The shoes belong to Khadijah's younger brothers, who lounge on the living room floor watching television as she and Khadijah pass by en route to the kitchen

The wide-open kitchen is saturated with sunlight. Mrs. Piaf busies herself with chores. Her skin is raw umber, slick and shiny, not unlike Ana Lucia's own mother's had been. Where Ana Lucia's mother wore kente headwraps, Mrs. Piaf dons a pink chiffon head covering which only leaves visible her pleasant face.

She places before the girls a plate of olive pastries and pink luster tea cups filled with steaming mint tea, then returns to her detailed cleaning, intermittently peering up to smile at Ana Lucia.

Khadijah blows ripples through her tea. "You're going to be late for work if you don't get going now."

"I woke up with the flu." Ana Lucia coughs listlessly.

"*Pobrecita*. Well, with the money you'll make today, you can buy yourself some proper medicine."

Ana Lucia sheepishly nibbles on a pastry, eyes closed. "He's going to call today," she confesses.

"He?"

"Yes. He. Him. Bobby. He's going to call. I don't know when. I have to be here for it."

Khadijah snorts jocosely. "No, you don't."

"Khadi, please."

"What would you seriously have me do? Go to work while you stay here chatting with your little boyfriend? What happens when my father comes home this evening? Men aren't allowed to call this house."

"He doesn't have to know I'm talking to a man." Besides, she thinks to herself, he's not a man, really. He's a boy. A perfectly intriguing boy.

Khadi grabs a pastry and begins chewing, one eye squinted, dramatically deliberating. "I'll see what I can do."

She stands, makes her way to the powder blue wall phone.

"Hola, que tal, Amoroso?" she says.

Mrs. Piaf continues sweeping, deaf to her daughter's conversation. Learning Spanish has never become the center of her preoccupations since fleeing Rabat.

Consequently, Mrs. Piaf doesn't understand when Khadijah explains that Ana Lucia must miss work today for proper treatment of her meningitis.

When she returns to the table, Ana Lucia puts on an exaggerated scowl. "Why?"

"Why not?" Khadijah shrugs. "Illness is the only way you can rightfully be excused from work. Besides that, it only makes sense. You let that boy Bobby kiss you, didn't you? That's the only reason you'd be letting him get between you and your money."

Ana Lucia stares into the tea cup at her lips, eluding a smile.

"Well, *habibi*, so be it," Khadijah says. "Now, all there's left to do is wait for the loverboy to call."

Waiting is an art Ana Lucia has nearly perfected after years of the closet episodes with her grandfather. She has learned that waiting is best bridled by the infusion of action.

Not big action, just small activities to bide the time while her blood churns between musings of Bobby. She and Khadijah listen to *Great American Speeches Volume 4* on record while playing cards. Mr. Piaf had given the record to Khadijah two short weeks before they left their estate in Rabat.

Khadijah lies sprawled out on her stomach on top of the bed, tossing her cards more languidly as it nears two in the afternoon. She falls asleep before they finish their sixth game of Rummy.

Ana Lucia's thoughts follow the soft drift of the snowflakes falling outside Khadi's bedroom window. She takes inventory of the little room with all its opulent markings—two lavish Indian watercolors, a prodigious oak sleigh bed, a gleaming gold candlestick phone—proof of the Piaf's prestige before Spain.

It was in this room five months ago that she and Khadijah got piss drunk. That day, Ana Lucia begged her best friend to shave bald her then waist-length curls.

Cut it all off. For God, cut it off! I don't need it anymore. I won't be angry. Lo juro por Dios. Lo juro. I don't want it anymore.

Hands shaking from alcohol, Khadijah submitted to her demand, cutting Ana Lucia's hair to a patchy pixie. Upon sight of herself in the bathroom mirror, Ana Lucia sobbed at the meaning of it all.

As the sapling is bent so grows the tree. Her life had fallen to rubble because it had started as such. And everyone to blame for it was dead. Cutting her hair had been a way of punishing the only person left to be punished.

Now, as she stares at her reflection in the window, Ana Lucia is pleased with how her hair has grown into a style now in mode, as though she'd purposely planned to look like one of those fun American girls with their shaggy Pageboys.

She shakes her wavy bangs from her forehead. It's not so bad now. Nothing is so bad now.

At dusk, Khadijah awakens from her nap at the sound of the azan, the call to prayer. It is a sonorous echoing which fills the apartment—the recorded chant of a voice of an Arab singer with an impossible penchant for wavering through sundry notes to land on the bluest one. His voice is a funeral procession.

Khadijah follows the procession, first covering her head with a gold scarf then taking her prayer rug to the living room. Ana Lucia watches, hugging the corner of the wall with her shoulder blade, as her best friend performs the sunset prayer ritual. Face down, then up; hands down, then up—a gentle rocking.

The words on her fluttering lips are as forged as her movements.

Khadijah doesn't believe in God anymore. Perhaps she never did; as a child, she was too consumed with her studies and extracurriculars—too consumed with *knowledge*—to ever consider her *beliefs*. What need has she for religion when she has science? For her, freedom from the concept of God has opened her to the possibility of everything. Though the possibility of everything is an attractive thought, Ana Lucia can't help but think how unscientific it is to live in a world of hypotheses without seeing any one idea through to its final end.

Whatever the reality, Khadi will not surrender the salah. Her refusal to publicly wear hijab is enough controversy for the Piaf household. If she foregoes prayer, her parents' assumptions about her will go tumbling down the slippery slope. Naturally, they'll conclude that she has lost her virginity, as everything in Islam begins and ends with a woman's virginity. They will conclude rightly.

Soon enough, prayer passes. Or rather, Khadijah passes it...like a kidney stone. Her face is plainly relieved when they return to the room.

Back in Khadijah's room, the girls lie side-by-side on the floor, biding their time to the soundtrack of Vincent Price's reproduction of the *Crime Against Kansas* speech by Charles Sumner. Ana Lucia can't help wondering if Kansas is close to Connecticut. To think of it, she's never really studied a map of The United States.

By eleven, it is almost a certainty that Bobby will not call. This is according to a pseudo-scientific probability scheme Ana Lucia has come up with in her waiting time.

Despite the odds, she can hardly suffer the thought of throwing her hand before her ace is possibly dealt. It seems to her hope and fear are eternally married in this way.

"Khadijah?"

"Yes?"

"What do you think?"

"About?"

Ana Lucia lies still, allowing her silence to gain weight. In the silence, yesterday's kiss raptures her whole imagination.

"You're talking about the loverboy," Khadijah says. "Well, I'd say that I'm not a betting person, but you already know I am. Where I'm putting my bet, it's best for you to go ahead and close your eyes. Tomorrow you'll be glad you didn't sacrifice your sleep for this."

Ana Lucia considers. Perhaps it is better to let him off the hook than to be let down.

"Alright then." She rises, heading for the bed. "I think I'm finished   now."

Bobby stands alone in the kitchen at five-thirty in the morning, holding the phone at the crook of his neck. His fingertips hang on the rotary dial.

Dom has retired to his room. Betty has retired to Bobby's bed.

He decides that he will sleep in the kitchen if he has to. He's reached his limit with Betty's blithe disregard for personal space. Taking seriously her new role as manager, she's been a dutiful little appendage to the band through the entire day.

Bobby breathes, contending with his nervousness. On the count of three, he turns the last number on the phone.

And waits, yesterday's kiss still on his lips.

"Hello," comes a chocolate milk voice on the other end.

"Hey. Hi. Ana Lucia? It's me."

"Hi," Ana Lucia whispers, clutching the phone, white-knuckled. Perfectly awake in an instant, she wonders if she was ever really asleep.

Khadijah awakens briefly then falls back asleep without ceremony.

Good. They are alone. All alone.

"It's me," Bobby repeats.

"I know."

"I hope it's not too early." He pauses. "I mean, I hope it's not too late."

"It depends."

"Yeah? What's it depend on, Ana Lu?"

The charming way he uses her name wrecks her coolness for a second. She turns over onto her stomach. "It depends on how well you can entertain me."

He gives a breathy little laugh. "You'll be entertained one way or the other. There's really no telling what's gonna come out of my mouth this time of morning."

"Have you slept?"

"Yeah. The day before yesterday."

She smiles, staring up at the ceiling and twisting her fingers through the loops of the phone cord. "We don't have to talk now. You can sleep."

"No, no. I really can't, see. I tried already. My mind and body are in agreement—I have to talk to you today."

Her smile widens. What a magnificent cold reading he gives from the script of her heart.

"So, um, yeah, what have you been doing?" he asks.

"Nothing. It was my day off today. I just listened to vinyl recordings. Serials, I mean."

"Yeah? What did you—I mean, what's your favorite show?"

"I don't have one. I prefer movies, really."

"Your favorite movie then?"

She doesn't know many English movies in their original titles. She and Khadi watched a bootleg version of *American Graffiti* some months back. Her supposed preference for movies had only been a method to propel the conversation forward.

"I like anything with Audrey Hepburn," she replies. "But you—what did you do today?"

"Nothing, really. We did a street show this evening. We just got home."

"How was it?"

"I don't know. Maybe bad. These things are never, like, *planned*. We go and play wherever, you know, and it's just so...so random."

"Random is bad?"

"It is when being surprised becomes the predictable part. Sometimes the shows are way decent, but sometimes it's just...*enough already*, you know?"

"I see." *Way decent...way decent...way decent.* There. She'll remember it for the next entry in her journal of American colloquialisms.

"We usually do about five random shows a week. We've been doing them for all six of the weeks we've been here, plus the last month-and-a-half we were in New York. What's that all together? Seventy-two shows? Something like that."

"Yes, I think so," she responds, though she hasn't a clue. Math isn't her strong suit. Perhaps it would have been if she'd ever taken a math class.

"No, wait, I think that's sixty, not seventy-two," Bobby says. "Whatever it is, it just gets a little tiresome after a while. But you know what I really want? I mean, what I really, *really* want?" He stops suddenly, recoiling from his swelling excitement. "Nevermind. I'm probably talking to much now, huh?"

"Tell me, Bobby." She adds to her voice a savory lilt. She lays her cheek against the pillow, imagining it to be his chest. "Tell me."

He hesitates. Then....

"I want us to take some songs from the greats—like some *What's Going On, Innervisions, Highway Sixty-one Revisited* type of stuff—and do our own versions. Like punk versions, you know? Stuff that'll make the kids nowadays listen. Like, show people what the world really looks like and how it could look if we'd just, you know, give peace a chance or whatever. I mean, we probably suck too deep to pull it off, and maybe I'm just frustrated that we haven't written any songs like that, but sometimes, I think, what's the point of any of it if our songs aren't changing anybody? I don't know; maybe it's enough that the songs are changing me in some small way. It's not like anybody here understands what we're singing about anyway. I guess this is just training ground, a place to make all our mistakes. I should probably stop talking now. I don't talk this much normally. Only when I'm nervous or afraid. You make me a little of both. In a good way. Fright awakens courage, right?"

Listening to his earnest voice, the sun rising in her heart brings a smile to her lips, though alongside it, a darker emotion has awakened inside of her. It is a familiar agitation, sparked by Bobby's expressed desire to have some great impact on the world. She knows too well the folly of such aspirations. Her parents and grandparents alike had become victims to that ambition.

The unsettling feeling at the pit of her stomach is soon disrupted by the sound of the dawn salah song.

Bobby pulls the phone back from his ear briefly, at the sound of a warbling chant on the other end of the line.

"What is that?" he says when the noise begins to fade.

"Nothing. It's nothing. My alarm. That's all it is."

"Wow. Must have woken up the whole house. Wait, you live alone, right?"

"Something of that sort."

"What about your parents? Where do they live?"

"They don't."

"They—they don't?" The realization of her words paralyzes his thoughts. His tongue is touched with the same paralysis.

"Don't worry yourself. It was a long time ago," she assures. "Things are better now. But your voice is very beautiful, Bobby. It sounds like autumn leaves when you haven't had much sleep. Maybe you could talk more."

He carefully considers his next words. "You know, when I said before that it was okay if you were dying to see me, I sort of meant it. Not in a jerk way or anything. Just, if you ever want to, like, reach out, I'll reach back."

Always reach back, he would have said if he didn't feel his words were already too large and too many.

"Don't know why I said that. Just felt like I should." Quietly bashful, he adds, "Was it okay?"

She says nothing to this end, but he is amazed to find that he can actually *feel* her smile.

Incredible...indelible...cen-cen-centripetal

"You're here to be a musician, right?" she says. "What about going to university?"

"I don't know if school's really for me. I'm sort of anti-school in the establishment as we know it."

"The establishment as we know it?"

"Yeah, you know—the system that kind of determines *what* you're gonna be before you figure *who* you're gonna be. They put you in these classes based on what they think you can do for society. It's like communism. As a good American, I had a duty to fight the communist regime, right?"

"Clearly."

"So, I fulfilled my civic duty and dropped out senior year."

She laughs. "In case no one's ever told you before, that was really stupid—going through all those agonizing years of communism without a diploma to show for it."

"Yeah, but it wasn't my fault, see. I was diagnosed with a bad case of truancy toward the end. It was tragic, really."

She laughs again, then forces herself to stop, before collapsing into another bout of laughter.

He grins, his foot tapping to a *Blitzkrieg Bop* beat. His nervousness and fear have dissolved entirely. It's an achievement he can rest with.

"Seriously, though," he continues, "I didn't drop out of school. I got kicked out after missing so many days. My mom got me back in so I could at least graduate. But you're right—I was stupid."

Stupid for not calling you back before now.

"Yeah—yeah, you were," she says with an audible ounce of charity, evidently perceiving the words sheltered inside his words.

"Hey, look, Ana Lu, I hate to leave you now, but I'm going to be dead tomorrow if I don't get some sleep now."

He is both pleased and awed to know that he can *feel* her pout as surely as he can feel her smile.

"Okay, well, um," she says, "well, goodnight."

"Chocolate milk dreams, Ana Lucia Vicente."

B
Pretty
On the phone, you are
Pretty
Everywhere, you are
Pretty
A universe of
Pretty
From Planet Pretty:
Population One

A
I like when you talk; don't stop.
Best not to give space for my words to begin.
The stories my words would weave
  may absorb more from you than what I can replenish.
So keep on talking, voice of milk and honey.
Your candy words will whirl around my head,
A pretty purple ribbon in the wind
Tying me up with thoughts of you for the rest of the day.

7.

"YOU UP, MAN?" Bobby hears Dom say when he wakes up.

"I think so," Bobby replies, his voice muffled by the pillow his face is buried in. "What time is it?"

"Just after one."

Bobby flips over. Dom sits on the edge of the bed, a cigarette dangling from his mouth.

"Don't worry," he says. "You can get out of bed now. Betty left an hour ago."

"You saw her leave?"

"Yep. She wanted me to get you up so you could see her off. I told her you were dead." He laughs out a smoke swirl.

Bobby smiles. Dom is too good an egg to have really said that, but the fact that he *would* have if not for his incurable politeness, is the reason they are best friends. And not just because he let Bobby take half of his bed when he knocked on his door at six in the morning like an orphan after he'd finished his conversation with Ana Lucia.

Dom hops up from the bed, grabbing a brown package from the table stand by the door. "You got some mail though. It's from your mom."

Bobby sits up, taking the box from Dom and tearing off the packing tape with his teeth. Inside, there are a bundle of projector slides, a cashier's check, and a hardbound copy of *Moby Dick*. Taped on the inside of the novel cover is a folded note. He unfolds it with the same conscientiousness it was folded.

My Darling Bobby,

Words won't adequately express how desperate I am to see your face again, so I will keep this part as short as possible. Dad swears he misses you even more than I do. What is more than infinity? You can try and figure out that one.

We had a marvelous dinner with Dominic's mother and father a few days ago. Mrs. Russo's cooking has gotten even better over the years. You can tell him that his mom is DYING without him. Her words verbatim.

A part of her still believes that Dominic's leaving was some sort of rebellion. She believes that she may have been putting too much pressure on him after what happened with Francis. All these years have passed, and the pain never really dissolves.

At any rate, Dominic's parents, your father, and I go about our daily lives in anticipation of your imminent return. Can you believe we are at T-minus forty-five days now? I hope the money I've sent will last you the entire month-and-a-half before you return. If you need more before then, write me. If not, write me still."

Bobby stops reading a moment, attempting to shake off the familiar sensation that he is suffocating in his own life. He can hardly rid himself of the feeling but reads on anyway.

I do hope you are finding all that you're looking for there. New York was its own adventure, but I'm quite certain that Spain will be the means by which you are finally introduced to yourself. Your truest self. Simply put, when you know yourself, you know a lot.

He stops again, breathes, counts to ten. Despite the dutiful obedience he's practiced almost his whole life, Bobby knows his quiet restlessness has been a constant challenge to his mother's mathematical life.

He continues.

Quite often it is on the road from domesticity to chaos that we find our true selves.

It is as Melville put it: "almost every robust boy with a robust healthy soul, at some time or other is crazy to go to sea." Perhaps, in some way, you felt you were almost too healthy here with us, too safe on dry land.

To only be exposed to the light—it is a tragedy. The best art is a rhythmic mingling of light and shadows, darkness and illumination. You have need of shadows at this time in your life.

I know Spain will bring that to you. And when it brings you home at last, you will have completely arrived upon the waterfront of manhood. No matter how it happens, I am proud of you.

I have enclosed the photographs for their nostalgic value. In times of distress, it is important to recall domestic life, the way things were. As for the book—well, to my great disappointment, you never got around to reading Moby Dick in high school. I had so wished you put more effort into your final year of school, but there will be time for that when you return for college. I only hope that in your spare moments, you will fit this reading in. It's quite a suitable story for your time now at sea.

That's all for now, my one and only. Dad and I love you endlessly. Remember to write. Call if you can.

With love,
Mom

"Everything alright?" Dom asks at last.

"Not too bad, I'd say." Bobby twirls the check between his fingers before holding it up in front of Dom's eyes.

Dom flicks the check with his thumb and index. "She say anything about how long you're planning on staying in Madrid?"

Dom speaks in regard to Bobby's plan to overstay his visa. It's a plan still without color, just a basic outline, an immutable edict to never move back to Connecticut.

His mother, a control freak of the highest order, has decided that his "rebellion" will fit into her timeline. She still doesn't know what Bobby knows: his greatest rebellion will be bypassing the times and seasons she has set for his life since he was born.

Bobby had heard it said once before that there were two things mankind has tried and failed to manipulate throughout the ages: nature and time. Neither can be bent for man's desire.

Torrential rains keep Bobby inside the apartment for the next week. He is unable to venture through the city, unable to see after Ana Lucia when she doesn't answer the phone the three times he calls. The hysterical rain gives the illusion that his apartment is drifting through a violent storm at sea. He sighs, staring out the living room window.

Time taunts him. Even when he tries to sleep it away, he is awakened for long stretches by his desire for Ana Lucia. He reaches for his guitar, sings over endless permutations of I-IV-V chords, yet he is unable to settle on lyrics that will give his feelings a right name.

The sun shines upon his face Saturday morning, awaking him with soft pleasure. He stares at the ceiling, relishing his good luck this day. Today is Los Reyes Magos— "Three Kings Day"—a celebration of the magi who brought the infant Jesus gifts. Fittingly, it is the day gifts are exchanged in Spain, a day more greatly anticipated than Christmas.

Five minutes before the opening of La Buena Vida, Bobby is excited to find that the venue is open on this holiday.

"Hi," he says to the bronze-skinned girl standing at the back door. He holds out the note he'd drafted three days ago. "Hola. Um, me llamo Bobby. Could you give this to Ana Lucia? I tried to deliver it to her apartment, but I couldn't get in the building. I don't think she's home."

The girl stares at him, heedless.

"Ah, shit," he mumbles to himself at the realization that she likely speaks no English at all. He holds the note a little higher and shakes it. "Por Ana Lucia. Please. *Por favor.* Por fa..."

He presses the note into the girl's hand and backs away, nearly tripping over his own feet as he retreats.

The Three King's Celebration begins in the streets shortly after six. Drawn by the lights of the celebration, Dom and Bobby make their way down to the parade, standing in the midst of the happy crowd. The fanfare makes jolly the otherwise frigid air: the blow of trumpets, blue lights hanging from bare branches, confetti coming down like snow in majestic free fall, three magi actors waving from one of the enormous floats. Bobby looks away from the actor seated in the middle of the float, uncomfortable with his face being painted a deep dark ebony. He supposes there is no historical context for blackface here in Spain.

When the crowd begins to splinter, Bobby and Dom go on their way, their steps rhyming as they make their way through the city. Dom lights a cigarette for Bobby and one for himself. They are on their way to meet Betty at the venue she has secured for them for the following Saturday.

The city is heavily marked by the Catholic imagination—murals of crucifixes, the sumptuous design of churches on every corner, streets named after Jesus, Maria, and Jose. Yet, a mile down, turning down the dim alley of brick storefronts, Bobby wonders if God is there at all.

At the end of a long stretch of venues, they catch sight of a couple in a raunchy routine. The *she* of the pair is on her knees. *He* is in her mouth. He is a steaming locomotive, thrusting back and forth into the tunnel she has made for him. They have no care that they may be seen. Or perhaps they want to be seen. Their kind of passion warps the senses.

Eyes squinted, Bobby can hardly believe his senses. The *she* is Betty Warner.

"Let's go, man," Bobby says quietly, setting his hand at the crook of Dom's arm. "Let's just wait somewhere. Until they're finished or whatever."

Dom says nothing in reply, unmoved by Bobby's hand. He watches quietly, his eyes aglow.

Bobby's eyes fall to the pavement.

When he looks up again, Betty and her partner are finishing up, still paying no mind to their surroundings. When she does spot them, Bobby and Dom turn their backs, as though oblivious.

"Young and Dom," Betty cries. "You're here! It's me!"

She rushes toward them, holding her trench coat together with one hand. Her lover follows behind her. Bobby's gaze moves to the sky, searching for invisible stars. Ambient light can be a real drag.

"How's the form, mates?" she says, taking hold of her lover's hand, gingerly swinging it back and forth. "This is Carlos. My man."

Carlos bows, looking up at them amiably.

"He don't speak no English, so— "

"I espeak a little," Carlos says. He gestures with his thumb and index. "*Un poco.*"

Betty looks up at him adoringly before turning her full attention to Dom and Bobby. "Glad ye finally made it. We've been waiting for ye a good fifteen minutes. This building here on the left is where Naïve'll be performing next Friday. I wanted ye lads to have a look-see beforehand. Are ye ready? *Vamos.*"

The four of them enter the venue, standing close to the door to avoid being jammed. The sweating crowd bounces with minimal rhythm, like fish caught on the hook of a fishing poll.

The rhythm guitarist onstage plays with outstanding vigor, his hands like the Road Runner's animated blur of feet. The singer, a screechy female with a rainbow mohawk, stands at the edge of the stage, bellowing lyrics Bobby only recognizes as "Personality Crisis" from the melody. He can hardly believe the music of the New York Dolls have made it to Madrid.

Bobby looks around in refreshed awe, taking note of the tune of the blue stage lights, the height of the stage, the grooves and splinters in the floor.

Between the music and his own thoughts, he can barely make out what Betty explains about the place.

Carlos soon takes her attention, leaning down to whisper in her ear. She smiles, stretching up to speak back in his ear. This Carlos, who Betty claimed five days ago would kick her ass if she entered their apartment, touches her arm with delicacy unbefitting her boorishness.

She turns to Bobby. "Listen, Young, do you want to learn Spanish?"

"Probably need to."

"Well, Carlos wants to have *intercambio* with ya. A language exchange. You help him with his English, he helps you with your Spanish. What do you say?"

"I mean, I thought..." Bobby lowers his voice. "I thought you said he didn't like you hanging out with guys."

"He's making an exception."

"How come *you* don't teach him English?"

"I told ya already, Young. He's got the machismo thing bad. He'll never learn anything from a woman."

Bobby glances at Carlos. His eyes are dark, typically Spanish, but they are neither brooding nor fierce.

"So, will you do it or not?" says Betty.

"Yeah, sure, whatever you guys want. But look, I gotta go."

"Where are you going?"

"Straight to heaven if I stock up on good deeds." He smiles. "Catch you later."

Ana Lucia can't remember if the name of what she wears this evening is dungaroos or dungarees in America; her mother used to call them *mamelucos*. Whatever the case, the ones she wears now are orange, corduroy, and the finest piece of clothing in her wardrobe. Beneath them, she wears a faux silk paisley button-up. She smiles. Bobby also wears a psychedelic paisley shirt, buttoned to the top.

Through her long bangs, Ana Lucia stares at his fingers as he monkeys with the carousel wheels of the movie projector. He wears ornamented silver rings on the thumb and index finger of his right hand.

The note he left with Khadijah at La Vida said to meet him in his rehearsal room at nine. Khadijah helped her fake a flare-up of meningitis, holding up a hot water bottle to her head in the bathroom for five minutes.

"What are we doing?" she inquires from the four-foot high speaker she sits upon, snacking on the corn nuts and cola he brought.

"Getting this projector together. For a movie."

"Where'd you get it?"

"From home."

"Avon home?"

"Yep." He nods, his drooping ponytail falling over the side of his neck.

"What are we watching?" she asks, pelting her feet back and forth against the speaker as she tosses another corn nut into her mouth.

When Bobby turns to her, his face is abruptly troubled. He rushes over, catching her foot mid-air before she can hit the speaker again.

"Sorry," she says, dropping her eyes, embarrassed.

"Don't sweat it, Ana Lu." He holds up a glossy movie mini-poster. "Have you seen it?"

She runs her finger along the outline of Audrey Hepburn in a nun costume. "No. I'm not really religious."

"Yeah, but it's Audrey Hepburn. It's the only one I could find here. I think it's, like, overdubbed in Spanish."

Bobby reaches for the light switch on the wall. The room is soon black, save the sprinkling of misty light shooting from the eye of the projector onto the screen. In time with the kingdom-come orchestration at the film's start, Bobby hops on the speaker beside her, the tips of his high-tops touching the floor.

"So, you don't believe in God?" he says.

"I'm not religious."

"Then you do believe in God?"

"Not necessarily. But I'm not..." She raises her chin, fishing for a proper word. "I'm not a royal atheist."

"A *royal* atheist?"

"I mean, a *real* atheist," she says quickly, shooing off her embarrassment. "There are energetic atheists—Nietzsche, Freud, Ayn Rand. I'm not one of them."

"Then, um, what are you?"

"I'm waiting. That's what I am."

He smiles, confused.

The word is *agnóstico* in Spanish, though Ana Lucia fears the word may be too easy a translation into English. First, the word may be a false friend. Second, *agnóstico* is such a typical word for Madrid's young, post-Franco resistance. Ana Lucia has never much wanted to *resist* anything; it'd be much more gratifying to surrender to a rationally satisfying answer to the business of life and death.

After one episode of being locked in the closet for five days, over which time she devoured Marx's *A Contribution to the Critique of Hegel's Philosophy of Right*, Ana Lucia came to agree that religion was merely an opiate for the masses. She was fourteen then.

At seventeen, after befriending Khadijah who met the idea of God with a yawn, Ana Lucia became convinced that disbelief was the real opiate. Khadijah seemed to use nihilism as a way to dull her senses, to avoid that ancient search for what transcended what could not be known with the body.

In recent months, Ana Lucia has been surprised of how often she can see the idea of "God" in the faces of human beings. Human beings like Audrey Hepburn, indisputably gorgeous in nun apparel— so gorgeous that Ana Lucia imagines it must be supernatural. There is always something in raw beauty that presents itself delightfully numinous, something that makes a person stare shamelessly, trying to gather the origin of such beauty.

And this boy next to her staring at her with puppy-wet eyes and contemplatively chewing on his bottom lip—this boy's prettiness is so supernatural, it's almost mythical.

"I know there's something bigger than what I can see," Ana Lucia says, watching him closely. "I'm waiting for it to reveal itself to me. Hunger in some way proves the existence of food." She shrugs. "And you?"

"Catholic. It revealed itself to me, I think."

"How?"

"Through evil mostly. Corruption's everywhere. The spectrum must have two ends, right? The opposite end to corruption is creation. God is creation and creator. All in one."

"Evil is the reason many people deny the existence of God."

"Yeah, I know. But I think they're wrong. Now, you have to watch the movie." He takes hold of her face, mechanically directing it back toward the screen.

Bobby lays his hand flat on the speaker, his pinkie finger nearly touching hers. Ana Lucia feels the attraction at their fingertips like the spark of metalworking.

Bobby stares at the screen straight ahead as his hand curves tentatively around her side.

Restless, his hand moves up her back until his thumb and fingers begin playfully touring the back of her neck. It's a gentle massage that makes its way to her hair.

She sighs, wooed. His fingers are not as skillful as her mother's had been when she plaited Ana Lucia's hair in the evenings before her father arrived home, but they are as warm and thin and appreciating.

Utterly charmed, Ana Lucia winds her leg around Bobby's.

"You're not gonna watch this, are you?" he says.

She shakes her head.

He stands abruptly, failing to untwine their legs. He makes his way to the stereo player, stumbling along with her at his side, as though running a three-legged race. She holds tight to his arm to keep balance. Their laughter is breathy, goofy.

He finally frees her to properly place a record on the turntable.
She returns to her seat on top of the speaker. A silky-voiced woman
begins an opening monologue about a man named Reverend Lee.

Bobby saunters toward her, holding up a book. "Hey, have you
ever read this before?"

It is a hardcover of *Moby Dick* with a vintage black-and white
jacket.

"Yes." The first time was in '74. The binding strings of the book
were exposed like ripped jeans by her tenth reading of it in '78.

When she takes the book from him, a pile of pictures cascade
onto her lap.

"What are these?" she says, straightening up the pictures into a
neat pile.

"Just old pictures. My mom sent them. She sent the book too."

"Can I see them?"

"For sure, whatever you want."

First up is a Christmas picture. The Christmas tree is tall, well-
trimmed, sparing on the ornaments, heavy on the silver tinsel. A
blonde-haired prince of a child sits at the feet of his mother. He is a
child so fair-looking, so similar to his mother, he could have been a
girl if not for his neatly-cropped whiffle.

Ana Lucia's face grows warm browsing through the pictures—
Bobby on the front lawn in his Sunday best, Bobby on a red bicycle,
Bobby at the dining table in front of a chocolate cake with one, two,
three...ten candles. The scenes and times change, yet he is never
without a smile for the camera.

There is something here, something in these old pictures that
brings out a deep yearning. Maybe a yearning to have known him
when these pictures were taken, to have held the baby with the
chubby cheeks, to have stolen a first kiss with the boy in the striped
shirt. Maybe a feeling that she knows everything that she needs to
know about him, accompanied by the sentiment that she wants to
know infinitely more.

The last picture is different from the rest. Bobby is fourteen,
maybe fifteen, sitting on a bed in an orange-painted room. That
exquisite arc of his upper lip is made visible by the fact that, for once,
he lacks a smile. In fact, he doesn't seem to notice the camera.
Rather, he is staring at the album cover in his hand. His hair is a
scruffy mop, brown and wild.

So wild, Bobby laughs now as he stands in front of her, his hand balled bashfully over his mouth. "That was my Dylan phase. I wanted the messiest hair I could get. I know it looks like shit, but that picture took, like, three bottles of hairspray and a half hour of teasing. It only stayed, like, ten minutes. My hair—it just doesn't work."

Ana Lucia touches her own curls. He doesn't know that his hair has always worked.

Still sitting on the high speaker, she looks down at Bobby in front of her. As he bites down a bashful grin, she feels a wish growing inside of her—just one wish for the deep dark wishing well. She wishes to know the story behind every picture he will take from this day forward.

Her face drifts down toward his, her eyes closed. He kisses the left corner of her mouth with excited compliance. The breath from his nostrils warms her skin as he burrows his nose into her cheek. It is mint and tobacco and myrrh. And the glow of Jupiter.

It is meditation.

Ana Lucia opens her eyes momentarily to see that both of their hands are linked together, suspended out at their sides like bat wings. She closes her eyes once more when he begins a rhythmic sucking of her bottom lip. He continues on to her top lip, with an added tug.

Bobby unlocks his left hand from hers. He needs that hand, *needs* it to hold her face, to direct it, to keep her lips on tempo with his.

She is still lost in the hymn of his lips when Bobby hits a rest. He holds his face in front of her, his eyes closed, waiting. She leads the meditation this time, stroking his velvet cheek with her own, coming closer, until her eyelashes flutter against his temple.

When it is his turn again, he kisses her until lava shoots from under the sea. There is lightning in the wishing well.

He takes hold of her waist, bringing her down from the high speaker. Her chest meshes against his, his hands hold both sides of her face. She circles his wrists, feels his hands and the tiny hair on the back of it. Deeper and deeper it goes, endless takes on a French kiss.

Madre mia...

It is a bold move, this swift shift from meditation to expedition.

Though they are fueled and ready for takeoff, Bobby suddenly pulls the key from the ignition. He ends with a soft kiss on her eyebrow.

He is teasing her.

Ana Lucia opens her eyes, focusing in on the little twitch in his eyebrow. She has super sight. She sees the jump of blood in his jugular.

"You never," he says between heavy breaths, "you never told me your age, Ana Lucia."

"What?"

"How old are you? I mean, yeah—how old are you?"

"Eighteen. I'll be nineteen in a week."

"Wait, you're not...are you still in high school?"

"I didn't complete high school."

That is to say, she never attended school at all, neither in Guatemala nor Spain. Her parents kept her out of school by conviction. Her grandparents, ostensibly out of the same conviction, though more likely out of fear that registering her for school would imply that they had taken on the full commitment of raising her until she finished.

"You didn't graduate? Seriously? How come?"

"I was fulfilling my civic duty." She reaches for his collar, unbuttoning his top button as he stares at her fingers. "I was fifteen by the time all of my family was gone. I had to work. It was fortunate in one way. I met Khadijah through work. You could say she's my Dom, I think."

Bobby keeps watch of her fingers, captivated as they move to his next button. As though her fiddling has an actual aim....

"So, this Khadijah girl is your best friend?" he says.

Only friend, she would say. Except she won't say. Nor will she say that her only friend is a peregrine species, one who garners her intrigue and loyalty but never her full comprehension.

"Yes, she's my best friend," Ana Lucia replies. "We haven't known each other since childhood, but we are alike. She moved here to Madrid in 1972, just a few months after I did."

"You weren't born here?"

"Central America. I was born there. Yes." Her eyes spotlight his protruding Adam's apple. It brings to mind a baby bird as he stares at her. "Khadi's from Morocco. Her father was a government official, so she received an ultra-proper education. She learned English, French, German, philosophy, science—all the subjects—from private teachers. There was an attempted coup to overturn the government in 1971, so her father moved the family out of fear. That's the ancient tradition of war and government—to displace."

Ana Lucia is immediately embarrassed by the look of awe her words inspire from him. She feels like an imposter, having synthesized her readings from the summer of '76.

"Anyhow," she continues, "a great deal of prejudice exists against Moroccans here. She's treated pretty awful most days. In her father land, she could have bought and sold most of the people in this city. But she never says who she really was...or is. That's what I love about her."

"See, that—that's what gets me about Dom too. He was always, like, the smartest kid in the class, but he was never a show-off, you know? In a way, Dom was, you know, displaced by war and government too. That's what brought us together. His brother Francis got killed in Vietnam a week before we met. It's weird, you know. I—" He hesitates. "The first time I met him, I just knew I'd spend my life for him."

Ana Lucia looks down at her own fingers. She has stopped fidgeting. "I don't understand."

"Don't understand what?"

Ana Lucia's eyes dart to the tiled ceiling. There is a word for it, for dual attractions; she can't bring the English word to mind, though she once read about it in an issue of *Time* a tourist left at the bar.

"The two of you are not...*you know*, are you?"

"Not what?"

"You're not—I don't remember the word. Are you—"

"Are we what?"

"*Una pareja.*"

"*Una pareja?* You mean gay?"

"Yes. That."

Bobby looks up, rubbing his chin thoughtfully, then deliberates. "I don't think so. I mean, as far as I can remember, no." He grins broadly, a departure from his soft, subtle smile. Grasping her wrists, he pulls her forward so that her forehead rests against his. His lips brush hers as he speaks. "But in case I am, will you be my disguise?"

Ana Lucia grins. "What do you suppose I've been doing this entire time?"

She reaches forward to feel the vibration of his Adam's apple as he laughs. It has the pulse of her propeller fan at home.

In this stance, his kiss becomes imminent, like frog preparing to leap from prod. But he doesn't leap; he murmurs.

"When are you going to let me see you?"

She looks away from him, in time with the flicker in her gut. "You see me now, don't you?"

"I mean, see you acting. I want to see you in a show. You know what they say about seeing the girl you like doing the thing she loves, don't you?"

"No, I don't."

"I don't either. But you are the girl I like, so...incidental fact, I guess."

She grows a little faint with pleasure. He makes little words so big.

The notion that *like* may reign supreme to *love*—it is a concept which hits Ana Lucia with a lusciousness as ardent as anything she ever learned from a book. Love is effectuated by obligation. Like is an indulgence. Possibly the sweetest indulgence.

"Seeing me in a show isn't possible right now. I don't have anything coming." Ana Lucia's fingers desultorily return to his buttons. "I've never had a show coming. Acting is really just a wild dream, a wind I haven't even begun to chase. I don't have training. I have no experience. Just desire."

He is quiet. Disappointed, she imagines.

"I like this song," she says when he begins to suddenly hum to the music. Though not untrue, her statement is a floundering attempt at nothing. An attempt *out* of something perhaps.

And yet, her words have hit an unintended target. He makes his way to the record player, delicately lifting the arm from the record. He wraps the record in a brown record sleeve before returning to her.

His voice is unusually amplified in the quiet room. "You have a record player, right? Here, take it."

He holds the record out for her, as though offering a paper-bag school lunch.

She receives it with the understanding that she will prop it up on the windowsill in her bedroom, stare at it, and think of him.

At least, until she can afford a record player.

The thing Bobby hated about the New York punk scene:

There, he became the teenager he'd never been in high school, the teenager who abided by one decree: in whatever you do, never appear as though you're trying.

Feigned nonchalance was key to survival on The Bowery.

In some ways, it seemed rock 'n roll was becoming a countercultural autocrat, not the mystic savior he'd imagined it to be since he'd first heard "Little Wing" and pondered for weeks what kind of magic a man had to practice to make a single guitar sound like three.

Still, Bobby and the band were bound by the law of the land. They restricted themselves to forty-five-minute shows with twenty songs, the crappiest sound systems available, and a ready answer for inquiries about what they did for a living: "We play for a shitty punk band."

Listlessness was law.

But today, Bobby has recovered his resolve to be glaringly intentional. Ana Lucia will know just how much he digs her. For the first time in a long time, it's time to give the appearance of trying.

When he arrives home, Bobby is surprised, though not soured, to find Betty sitting on his bed for the third evening in a row.

She balances a wig on the tip of her index finger, combing through it meticulously. Three more wigs lie on the bed beside her—a black, a blonde, and a green one.

"You're still here," Bobby says, quietly setting his house key on the dresser beside the high stack of Naive's own recorded tapes they pass out after every show.

"Indeed I am. But I can go if you'd like. Dominic will let me stay in his room if you are opposed to another night. You have only to say the word, Young."

She meets his eyes quickly before returning to the primping of her wig.

Bobby picks up the black wig, taking a seat beside her. "Stay." He begins running his fingers through the wig, taking out the snags with sharp crackles. "It looked like you and your boyfriend were doing alright."

"I plan to keep it that way for as long as possible. We love each other best by avoiding one another. Not for long stretches though. We're somewhat addicted to each other, I'd say."

Bobby stops to glance at her. He marvels at how she appears simultaneously older and younger with deep, violet circles beneath her eyes but fuller cheeks without her usual burgundy blush. Her skin is the color of a seashell, dotted by a few small acne blemishes. Her blue irises float liquid in sterile whites.

Bobby looks down at the wig in his own hands, disturbed by where her cotton candy pink lips were earlier this evening. He feels guilty for her cluelessness.

"Carlos is my greatest strength and my biggest vulnerability, you know?"

"I guess that's love."

"Only to someone who's never loved before. Love isn't an addiction. Love makes you free. Real blessings don't come stocked with curses, you see. That's what Mama Warner used to say anyway." She stops to look over the condition of her wig. "I think ye lads will get along fine when ye do your language exchange. Carlos is quite the encitin' soul. Just one thing he's got going against him: he's a fecking guard."

"A what?"

"A fecking gu...a policeman. He's a policeman."

"How old is he?"

"Twenty-five. Why?"

"How old are you?"

"One hundred and forty-five. Why?"

"Because, because—" He abandons his reply, his finger caught in another tangle in the wig. "Hey, look, I need a favor."

Her eyes turn to him, inspired, naughty. "What kind of favor, Young? You have a hankering for my favors now?"

"Not a favor, just a suggestion."

She wears candidly her disappointment. "You're gonna tell me or need I guess?"

"Do you know any places around here that give, like, acting classes or theater or something like that?"

"No."

"You didn't even think about it."

"'Course I didn't. I don't think acting's right for you. You don't have that thespian spark."

"You don't even know me."

"Nor you me," she says. "Yet, you're asking for favors so soon."

"Look at it as a trading of favors."

Her eyes squint at him in a burlesque expression of enmity. "Give me three days. I'll find you something...ya little gobshite."

8.

FROM TIME TO time, Bobby thinks about the idea that his virginity wasn't taken or lost.

It was fixed.

Fixed by a girl named Joy, who laughed when his cousin Kyle made that same tired joke about Bobby showing up late to his deflowering ceremony. Not to worry, she said, Joy would fix it. Red-headed Joy—Savannah-born, ready-and willing hostage of The Punk Scene since 1977—"fixed" him on her polka dot couch. Afterward, she raved about his performance with such Southern hyperbole, he was pretty sure he'd only done an average job. He promised to call, but he was sure neither expected him to. They didn't exchange numbers.

Being with Joy taught him how easy it was to drink the water and forget the glass. Though he had a few more drinks after her, his Catholic conscience never let him get away with the kind of compartmentalizing that insisted some girls were for a man's heart and others for his body.

He never found out Joy's age nor her last name, though he was pretty sure she was in her mid-twenties—just young enough to excuse taking the virginity of an eighteen-year-old, while old enough to be a little embarrassed by it.

Betty exudes the same elusiveness concerning her age. Bobby figures she is older than him, but how much older, he can't really be sure. Still, he has made up in his mind that there will be no "fixing," despite how silkily she unravels his annoyance with her and despite the fact she sleeps in his bed bare-chested for the next three days.

Nevertheless, Betty does convince him that she is a kind of fixer. Aside from lining up two more proper venues for Naïve, she offers Bobby three additional fixes:

First, she finds for him the theater class he requested. The class is scheduled to begin the first of February and will continue twice a week through June. Not a bad deal for the money, Betty says. Still, it's one half of the money his mother sent, gone in a flash.

He recovers after seeing the amazement in Ana Lucia's eyes when he hands her the class syllabus as an early birthday present.

The second thing Betty offers is her departure.

"I'm going on my way now," she announces unexpectedly the morning of her eighth day staying in his room. She holds a plastic bag bloated with clothes and wigs over her shoulder, like some Davy Crockett sojourner. "I'm going back to the boyfriend."

"Are you gonna be okay?" he says groggily from the from the floor where he has slept every night for the past week.

Betty purses her lip, then turns from him. "Have fun in your acting class. You never know who may cross your path, eh?"

After she walks out, Bobby notices she has left a long black wig on his bed. He picks it up and twirls it on his index finger, half-smiling at how intentional she is in leaving her mark.

The following day, Betty makes known her third good deed, calling the apartment to say that she has arranged for Bobby to meet with her boyfriend Carlos for their first language exchange the following Monday.

They meet in a small bar in La Latina. In the orange bar light, Carlos's hair is chocolate, his eyes more apple green than brown. He has a full beard—he is a *real* adult. His lips are relaxed.

"Hello, I Carlos," he says, reaching out his hand to shake Bobby's.

Despite his initial fear of meeting with Carlos, Bobby is quickly pacified. He may have a friend in the guy. And not just because Carlos abates his nervousness with an English worse than Bobby's Spanish. Between all his mismatched conjugations, Carlos is something of a comedian in his native language.

The next day, Ana Lucia laughs as Bobby relates Carlos's jokes to her as best he can in Spanish.

It is afternoon, a half hour before Ana Lucia must arrive at work. The China blue sky hosts puffs of cotton clouds as the couple sit at an obscure rooftop restaurant in La Latina. Dry plants scale the half-walls. A Polaroid camera hangs around Bobby's neck, his auxiliary companion for the afternoon. He hopes that pictures will offer him the thousand words they promise. He hasn't written a decent lyric since New York.

Since leaving the apartment, he's only taken pictures of the winter-brown ferns and the passing cars on the street three stories down from the ledge.

When he begins stuttering out his order to the waitress, Ana Lucia takes over and orders the *menu del dia* for him, her Spanish flowing like water—*ensalada de casa, paella (sin carne, sin mariscos),* and *platano (no chocolate, por fa).* And a bottle of wine that neither drinks but instead take turns quietly spinning as the other speaks.

Bobby stares at her sparkling teeth as she laughs, turned on by the notion that she sees from greater heights than he does, that she knows heaps more than he does about a million things. He is further aroused by the fact that despite the weight of her knowledge, there is something he could give to her so heavy she would lose every thought in her head...if she'd ever let him.

Bobby holds in his hands his pristine copy of *Moby Dick.* Ana Lucia's copy is falling apart at the seams, most of the pages held in place by her tight fingers.

He stares at his perfect book and lights a cigarette. She has read the first five pages to him, though he has stopped her twice to recount a story of his meeting with Carlos.

Now, she looks up at him to confirm that she can continue on with reading.

He nods.

As Ana Lucia reads, Bobby stares at her mouth. Her canines protrude slightly. She's got Joan Baez teeth. His eyes move up the side of her face. Her earrings are mismatched, one large and square, the other a silver triangle. He wonders if she knows. She must. She knows everything.

"You ever been with a guy, Ana Lucia?" he asks.

She looks up from her book. "I thought I was with one now."

Bobby laughs. "No, I mean, like, have you ever—you know—*made love* with a guy or whatever?"

"I haven't," she says. Feigning nonchalance, she pretends to silently read, then asks, "What about you?"

"I haven't done it since I landed in Madrid."

"What about on the plane?"

"What?"

"Nothing. So, you're saying your cookie jar is currently empty?"

He mulls briefly over her cookie jar symbolism. "Yes. Wait, no, not *empty*. Just closed until...." He meets her gaze. "...until, you know."

Eyes falling back to her book, she bites her bottom lip to banish a bashful grin. "So, um, do you ever eat your own cookies, you know, from time to time?"

"That some strange way of asking if I masturbate?"

She smiles broadly, unable to control herself.

"I haven't done it since I left Avon. Didn't do it on the plane either, in case you were gonna ask."

This time, she laughs so loud, the waitress looks at them from across the rooftop.

"It's a pretty lonely practice, if you think about it," he says, taking a drag from his cigarette "If sex is reaching the highest place of unity with another person, playing by yourself—or *with* yourself or whatever—is kind of counterproductive."

"So, what made you close it—the cookie jar, I mean? Reasons of religion?"

"Yeah, that was part of it."

She only nods. She begins sketching on a napkin with the tiny pencil the waitress left behind.

"And you?" he says.

"Me?"

"Your cookies, I mean. You ever eat your own?" He shakes his head, freaked out by how odd the metaphor is starting to sound.

"My cookies are...fresh-baked." She sketches faster, brushing the lines of her drawing with her pinkie finger.

He stops to consider her meaning. "Forgive me, Ana Lu, I got no idea what the heck that means."

"It's just to say that I started puberty late, so I haven't followed an average timeline for sexuality."

"You started puberty late?" He leans forward, absorbed. "How late?"

Ana Lucia flips over her napkin. "You want to know so much today."

The Little Saints

"Case you didn't catch it, Ana Lu Magoo, I want to know everything about you every day."

Beguiled, her cheeks awaken to shimmering gold. "Sixteen years old," she says. "You can draw your own conclusions from there."

"Interesting."

When she looks up from her book to see his reaction, he is sucking on his top lip, his eyes lifted to the clouds.

"Is everything okay?"

"Copacetic," he says, folding his hands in his lap. He brings his gaze back down to her. "It's just—I don't know. You starting puberty late is kind of a turn-on. Like, everything you have is brand new or something."

She pauses briefly, then begins reading out loud again, sheepish. Cute.

"Should I stop now?" she says suddenly.

"What? No, no don't stop. I'm paying attention. Promise, I am." He reaches for another cigarette in his coat. "I just think this Melville guy's writing style is hilarious, that's all. This dude had to be a real joker back in his day."

"The book wasn't published until ninety years after his death. He couldn't find a publisher for it during his time."

"Seriously?"

She nods.

"Guess there's no guarantee for artists, huh? All depends on who the gods are at the time."

"Does that give you fear?" she asks.

"About my music?" Bobby turns his face, to think and to funnel his cigarette smoke toward the rooftop ledge, away from her. He stops to consider if she should know how deathly afraid he is of being unknown. "I don't know. Maybe. I probably keep myself too busy to realize I'm afraid. What about you? Are you afraid?"

"Afraid of what?"

"Of not making it?"

"Not really."

"Then you have faith, Ana Lu. Even if it's not faith in God."

"No. I don't think that's it."

"What else could you call it then?"

"I'd call it—" she holds higher the book in her hand "—a story. *Moby Dick*. We should return to it."

She doesn't look at him to confirm this time. She simply continues:

Consider the subtleness of the sea; how its most dreaded creatures glide under water, unapparent for the most part, and treacherously hidden beneath the loveliest tints of azure.

She stops abruptly, closing the book.

"I want to say, there *is* one thing that I'm afraid of," she says.

"Yeah? Tell me."

"I'm afraid of succeeding at something— at *anything*—and having no one to be proud of me."

Bobby is wordless at the statement. The song suddenly playing in his head—a Marvin Gaye song—is the only thing he really wants to say: "Come Live with Me, Angel."

Come, be with me, Ana Lucia; You'll be proud of how proud I can be of you.

Before Bobby can reach for her hand, she pushes back her chair and stands. "I should go. I'll be late if I don't leave for work now."

Bobby breezily flicks away his cigarette stub and reaches for the camera hanging around his neck, directing it up to her and snapping a candid photograph. The camera quickly spits out the picture.

"What did you do?" she says, reaching for his camera from across the table.

He pulls the photograph from the exit slot and begins waving it. "I don't know what you speak of, Ana Lu. Now give me a kiss before you go, will ya?"

The corner of her mouth swerves up, amused, shy.

Bobby encloses her hand in his, gently balling her fingers into his palm. "Hey, you ever kissed a boy before?"

"What would you call the other day in your rehearsal room?"

"I'd call it me kissing you. That day *and* the first time."

He stares at the picture, the white cloud of the Polaroid fading. In it, Ana Lucia's pink mouth hangs open, surprised. The camera flash has achromatized her skin, presenting her olive as ivory.

"So, um, you ever kissed a boy before?"

"Have you?"

Bobby laughs, fitting the photograph into the inner pocket of his coat. "Don't be late for work, Little Lu."

Ana Lucia brows raise, clearly bewildered by how easily he backs out of the conversation. She stands. Bobby turns over the napkin she has sketched on, staring at what seems to be a snake. The snake is bleeding from its eyes, though the sketch is so abstract he can't be sure. She quickly grabs the napkin from him and places it in her pocket.

She bites her lip, smiling. "I have to go now."

He watches her walk toward the exit, wishing there were no other patrons so he could feel free to snap a picture of her backside. He turns his attention back to the picture in his hand, though the sight of her beautiful bottom is still printed in the space behind his eyes. While his mind swims in take after take of her posterior silhouette, she is suddenly in his lap, having made a bold turn from the exit and back to him.

Bobby notices the meagerness of her hands as she holds his face between them and dips down to meet his face with an uncertainty so naively sexy, he'd happily trade all of twenty-six-year-old-Joy-from-Savannah's patient, detailed first-time instructions for Ana Lucia's simple exploration.

With her lips, she contemplates his hairline, the taut skin at the underside of his jaw, the slopes on either side of his nose. She is a creative genius.

She makes him wait in trembling for her lips, for her tongue to do a sea dance with his. She's good—*so killer good*—at this. Would that he could eat her up.

This is the moment he realizes consciously that he needs to have sex with her. Not as a passing thought, not as pondering of what could be, not as the frivolous business of his imagination. No, no. Being with her is now a necessity, something without which the future loses its color. From this point forward, he knows the feeling will be with him perpetually, like white noise, like oxygen in his blood.

As soon as he comes to the realization, Ana Lucia backs her face from his, pride making her lips tense and trembling.

"I've kissed a boy," she says with an inebriated sing-songiness to her voice.

He smiles, pulling his lips inward to lick them, to taste her one more time. "Yep, you have. I'm proud of you."

A

I'm proud of me too.

9.

DURING THE FIRST five, maybe six, closet episodes, Ana Lucia cried quietly in the closet, tears crawling out between her fingers as she breathed in spurts. The greatest terror came not from the darkness itself but rather, from not knowing when the episodes would begin. Or end. In this way, the old adage failed—ignorance wasn't bliss.

In time, pride did its good work in her. She began to see herself as the heroine of a Brothers Grimm fairytale—she resolved not to let the evil grandparents win. She made her own Rules for Survival, practical skills for staying alive until the great arc of her tale arrived.

Ana Lucia grew strategic, imagining herself to be a miniature spy. During her free time outside of the closet, she made clandestine, fidgety-eyed trips to the closet, storing away cookies and biscuits inside her coat pocket which hung inside. She managed to also keep hidden away a finger-sized flashlight in a pair of old, brown loafers she kept in there. After replacing her grandmother as the house cook three months after her arrival, Ana Lucia felt safe hiding her grandmother's black sauce pan and its glass lid behind an empty brown box in the closet. She used it as a port-a-potty, squatting over the pan when necessary and covering it with the lid when she finished. The lid was the genius part, really. Dying by the inhalation of one's own fecal matter seemed too dismal an irony. It would be accidental suicide. There were better ways to die. She'd learned as much from her parents.

Time passed and her body grew slowly—by age fifteen, still no menstrual period, knobs for breasts, hairless as a sphynx cat.

Where her hips did not expand, her mind did. If the mind could flourish, all things were still possible. Nothing that could be perceived could be perceived without the mind. Feeding her mind became the crux of her method for survival.

And so she needed books, more books than the ones she arrived with in Spain. She would get them however she could.

She would have signed up for a library card if her grandmother hadn't confiscated her passport the first evening of her arrival. She'd briefly considered stealing books from the library but didn't want to risk getting caught.

So instead, Ana Lucia stopped by the used bookstore in Malasaña each time her grandparents sent her to the supermarket. She quickly learned to bargain shop so that she could use the leftover change to buy a different book from the bookstore each week. She wasn't much interested in Spanish literature. She was sure Spanish novels were entertaining enough, but they didn't have the power to transport a girl the way English-language novels did. She trained her eyes to spot English words in the rows of Spanish novels on the shelves. If she searched hard enough, she could usually find one, sometimes more during the summertime when tourists donated their English books to the store.

She bought the books no matter their condition. Ripped covers, sticky edges, urine-colored pages. For what they contained, they may as well have been gold-plated. After handing the bookstore keeper a shaking handful of pesetas, she stuffed the books into the slit she'd cut in the inside lining of her winter coat.

From time to time, people on the street would ask why she wore winter coats in the summer. She ignored them. All that mattered was that her grandparents never asked for receipts or counted their change.

Ana Lucia's books stayed in the lining of her coat until she was sent to the closet. Each time she grew excited for the treasure she had buried for herself. The English words skyjacked her imagination, bathing the pitch-black space of the closet in technicolor movie scenes—ol' Huckleberry Finn lazing in the woods with Jim, reading about kings and dukes and earls and the like; Laurie stomping off to the river and angrily rowing his boat away after Jo so stupidly rejected his proposal; Rose meeting Troy on the front porch of their house, ready to speak to him after six months of silence. The readings all made her feel so *American*, as though she was the product of the greatest nation on Earth, where free speech wasn't a crime and free thought wasn't a luxury.

Ana Lucia grew fixated with the creations of her own brain, wishing she could find an efficient way to keep her little flashlight on while simultaneously holding a notepad and a pen.

Outside of the closet, her grandparents addressed her without ever using her name. It was a courtesy she extended to them as well. She didn't know what she would call them anyway.

It was better that they didn't address her as though they knew her. They had no idea about the mind that danced or the feet that deliberated before entering a room.

Not counting the times she whispered to herself in English to make sure that she kept her English sharp, Ana Lucia was mostly quiet. Still, she was never invisible to the eyes of a man who wanted see what he could control, to prove to himself that he still had a voice, though it had been silenced through the years of slave labor in Franco's political prison.

Her grandfather was one of those men who grew old in an ugly way, not with a welcoming burliness and jolly laughter. He made clear to her that he owed her nothing and that she should count it a mercy that he did not force her to attend school like the other poor, brainwashed adolescents. He further "blessed" her by allowing her to sit as his feet as he recounted his early years in the Confederación Nacional del Trabajo, when he warded off the constant threat of Franco's regime. He also recalled the days in prison camp when he was chained to five other men and after twenty hours of work, was forced to sleep standing up, still chained to his fellow prisoners. He claimed that the only language the Franco regime spoke was blood. Had he been smarter, he would have learned their language earlier. He would have armed himself with a rifle and blasted the heads off a few of Franco's guerillas. He'd had friends who'd done it, and they were sent to execution with the kind of glory which doesn't spread far and wide but is immortal to all those who hear of it.

It seemed to Ana Lucia that as eager as her grandfather was to teach her, he was even more eager to rule her.

Remove the hair from the drain
Clean behind the stove this time
Wipe the throat of the toilet in the morning
More Jack now

The latter request was rarely spoken; he simply jingled the ice in his empty glass. Even if it were a possibility, Ana Lucia would never have denied him the request for more liquor. The hard brown stuff was the only thing that filled the gaping hole in his soul, the only thing that made him sometimes clasp his hands over his globose stomach and laugh.

At times, she almost laughed with him, imagining herself sticking a pin in his abdomen and watching him sail away like a wild, deflating balloon.

Ana Lucia wondered if that was how young slave girls entertained themselves, serving their masters. It was fair to think of herself as having some kinship to young slave girls. Her ancestors on her mother's side—the Garifuna—were taken from West Africa as slaves, though, to be fair, they were never *actually* slaves. Besides that, slavery was outlawed in Guatemala in 1823. One hundred and fifty years seemed like ancient history to Ana Lucia, though she wondered if any practice could really be considered ancient which hadn't been dead for as long as it had been alive.

She sometimes considered the idea that her father could have been her mother's master if the Spanish ship that carried the Garifuna slaves hadn't shipwrecked, the survivors narrowly escaping two hundred years of slavery.

Truly fate was giving her parents a coy wink, for anyone who knew them couldn't deny that it was her mother Katina who did the owning in their relationship.

Several times in the closet, Ana Lucia imagined what her parents' first meeting must have been like. Her father Javier, having recently completed his post-graduate teaching internship at the University of Chicago in 1960, moved to Livingston, Guatemala on an abolitionist's mission. Javier regarded as slaves the functionally illiterate, those who could have no say in democracy for their ignorance. Javier had left Spain while his father was still in the labor camp, taking with him Luis Rafael's radical ideas and mingling them with the burgeoning American counterculture.

Ana Lucia liked to imagine her father's awe upon meeting twenty-one-year-old Katina in that small coastal town that held every shade of *negro* from bagel to indigo. Katina Moreira—a Garifuna with skin the color of an acorn, who not only knew how to read and write Spanish and Garifuna, but had such a penchant for business that she alone had kept thriving her parents' beachfront restaurant for the two years since their passing.

Ana Lucia believed that they had met in that restaurant, when her father Javier came in for a drink after a long day tutoring ten-year-old boys. He hadn't expected to find a proper Garifuna celebration—costumes, congas, coladas.

Surely Javier had fallen in love watching Katina dance punta in her flowing white skirt and white head wrap. The magic of punta was all in the educated motion of the feet, in how a subtle scamper of the heels could make the whole body vibrate. Javier studied Katina's sage hips and genius bottom as they rolled, knowing that it was true—dance was a perpendicular expression of a horizontal desire. Oh, how watching her must have brought an incurable fever to his blood, a temperature so high it kept him in delirium long enough to approach the most beautiful woman he'd seen in his life and ask her for the chance to get to know her. Just a chance.

Una oportunidad, ya está. Nada mas, princesa.

Just one walk on the beach, to the tune of the remote Primero and Segundo drums. He got to know her fast and got to know her well, for eleven months after meeting, Javier and Katina welcomed Ana Lucia into the world.

Javier integrated quietly into the Garifuna community, as quietly as a Spaniard could. Being a linguist, he mastered the Garifuna language in a matter of months, which enhanced the pursuit of his mission to educate the dark illiterate of the region. He was, for all intents and purposes, a blue-eyed, sable-haired Garifuna. And so, Ana Lucia always considered herself singularly Garifuna. She even made a nine-year-old's solemn promise to never abandon her roots after watching *Imitation of Life* to advance her English; despite having inherited her father's skin-tone, she would never betray her mother and her people like foolish Peola.

The promise was sincere, but Ana Lucia thought of it very little by age fifteen. She couldn't afford to fight for her life inside the closet while simultaneously fighting for racial identity.

Instead, she focused on other memories of Javier and Katina. They were a philosophical pair. She remembered once hearing her father tell her mother that it was quite possible that this life was simply a dream, that in our supposed death, we would be awakened to a body that had been in suspended animation for the span of our lifetime—just a few seconds in the dream world.

This theory ever-present, it became exceedingly difficult for Ana Lucia to determine what was real—her dreams, her memories, her readings, or the world outside of the closet. Perhaps they were all real in some way. In other ways, none of them were.

The part of reality most confounding was Ana Lucia's inability to tell day from night during the closet episodes. Darkness became the light in constant blackness, like the exception that swallows the rule. Darkness became her womb.

Except that time in May of 1976, when the light cut suddenly into the darkness like an ice-cold blade. The closet door flipped open, and her grandfather stood on the other side, his orangutan belly taking up most of her vision as she sat crouched on the ground beside her books.

"Stand," he commanded.

She stood.

"Where is the money?"

She said nothing.

"You'll answer me."

"You'll answer him," her grandmother said. Her voice came from behind Luis Rafael, his body a thick wall between grandmother and granddaughter. "Where is the change from the grocery store?"

"I lost it."

"You're lying," her grandfather shot back. His monster stomach moved closer to her. "Tell the truth. For once in your fucking life, tell the truth!"

She did not answer, *refused* to answer for the guerilla ghosts he spoke to.

When she did finally speak, she managed, "I don't want to—"

I don't want to be afraid of you. I don't want to find my only satisfaction in boiling tea water for you in the same pot I shit in. I don't want to pray for your death so often as I do.

Should He exist, I don't want God to ignore me anymore.

"—don't want to make you angry." She said the words fast enough to avoid vomiting on them. "If you give me time, I can—"

"What did you buy with the money?"

As if his eyes were guided by The Accuser himself, her grandfather's gaze settled on the pile of three books by her foot.

"Books," he said assuredly.

He immediately turned from her, walking off and leaving her to gaze upon her grandmother. Ana Lucia observed her grandmother's tired face, soft lines drawn across papery skin, her silver hair tucked into a bun so tight, it seemed to smooth out the lines on her dove-white forehead.

Ana Lucia's gaze was shaken loose from her grandmother at the sound of a first gunshot. She would learn later that he had shot the living room vase. The flowers exploded through the air and landed quietly on the floor as though a wedding had taken place.

She hadn't time to move before Luis Rafael showed up with the pistol pointed at her in the closet.

"I speak blood," he said. "Don't you know that I speak blood? I told you already. I told you!"

That's when he shot. Shot three good times, fire exploding from his pistol, hitting his target with assassin precision. The sound was so loud, it was all she could think of before she realized that she hadn't been shot dead.

Instead, her grandfather had killed the books.

He shot holes in them, the pages bursting out like confetti in smoke. The shrapnel from one bullet grazed her ankle, though she did not feel the pain as she bent over to frantically examine the books. Her grandfather stomped off.

For the first time in front of her grandmother, she cried, curled her wasting body over the books, protecting what was left of them. She cried for the attempted murder, for the partial-draining of her life blood. She cried, afraid of what he might do to the remaining books if he found them.

Accustomed to the madness, perhaps encouraging it for the guild—Ana Lucia's grandmother had one thing to say to her as she mourned the loss of those three printed worlds.

"Let him be. If you don't bend to him, he will break you. And who will know about it?"

The words stopped Ana Lucia's weeping, her wailing smothered by truth.

She realized then that she was a little tree in an empty forest. Take an ax to her root, timber!, and—

Silence.

Should her grandfather murder her, no one would report her death, for there was no one around who knew about her life. It was the scariest thought conceivable for Ana Lucia—to die unknown to the living.

Still, she was fifteen then. It wouldn't be too much longer before—

10.

AN ANONYMOUS SAVING GRACE keeps Ana Lucia generally sane, except in those moments when, like a searcher's flashlight in the murky forest, the reality of what happened comes to mind. In those moments, her chin falls toward her chest, her eyes close, and she shakes her head, as though waiting for a cold headache to pass.

Today, her chin is raised. The theater class Bobby signed her up for begins in a matter of minutes.

Ana Lucia walks in the simple university classroom and notes that she is one of only five students. At nineteen, she is the youngest in the class.

The teacher is male. The recessed lights ahead create a spotlight on the porcelain skin at the crown of his head. His name is Pedro Ramirez.

His speech is rubbish, really. His lisp makes deciphering his greeting a translation pursuit. Ana Lucia is able to determine that he wants them each to sit in one of the gray chairs that form a circle in the center of the room. With fairy waves of his hands, Pedro stands outside of the circle giving scattered details of what they will do in the course—something about executing improv exercises, preparing for short plays, and learning proper stage etiquette. He warns that it will be an accelerated course. Ana Lucia fears that if the course moves as fast as his speech, she may be unqualified for it.

As she ponders these things, Pedro speaks with sudden clarity. "I know that I have fooled many of you with such vernacular," he says. "It is my hope that my students also shall become masters of foolery. In which case, I will have done my job well. In these months, you will not become masters of theater, but I trust that you will understand the dynamics of metamorphosis, the art of becoming what you never thought possible."

A smile rises inside of Ana Lucia. This is where she belongs.

Pedro soon affords the students the opportunity to introduce themselves.

There is a man named Jose Martinez. The other man introduces himself as Franciszek Jez. He wants to be called Jez. There is a brunette named Lucinda, a red head called Paula.

When the blonde's turn comes to introduce herself, she smacks her maroon-stained lips before resolving to a Duchenne smile. "My name is Skylark Warner. Ye can call me Lark."

Another smile rises in Ana Lucia. She can still recognize English-language accents when she hears them. Skylark Warner is Irish.

Ana Lucia arrives home to find a gift sitting on the welcome rug outside of her apartment. It appears to be a ceramic cast of a panda bear. When she kneels down to pick it up, she finds that the head is detachable.

It's a jar, filled to the brim with an assortment of fresh cookies.

Tagged to the inside of the panda bear head, there is a handwritten note.

Can't get my mind off cookies now.

It's all your fault, Ana Lu.

Yours,

Bobby

Ana Lucia grins, carrying the cookie jar to her bedroom and rummaging through the sweets as she sits on the mattress. She chooses a peanut butter cookie first and takes a bite, looking blithely out the window.

Her eyes dart to the floor. There lie the canvases she had intended to destroy this morning. The oil painting of the woman and the bloody forehead. The one with the man whose guts billow out of him stomach. The woman whose brains bleed from her temple. All the works of her hands.

Her eyes turn back to the window. The light mist outside turns into a slow rain.

She blinks as the clear rain drops change to scarlet. They fall sluggishly down the window, thick drops of blood. It is raining blood.

She closes her eyes, hoping it will go away in an instant.

It won't.

Ana Lucia tastes the blood in her own mouth. It is as sweet as the peanut butter cookie. It coats her throat as it goes down. She begins to cry tears of blood. They slide swiftly down her cheeks, runny as dye.

Oh, the blood that was shed—the blood that once covered her hands, that once spray-painted the car window. Oh, the blood! The never-ending blood!

Ana Lucia's chin falls to her chest. She need only wait. This image too will pass.

11.

AT THE START of his third language exchange with Carlos, Bobby recognizes he will shortchange his partner this go-round. Carlos would probably be better off talking to the bartender, who speaks decent English from a year spent in London. At least, he could listen to Carlos, offer some corrections. Bobby cannot.

Unable to arrest his thoughts, Bobby follows them as they dart off in every direction.

He remembers the simple message Ana Lucia left on his phone last night.

"I can't talk, really," her quiet voice said. "The class was good. I was hoping you could tell me what a Skylark is?"

He called her back to tell her that a Skylark was a cool car. It was around one in the morning, after he'd arrived home from Naïve's third show of the week.

"A-hoy, this is Bobby C. Am I on the air?" he'd joked when the phone picked up.

"Who the fuck is this?" came a male voice on the other end. Though it was an Arabic accent, the English was impeccable, regal even.

Bobby's stomach dropped. "I'm—my name is Bobby Carter. I—"

"Who are you, I said. And who are you calling for at this hour?"

As the man began suddenly calling out to someone else in Arabic, Bobby hung up.

It was a right number, Bobby was sure, but he wouldn't chance calling it again to confirm it.

He lay in bed pondering whether Ana Lucia had moved (no, she liked him more than that), had a Saudi boyfriend (well, she *was* more private than any girl he'd gone with), or if she lived with a relative (was she, like, half Arabic?).

He'd only called her to hear her voice, but he had planned to tell her about how he'd screwed up the show that evening when someone threw a lollipop on the stage and hit him in the eye, causing him to tumble off the stage. It was mostly true, except the falling off the stage part—that was just to get a laugh out of her. Six weeks knowing her, and he'd say just about anything for that laugh.

Plus, he'd formed a list of questions that he would find some clever way to insert in the conversation.

How was your day? *Did-you-miss-me?* What side of town did you grow up in? *How-did-your-parents-die?* Have you ever been in love? *Do-you-ever-have-the-kind- of-wild-thoughts-about-me-that-I-have-about-you?*

"How is America?" Carlos says, scattering Bobby's thoughts like dust.

"I'm sorry, what?" Though he has been staring at Carlos from across the little wooden table the whole time, he hasn't *seen* him. He has almost finished his pint of pale ale. Bobby hasn't touched his own. He hadn't planned to. Carlos insisted on treating him to one.

Carlos laughs. "I say, how you like America? Es good?"

"Oh, well, um, yeah, I like it. Maybe-maybe you and Betty could go there one day. She said—" He stops, staring up at the bizarre Victorian bed lamp hanging over their table. "You should go. If you ever want."

"Why you madru—" he searches for the English word. "Why you move here?"

"I don't know. Just wanted a change."

Carlos nods, pensively closing his bottom lip over his top. "How much you know about Betty?"

"Not much."

"You know she come from Ireland?"

"Yeah. But *she* didn't tell me. Her accent did."

Carlos takes the last sip of his ale, amused. "I give you fear, Bobby? Betty tell you I'm—*como se dice celoso?*"

"Betty didn't tell me anything about you. She doesn't—we don't talk. Not really." Bobby wonders if liars also stutter in Spanish.

"Bueno, Bobby, you should ask her why she come here to Madrid. Her history es...es incredible."

"How do you mean?"

"She has no family anymore. They all...they die."

"What?"

"She come here to forget them." Carlos pivots in his chair, calling for the bartender's attention. "Excuse me, hombre, I have question. How you say *celoso* in English?"

"Jealous," the bartender replies in an offbeat British accent.

"Yealous?"

"*J-j-j*ealous," says the bartender, kindly correcting that baffling J.

"Ah. Vale. Thank you." Carlos turns back to Bobby. "Betty tell you I'm jealous man?"

Bobby coughs, attempting to clear the apprehension from his voice. "Not really. We don't really ta—"

"I'm not jealous man. Her problem is she have no trust, poor girl. I love her a lot. Big, big love I have. But she don't feel it. Why? Because I'm police. Police kill her family."

"What?"

"I'm police. *Policía.* How you say that?"

"No, I mean, you said the police killed Betty's family? Why?"

"Why? *Oof...*good question, friend." He rubs the hair on his chin. "Religion. Always religion."

Carlos points to Bobby with his finger held out in the shape of a pistol. He slams his opposite hand down onto the table to simulate the firing of a gun.

Bobby flinches, his full glass of ale quakes. The pound has sent a shudder through the table that vibrates from his wrist through to his funny bone. The awful tickle climbs up and down his arm and back, even across his chest. The rattling feeling stays with him for the rest of the exchange, as though something has physically entered inside of him.

Something like a parasite.

He wonders if the feeling will go away. One thing he knows: the shaking won't move unless he moves.

Bobby stands. "I'm sorry, I should go now."

The shaky feeling is still there the following evening as Bobby sits alone in the living room. He watches his fingers tremble on the arm of the couch.

He is convinced of one thing now: he is the only one in the world who hasn't been displaced by war or government or...or anything. He has moved here on his own accord.

He has had one oddity in his life—his father was the stay-at-home parent after he retired from his work as a traveling salesman. Yet, even this so-called switching of gender roles was becoming fashionable.

None of the greats had fashionable beginnings, forget about easy lives.

Lennon's father ran off to be a merchant at sea before he was even born.

Johnny Cash was so poor he had to work in cotton fields before he landed a record deal.

Elvis and his family lived in a one-room apartment in Memphis.

Last year, schizophrenia had taken out Donny Hathaway when he jumped from the fifteenth floor of the Essex Hotel.

In his whole life, Bobby has suffered two cavities. Maybe he would have broken a bone if he'd been interested in football like Willie Nelson. No wonder he can't write a decent song.

The ringing of the phone interrupts his thoughts. He walks to the phone, weary.

"How was your acting class?"

"Betty?"

"Tell him what he's won."

Bobby smiles softly. "Hey, look, I want to catch Dom before he leaves the house. If you want the wig you left, I can give it to you next time I see you. I gotta go now."

"The wig is yours. How was your acting class?"

"I didn't go. The class was for somebody else. I really should go now."

"A girl?"

"Yeah."

"Must be quite the lass. What's her name?"

"Marcia Brady. Catch you later, okay?"

Bobby hangs up the phone, watching his shaking hand vibrate against the receiver.

As he enters Dom's bedroom shortly after ten, his mind has returned to his *Leave It to Beaver* life and he wonders if it is possible to absorb someone else's pain.

Dom sits shirtless on his bed, preparing a joint. "What's up, Bobby C?" he says.

Bobby approaches the edge of his bed. "Just wanted to talk to you. The pink light's been on like every night. Thought I'd catch you when I could."

A faint smile flickers at his mouth. "Nothing compared to you and that Ana Lucia chick. You're gone even when you're here, dude."

"Well, I'm here now. Completely here."

"Yes, you are," Dom says. "Have a seat, young blood. What's on your mind?"

"Nothing, really. Just...you ever think about Francis?"

Dom sprinkles herbs into the paper for the next joint, seemingly unruffled. "There's not a moment I don't. Why do you ask?"

"I don't know. I was just wondering what you think about when he comes to mind or whatever."

"Sheesh, dude, I don't know. Vague shit. Just how he was."

"You ever think about how he would be now?"

"Not really. I don't like thinking about that." He fastidiously rolls the joint strip. "What makes you ask all of a sudden?"

"I just never did. I care though." Bobby looks from Dom's busy fingers to his sapphire eyes, then adds softly, "I care a lot."

In that moment, a stout silence hovers over them. Bobby remembers the pictures he saw of Dom's brother Francis. He was tall and curly-haired like Dom with a rowdy grin. Bobby always imagined Fran as the type who could never get his fill of telling raunchy jokes, playfully throwing footballs into the backs of little kids, and waxing cherry red cars.

Dom licks the edge of the joint strip, sealing it. "They decapitated him. The Vietcong did. With an ax. That's what the medical examiner said. Probably took more than three blows to completely sever it. They never found the head though. Dad and Mom argued about whether to cremate him. Dad wanted to. My mom couldn't do it. She wanted his body intact. She couldn't understand how God was supposed to resurrect him with his body in ashes."

Bobby nodded. Having named her two sons after the two great thirteenth century Saints, it was no surprise that Mrs. Russo's thoughts were continually on the World to Come.

"My father ate her fucking head off for bringing up the idea of the afterlife. He was all like, 'If there is a heaven, I hope Fran never sees it. Who would want to spend eternity with a God who'd let this happen to His own children?' They started screaming. He called her a fucking bitch and everything. That was the first time I ever heard my folks argue. Can you believe that?"

"Dude..." Bobby touches his neck, awed by the dew and the warmth of his own skin, of his own life.

"There were days, you know, when I used to have this anticipation for him like he could still walk through the front door. When I lost that, I knew he was gone for good."

"When did you lose the anticipation?"

"Last year, I think. Somewhere in there."

Bobby's hands go cold and wet against his warm neck. Shame. Shame. Dom had lost his brother shortly before they met, and Bobby hadn't considered the tight jar of secret pain he kept in the center of his chest. He hadn't considered how full that jar was, hadn't asked about it.

He had yet to seriously contemplate Ana Lucia's secret jar, the one she must be keeping for her dead parents.

Dom laughs to himself. "You know, Fran used to take me out to the shed by the woods near our old house in New Canaan. We'd just sit there for hours shooting the shit. He used to chew tobacco like a fucking horse. He'd been doing it since he was fifteen, and Mom fucking hated it. But whatever—he was Francis and he always told me he couldn't be anybody but himself. Anyway, this one day, we were sitting there in that shed and it was raining like a bitch, and he just randomly goes, 'If I'm ever not here to tell you this, I'm telling you now: Live your life for you, Domino. Live it for you and only you. Happiness is the end-game.' I was only, like, eleven—he was seventeen then—but he already thought I was too much of a punkass about everything. Especially when it came to Mom. He was probably right."

Bobby closes his eyes. That feeling has hit him again—that transcendental awareness he had about the new kid Dominic Russo the moment Sister Katherine Thérèse introduced him to Bobby's sixth-grade class. He'd give his life for the kid.

"The love doesn't die, you know," Dom continues. "It's God's trick. Love is everlasting, but people aren't. That fact is smack dab between a blessing and a curse."

Bobby opens his eyes, dazed by his words. Dom limply holds a joint in his hand, his eyes wet. There is something so soft about him now, it seems as though his skin will bleed at touch.

The parasite is stirred. Bobby holds his hands together to keep them from shaking.

"Anyway, Bobby C," he says, casually sniffing and wiping at his eyes, "let's go get something to eat. I'm not planning on depressing you anymore tonight, no matter how bad you want it. You don't need my pain. You'll get your own soon enough. Everybody does."

La Primavera

ربيع

Le printemps

Earrach

Bamvua

Spring

B

I wonder:
How love makes you lazy and hyper
all at once
How it makes you want
to reach for the stars and gaze at them,
all the same

Te quiero—

It is to say,
I love you
It is to mean,
I want you

For me, For once
Those Two meanings
Are One

And the Same

A

The old fear is dead
Or perhaps sleeping
But static
All the Same

That old fear of nonexistence,
Gone
Gone now because I see you
Seeing me
And I exist

Losing my breath and my brain,
I consult My Heart
She is not yet misspoken
She teaches me how to touch you

The Little Saints

She shows me how to absorb your touch
How She loves to play!

This Heart of mine, She is made of glass
—a goblet overflowing
Rose Wine
My faith in Her has billowed and bloomed
—how brave, My Heart!
This faith is losing its cutting edges
This—this is the faith you give me.

El amor y la fe son iguales.

12.

MARCH HAS COME.

Ana Lucia's hair is bob-length—it grows like a weed. Bobby likes to wind his fingers through it like jute. She would be lulled to sleep by his fingertips on her scalp, if not for the solar storm glow in her heart that causes anxiety at the thought of missing a single second of him.

For all of what Ana Lucia finds to be a typical punkness he advertises, Bobby is gorgeously domestic, using an old T-shirt to lick up the dust on the table and floors, setting up a small space heater to keep them warm in the rehearsal room at La Fábrica. He brings scratchy blankets and lumpy pillows to put together pallets on the floor for reading, for watching movies on the projector, or for listening to music on the record player. It is also their private space to recount their days—Bobby's steadily-increasing shows and Ana Lucia's acting classes. Ana Lucia brings with her stories of the girl named Skylark, who brings with herself more impulse than talent, most days flapping around like a weather vane in a tornado. From Bobby's exchanges with Carlos, he brings new Spanish phrases and jokes.

In one of their times together, Bobby brings Ana Lucia a long, black wig. He doesn't explain where he got the wig from but says maybe she can use it to help get her into character one of these days.

She smiles. Maybe she will use it.

When they aren't talking, they are listening to the albums Bobby brought from home, to songs once banned in Spain. Her favorite is *Just Like a Woman* by Bob Dylan. She is impressed by the words, though Dylan's voice brings to mind a slow train whizzing past corn fields. Roberta Flack also sings the song, her voice cool and woody like the inside of a Spanish guitar. It makes Ana Lucia feel as if the voice is coming from within herself. Robert Plant's voice crowing about the land of the ice and snow comes from without, like a shooting star. Ever-allegiant to his punk sensibilities, Led Zeppelin is Bobby's guilty pleasure.

Today, *Willy Wonka and the Chocolate* factory are background noise as they continue their reading of *Moby Dick*.

Bobby lies on his back in the middle of the floor, hands behind his head, as though bathing in the sun. Leaning her back against his propped-up knees, she sits cozily Indian-style upon his stomach. He shifts from time to time, his body rocking from side to side like an overpowered canoe, but he swears he can handle her full weight on his diaphragm.

Ana Lucia holds up the book for him to read out loud. His is still in mint condition, the smell of its pages exciting her with the remembrances of bookstores—stewards of all the worlds and universes she'd ever know.

When he reaches the end of a chapter, she says, "Are you paying attention to what you're reading?"

"Sure am, baby."

She laughs, staring lovingly at the bit of extra skin beneath his chin she can see only from this position above him. The skin folds like dough when he smiles wide.

Ana Lucia pokes her finger into his little chin fold. "Did you call me baby?"

"Yep. Hope that's not too Casanova for you, sugar," he says, still grinning with squinted eyes, as though truly staring at the sun. "Anyway, I've been thinking, maybe you and me should go out to sea together."

"To Melville's sea?"

"Well, yeah." He shifts, tipping the canoe again for comfort. "I can't stay here much longer."

Her fingers go cold. "You can't?"

"It's not that I don't want to," he says, taking her hand and concentrating on her fingers as he plays with each one. "Or maybe it is. I feel like my time is up here. I feel it deep in my soul, you know. Like how I felt in New York. I just knew there was no more sand left on my side of the hourglass."

Ana Lucia looks up at the projector screen. She sees the taffy colors of Willy Wonka with overcast eyes; the toddler giddiness they brought is gone.

"On top of that, my visa's expired. I'm officially an illegal alien."
He laces her fingers through his. "But I've been thinking on it. We
should leave together. I have enough money for both of us to take a
plane to Italy. We'd have to figure out the rest after that, but I heard
it's pretty cheap to live there and you could basically go to the mom-
and-pop pizzerias and they'll give you their leftover food for free. So,
it isn't like we'd starve."

"And for shelter?"

"Tee Pees. Like the Indians, you know? Me and my dad made
one once. It doesn't take a lot of material, just skill. The weather's not
bad in Rome. My mom spent a year there before college. Plus, if you
speak Spanish, it won't be so hard to learn Italian. When we get
there, we could—"

"Bobby?"

He gazes at her with bird-bright eyes. "Yeah?"

"You're a little—how do we say it?—*chalado* today, yes?"

"Got no idea what in the world you said."

"Chalado is to say 'crazy.'"

"Hmmmm..." He pseudo-ponders the meaning, a grin on his
face so lazy he looks as though he might fall asleep. "They say it
makes you a little...chalado."

Her stomach bucks. The taffy colors are loud again as she
contemplates the "it" that makes him crazy. "What will you do about
your music if we followed your crazy plan?"

"Who knows who we could meet? I mean, maybe there'll be a
big-time director there, and he'll want you for his movie. He might
hire me to do music for your movie. If nothing else, the inspiration of
just being there would be worth it. You could take your sketching to
the next level. I mean, Picasso started there, right?"

"Picasso was from Spain."

"Yeah, I know, but—" he pauses. "From Spain? Really? I must've
just assumed that name was Italian. It sounds a little Italian, doesn't
it?"

"Are you searching for turbulence, Bobby?"

"Turbulence? Not really. Just some kind of upset to the daily
routine."

She would have said, "*Tranquilo*, Bobby. If life is a cruise ship
for you, you shouldn't wish for a battle ship." She would have
explained that her life started by the sea of Livingston. She would

have told him all about the sea and the things that the sea brings, that it brings sharks, not whales. And sharks only speak blood. If you don't speak it too, your own will be poured out like mop water in backyard grass.

She would have explained this to him, but she couldn't. Just couldn't.

"What do you *really* want, Bobby?"

Bobby closes the book and lifts himself up, still holding her against him when he is on his feet. He slides her down himself like a pole, kissing her mouth quickly.

"I don't know what I want," he says. "I just wish I could play you one of my songs and it would really mean something to you. The way *Subterranean Homesick Blues* made me want to, you know, really get born or whatever. I mean, I was late to it—heard it for the first time when I was thirteen—but it makes you realize that there's got to be something more to do here than just exist. Nothing I ever wrote could do that for you. For anybody, really. The thing is, you can't really give what you don't have. There's never been anything to talk about on Easy Street."

"Easy Street?"

"Where I've lived my whole life."

"It's in Avon?"

He laughs faintly. "It *is* Avon."

Bobby turns away, walking over to the projector to put his fingers in front of the lens, shadow puppets showing up in front of a slobbering Augustus Gloop. She fears for a moment that he might be gearing up to leave.

"You should play me a song?"

"What do you wanna hear? You ever heard of The Who?"

"I want to hear you." She smiles, brave. "Your voice is the only one I ever want to hear, really."

For humility's sake, his eyes alone smile. He produces a piece of gum from his pocket, pries her mouth open with his thumb and index, setting it on her tongue. It's strawberry flavored.

He goes thumbing through the pages of *Moby Dick*. "You don't have any brothers and sisters, do you? I mean, if you did, you would've told me about them, right?"

"No to brothers and sisters. Yes to other question."

"That's something we have in common then."

"Honesty?" She smiles, willfully dense; she can deflect as well as he can.

"Being an only child," he returns, meeting her contrived doltishness with a humored shake of his head. "My mom had me at forty. She couldn't really have any more after me."

"My mother would be forty now."

"No kidding? How come your parents didn't have more kids?"

"I think they believed they were doing the responsible thing for an overpopulated world."

Being alone for as long as she has been, Ana Lucia is sure it was the least responsible thing they could have done.

Yet, now, in some strange way, Bobby has become a brother to her.

Bobby weaves his fingers through hers. "Ana Lu, guess what?"

Having begun blowing a bubble with her gum, she simply raises her brows.

"I have something to tell you."

Her brows raise higher as she blows the bubble fatter.

"You already know what it is, don't you?"

She shakes her head, the bubble dangerously large. The Willy Wonka candy-laden wooziness is in full effect.

At the moment Ana Lucia is sure that the bubble can't gain anymore surface, Bobby quickly moves his face forward, popping it, splattering the sticky, rubbery gum all over the center of her face. Immediately, he begins clearing the gum off with erotic kisses. He moves down her face until the slow skim of his teeth on her neck works in quiet agreement with his hand sliding around her waist. Hoisting her up, he drives her to the wall behind them. When her head meets the wall, Ana Lucia is hemmed but unfettered, ready and willing to be consumed, to be eaten up like Veruca Salt's monstrous lollipop.

Bobby's desire rises for her like a periscope from beneath the water. To Ana Lucia, it seems his erection is rising like its own separate entity. In this way, she feels like a snake-charmer.

As he holds her face to keep her as his, she wonders if he has any control at all over what his body does. She considers what would happen if they stayed kissing this way all night. Would the "periscope" eventually slip back under the water?

With the same autopilot absence, his knees bend up and down while his faintly quivering hands toy with the button on her jeans. Her body throbs and clenches. She wonders if it's normal, this kind of delicious pain, like a rush of water pushing through a valve, threatening to burst the pipe. She is aware that Bobby—this vessel of hot blood and warm-honey breath—is the only one who can empty out the pain. The thought of his piercing through her tension throws her into a frenzy. Charging closer, she pulls his waist to her, braiding her body to his as tight as she can.

Guilt soon checks her excitement.

The fact is, Bobby has been an open book. She has not. He doesn't really know her. He can't. She hasn't told him the one thing he needs to know about her.

Tragedy the Second.

Ana Lucia closes her eyes, attempting to pull her attention away from the guilt and place it back on his thick lips that take her neck like a ripe peach. It is a wonder, how sex—the magic, unknowable rune—will be a reality in a measurable time. More of a wonder is how bold and unafraid she is with him as her fingers cling to his hair and her mouth moans.

Yet, most persistent is the prattling prosecution in her head, despite the fact he has begun unbuttoning his own shirt.

He doesn't know her. He doesn't know about May 21st or the person she was that day three years ago. The person she was that day has not shown her face since, but is likely swimming through her blood like a latent virus.

Should Bobby know about who she was or what she did that day in May, his fingers wouldn't be prying to pull down her jeans with an eagerness to know what her inner flesh is like. He would know it is not warm or wet or soft. It is dry, cold, hard. Unflinching at the sight of death. He doesn't know that. He doesn't know *her.* Making love would be a lie and she, the liar.

"Bobby, I," she pants in his ear. "I need to—I have to—"

Before she can make out the words, there is a ferocious blast, a sound that seems to shake the room with the same ferocity of her grandfather's gunshots in the closet. The prattling of the prosecution in her head is quieted by the blast. The sound echoes down her spine.

When she opens her mouth to speak—to react—she finds she cannot.

Bobby has only reached the third to last button of his shirt when he begins tugging at Ana Lucia's jeans.

"Bobby, I," she pants in his ear. "I need to—I have to—"

Her words are punctured abruptly by a blaring sound from the room next door. Ana Lucia freezes. Bobby jumps but settles down at recognition of the sound.

"It's okay," Bobby says quietly through his lapsed breath. He looks down at his hand curved around her side. Through hormone vision, the skin of his hand is Super 8 grainy. Still out of his mind, stiff but floating, he swallows down the bubble gum he has lapped off of her skin.

Her face, though stricken from the blaring sound, has never been so pretty in his estimation. Her lips are ruby, thoroughly worked and worn.

He angles his face down to hers, cheek to cheek, whispering in her ear, "There's this other band that rehearses in the room next door sometimes. Their amp is really sucky. Sounds like World War Three every time they turn it on."

Her eyes hardly move. Her chin soon drops to her chest, ashamed for what was about to happen.

He takes a single step back from her, embarrassed. "I hope you're not, like—was it, you know, too much or whatever?"

She says nothing. He looks down at his yet insistent erection.

Bobby slinks away, easing a cigarette out of his pocket and rebuttoning his shirt. He leans against the large speaker as he lights up and looks at the projector screen; the Oompa Loompas are shining the golden geese eggs.

"I know you probably won't believe me, but I wasn't trying to fu—" he blows out a swirl of smoke "I wasn't trying to make love or whatever. Not here like this. I respect you. A lot."

With her face still pointed down, all the eager blood of Bobby's lower region rushes to his face.

"It's not that I don't want to." He scratches his forehead, embarrassed. "I want to more than I ever have in my whole life."

Bobby coughs. He imagines that the pluck of a harp would give proper texture to what he's been practicing how to say for the past week.

"Listen, you're like the first thing I think of in the morning and the last thing at night," he says. "You—you're the thought behind every thought. I mean, you can tell that, right? You can tell that I—"

That I love you, he would say. He would explain how a priest once told him that if he could see everyone the way God sees them, he would worship at their feet.

I think I see you the way God does, he wants to say.

But he won't say it—he can't. Not with her still standing against the wall unmoved.

"All I want to say," he starts, "all I want to say is that I wasn't trying to get you to do anything you don't want to do. I think, you know, to show you how I feel about you, we should be, you know, married and stuff like that before we—"

In fantastic irony, Veruca Salt is singing that she wants *it* now. He laughs to himself, approaching Ana Lucia and linking their fingers. "Man, that girl is annoying, isn't she?"

Her only response is the rise and fall of her chest. Defeated, he releases her hand.

Her arm doesn't fall to her side. Instead, it hangs in the air like a swanky department store mannequin.

Bobby's eyes widen, his breath jumps. "Ana Lucia?"

Her hand remains a pendulous branch, the fingers slightly curled, as though his touch has molded her like candle wax.

Bobby takes her face into his palm, turning it up to him. Like her hand, her face stays in the position he moved it to. Her eyes subtly flicker. She is still there on the inside.

He thinks of his mother, how she handled her clients. He will put away himself and imitate her now.

He wrests her shoulders. "Ana Lucia, can you say something? I'm gonna find a phone, okay? Don't worry. I'm gonna take care of you."

He pushes back his hair, trying to recall the Spanish emergency number, when suddenly, her face lifts. She blinks three times.

"Ana Lu," he says.

She watches her own arm as it moves down to her side, seemingly mystified by her control over it.

Her eyes roam the room, her mouth agape. "I need—"

"What do you need?" He reaches for her face. "Tell me what you need, Ana Lu."

"I need to go home."

She steps forward, allowing his hand to fall from her. She walks past him, not turning once to answer his questions that follow behind her

B

Please
Come back, I need—
I need to hear from you.

A

You can't hear me?
It's a wonder
Sometimes I'm so hollow,
I echo like a gong.

13.

BOBBY HAS FOUND that the best way to stagedive is to jump, not fall. There is better insurance for one's life that way.

Today, he decides to fall. Backwards.

He has never loved anything like he loves the crowds that catch him. He once had to explain to his mother that this is how strangers become family.

Kyle and Dominic continue playing, as Bobby is passed through the crowd, his guitar strapped to his chest, the microphone in hand. The shower of bright Par Cans shrouds his vision like the Northern Lights, giving the illusion that he is floating through space. Yet, like a stone he sinks into his own thoughts until he hears his own singing as through a glass door.

Every free moment since the incident, he has argued with himself over whether Ana Lucia's sudden paralysis was a single event or an ongoing matter she's kept hidden. He would have asked her himself but he couldn't find her at home or work. There is one other person he knows he can consult for reliable answers, but he is in no mood for a four-hour conversation. His mother would ask every question she could think of, predict the worst for his "little friend," ask him whether he wanted to really get himself involved with this girl—a question so belated, annoyance would swell his chest like fast-rising dough.

Therefore, Bobby ponders alone Ana Lucia's paralysis. If it was a singular event, perhaps just a mis-crossing of otherwise functional wiring in her brain, the moment might be something they could laugh about some day.

Or not. Whatever the case, at least they'd be able to move on.

If there is something more permanently wrong with Ana Lucia, it would ruin the whole love endeavor.

No, no. It wouldn't ruin it. Nothing could ruin it.

If something is wrong with Ana Lucia, he'd have to help her. He'd spent most of the last eighteen hours imagining what form this help would take, keeping himself awake with absurd visions of himself emptying bed pans and taking midnight temperatures. No question about it, love would no longer be free; it'd be anchored down by obligation. It'd be fantastically strong but indisputably shackled.

Surfing over his audience like this, their hands propelling him along like a sea current, was normally a reliable way to forget the real world. Right now, it is no way to forget Ana Lucia.

Or love.

Love makes him sigh restlessly at show's end, as he walks out of the venue with Dominic, Kyle, Betty, and Carlos.

Betty is atypically punk this evening, in jeans and a loose white blouse. Her brown wig is straw-straight with blunt bangs that nearly cover her eyes. She is matching Carlos's reserve.

Bobby holds his hand to calm it. Every thought of Ana Lucia moves the perennial quiver in his hand to his spine, makes him want to jump out of his skin and leave his whole body behind. He's never missed a girl so desperately that he was so terrified to see.

He stuffs his rock-cold fingers into his pockets, as Betty and Carlos lead them from the venue. They weave through a maze of outdoor restaurant tables with umbrellas and steel chairs. Bobby looks down at the various women at those tables, so similar, sitting crossed-legged and lackadaisical, some tipsily rubbing their shoulders against their companions. Laughter pours out from the open doors of the tiny television-lit bars on the narrow lane they pass down. The lane finally opens up to a larger square of restaurants.

"Carlos has never seen a stage dive before, have you, love?" Betty says, sauntering between Carlos and Bobby. Dom and Kyle are their bookends. "He thinks you are a god, Young."

Carlos glances at Bobby, almost suspicious. "You not have fear when you do that?"

"Sometimes I do."

"Then why you do it?"

Betty pinches Bobby's arm. "Fear ain't a good enough reason not to, am I right, Young?"

"Yeah," Bobby replies. "Yeah, you're right."

That settles it. He'll go see Ana Lucia as soon they leave Betty's apartment.

"But if the arm break or the leg break, what you do?" Carlos asks.

Betty laughs. "You mean like the guitar strings he broke tonight. Three guitar strings in one night, Young. You're setting records."

Bobby smiles, looking down at the cobbled street and fingering the coiled, broken guitar string in his pocket.

"You give no answer," Carlos insists. "What you do if you break the leg? Or the head? What you do then?"

"I don't know. Just have to pray it never happens."

Hardly satisfied with the answer, Carlos offers him a cigarette as a barter to keep the conversation aloft. "But if it do break?"

"Then it's over for Jimmee The Youngster," Betty says. "He can't go to the hospital. Unless he wants to get deported. How do ya feel being an *imigrante ilegal?*"

"We close to your place or what?" Kyle interjects. "Shit's a lot farther than what you said, Betty."

"Quit your olagonin', will ya? The flat's right there." She points to the four-story, beige-stone apartments stacked above a row of bars.

Kyle's complaint isn't one of tired feet; it was a question of how long it would be before he got to the hash Betty had promised with a special assurance that Carlos keeps dope for days, despite his being an officer of the law.

Soon, they are inside Carlos and Betty's small living room. To Bobby's surprise, it is neutral, pleasant, hygienic even. There is a green accent wall, a pear-colored couch and ab ebony end table from which whirls of smoke rise out of a glass of cinnamon incense. Standing at the end of the room is a winding staircase, winding like Jacob's Ladder up to who-knew-what.

While Dom stares curiously at a skyline painting on the wall, Bobby looks down at the cigarette between his fingers. It remains unlit. This morning he promised himself that he would give up smoking for Ana Lucia, in some way bargaining with God to keep her in his life.

"I'm going to change out of this shit," says Betty, halfway up the stairs, already unbuttoning her blouse. "I'll grab the hash too."

Dom, still quietly focused on the skyline painting, says, "Nice picture."

"Yes. Betty make it by her own," Carlos says.

Kyle lights up a cigarette. "So, Betty Bo Peep can paint? Whod've thunk it?"

"Hey, can I use your bathroom?" Bobby half-smiles at Carlos. "Dónde está el baño?"

"*Claro.* Come, I show you."

He leads Bobby up the winding staircase. There are two rooms at the landing, the bathroom immediately at the top and an apparent bedroom to the left of it. Carlos heads into the bedroom with Betty.

Inside the bathroom, Bobby pees as quiet as he can, planning what route he will take to Ana Lucia's house when he departs. As he washes his hands, he stares at the three condoms lying at the corner of the faucet top. It reminds him of the urge to release that has been sitting inside him like a little coal burning him numb.

And if the quiet urge isn't enough, Carlos and Betty are teasing his libido with the carnal sounds coming from their bedroom. Bobby sighs, shaking his hands dry.

Outside of the bathroom, he finds that the sounds are not the end-song of ecstasy. Rather, they are an opera of rising tension. Betty and Carlos yell in Spanish, a Spanish too involved for him to understand and too intense for him to do anything other than quietly descend the stairs.

"What's up?" Dom asks, meeting him at the bottom.

"I'm not sure," Bobby answers, looking down at Kyle searching through the car magazine on the coffee table. "You can probably make it out a lot better than I can."

Dom walks up to the center of the staircase. "Sounds like he's pissed about us being here," Dom whispers, looking back at Bobby. "He doesn't want to give up that much hash. Plus, I guess he's mad about the clothes she's changing into. He's threatening to kick her ass if she doesn't change. Shit, dude, this is so...*stupid.*"

Bobby and Dom stiffen at the whip crack of palm against skin.

Dom skims his top lip with his teeth. "What are we gonna do?"

Kyle looks up from the magazine. "Stay the fuck out of it is what you're gonna do."

The Little Saints

Bobby immediately concedes that perhaps his cousin is right, but it's all negated by the fact that Kyle has no soul.

They flinch at the next rumble and roll which makes the ceiling tremble.

"We gotta do something," Bobby says, starting back up the stairs. "I mean, we can't do *nothing*, right?"

"Stop trying to be a fucking hero, Bobby. Sit your lily-white ass down."

"I'll go with you," Dom says, his gaze travelling to the top of the stairs.

At the door of their bedroom, Dom turns the knob, letting out a shaft of gold light and tentatively peeking in. Bobby pushes the door open completely, his eyes sweeping the room in snapshots.

A curiously unruffled queen bed in the center of room.

Betty's wig beside it like a large rodent.

A baggie of desert-sand colored hash on the dresser.

A scarlet accent wall, ominous.

Crouched against the wall is Betty in mismatched bra and panties. Carlos hovers over her, his hands falling from her neck as he looks back at Bobby and Dom. His fingerprints on her neck linger, violet bruises between blushing red and white skin.

Betty wipes at her nose, smearing blood across her upper lip.

Dom intersects the awkward quiet. "Hey, dude, what are you doing?"

Bobby steps over to the other side of the room, wedging himself between Betty and Carlos. He examines her neck with his fingers, astounded by how soft she is.

"No la toques, puta madre! She okay. You listen me? She okay. You go."

Bobby ignores Carlos's noise, directing his words to Betty. "We're gonna go now. You should get your stuff. Stay with us for—"

Carlos wrangles the back of Bobby's shirt like a leash, the collar stitching coming apart like the sound of a zipper. "You listen me?"

Carlos jerks Bobby up from the floor and wrestles him onto the bed, pinning him down. The obstinacy of his muscle weight outrivals Bobby's height. He blinds Bobby with a sucker punch to the eye.

The pain shatters any logical thought in his head until he can only hear Betty's cries as she marches over to Dom and shoves him. "Why are ye in here? I told ye I was coming back down!"

"Bobby's trying to protect you!"

"Get out of my way, you feckin' ape!"

As Dom and Betty's feuding grows more frantic and adolescent, Bobby and Carlos fall off the bed to the floor. At landing, Carlos's hands circle around his throat, choking Bobby until he begins to gurgle.

Tossing Betty aside, Dom grabs Carlos's shoulders, snatching him off of Bobby. As a shoving match ensues between Dom and Carlos, Bobby rises to his feet.

He watches Carlos deliver punch after punch to Dom, pushing him out of the room to the top of the staircase. Dom wobbles, gripping the rail to keep balance.

Betty claws at Bobby's back as he rushes to Dom's aide. With beastly instinct, Bobby curves his arm around Carlos's neck in a choke hold.

In an attempt to loosen himself from Bobby, Carlos pivots violently.

Bobby does not see the fall, for his eyes snap shut in fear. Instead, he hears the potato-sack tumble down each stair of Jacob's Ladder.

With a siren scream, Betty flies down the stairs to where Carlos's body lies across the two bottom steps like a roadside deer.

Bobby and Dom watch wordlessly as Betty tends to him. Bobby's eyes focus in on the milky white flesh of her curling stomach as she crouches down beside Carlos.

Supporting his head with the palm of her hand, her blue eyes flare up at Bobby. "Biggest mistake of your life, Young. Biggest mistake of your fucking life."

 ───⊙❨⊙❩⊙───

Betty's chronic sense of melodrama keeps her from saying that Carlos isn't actually dead for what feels like a full ten minutes as she lies over his motionless body as though hugging a casket. During this time, Bobby begins basic calculations of the money and time it will require to buy two same-day plane tickets back to Connecticut and convince Ana Lucia that if she leaves for America with him today, they can straighten out later the logistics of starting a life there.

The incomplete calculations remain in the back of Bobby's head an hour later as he, Dom, and Betty sit around their kitchen table in

Lavapies beneath dusty orange lighting. Betty wears the white tank top and green corduroy miniskirt she threw on as they rushed out of her apartment forty-five minutes ago.

Kyle stares at them weakly as he leans back against the kitchen counter, offering his commentary through puffs of cigarette smoke. Bobby is surprised Kyle has yet to congratulate him for nearly killing someone in this here fight, his first ever real-man fight.

Dom and Bobby turn circles around the same ring of logic, launching into litanies about how righteous and inevitable what they did to Carlos was.

Just righteous.

"Where we're from, guys don't do that to women," Bobby says, staring at Betty's neck, the once plum-colored bruises having darkened to rotten-apple brown.

Kyle snorts. "Right."

"They do it," Dom adds, "but they don't get away with it."

"Like you'd know," Kyle mumbles, another ghost swirl of smoke floating out of his mouth.

"Not if anyone sees it. It's just—"

"It's fucking wrong, is what it is," interjects Dom. "And letting a girl get beat up—it's bad church."

"You wanna know bad church?" says Kyle. "Bad church is how you're about to get your ass banned from Spain. That's if anybody can even bail you out of jail."

Anger, like a hot billow of smoke, inflates Bobby's chest. "Could you just shut up? Please."

Kyle's own anger rises, then sinks. Quietly scooping up his pack of cigarettes from the counter, he smirks. "Have fun figuring out your lives, kiddies."

He heads out the kitchen, leaving them with the sound of his bedroom door shutting.

"Let's call the police, tell them what happened" Dom says. "They can straighten it out."

Betty lets her head fall heavy into her hands. "He *is* the police. Or have ye forgotten? This ain't the land of the free and the home of the brave. This is Spain. Do ye not realize that democracy and justice are infant concepts here? Ye really think ye'll have an iceberg's chance in purgatory of gettin' out of this one?"

The boys' eyes fall to the table in quiet musing. Bobby thinks back on the rushed choice they'd made an hour ago to anonymously call the ambulance before jetting out of Betty's apartment. It was all Betty's idea, really. Nothing was broken that they could tell was broken, she'd said. He was as good as sleeping, she'd promised.

"Well, there are two things that are certain," Betty deliberates. "Number one, I'm going to have to move in here with ye until I can find something for meself. I can never go back there."

Bobby and Dom exchange quiet glances.

"Oh fuck the both of ye, ye selfish eejits! It's me who just lost the one person I've been able to depend on since I moved to Madrid."

"He doesn't love you. A man who does this doesn't—"

"How thick are ye? *I'm* the one who told ye that he doesn't love me. And I don't love him. Not every relationship is about love."

"You said two things were for sure," Dom jumps in. "What's the second thing?"

"The second is that Young here had better find a place to go. When Carlos wakes up in the hospital and gets his wits about himself, he's going to talk to his police friends and they're coming after ye. Don't ye doubt it."

"Just tell them the truth, Betty, that Carlos was beating you and Bobby was only trying to defend you."

"Shall we have this conversation once more for fun? There will be no justice for the American tourist who's tossed Spanish law enforcement down a flight of stairs. To top it off, the truth may have worked for a legal resident. Illegals aren't shown the same mercy."

Relenting to her cynicism, Bobby asks, "So what do I do?"

Betty's response is chopped by the violent knocking at the front door that turns their eyes to saucers. Bobby's heart begins a stampede.

"First thing you do is get out of here as fast as you possibly can

Sylvia Plath asked it first on paper, so Ana Lucia doesn't consider herself a great philosopher when she wonders out loud if there is no way out of the mind.

She has learned that while there are several ways to flee the body, the only time an innocent soul can escape a tortured mind is when death at last clips the thread of life. Then again, who could even confirm that?

During her episode with Bobby the other day—the sixth of that kind that she has experienced in the last three years—there was a semblant detachment from her body, yet there was no disengagement from her mind. She could see Bobby, his movements, his pretty mouth speaking words of what seemed to be love, a love that made him too nervous and pink to express it clearly. In her own mind, she was reaching a hand out to cup his face, to ask if love had made him so blind that he couldn't feel her anticipation for him in every moment. Yet, her reaching for him was happening too slowly for Bobby to perceive it. She just needed a minute to take back possession of her body. A minute or ten—she wasn't sure.

He thought she wasn't there. But she was. It was just—just that her tongue was locked, held down by some invisible monster that had entered like green vapor shortly after *Tragedy the Second*.

"I'm here, Bobby," she'd wanted to say. But her tongue was too slow. So, she'd repeated it in her head. *Here. Bobby, I am. I am here, Bobby. Am Bobby Here. Am I here, Bobby?*

Ana Lucia cried the whole night through after the episode. The seal was broken, and all of the ugly madness had come oozing out like infection.

She couldn't speak on the illness with certainty. She'd diagnosed herself a few months ago with the help of Khadijah, who'd read her an article in French about the disorder. It wasn't schizophrenia. Not narcolepsy. In French, it was being referred to as *maladie du pays*.

Ana Lucia can hardly pronounce the phrase, let alone explain the term to Bobby in English. She knows she is incapable of explaining to him how she exhibits symptoms of shell shock without explaining the war she once fought.

Now Ana Lucia sighs as she turns over beneath her blanket at two in the morning, considering what can be done. She wonders if she has the strength to maintain silence on the matter, leaving the situation suspended in mid-air like her arm had been that day. She'd have to bear never speaking to Bobby again.

She turns over once more, and her doorbell rings. Whether by instinct or process of elimination, she knows it is Bobby. She is thankful for the good monster that takes over, the one that won't let her avoid answering.

Bobby stands at the door, hands tucked into his coat, black sunglasses shielding his eyes the way they had the first night she'd met him.

In an unexpected turn, fear flies away in an instant, birds moving to the warm South.

Everything is okay.

His face makes it okay. She has become so accustomed to that face, it is like looking at her own reflection. Her own reflection in the noonday sun.

"Bobby."

He brings his face to hers, nipping her lips for a single molasses-drift kiss. The kiss is a parenthetical statement, an aside from the former chaos. She feels his thick sigh on her cheek; it seems he hasn't exhaled since he last saw her.

"Are you okay?" he asks quietly, taking a small step back from where she stands hugged against the doorpost. "I've been three seconds from losing my shit all day. Tell me you're alright."

She nods, the mixture of his body heat and the cold from his leather jacket making her thankful to feel any and everything right now.

"What happened?"

"It was nothing. Really. It happens sometimes when I don't get enough sleep. It's happened since I was small."

His eyes glow. "Why did you run?"

"Embarrassment."

"Are you lying to me?" He holds his arm up against the doorframe, further encompassing her in his hot-cold cloud.

She looks away. "Why would I lie?"

Bobby blinks, evidently unsure what to do with her answer. "I don't know."

Her lie hangs over them, its presence palpable but not visible. In the end, he can't prove she's lying. And he won't try. As with all her evasiveness, he's still waiting patiently for her to let down the drawbridge from her princess tower.

Bobby takes a step back, his face abruptly distressed. "Listen, Ana Lucia, I-I need to know, will you marry me?"

She half-smiles, stepping out onto the doorstep in her make-shift night gown, a green dress printed with dragonflies. She watches his bemused glance at her neon pink socks.

"This feels like déjà vu," she says. "I think those were some of the first words you ever spoke to me."

"I'm not joking this time."

"You were only joking the first time? I'm wounded"

"*Wou*nded."

"What?"

"The word's pronounced *wounded*," he says. "Like, uh, like with a double O. The word you said, wound, is like—it's the past tense of wind."

"Oh."

"Listen, Ana Lucia, I need you." He pushes up his sunglasses, revealing a racoon-ring around his eye. "I would never ask you for something this big, but I have to. I could go to jail, I could leave this country, but I can't leave you. I thought about it, and I just can't do it."

"You confuse me."

"I don't mean to. I'm gonna tell you. Just—I'm gonna tell you everything."

And so he does, between sighing and nervously pinching the bridge of his nose.

There is Betty, Naïve's manager. Carlos, the Spanish intercambio guy. A beating. An intervening. A fight. A fall down the stairs. An escape. A need to get out of it. If Ana Lucia could just, just...please.

"How did you get out of the flat after you heard the knocking on the door?" Ana Lucia breaks in, her words halting his sudden pacing.

"I jumped out of my bedroom window. Third story. I landed on my hands to brace the fall." Bobby draws up his coat sleeve to reveal his knotted, blushing wrist. "I think it's sprained or something."

Ana Lucia runs her fingers over the bones that protrude like tree roots. "Did you push Carlos down the stairs or did he fall?"

"He fell. I think he fell. Shit, I don't remember. It happened super fast. But it was the right thing, you know? Betty's a pain in the ass, but no girl deserves to be hurt like that."

Ana Lucia stares spellbound at Bobby, still holding his wrist. Her Bobby—her flustered young gentleman, protector of the honor of all womankind. Her eyes move to his free hand blindly pulling his jacket zipper up and down.

"I'm going back to The U.S.," he continues. "I have to go now. But I want you to come with me. We could, like, get married or whatever, and you'd be legal there. We could go anywhere. I mean, we could go back to Central America if you want. Whatever you want, Ana. I'll do whatever you want if you come with me."

"Carlos was hurting his girl? Tell the police that. Tell them he hit you first."

"But, I mean, you don't want to go with me to the U.S.?" He goes pink-faced again. "I understand. You don't know me all that well. I get that. I get it"

"It's not that. Madrid is where I should be right now." She trails off, the words themselves discovering the revelation.

"Marry me here then, Ana Lucia. Marry me now. Tonight."

"Tonight?"

"We don't have to leave the country. I'll be an automatic Spanish citizen if we're married, right? I'll be able to fight this thing with Carlos if I'm legal. And I can be with you. That's all I want. You were like the first thing on my mind when Carlos fell. Can you believe it? I wanted to run away, but I couldn't. Our time's not up yet, Ana Lu. We haven't finished the book yet. We've got at least two hundred pages left in *Moby Dick*." He breathes a quiet laugh. "I just...I feel it in my bones. I feel you in my marrow, Ana Lu. I don't know if you feel it, but I—do you *feel* it?"

Ana Lucia is quiet, considering how to respond to his lifted brows and folded lips. If she has learned nothing else from her years storing food in the closet, it is that what is kept hidden too long spoils. She must tell him that she loves him too.

Perhaps she cannot say it out loud. But she will show it.

Slowly working down the zipper of his coat, she slides her hand inside, settling her hands on his waist.

Magic—the same magic from the first night he held her in the same place.

"This probably won't work," she says.

Along with her, he stares down at her hands on his waist, staggered by her touch. "I know it might not work, but..."

"Okay." She nods quietly. "Okay."

"You alright?" Dom asks, ushering Bobby and Ana Lucia into the apartment. He uses his hand as a visor against the seven o'clock morning sun.

"Yeah. We're okay," Bobby replies, draping an arm over Ana Lucia's shoulder. "Ana Lucia, this is Dom. Dom, Ana Lu."

Dom's eyes are fixed on Bobby. "What the fuck happened, man? Where did you go??"

"I'll get into that in a second. What happened when I left?"

"It was Carlos at the door."

"Carlos? What'd he look like? Did he bring the cops?"

"No, but he was coming for you, for sure. He had this giant, *Tom-and-Jerry* knot on the side of his head. When he found out you weren't here, he just wanted to talk to Betty. Him and Betty talked alone in your room."

"And then what?"

"Not sure. I couldn't hear anything. He didn't, like, fuck her up or anything. They just talked. He left first, then she left, then I left. I just got back ten minutes ago."

"Where'd you go?"

Dom shrugs. "Just went around."

"Oh."

Ana Lucia watches them nod slowly in sync, neither requiring or offering further explanation.

"Well, I gotta use the bathroom. I've been holding it since we left Betty's apartment. I swear, I'll tell you everything." Bobby turns to Ana Lucia. "I'll be right back, okay?"

Bobby trots off, leaving Ana Lucia in a cold little airship with Dominic. His eyes hang briefly on her with the solemn concentration one gives to a serious birthday candle wish. It occurs to her that he might be wishing she would go away. His gaze flees her before he steps quietly backward out of the zeppelin, turning his back to her and retreating down the shadowy hall.

As Bobby stands at the toilet, the sound of his seemingly never-ending stream of urine suddenly intermingles with a swish of water in the bath beside him.

He draws back the bath's blue curtain to find Betty sitting in the tub, her breasts wavering over the water like lined safety floats.

"Betty."

"Young. Give me that towel, will ya?"

She points to his navy towel hanging on the door. Thoroughly addled, he manages to mechanically hand her the towel, angling his face to the ceiling, though the print of the storm-cloud bruise beneath her breast does not dissolve in his mind's eye.

"What's going on?" he asks.

"Could you be a little less vague?"

"Dom said you were gone."

"I was. I came back an hour ago. He wasn't here when I arrived. I'm not sure where he went in the meantime. He's an elusive one, that Dominic."

"How'd you get in?"

"Did it not enter your imagination that Kyle would let me in?" She laughs. "I took your key off the kitchen counter before I left."

"What about Carlos?"

"What about him?"

He brings his eyes down to the sight of her wiggling in his towel to get fully dry. "Good grief, Betty, can't you just—it'd be pretty righteous to know if the police are gonna kick down my door."

Her back still to him, Betty grabs his lotion from the bathroom sink. She opens both sides of the towel like a cabinet to lotion herself.

She is shameless, just shameless, testing if Bobby will have the self-control to not stare at her in the mirror that hangs upon the bathroom door right in front of them. As though at the sight of a naked woman, this docile vegan won't become a barbarous carnivore.

Bobby feels his pulse in his face, his thoughts stumbling. He thinks how long he has held this combustible liquid inside of himself—six unreal months, since New York, actually—and how much he needs to just do the thing, to just get it over with already, so he can be a normal human being again.

From the mirror, she catches his shining eyes before he looks away. "You needn't be worried. I've settled things with Carlos."

"You're back together?"

"No. I told him that I'm no longer interested in a relationship. I told him that I was interested in someone new, someone who would never lay a hand on me." Towel closed, she turns to him again, taking a provocative step forward.

"Me? You told him you were interested in *me*?"

"I did. Never had a man fight for me the way you did. Even if it's the dumbest thing you ever did, it was the sweetest thing ever done for me."

"Come on, Betty."

"Don't worry. He won't come after you now. Ingrained within him is a barbaric desire to win his property back. Sending you away won't prove that he is the worthier man. He believes he can win my heart back with his Spanish charm. In his mind, nothing can outrank the wiles of a Spanish lover, especially not a dumb American boy's wooing."

A petite knock at the door draws his thoughts away from the question of how this could possibly make sense in Betty's head.

"Bobby?" Ana Lucia's little voice chimes through the door.

Bobby gestures at Betty with wide eyes, pleading with her to be quiet. Best he not be seen in this compromising scene.

Bobby cracks the door open, slipping out so that Ana Lucia cannot see Betty. At the same time, Dominic steps out of his room, joining them in the dark hall.

"So, um, did you tell Dom?" Bobby asks.

She shakes her head, a shy little thing.

Her timidity feeds his bravery. "Hey, so listen, man, we're married—Ana Lucia and me."

There is a slight lift of Dom's left eyebrow.

"We got married. Early this morning."

"Bullshit."

"True shit." Bobby turns a penitent eye to Ana Lucia. "I mean, it's true. Ana Lucia is a citizen and now—"

"Bullshit," Dom says again. His eyebrow has lowered. "There's no way. Bobby. How'd you just get married on the spot here, huh? This is Catholic country; it ain't Vegas, dude."

There is something irritating about Dominic's pragmatism, something that registers almost *feminine* to Bobby, as though he is listening to his own mother and her scorn for all things unimagined. It isn't long before Bobby is irritated by his own irritation with Dom. Their relationship has always been cream.

"Dude, I'm not yanking you. We got married. We worked it out. Ana Lu's got this friend Khadijah, and—"

"Well and good, Bobby, well and good. But I bet you didn't know divorce isn't legal here in this great post-Franco democracy, so what are you gonna do about that? What are you gonna do when it's time to go? If you're not bullshitting me, you're gonna wish you were."

"We haven't talked about everything yet," Ana Lucia tries, "but we have—"

"I'm talking to Bobby here, if you don't mind."

Bobby is frightened by the lumps in their cream, by the quick rise of indignation in him and the involuntary wrinkle of his eyebrows.

There descends upon them a silence so large, it might suffocate Bobby.

"Say what you really want to say, man," Bobby says, daring to puncture the bubble.

"Don't have anything to say."

"Yeah, you do. It's okay. Just say it."

"Alright then, fine," Dom says. "Listen, I know you, dude. I know how you are and we both know how this is gonna end, so there you go. That's all I'm gonna say." Dom pushes his hair back from his face with the palm of his hand. Bobby sees a muscle in his jaw jump. "You should probably just pack your bags and everything. You have a wife now. There won't be enough room once Betty comes back anyway."

The dining room table in Ana Lucia's apartment is arranged with the same meticulousness his mother sets the one at his house in Avon. It's a small table befitting a small dining room, though the adjoining living room is slightly larger. The walls and furniture are taupe, chestnut, and walnut, matching the scent of coffee in the air. Bobby stands beside a velvet sofa, next to Ana Lucia.

"You must—" Bobby coughs. "You must've gotten a really good deal on this apartment. It's a lot better than anything that we could afford."

She nods, her eyes turning to the ceiling as she walks forward, past the couch, to a short hall with two open rooms on the right and a bathroom on the left. His suitcase knocks against the wall before they reach the first bedroom.

It is a sunshine room in shades of lime and pineapple. Groovy flowers are printed on the bed comforter and pillows. Beside the bed stands a strong mahogany dresser and above it two oval mirrors. The room is a Brownhill furniture display.

Ana Lucia walks past the room.

The room she takes him to is naked in contrast to the last.

No, not naked. *Nude.*

In the center of the floor, there is a thin blue mattress over which a dark blue fitted sheet is stretched. The solitary mattress resembles a Greek pool with four pillars of books stacked thigh-high around it.

Bobby sets down his suitcase at the room's entrance. "So, I guess we're sleeping in separate rooms? Are you not—" he stops, configuring his thoughts. "I hope you trust me. I wouldn't—"

"I trust you." She looks around, notably avoiding his eyes. "This is my room. We'll both sleep here."

"What about the other room?"

"It's an extra room."

Bobby slides a cigarette out from his inner coat pocket before pressing the heel of his hand against Ana Lucia's forehead, as though checking for fever. "You alright?"

"I'm alright." She stares up childlike at the cigarette between his fingers. "Maybe. No smoking in the house. Please."

He tucks away his Marlboro, embarrassed. "Yeah, yeah, for sure. Whatever you want."

She looks at him with a hesitancy that matches his own. They are strangers to this new life.

"I have acting class in an hour," she says.

"Oh, yeah, that's right. We can talk when you get back then, figure everything out or whatever."

"Okay." She clasps her hands together as she moves backward toward the door. Her heel hits his suitcase at the entrance, causing her arms to flail as she catches hold of the doorframe to keep herself from hitting the ground.

Bobby tries to contain himself but can't help holding his stomach as he bursts into laughter. Her own expression blossoms to a smile so big and bright it clears away the awkward shadow that has loomed since the night before. Their unalloyed joy moves him to embrace her.

"Just don't smoke in here, that's all," she says, pinching his back playfully and stepping back from him.

He motions at his forehead, doffing an imaginary sailor's cap. "Ay, ay, Ana Lu Kung Fu."

Ever-curious but rarely a spy, Bobby certainly feels guilty when he finds himself in Ana Lucia's closet twenty minutes after she departs. Not guilty enough, however, to keep himself from looking through the stack of paintings he finds at the back of her closet.

Some are images on canvass. Others are painted onto construction paper. They are all fine pieces of art. He only knows this because, though he has never been a particular aficionado of art, each piece causes his head to cock father to the side in wondrous scrutiny.

His stomach first jumps at the gruesome ones. They are mutilated bodies, streams of blood, lifeless bodies. Yet, they are painted without dark shadows. Their colors are vibrant, their lines erratic but drawn with a decisive hand. In contrast, there are several pictures of dreamy faces, of houses, of skylines, of sundry scenes. One scene he recognizes from their reading of *Moby Dick*. It is Tashtego falling into the sinking head of a sperm whale.

At last, Bobby happens upon the last painting. He cannot tear his eyes from it. It is the only one of its kind in the collection.

It is a drawing of Ana Lucia—age nine, maybe ten—standing beside a harbor between two people who are evidently her parents. He stares at her thin legs. He can tell she's just hit a growth spurt by the way she stands on them with the wobbly, bent-knees of a colt. Judging from the little sketches she has made in the rehearsal room, he assumes she has drawn the picture.

Though the color scheme she has used is sepia, he can make out that her mother is dark-skinned and her father is fair. Bobby stares harder. So she is a—what was that Cher song?—a *half-breed?* Yet, between the two of them she seems so *whole.* He's never seen that smile on her before.

The picture explains so much and leaves questions to ponder as he takes a walk to clear his head and avoid the swelling desire to meddle until he turns the house upside down to find out everything he can about her. Still, he takes care to put the paintings back as he found them. He will be patient.

Soon, he leaves the house. He walks alone, the sun loafing at the horizon, his own eyes at half-mast for not having slept for almost two days now. As he approaches the metro station, he decides he'll hop on the train.

At the turnstile, he pulls out his wallet to find that what cash he had was spent on food this morning. Wearied beyond reason, he takes a quick look around, before hoisting himself up by the turnstile columns, and swinging his long legs over the entrance. He rushes to the approaching train.

From the time he spent on the New York subway, he's developed an uncanny ability to sleep on a moving vehicle with the alertness of a cat.

The bumpiness of the ride rocks him only halfway to sleep. He chooses to dream though, to dream of much earlier in the day when he and Ana Lucia stood outside of Khadijah's house at three in the morning.

Ana Lucia explained Bobby's plight to Khadijah. Khadijah only stared at him as Ana Lucia talked.

To his surprise, Khadijah had an immediate plan. She knew someone, a clergyman who could make a marriage happen in no time.

Within an hour, they were at a Muslim imam's apartment. The inside of his apartment was decorated in a strict green and white theme. The iciness of the rooms reminded Bobby of the planet Krypton.

The imam was dressed in a white robe himself. If Bobby wasn't mistaken, the man wore winged eyeliner.

"How are you?" Bobby tried asking the imam.

The imam only raised his brows.

"He speaks Arabic, Bobby," Khadijah said.

"Oh." Bobby paused. "Why is he doing this for us?"

"He believes in the cause of marriage for all people."

Bobby looked at the imam's winged eyeliner again. A million questions vied for his attention, but he could only think to ask, "Will it be legal? This almost seems too simple to be legit. Plus, I mean, I'm Catholic, not Muslim."

Khadijah sighed, annoyed. "According to Mishkat, the best wedding is that upon which the least trouble and expense is bestowed. Answering your other question, we wouldn't be here if it weren't legal."

"But, I mean, I want to stay Catholic."

"Then you will, won't you?"

He nodded. What more was there to say?

Khadijah spoke to the imam for a bit in Arabic as Ana Lucia and Bobby stood in the middle of his living room.

She didn't bother interpreting their exchange before the imam and Khadijah took Ana Lucia behind an ivory veil which hung down the center of his living room.

Not knowing what to say, Bobby stood silently beside the semi-transparent veil, waiting for Ana Lucia. He could see Khadijah working on her makeup and the imam designing something on her hand. The design liquid smelled like maple syrup.

The imam and Khadijah were the first to come out. Ana Lucia followed.

Her hands were decorated with brown swirling figures. Bobby noticed the design as she reached up to touch the red veil lying over her hair. She looked up at him with true bridal ardor, her face dusted in a powder that concealed the adolescent dewiness of her skin and replaced it with a porcelain mystique. Thick black eyeliner rimmed her eyes, highlighting what an exotic doll she was. Were her eyes really brown? Gosh, they were silver or bronze or some stone he couldn't place. Her mouth was bare, a pale carnation.

"Right now," he wanted to say, "you are the most beautiful woman the universe and time have ever known."

He wanted to say something like that but found that he couldn't. There really were things so beautiful they could silence a man to tears.

The imam made them kneel in front of each other and spoke words neither could understand.

Khadijah followed it by making them repeat Spanish vows.

Novio Roberto Carter, tomas tu a Novia Ana Lucia Sará Érei Vicente-Moreira como tu esposa, prometes amarla, respetarla, protejerla abandonando a todo y dedicandote solo a ella.

"I do," Bobby said, his head tilted to the side, engaged again with Ana Lucia's fantastical beauty. "Yo, si."

Ana Lucia followed with her vows and Bobby became Mr. Cloud Heart as he considered how boss it would be that with the addition of Carter, Ana Lucia would have seven names in total. He'd once heard a priest back home say that seven was the number for completion.

Khadijah said to Bobby, "For this to be complete, you will need to give Ana Lucia a gift. It's tradition."

"I really don't have anything. I didn't know I needed anything."

"Be creative."

It was then that Bobby remembered the broken guitar string in his back pocket. He pulled it out and took special care tying it in loops around her ring finger.

The imam smiled for the first time since they arrived. He pronounced the final words. He went off immediately for a Kodak.

Staring down at Ana Lucia, Bobby saw Christmas morning. He took her face between his hands and kissed her until they were both so dizzy, they had to hold hands afterward to steady themselves.

At that dizzy moment, the imam stood in front of them and took the picture, the flash nearly blinding them both.

Now, Bobby wakes on the train to another flash behind his eyes.

He opens them to find it is the light of an officer's flashlight in front of him.

"Hey," says Bobby, lifting the back of his hand to guard his eyes.

The officer clips off his flashlight. Beneath a filter of neon light blobs, Bobby sees that the officer is blonde with a cinnamon mustache. He is taller and thinner than Bobby himself. Maybe just a couple years older.

Though the officer does not speak lightning speed Spanish, Bobby cannot make out most of his words.

"I don't speak Spanish very well. I'm sorry."

The officer taps his flashlight against his palm. "You have your ticket?" he says in Russian-accented English.

"Ticket?"

"For the train."

Bobby straightens up, patting his jeans pockets. "Listen, I—"

"Identification?"

"What?"

"Where's your identification?"

"Um, it's—" He pulls out his expired visa. He sighs, resigned. "Here you go. It's all I've got."

Bobby places his visa in the officer's hand, blinking his eyes as if to wish away the officer's ugly frown.

14.

THE CLASSROOM IS spider-black, save the ring of saffron-flamed taper candles which the students hold. Having found the candles in his desk drawer, Pedro, the course instructor, passed them out at the start of class.

From the center of the circle of students, Ana Lucia stares at Skylark, the electricity of this makeshift Colosseum making them both solemn as gladiators

Skylark's face has been painted onyx, a last-minute courtesy of Pedro, who just knew-*knew*-knew that her slicked-down, white-blonde hair and white princess vest would make her acting one-dimensional without a compelling contrast. It only followed that he had-had-*had* to dust Ana Lucia's face with white power from the unmarked cannister he carried in his shoulder bag. It would suit well the black wig she donned—the one Bobby gave her.

The exercise today is a one-on-one experiment Pedro conceived fifteen minutes ago when the need for his students to develop greater emotional accessibility became abruptly evident to him; he saw it in their vacant eyes. There could be no better way to put them in touch with their emotions than to let them loose in this man-made arena, script-less and prompt-less. Their emotions would build the story. He would begin the exercise with Skylark and Ana Lucia for no other reason than the fact that they both spoke English and he loved practicing his withering English with them.

So, here they stand, unsure of how to begin. Determined to impress Pedro, Ana Lucia makes the first move. She takes a laggard walk around Skylark, eyeing her from head to foot, wishing to convey some emotion that has yet to seize her. She puts on an exaggerated sneer.

The Little Saints

Skylark quickly drops to her knees and clutches Ana Lucia's wrist, her black-painted skin causing her eyes to glow like a comic book villain.

"What's this on your finger?" she says, pinching the guitar string wrapped around Ana Lucia's ring finger. "Is this some excuse for a wedding ring?"

Ana Lucia looks to Pedro, waiting for him to rebuke Skylark for breaking the rules. He says nothing.

Ana Lucia looks back at Skylark, a beggar at her feet. "This is my—"

Pedro cuts in from outside the circle:

Don't copy your partner. Only be yourself. Yourself. Your. Self. Be.

Discomfited, Ana Lucia breathes, everything inside of her going quiet and arthritic. Again, she is forced into a self she is supposed to be, a self known neither to the outside nor the inside. She wants nothing more than to act out some other self, per usual. That opportunity has been keeping her coming back to this class.

Ana Lucia looks down at the candlelight flickering in Skylark's eyes. It is an evil twinkle, really. Skylark sees how cramped Pedro's instruction has made Ana Lucia. She stands, drawing close to her opponent. To Ana Lucia, she smells like tobacco and cherry bubble gum.

"A young thing like you got no business being married," says Skylark. She dusts her finger along Ana Lucia's collarbone. "You'll find that out soon enough, won't ya? Marriage is the great un-veiler. So who is the lucky lad?"

Ana Lucia's stomach quivers. Skylark's touch is experienced. She instigates an urge similar to the one Bobby gives her, except this one makes Ana Lucia feel as though she might gag.

"I'm quite surprised that you could find a man to love you," Skylark continues, massaging Ana Lucia's neck. "You don't impress me. Not one bit. What is your allure? Your face? No, it can't be. Your face hardly lovely. Could it be your mind? Doubtful. Your words give away how unsexy your mind is. Ah, but I know what it is. It's the pink pearl of great price you've kept all to yourself, isn't it? Isn't it?"

Pedro again:

Enough words, Skylark. I want to see you. You. Just you.

Skylark retreats a step, skimming her back teeth with her tongue. She moves forward once more, taking the back of Ana Lucia's neck with just enough pressure to cause her to feel she might collapse if not for Skylark holding her up. Her free hand falls to Ana Lucia's lower back as though initiating a slow dance. She begins tenderly lowering Ana Lucia to the ground as a man laying his virgin lover upon their verdant bed.

Skylark's eyes are impenetrable wells. Ana Lucia's gaze darts to the circle of students. She can't find Pedro.

Instead, she hears his voice above her like the voice of God:

Let it happen; don't fight it. Life doesn't play by a script. Please don't fight it.

Ana Lucia is sure she has heard these words within herself thousands of suns and moons ago when she met death for the first time, the time she was first carried off by alien arms.

Skylark lowers her entirely to the ground, straddled over her but delicately cupping the back of her head.

She leans down, whispering into Ana Lucia's ear. "The pink pearl of great price. That's all it is. It is an intrigue that will make a man give all he has to know its worth. But once he knows, his curiosity will fade. Yes, it will. But what a bore all this has become. Let's have fun, shall we?"

Skylark quickly pulls her lips away from Ana Lucia's ear, though she is still loosely mounted on Ana Lucia, her knees pressed to the ground on either side of her. She reaches into her back pocket and pulls out something imaginary, something she holds up above Ana Lucia like a butcher knife. She violently brings her hand down, stopping short of pounding Ana Lucia's chest but causing Ana Lucia's blood and bones to shudder. Skylark mimics removing the knife from Ana Lucia's flesh and repeats the faux stabbing in double time, screeching out a rendition of *Psycho*'s shower scene violins.

Ana Lucia's inner light blinks in and out. Her eyes go cross. Her skin loosens, making way for her soul to take a familiar ascent. It is happening. Here in this class, it is happening again. The effect of the *maladie du pays*.

Except it is not happening. Skylark is standing now, laughing like a hyena. Pedro has turned on the lights. The students are moving, each blowing out the candles they still hold. Ana Lucia can move her eyes to follow them. She hasn't lost control.

Except tears are dripping down her face. She can't control that. She crisscrosses her arms over her chest from the ground where she still lies, holding herself like a child, the way she used to when she longed for her parents. Yet now, all she wants is Bobby.

All she has is Pedro. He kneels down beside her, helping her to sitting position.

Qué maravilloso! You have done it, Ana Lucia. I believed every word you haven't say.

Peering through the gaps between the jail cell bars, a stinging tear cuts a rivulet down Bobby's cheeks. He brushes it away quickly. He's just tired. Not weak, just tired.

Bobby occupies the cell alone. To keep from gagging at the slippery pile of feces on the toilet seat beside him, he stares at the lone cop sitting at the desk outside. The man is a different officer than the one who brought him here but probably the same age. Since allowing Bobby a single phone call, the officer has ignored Bobby.

Bobby tries pushing away the thought that he should have asked the officer if he could make a trans-Atlantic call to his parents. He hates that at nineteen years old, he feels so much like an inconsolable child, up well past his bedtime.

His eyes cut to the clock behind the officer. Forty-eight hours have passed since he last slept. He closes his eyes, resigning himself to sleep standing up.

Until footsteps and a voice jolts him back to consciousness.

"Well, well, Young. Can't keep yourself out of trouble for a single day, can ya?"

Betty has spoken. Dom stands beside her, his shoulders hunched forward in his leather jacket. He is shaking his head, though Bobby can't tell if it is in pity or condemnation. Not that it would matter. They haven't properly reconciled from earlier today.

Bobby can think of nothing else to say, except, "Why did you bring her?"

"I didn't."

"Oh, *please*," Betty inserts. "Ye are blessed to have my company. I'm the only chance you have of getting out of this. I got you out of it the first time when you almost killed Carlos."

"You think you could talk any louder?" Bobby says, quietly hanging his head against a cell bar.

"These bastards don't understand a word of English. Now, how do ye lads suppose I'm going to solve your little problem?"

"Betty," says a Spanish voice.

The Little Saints

A dog-tired Carlos enters. He moves to stand beside Betty and Dom. The left side of his face is bumpy and violet, his hair and shirt equally ruffled. The officer acknowledges him with a nod. They are police buddies.

Bobby's stomach flips. Dom's gaze hits the ground.

Carlos pays neither of them any mind, immediately taking Betty's face between his hands. He kisses her face, targeting with his lips all of the bruises he created the night before. Betty closes her eyes, relishing his consolation, a fiend for his touch. Dom and Bobby watch them with wonder, as though viewing a most lavish religious ceremony.

"Baby," says Carlos. He continues in a delicate Spanish that seduces even Bobby's ears.

"No, no," Betty says, shaking herself away from him. "You must speak English. You're not going to get better unless you can speak in English when you're emotional. It's the only way."

He yields. "Why are you here?" He glances at Bobby, then back at her. "This boy hurt you?"

Bobby is stunned by the irate energy of his own tired blood as it rushes to his face.

"You hurt me, Carlos," Betty says. "You are the only one who can hurt me. You kill my *soul*, Carlos."

"I'm sorry. I never hurt you again."

"Sorry isn't enough."

"What you want from me, *reina*? I do it for you."

"I'll never come back to you, so you can put it out of your mind."

Carlos's eyes turn down, attempting to soak in a reality too dense for his imagination. Despite the bruises Carlos has marked her body with, Betty is clearly the one in control, having laid claim to his soul. Bobby looks up at the ceiling, arriving suddenly at a revelation—abusers are never really in control, for they cannot control themselves.

Betty grips the cell bar, her hand settling just below Bobby's. "Besides, I've fallen in love with someone else. We both knew I would eventually."

"Who you love, Betty?"

"I told you already. You can't see it?" She grazes Bobby's pinkie with her own.

Bobby moves his finger. "What are you—"

"With this?" Carlos gives Bobby a nasty gander. "You fall in love with *this?*"

"He's the man I want."

Bobby scuffs his feet against the cement, a juvenile stomp. "Betty, what are you *doing?*"

Carlos has a sudden combustion of dramatic Spanish. Betty talks back with him in a trembling voice. This is apparently the climax of their opera. When the lights come up, Carlos lifts his head, his eyes become wellsprings as they meet Bobby's.

Carlos grips the bar beside his head.

"I need five minutes. I get you out. You have debt with me. You pay me tonight."

❦

Bobby knows the key is under the doormat when he arrives at Ana Lucia's apartment at half past four in the morning. He's not sure how he knows the key is there, but the fact that he does makes him feel that he knows Ana Lucia in some way that goes beyond the natural course of learning someone just over four months. He's convinced that she's God-made for him and that their union is as much knit in the design of the universe as the stars and galaxies.

As he turns the key in the door, he feels his frog heartbeat through his neck. He is faint with anticipation of seeing her. And exhaustion.

Bobby enters in to find Ana Lucia standing in the spotlight the moon has made for her in the living room. He joins her in the spotlight, noting the white powder edged around her face. Seeing his face, she doesn't open her mouth, just her arms.

If not for her arms around his waist, he would sink to the ground.

The alertness of her muscles gives away that she hasn't fallen asleep. He imagines that like a preying tiger, she has been pacing for him.

"You're here," she says.

"That's true," he says, holding her tighter to himself. "I'm here."

"I'm sorry."

"What do you mean?"

"I'm sorry for saying, 'Yo cago en la leche de tu puta madre' the whole time you were gone."

He smiles, confused. "I don't know what that means."

"It means I shit in your whore mother's milk."

"Oh."

She nods, her lips pursed.

"I still have no idea what in the world that means."

"It doesn't make a lot of sense in English," she says, "but it's the worst Spanish curse. I'm sorry. I didn't even mean it. I thought you left me. Forgive me."

He laughs, kisses her forehead. "It's okay. Just promise you'll never poop in my mom's milk. She's already a little allergic to dairy."

She smiles this time, her light the envy of the moon. "I promise. But are you okay?"

"I'm good now. I mean, I don't have any money anymore, but—"

"You were robbed?"

"Kind of. Can we talk about everything tomorrow?"

She nods, perhaps exhibiting such submissiveness from excitement that he'll actually be *here* tomorrow.

Here in manic Madrid, the capital of born-again Spain. Here with Little Miss Sleepy Head in a dragonfly dress and neon pink tube socks.

On the mattress in their bedroom, he lies on his side, one hand on the side of his face and the other resting against her warm neck. He measures her pulse as though counting sheep. Still fully clothed in his wedding attire—a Ramones T-shirt and black jeans—it is Here in the capital of the world that he finally falls asleep.

15.

BOBBY GAVE AWAY what remained of the last check his mother sent him to get out of jail.

He says she won't send him another check for a month. That is, if she sends anything at all, considering he's overstayed his visa.

To earn money, Bobby does solo street shows. With buckets of change, he pays for everything they need. He cleans. He cooks.

She cries.

Every day.

In private.

She hasn't been taken care of since she was ten years old. She is afraid to close her eyes, afraid to wake up from this dream.

For a boy unaccustomed to lack, Bobby lives their life of potato soup and cold showers with saintly patience. He brings a touch of ingenuity to their poverty, so that being poor doesn't seem so expensive. One night, as they recline Indian-style on the living room floor eating sauce-less spaghetti, Bobby jumps to his feet, rushing to the bedroom and returning with a Virgin Mary candle. Retrieving a lighter from his pocket, he lights it and turns off the lamp. He is preserving electricity, but not just that, he is preserving their magic. When she opens her mouth to comment on it, he leans forward, kissing her with velvet lips and whispering a "shhhhh." She looks down quietly, blissfully at her noodles, realizing that he is even frugal with their words in order to enjoy the richness of being and being together. Love is a language without words.

And he—he is like a water lily, floating gently without any respect to what dark waters may be beneath. It is of great interest to Ana Lucia that he seems to know how to be poor without ever having been poor a day in his life. There is no synonym to poor.

Though there is sometimes no dinner for the poor, there is often dessert. Ana Lucia imagines that making love is a meal more prized among the poor than anyone in the whole wide world. Honestly, fuel is needed for the tank, and if it can't be bought, it must be made. It's no wonder that the poor population multiplies so rapidly. Sex is the one sacrifice even the shrewd poor will not make.

Yet, Bobby has been making that exact sacrifice without complaint.

Until one evening he comes home from a street show, holding a card in his hand. He hands it to her quietly as she toys with her hair in front of the full-length mirror that leans against a wall in their bedroom.

Ana Lucia stares at the card in her hand, then back at him.

At the top, the card reads, *Santa Teresa de Ávila, ruega por nosotros.* On the card is printed a picture of Saint Teresa of Ávila. She is strewn out on a divan, her face raised to heaven. An angel flies above her with a spear pointed at her heart. Her face, though pained, holds a hint of euphoria.

Bobby is smiling. "I found it on the ground outside the apartment, just sitting on the sidewalk like an angel put it there."

"What is it?"

"It's a prayer card. It's the ecstasy of Saint Teresa of Ávila. You must've heard of her. She's from Spain."

Ana Lucia turns to him, so that they stand face-to-face in front of the mirror.

"She was a mystic," he says. "Like, she had all these experiences with God that were supernatural. She physically felt God, all of His pain and pleasure for humanity."

She meets his eyes. "She looks like—"

"Like she's having an orgasm or something?" He smiles with a bit of mischief, though he doesn't mean to. "I know."

She looks again at the picture, confused.

"It's really a divine thing. The experience, I mean."

She wonders if he purposely leaves ambiguous the experience he's referring to. Her stomach flips.

"I know it looks like sex. I guess sex is just the shadow of what's to come. God is the light, the real thing. We get the light when we reach heaven. Heaven will be beyond orgasmic."

She laughs. "You're saying Heaven is sexy?"

He scratches his head, thoughtful. "No, I'm just—I'm saying sex is heavenly." He hesitates. "I know you never had it, and maybe you're scared, but I hope...I hope you know I don't just want *it*. I want *you*. If you knew what just being in the same room with you does to me..."

She looks up at him in the mirror. He takes the card from her, stares at it. All is quiet. She can hardly wait for what he will say next.

"I want to make your face look like that," he decides. "I want to make you see God, heaven, the angels—all of that." His eyes fall. "I'm not saying I know everything your body needs, but I swear, I'll figure it out. I'm gonna give you everything I ha—"

Ana Lucia offers up her mouth, halting his words. He takes her waist, the waist that has always been his, squeezing it with enough pressure to bring a touch of St. Teresa's beautiful agony to her face.

She twines his worn gabardine vest between her fingers. This is the most *pressing* kiss they've shared—she pressing her lips like a mad woman against his and he pressing his palm against her back, pushing her breasts against his chest until through thin T-shirt, skin and sinew, she can feel his heartbeat. The rapid and steady thumps narrate the tale of a man in love fallen. She is stricken by how easily she falls in love with him falling in love with her.

She may very well be falling in love with the fact that his heart beats so strongly, that he is present, that he is alive. For an instant, she misses her mother and father. Joy and sadness meet in the center of her chest like salt water to spring water, threatening to break her heart clear down the middle.

She breaks the kiss, turning to look forward into the wall mirror that sits in front of them. Their reflection strikes her as oddly quaint —her in that vintage dragonfly-print dress, her wavy bangs grazing her forehead and him in a simple white cotton T-shirt, his hair inadvertently side-parted back into a ponytail.

They are Rockwell's *Boy-and-Girl-Gazing-at-the-Moon* quaint.

She meets his gaze in the mirror, tilts her head to the side, and grazes her own neck with her fingertips, guiding his eyes to the place where she wants him to kiss her. She trembles—her body can hardly wait for what his hands will say in response. He glides his fingers around her neck with vampire finesse before his lips meet her skin, kissing her with quiet power.

She detaches herself from him again, lifting her eyes to the mirror and her hand to her shoulder, testing that this is no fluke. Bobby unbuttons the top buttons at the front of her dress, creating enough slack to slide it down and expose her shoulder. This kiss is more of a gentle bite than the other, though it turns to avaricious sucking. She watches her own eyes widen in the mirror.

This becomes the game they play. He looks in the mirror for her direction, and she responds with her hand, touching her cheeks, her eyes, her arms, her knees, until at last, she cups her own breast.

"I'm going to make love to you now," he whispers, cupping his hand over hers. "I hope that's okay."

All is quiet for a moment. He looks at her, searching for an affirmative.

She is ready.

She thinks she is ready.

She knows she is not.

No doubt, she wants to see heaven, the angels, God—the "all of that" Bobby speaks of. Still, Ana Lucia doesn't know yet if she believes in God, and in moments she is almost sure He exists, she finds herself breathing little prayers: "Please let this last forever"; "Please keep this the same always"; "Please don't let the monster inside of me destroy this." Despite how well their lives work together, she recognizes that she has the combustibility of an aerosol can.

Ana Lucia takes Bobby's hand from her body, setting it down by his side staidly.

His eyes blink at the sudden diffusion. "You don't want it?" It as though he is asking if she doesn't want heaven. "You really don't want to?"

"Not today," she says.

Bobby's eyes flutter again. "Okay." He backs himself from her, as though he can keep her safe from his flooding desire. He looks down at her bare feet in the mirror when he says, "Don't sweat it. Like, seriously. Because, you know, I...I *love* you, okay? I wanted to say it in the rehearsal room that day, but I was too scared. Plus, love seemed too small a word to sum up everything I feel for you. Maybe I could've said something like 'I supercalifragilisticexpialidocious you,' but that would've been too complicated. What I feel for you—it's the most simple thing on earth, really. I guess 'I love you' will just have to do for now. And I'm not blowing sunshine up your skirt, so—" he looks away, flushed. "So, that's that."

She touches her dress, trying to gain the meaning of the phrase.

"And look, Ana Lu, you don't—I don't—" He stops, skimming his top lip with his teeth. "You're not just tolerated or accepted here. You *belong* here. With me. Marrying you wasn't an accident. Just thought I should say that."

Perhaps to spare her the awkwardness of immediate reciprocity, he begins searching for a place in the room to put the Saint Teresa prayer card.

Inside her, words well up—

I don't just belong with you, I belong to you.

The words remain a nervous, dizzying breath in her throat.

Sighing the wind and the words, Ana Lucia decides that it is more profitable to pray silently: "Please, please don't let the monster inside of me ruin this."

B
So, you don't love me?
I'll try to convince myself of that for the moment
Better to be surprised by a false premise
Than a failed wish

And yet...
I know what I know, True Blue Ana Lu
It is much harder
To unknow than to know
Much harder, much-much harder
To un-see than to see
That sold sign on your heart
Which hangs just for me

A

Love spoken aloud is

A promise.

A promise is

A debt

A debt is

An Obligation

Obligation is slavery

A slavery

To which I can never return

16.

THERE WAS MORE blood inside of Luis Rafael than Ana Lucia could have ever dreamed, despite how many times he spoke of blood. May 21st —the last day of his life—she realized that he had always been nothing but a bag of blood.

After her grandfather's blood was spilled, Ana Lucia glanced from the burgeoning pool of blood to the knife on the kitchen floor, unsure of her next step.

She stood alone in that kitchen like the orphan who her grandparents had first picked up from the airport.

Today, as she walks home from La Vida, Ana Lucia searches herself for the answer she'd asked when the knife first sunk into her grandfather's gut.

It is the answer to why. Ever since *Tragedy the First*, the question has been the same.

As Ana Lucia looks at the line of trees on the sidewalk, her vision blurs, as though looking out of a subway car.

The answer to Why should never be found. No, it should never be found. It's not for a person to know. For if a person knows the answer to Why, his search is over. When the search is over, it is surely time to die.

But Ana Lucia doesn't want to die. She's only five steps away from her apartment building. She wants to live.

In her apartment, she can share in the lovely ignorance of a boy who doesn't know Why and has no reason to ask Why. If she can make it to him...

If the prayer will work again.

"Don't let the monster come out," she prays to the unknown God. Maybe He is in the copper moon, holding the answer to Why on His hip.

The copper moon is increasing in size at mutant speed and along with it, the visions in Ana Lucia's brain. The visions bloom and bulge, taking up the expanse of her mind, visions of a punctured throat and an exposed heart with one beat remaining.

The visions are pushing to the surface, the monster is reaching his hand up through the dung. She tries to will herself from walking up the apartment building stairs to her unit, but she cannot. If she stops, she will be caught suspended outside. Who will know what to do with her?

Entering her apartment, she knows there are only a few minutes left before control will be gone and her body will be locked inside the prison of her mind.

Hearing Bobby rustling with something in the bedroom, she decides she must go to him. She must urge him out of the house, so he won't be witness again to her *maladie du pays.*

In the bedroom, he stands next to her pillar of books. A pair of her word-tattooed sneakers are beside his feet. He holds the one drawing of her parents she has managed, the one where she stands between them by the sea.

Fear meets possessiveness, producing an alien anger in Ana Lucia.

"Why do you have that?" she says, snatching the drawing from his hands.

His brows squinch. "I found it. How come you never showed me this? You were a gorgeous little girl. I'd would've found a way to kiss you back then."

"Why are you doing this?"

"I didn't mean to go through your stuff." He tries smiling. "I'm just obsessed with you, Ana Lu, that's all. I found the paintings before, and I was really—I mean, some of them really freaked me out, and I don't know what they all mean, but I know they come from the kind of genius anybody would chop off his ear for. I knew you could sketch—I've seen you doodling or whatever—but I didn't know you had *the gift,* Ana Lu. Not until I found the paintings. People like me work sun up to sun down hoping for a little bit of talent, but other people—people like *you*—were born with the gift. You got the gift free of charge, Lu."

Her mouth tightens, though she is aware that anger has not done the tightening. It is the monster, the one who will soon take over her whole body.

Bobby reaches tenderly for her waist. She shoves his hand away with what control remains.

"Get out," she manages, saliva at the corner of her mouth.

"You're serious? Ana Lu, what's up? What—"

"I told you to get out. I mean, get out." Her breathing is a hot kettle. "You can't stay here anymore. I don't want you here."

"Calm down, okay? I'll put it away."

Poor Bobby. He can't see it—there's no putting it away. It's out.

She begins pushing him at the center of his chest, cursing him in Spanish, staring at her strong hand as it pushes him to the front door. She cannot look at his eyes for fear that her mercy might be misguided, that she might let him stay.

"Out, Bobby! Out!" she screams, shaking her shoulders from his grasp.

"Ana Lu—"

One more push and he is out the door. She slams and locks it behind him.

What is left of her can only feel grateful that she got him out before she becomes a wax statue again.

What is left of her won't ask Why. Being trapped in her own body like this with no escape, asking Why would be too dangerous, for the question of Why will surely always be bigger than any answer to it.

B
I–I...

A.
You-I...
—We—
We were always standing
on a shaky footbridge.
Today, you sink into the quagmire
Bare-foot
Now, I've done all I can do to save you from the reeds
Trust:
You've done all you can do to save me back

17.

BOBBY KNOWS THE relationship is dead when he doesn't hear
Ana Lucia's voice on the seventh day, the day of rest. Day Seven is
the day to put it to rest.

He should have known it was over on Day One, when he
returned to the apartment the day after she kicked him out and found
a note saying that he should gather his belongings and leave his key
under the mat. The fact that the note was type-written said it all.

Still, he didn't *know* it was over. He'd never in his life had any
reason not to hope.

Ana Lucia was clearly sick in her mind. Still, he hoped.

Too weak to fight anything but the good fight, he didn't ask for
his bedroom back from Betty when he returned to the apartment he
shared with Kyle and Dom. Instead, he slept alone on the living room
floor. That second night, Dom came to visit him, sitting on the floor
beside him, swapping out records on the turntable until nine in the
morning. The last song landed on Gilbert O'Sullivan's "Alone Again
(Naturally)."

By the evening of the sixth day, Bobby had considered it divine
revelation that faith without works was dead and that he'd be dead
soon if he didn't get the chance to see her. Visiting her at her job was
an order from God so far as he was concerned.

So, he went to La Vida on the seventh day. He was planning to
tell her that hard times were inevitable and that there was a difference
between peaceful coexistence and true unity, that love is a contact
sport, that love finds you in your safe spaces, and that he just wanted
to love her, even the not-so-well parts of her. He was going to tell her
that he'd wait for however long it took for her to take him back,

which maybe wasn't true, but had to be true because he'd be dead if she didn't let him back in soon.

Though he stood in front of her at the bar as she mixed a drink, he didn't get to say any of those things to her. She refused to look up at him, though he repeated her name five times.

Five times.

He began to count her eyelashes as she looked down at the drink she was making. He got to seventeen.

"Leave it alone, Bobby," he heard the moment Ana Lucia went off to deliver the drinks she'd made.

Looking to his left behind the bar, he saw Khadijah.

"Just leave her alone," she said.

Breathless, he asked, "Is she okay?"

"She'll be better if you just leave her alone."

The only option Bobby had left was to beg. Though he'd never actually begged for anything in his life, it wasn't pride that kept him off his knees. It was the physical reaction he was having. He could feel convulsions travelling up from his stomach to his face.

He held them in until he arrived home, where he cried until his face was disfigured by sadness when he gave himself a quick look before he headed to the bar where Naïve was scheduled to perform that evening.

Now, Bobby sits in the basement of the venue, exceptionally cold and dry after an hour performance. He wears the stare of a belligerent drunk as he watches Betty snort a line of coke from the little table which sits between them.

Dom looks sad as he snorts his line. It occurs to Bobby that maybe Dom normally looks this sad. Perhaps he was just too happy to ever notice that the kid's eyes have always been clown-droopy.

Bobby had practically begged for this kind of pain. He'd once thought it would merit him the inspiration to write a decent song. It didn't. This depression gives nothing. All it does is steal and steal and steal—

"What a fecking sourpuss," Betty says suddenly, pinching the punch-colored tip of her nose. "I can't take it. Why don't you jump off a bridge and die already?"

"Why don't you mind your own damn business," Bobby retorts.

"I was. But you come here with this bullshit, and my high is completely fucked." She slams her hand on the arm of her green velvet chair. "You lost your little woman. So the fuck what? There are worse things to lose, you know. How about losing your whole family in one big swoop? Try being on the street and watching the fecking guards shoot down your mama, your step-pa, and your little sister when they walk out of Mass because of some fecking religious love spat between the Protestants and the Catholics. Try having your sister bleed to death in your arms asking for mama who's already fecking dead. Try it, will ya? Then, come and tell me if you still feel anything about some lass leaving you."

"I'm sorry, Betty," Bobby says. "I didn't mean to hurt you." He lowers his eyes for her loss. Following his show of pity, a fleeting pang of hatred brings a twitch to his eye. Why should he apologize for his pain? Moreover, why does she make it so difficult to decipher between her need to be constant queen—even the Queen of Pain—and her sincere emotion.

"I'm not religious," she continues. "I believe religion makes victims of us all or maybe we make a victim of it—who knows?—but whatever the case, you owe me a penance, Young. Your penance, then, is to be grateful for once in your God-blessed life. I swear to the good God in heaven, that I'd kick your teeth out for being so selfish if I didn't love ya so much."

He stares at her, wordless, sinking down and disappearing inside of himself until he is back at the apartment at one in the morning, standing in the kitchen, clutching the phone. The last number is a one on the rotary. Thank God.

It's seven in the morning in Connecticut. For sure, his mom has just gotten out of the shower.

"Mom."

"Bobby?"

"Yes."

"What's going on? Are you okay?"

"Yes."

He imagines that she is taking a seat on the edge of the bed beside his sleeping father. "You got my letter then, didn't you? Dad and I are really, really worried about your staying past your visa. I thought we had an agreement about the time you were going to be away. I'm between a rock and a hard place here." She stops. "Are you okay?"

"I'm okay."

"You're crying. Honey, what in the world is going on? You're scaring me. Talk to me."

"My girlfriend." It is all he can say and is likely as golden as a child's first words to his mother. He's never said the two words together in front of his mother. On top of that, the word is all wrong. She isn't a girlfriend. She wasn't even a girlfriend when she was just his girlfriend. A word like that was too hokey for a girl like her.

"You have a girlfriend, Bobby? That's what's keeping you there, isn't it?"

"I shouldn't have called."

"Please don't hang up. Please." She is begging in a whisper. "You called for a reason. Let's talk about it."

Nothing left to do, he tells her about Ana Lucia. He skips over the sacred details—the preciousness of what she is, what she looks like, the fact they are married—but he tells her of the episode in the rehearsal room when she went paralyzed and about this second time when it seemed like her skin was growing tighter, as though she was being closed into herself, even as she forced him out of the apartment. When he is finished explaining, he stops without ceremony, letting silence be his mother's cue.

"Bobby, can you hear me?"

"Yeah."

"I don't want to scare you and I'm not supposed to diagnose anything so I'm not technically, but—"

"Can you just say it, Mom?"

"—but it sounds like catatonia, Bobby. She was in state of catatonia. She exhibited signs of waxy flexibility the first time. And I'm willing to say she was close to it again when she made you leave, the way she was behaving so frantically. I know that can be really scary, but trust me, if this is what I think it is, it was more scary for her than it was for you."

"Catatonia?" he says.

"Listen, it's awful coincidental that you've met someone who's exhibiting this kind of behavior. A couple of weeks ago, I was browsing through the Diagnostic and Statistical Manual of Mental Disorders we received at the office. There are a lot of new discoveries. One of them is giving greater insight into Post Traumatic Stress Disorder. It's mostly related to what we normally call shellshock. Do you know what that is?"

He nods, hardly concerned that she can't see him.

"It's now diagnosable in the general population. An assortment of traumatic events can lead to this, not just war. It's—" She breaks for a second. "Listen, I don't want to terrify you. Obviously I'm not able to diagnose anything from here, but it is a theory, barring that the young woman is not generally schizophrenic, which is a whole other beast that you wouldn't even want to begin to think about."

He is shaking.

His mother continues. "I want you to know that I am very sensitive to what you're going through, but please be aware that this is probably a blessing, Bobby. Frankly, I don't think you have the emotional capacity to deal with a girl who is exhibiting this kind of behavior. You're nineteen years old, honey; this isn't time to get tangled up. Give yourself a chance to be free, Bobby. There will come a time in your life when commitments will sometimes impede on your happiness. Enjoy being uncommitted and free to roam."

"It's too late for that. I'm already committed."

"Only in your mind, Bobby. I know it doesn't feel like it right now, but this too shall pass. It always does."

"On paper too. I'm committed by law too."

"Excuse me?"

He sniffles. "She's more than my girlfriend. I married her."

"Oh, Bobby, please don't tell me that. Please."

"I have to go, Mom."

"Bobby—"

"I really have to go, Mom. I love you."

Ana Lucia has thrown up every day since Bobby went away. She vomits yellow saliva in the bathroom of La Buena Vida Saturday morning, the second week since her Milk and Honey dried up. She has dreamed of her father, white horses, and rattlesnakes all week.

Passing time is not the worst part. The worst part is feeling Bobby's love like a radio signal reaching for her over the distance between them.

"He's not coming back." Khadijah says in passing as Ana Lucia returns from the bathroom and stands behind the bar counter.

"I know," Ana Lucia replies, looking down at Khadijah's hands as they prepare a café con leche.

"No, you don't. You still think he's going to try again. He won't. You broke him."

Ana Lucia looks up at her friend. Khadijah does not look back, staring instead at the drink she stirs.

"I don't really know you, Ana Lucia. You're my best friend, but I can't say what your favorite childhood game was, where you went to school, who first infatuated you. I was very interested in you the first day you showed up at La Vida to work. You looked so sad and so lost and so beautiful, I thought you might be from my country. Maybe you came over the same way that I did. Maybe you passed through cold waters up to your knees with one bag and a little brother in your arms. It turned out, you didn't, but I figured out that you had passed over some high sea the day you begged me to cut off your hair. You were asking me to get rid of your past. You didn't understand then that the past goes nowhere. The past is settled, and if you believe in fate, so is the future. All there is left to do is accept it.

"He won't come back to you. You have to learn to live with that, the same way that you have to learn to live with whatever happened to you before we met. Bobby's gone. I suppose that if you're going to lose everything, the best time to lose it is when you're young. Should war send you from your homeland, should you be stripped of your fortune, should you lose the love of your life-it should happen when you're too young to feel that you ever had any control over it. When you're a true adult, you'll feel that you could have done something to stop it—the way my father feels when he looks at us and remembers that he'll never be able to return our past life. Best thing you can do is make peace with your lot, habibi."

Khadijah walks off to deliver her lukewarm café con leche. She has drawn the curtain. The curtain is drawn.

Unfortunately, Ana Lucia is not dead. Her hollowness doesn't equate to death.

Hollowness is a vulnerability. It creates space for her insides to teem over with memories of tragedies so fantastical, she titles and catalogues them most days as mere fiction.

Today she remembers them as real life.

June 5, 1971

Tragedy the First

The "horse" Ana Lucia's father drove was white. It was a
Mustang, arguably the coolest American car made in '64. Javier had
splurged on it with the earnings he'd put away during his three years
student teaching at the University of Chicago.

Ten-year-old Ana Lucia sat in the backseat of the Mustang,
staring out at the winding highway, a curtain of white-frosted
mountains in view. To Ana Lucia, they were monolithic knees. She'd
been reading Robert Frost for the last three weeks. As they drove,
Oliver Twist was the literature of the day.

Her mother and father listened to her read from the novel out
loud, having turned off the radio a half hour ago to give her practice
time for her English.

Ana Lucia looked up periodically from her reading to glance at
her mother's profile as she peered at her father.

Smitten was the proper word to describe the expression on
Katina's face as she observed her husband steering his prized car.
Ana Lucia had learned the meaning of smitten a month ago. She
memorized it as the past participle of smite, which meant to defeat or
conquer. Therefore, being smitten was what happened when love
conquered a person.

Ana Lucia was also endeared with her father that late afternoon.
He had finally made the decision to allow them a vacation in Antigua.
Katina convinced him to do so after three nights in a row, Ana Lucia
had climbed into their bed complaining about dreams of masked-
men coming to murder them in their sleep.

The nightmares had come after Katina and Javier sat her down to
warn her about an old danger that was brewing anew. After months of
withdrawing their surveillance, the military government were again
covertly monitoring Javier, taking special interest in the radical growth
of his extra-governmental education program. For a government in
the midst of a civil war with its uneducated and impoverished
population, Javier was becoming a threat in the ranks of Che
Guevara, as much a menace as the herd of Communists executed in
the United States some decades prior. The possibility that Javier
would suffer Guevara's fate was hardly lost on him.

Perhaps her father never considered whether there was sufficient benefit in Ana Lucia knowing his vulnerability. He couldn't hide anything from his *chiquita*.

For the moment, those worries were consciously left in Livingston, her mother having shut down their restaurant by the sea for the length of their vacation. Now, there were only blue skies, a white mustang, and an old copy of *Oliver Twist* in an olive-colored paper jacket.

"Although Oliver had enough to occupy his attention in keeping sight of his leader," Ana Lucia read, "he could not help bestowing a few hasty glances on either side of the way, as he passed along." She paused. "This one's hard, Daddy. Did your father make you read this when you were ten years old?"

Javier caught her eyes in the rear-view mirror. For young Ana Lucia, his expression proved undecipherable.

"His father didn't make him read anything," her mother said, looking back at her. "He wanted to. Your father was a most perfect child, weren't you, Javi?"

Javier smiled softer than was his habit. "My father wasn't around to make me read when I was old enough to read difficult text."

In that moment, it occurred to Ana Lucia that she didn't know anything about her father's childhood.

"You were an orphan, like Oliver?" she asked.

"In one way, I was."

Katina looked at him, her smitten gaze slipping into a careful study of his countenance.

"Is that why you loved Mommy?" Ana Lucia probed. "Because you were both orphans?"

"You're trying to find a way to avoid reading, Lucita," Katina interjected. "Now, let's start again."

Ana Lucia brought her book back up to her eyes to read but lifted them back to the rear-view mirror when her father spoke again.

"My father didn't die," he said. "He had to go away for a long time when I was nine years old. He was sent to a prison camp."

"What was his name, Daddy?"

"His name was Luis Rafael."

"Do you remember him?"

"I do. But I didn't know him. I only knew about him from what neighbors told me."

In the mirror, Ana Lucia caught the furrow of her own brows. "Did your mother leave you too?"

"No. She was never really there though." He laughed, rueful. "Begin the next paragraph, Lucita."

She began reading aloud again. She read in the way her father hated—smoothly but without comprehension. She could hardly pay attention to the words, too busy putting together a childhood for her father. She knew he was from Madrid but little else. She knew *what* he was—a revolutionary, an altruist—but she had yet to know *who* he was outside of that.

Ana Lucia emerged from her musings with the blast of blinking blue lights behind the car.

The corners of Katina's eye turned down. "Are we going to stop, Javier?"

'I think we don't have a choice," he said, his voice composed.

He directed the car over to the side of the road, beside a plane of dry dirt and scattered grass. The police car fit itself behind them, so close it almost tapped the Mustang's bumper. Two officers stepped out of the car, twins in their midnight black attire and guard hats. One approached the passenger's side, the other stood on her father's side.

"Step out of the car," they said in Spanish.

Her parents exchanged a glance, a tacit agreement to comply. Her father looked back once at her, bidding her to silence. He sent her a kiss with his eyes.

Ana Lucia's attention fell immediately to *Oliver Twist*, desperately attempting to fade out how much the police officers resembled the men in her nightmares as they took her parents to the side of the road.

"Stop thief! Stop thief!'" Ana Lucia read quickly, as though reciting a prayer. "The cry is taken up by a hundred voices, and the crowd accumulate at every turning."

Ana Lucia tried to make her voice drown out the low arguing outside of the car.

We're not fleeing from anyone. We've done nothing wrong. You don't have the right to hold my husband and I.

Shut up, black bitch.

Ana Lucia read on, tears wedging themselves through from the corner of her eyes. "'Away they fly, splashing through the mud, and rattling along the pavements: up go the windows, out run the people, onward bear the mob, a whole audience desert—"

I'm Javier Vicente. If you want me, take me. Only me. Don't touch my wife.

You don't decide who we'll take. Now, shut your fucking mouth and put your hands behind your back.

"—Punch in the very thickest of the plot, and, joining the rushing throng, swell the shout, and—"

We'll go with you. Just, please don't—

The crack of the first gunshot went up like an angry firecracker. Ana Lucia's shoulder's quaked as she slid down to the car floor, her heart running wild.

Katina's scarlet scream was dulled to Ana Lucia's ears by the glass of the car window.

The second gunshot ended her screaming.

"—lend fresh vigour to the cry, 'Stop thief! Stop thief!'" Ana Lucia read, wailing the words.

She stopped when she heard the car door open. She listened to the officer anxiously rummaging through the glove compartment, evidently unaware of her existence.

When she could no longer keep herself from breathing, the officer turned to investigate.

Finding her crouched in the back, he blinked, oddly nervous. Ana Lucia could only pay attention to his Mr. Potato Head mustache that twitched as he spoke.

Looking up at the officer, she could see the window out of the corner of her eye. A splattering of blood—her parents' blood—crawled down it like crimson rain drops.

"What's your name, little girl?"

She didn't respond, clutching her arms tighter around her knees.

The officer reached back to take the open book lying on top of her knees. "What are you reading?"

The twin cop opened the driver's side door, immediately stunned by Ana Lucia. He looked to the first officer in the passenger side. They came to an understanding with their glances.

"There's been an accident with your parents," the second officer said. "Everything will be okay. It's very important that you close your eyes now and stay very calm. We'll have to take you to our car."

"Do you hear us, little girl?" said the first officer.

Her heart running in her chest like a brown hare, Ana Lucia only nodded.

The officer in the passenger side came to her, opening her door. She noted immediately the gold and brown rattlesnake tattoo on his hand as he reached his arms down to her, lifting her like a bride at the threshold.

"Close your eyes," he said.

In fear, she obeyed, resigning herself to his arms, as though giving up her spirit to the wind. The dark behind her eyes gave her senses of the blind. The peppery scent of the officer's skin, the painful firmness of his hand beneath her thighs, the ferocity of his breathing—all painted a picture her eyes did not see.

The officer laid her down in the back seat. She breathed.

"We have two suspects here," the officer said, the static of his police radio almost obscuring his voice. "Both have sustained gunshot wounds to the head. The use of deadly force was used for resistance of arrest. There is a child, unseen to us initially. We'll need to contact the next of kin as soon as possible."

At those words, little Ana Lucia didn't open her eyes, but in her mind's eye, she saw her parents lying side-by-side on the ground, bullets lodged in their foreheads like red Hindu dots.

18.

Bobby has given up singing. He is yelling now, proving true the punk stereotype he'd been intent on invalidating.

The thing is, he can sing and sing well. Naïve knows it—that's why they've been shooting him confused looks throughout the set. The audience doesn't know it, but they don't care. They don't care about anything.

They don't even care that mid-way through one of the band's original songs in A minor, he arpeggiates an ugly A-major chord as an introduction to "Comfortably Numb."

Dom's drums go weak and Kyle's bass fades out. The two of them stare limp-eyed at him.

Now, he is singing. Not singing well but singing. His eyes are closed. He is sleepy. The song was always the sound of twilight to him. He's happy to finally be sleepy. Maybe tonight he will sleep, even rest. He's given up. There will be no more agony; agony is only a struggle against the pain. Now he accepts the pain like a second skin.

In this way, there is no pain, there is just *him*. He is receding....

That Pink Floyd lyric is the last to come from him, as he unstraps his guitar and walks quietly off the stage. The audience is so loud, they are their own music. Only a few notice his departure.

Even Betty, standing in the midst of the crowd, doesn't dare stop him in his sleep walk toward the door.

It is at the door that he sees her, the her that can't be unseen.

She wears a wig, long and jet-black. She is dressed in a faded black shift dress a half size too big and white-striped navy Adidas.

It seems that in disguise he knows her better than he ever has. It is a knowing that can't be unknown. It is love.

When she sees him, she scurries out the door, where a light rain falls oblique onto the midnight streets. Bobby follows.

She walks fast. Not too fast though. Just fast enough to give him the chase a man needs.

Though the walk is long, it is a walk guided by one visible star in the sky. To him, it is the star of Bethlehem. The "Comfortably Numb" solo plays in his ears, giving drama to his steps. Bobby realizes he is not following her so much as they are being led through the city to a park they once visited together in the daytime. The park is now vacant. It is Parque de El Capricho. Literally, the Park of Whim.

Yet, there is constancy in the moist grass beneath their feet. Soon, they find themselves beside a small pond. The wise willows hang over it, stopping short of grazing the ripples, just flirting with the idea of a wet touch. The infant cherry blossoms boast of how well they know love in their youth, how they understand that love has its cycles and how there are days to be clothed and seasons to be gloriously nude. Not in winter is their nakedness discovered, but in springtime, when their gorgeous petals are finally free for all to see.

"Stop," Bobby says to Ana Lucia. His excitement has overcome him. The slight rain has eased up. "Stop there. Please."

She stops. He can't believe the control he has over her.

Her long black wig swings over her shoulder when she turns to face him. Tears stream down her face like falling stars.

He steps toward her so that he stands as near to the pond as she.

"I know why you left," he says.

The stars continue to fall. Some ancient world is coming to an end.

"But I also know why you've come back," Bobby continues. "The divide is gone, Ana Lu. It's gone. You and I aren't two different people anymore. I feel everything you feel. And I understand why you left me. After you did, I saw you like this doe running through the forest. I felt like I wanted my doe back. But I don't want to cage you, Ana Lu. I want you to be free. I want you to know that you're free to give or not give me whatever you want. Even if...even if you're, you know, sick. Sick in your heart, I mean. The decision to share your pain with me is yours. It'll always be yours."

A large tear slips down her cheek, a flash of lightning among the falling stars. "You don't know everything, Bobby."

Bobby tightens his hand. The words scare him.

She meets his eyes. "I want you to know everything."

B

Tell me

Tell me everything

A

Tragedy the First comes first

You listen to it like a children's book—with open mouth and diamond eyes

Does it makes you think

My life has been clinching for the kill

Since Day One?

Me too.

I think so too.

You want to hold me now, kiss away my pain.

But there is more left to tell

Tragedy the Second, I've named it

As though it were a story not my own

Now, it is a story that will be your own

If you are brave enough to hear it.

B

I'm brave enough now

Tell me

Tell me everything

May 21, 1977

Tragedy the Second

After the incident where Luis Rafael murdered the books, shooting bullet holes through them in the closet, Ana Lucia knew her own death was imminent.

She never once feared that her grandfather would kill her—she was too good a slave for that. Instead, she understood that if her brain had no outlet, her body would decay. It was only a matter of time.

After burning her secret stash of books, Luis Rafael changed his method of locking her away. Before, his ordering her to the closet was erratic, sometimes based on his mood, other times based on some lesson he deemed important for her to learn. After the books, he stuck to a schedule—five days in the closet, two days free to prepare food for the week and clean the house.

The first time Ana Lucia considered that there may be a God with a vested interest in her salvation was the day she came across a stack of her grandmother's diaries. That day, her grandfather had tasked her with organizing her grandmother's closet. The diaries were something she could read, another reality into which she could escape.

Ana Lucia hid the diaries one at a time in the closet, with the same cunning she hid the novels she brought home. She generally read one journal a week, trading one out for another.

There were forty diaries in all, the first dating back to February 1929 when Maria Teresa Obregón had received a black leather-bound journal for her fifteenth birthday.

Having been held by her grandparents five years, Ana Lucia didn't find out that her grandmother's name was Maria Teresa, not *mujer*, until she saw it signed in pretty cursive at the end of her first diary entry.

The first two years of Maria Teresa's writing were an exercise in the mundane. Maria Teresa recorded what she ate, what she wore, which chores she was in charge of. She even wrote about writing.

Something changed in Maria Teresa when she was seventeen. Her entries assumed a new voice, a more urbane one. She'd met a twenty-year-old shoeshine boy named Luis Rafael Vicente.

She admitted to being drawn to his stoicism, to the fact that he didn't care to look at her or any woman, even the most beautiful ones. She'd found out that he was a virgin—the only one over eighteen she knew—and she became determined to have him, to get him all alone in the woods near the edge of town and wheedle him with her soft voice and words.

It took six months of offering, but she finally managed to get him to take her body. After months of stealing off with him, she wrote of her dissatisfaction.

Luis Rafael is passionate during love-making, yet I can tell his passion is not for me. It's for something else.

He is passionate for life and he relieves his passion through me.

He has joined the Confederación Nacional del Trabajo. It has given him reason for life. He is no longer utterly apathetic. Except with me. He saves his listlessness for our conversations.

I hope this won't last.

Absorbing the disdain Maria Teresa held for Luis Rafael through her words, Ana Lucia thought of her grandmother with fondness for the first time.

In the closet, she continued reading in suspense, reviewing her grandmother's life like a movie.

Five months after her first encounter with Luis Rafael, Maria Teresa found she was pregnant with their first child. She wanted to dispose of the pregnancy. He wanted to marry her.

He wants to be married in the church. He doesn't hate the idea of God the way I do. He only hates the government. I try to tell him about the number of victims the Church and God have made. He tells me God is the victim, His name slandered not by those who take it in vain but by those who use it with a purpose—a purpose to destroy.

I don't know if I agree with him. But I love the way he talks. I love him. We will marry in the church.

Her first child, Josefina was born August 17, 1932.

Maria Teresa had two more children—Ana Lucia's father born in 1934 and another child named Carmen born three years later—before Luis Rafael was sent to prison as an anarchist in 1943.

Ana Lucia felt herself grow dizzy seeing her father's name in print and thinking about the two aunts she had never known about.

Maria Teresa's comments on the children were mostly tedious narratives, except one passage she wrote in 1952. Luis Rafael was still locked away.

The Little Saints

My children are little people now. Their personalities have developed, and I can't help but feel a sadness for what I see. I can predict their futures. It is a pity what they will become.

Josefina will depend on a man to save her. What she doesn't see is that she doesn't have the looks to reel in the kind of man who will save her. I will let her believe it is possible though. It's a good distraction from the prospect that she will grow up to be poor and desperate like me.

Carmen is fifteen and walks around aimless. She doesn't know what she wants out of life. For this reason, she will get nothing from life.

Javier is much like his father. He has left to go to university in England. He says he will go to America after that. He is too intent on finding a land where he can be a hero. Poor child. Poor, poor child. He hasn't learned the lesson of his father yet.

Ana Lucia shuddered to think her grandmother had prophesied her father's fate.

Perhaps Maria Teresa's bitterness made her the prophet she was writing that entry. She'd gone through years of heartbreak with lover after lover. She had no access to a civil divorce in Franco's Spain. No man was willing to live with her in light off her circumstance.

During her seasons of brutal loneliness, she wondered whether she ever really loved Luis Rafael or had simply been seduced by his aloofness.

He was so quiet back then, so mysterious. The quiet ones will always deceive you. You never have access to who they really are, although you believe you do. What you see in them is merely a creation of your own ego and desires.

When Luis Rafael's prison sentence ended in 1968, Carmen and Josefina were gone, both having married. Maria Teresa had grown not only to accept being alone by then, but she had learned to love it. Luis Rafael was an intrusion.

I wish he were the quiet man he used to be.

He has stopped believing in God. Unlike me, he is loud about his unbelief. It's pure vanity. What need is there to be loud about something that does not exist for you?

He is angry that Javier has left the country. I asked him what he expected. He has been gone twenty-five years. Did he expect Javier to stay with us forever?

He looked like he was going to hit me when I said it. He didn't. But now the fear is there and it is worse than a punch.

The entry on July 23, 1971 was the first mention Ana Lucia saw of herself.

Javier is dead. He was shot down after resisting arrest as a Communist. We know the truth. Civil war has persisted in Guatemala for years. He was one of the many revolutionaries the government assassinated.

I breathed a sigh of relief learning about his death. For too many years, I didn't know where he was. Now, I do. Knowing is an elixir.

When we received the letter in the mail, we learned also that he has a daughter named Ana Lucia. We are the next of kin. Luis Rafael insisted that we take her.

I am sixty-three. He is sixty-six. Though he considers himself strong from all his prison labor, we are old now. We have no need for children. He is only looking to replace the children that ran out on him in his absence.

Ana Lucia read little in her grandmother's journal about the abuses they inflicted on her. Yet, the very last journal entry she wrote, written just three months before Ana Lucia read it, suggested an awareness.

Luis Rafael's ways no longer bring me fright. I know he won't hurt me. He doesn't care enough to. And I no longer care enough to hurt him. Should I find a new man, it will be because it is what I want, not because I seek revenge. I no longer seek anything in regard to him.

He loves the girl. In his own sickening way, he loves her like his own children.

His abuse is a means to keep her near. If ever he gives her freedom, he is afraid she will leave like everyone else.

It doesn't matter that I am still here. It seems to me that we are waiting. Waiting. Waiting.

Waiting to see which of us will die first.

I don't want to wait any longer. I must go on my way. I must go soon. Or I will be the first to die.

I am leaving. It will happen soon.

In the darkness of the closet, her grandmother's words illuminated by the small flashlight, sixteen-year-old Ana Lucia knew it wouldn't be long before the end.

The Little Saints

Ana Lucia was let out of the closet for her two-day reprieve three days after reading that last passage.

It was May twenty-first.

When she stood in the kitchen cleaning the stove, Ana Lucia watched her grandmother come in for a glass of water. A wave of mercy for the old woman washed over her. For the first time, she saw Maria Teresa for who she was—a woman made lonely by her selfishness, awkwardly turned in on herself so that all she saw was herself and all that life had denied her.

She followed her grandmother to the living room when Luis Rafael called for more whiskey.

Carefully, Ana Lucia poured the liquor into her grandfather's glass, her curious eyes on Maria Teresa as she took a seat in the chair beside Luis Rafael.

She took a sip of her water, then said, "This is the last day."

Luis Rafael took a sip from his glass, unruffled by his wife's words.

"This is the last day, Luis."

This time, he gave her the courtesy of a narrow-eyed glance.

"I'm leaving you," she said, placing her glass on the end table beside her chair.

Luis Rafael took another sip, his eyes moving back to the television program he watched.

"It's not that I don't love you anymore," she continued. "It's that I never did. I believe you never loved me either. Nothing is lost."

Luis Rafael looked to Ana Lucia. She had backed herself to the entrance of the living room.

"Are you taking the girl?" he said.

"I don't intend to." Maria Teresa also turned her eyes to Ana Lucia. "You should let her go free. She's nearly an adult. She can care for herself."

Ana Lucia could have cried. For hatred. For love. For freedom. For the everything-ness and nothing-ness of a liberty that should have always been hers.

"I've been trying to save us by being quiet," Maria Teresa said. "There is no us. I was trying to save something that never existed. But individually, I can save what's left of you and of me. By leaving. It's the only way."

Her grandmother had hardly spoken over the years. Ana Lucia was surprised to find she was as much an artist in speech as in writing.

Maria Teresa further ornamented the artistry of her words with a quiet departure. She went off to her bedroom, shutting the door, as to say the conversation and the last forty-five years of her life were finished.

Luis Rafael drank to her decision. Drank to the sitcom on the television. Drank until he fell asleep in his living room chair.

For the first time, there was no one to tell Ana Lucia what to do with the rest of the evening. She saw to it that everything was clean and cooked before retreating to the tiny bed-less bedroom that had been loaned her the past five years.

The room seemed to breathe on her a cool sigh of relief.

Ana Lucia lay on the floor, flushing down the excitement of an unreliable freedom.

She began to wonder whether she should go to her grandfather and awake him so that he would not spend the night alone in the living room. It was a painstakingly hard decision to make. If she woke him, he might be angry enough to throw out even the suggestion of letting her go. If she didn't wake him, he might wake up with a cramped neck and the suggestion of her freedom would sink back through the hard earth from whence it came.

As she contemplated her options, she heard the first blast of gunfire. It came from across the hall, from the room where her grandmother slept.

Ana Lucia bolted up, her breath eluding her.

She didn't stop to think whether investigating the gunshot was safe. She knew it wasn't. But an end had come, and she had to know what that end was.

She walked softly across the hall, looked into her grandparents' open bedroom, and felt her own mouth fall agape.

Like a Rorschach inkblot, blood was splattered on the wall. Maria Teresa lay face down on the floor, a trail of blood curving like a lizard tail from her forehead.

Luis Rafael stared down at his wife lying at his feet, his pistol dangling from his fingertips. He looked up at Ana Lucia, his lip sagging, feeble.

Ana Lucia darted off, awakening her grandfather from his stupor. He ran after her, fantastically swift in his madness, outrunning his age and creaking knees. He blocked the front door, forcing her in the kitchen next to it. Winning their brief game of cat and mouse, he hemmed her against the counter with his monstrous belly. Calmly, he laid his pistol on the counter beside her, trading it out for the boning knife he'd grabbed from the sink.

"It's over now," he said, backing from her, the knife pointed at her.

Ana Lucia shook her head, licking away the salty tears above her lips.

He shook the knife at her. "Everybody's gone now. Javier is dead. Josefina and Carmen have run away. Now, you—you also get to be free."

Her gaze fell limp on him. She understood now his words.

In her crying, she had not realized that he was not planning to plunge the knife through her chest. He was handing the knife to her. A gift.

Ana Lucia stared at the knife.

He shook it again, his kind offering. "Free yourself."

Grabbing her hands, he placed them over his, so that together they held the knife up like a torch.

"Free yourself," he commanded.

She shook her head again, tears moving faster down her cheeks.

"Free yourself or I'll free you."

Never—never, never, never—had she consciously looked into her grandfather's eyes. At that moment, she did. Their color and intent were steel. They told her what she needed to know: the decision was hers. She could choose to slaughter him or choose to be slaughtered by him.

She tried to understand, tried to see the knife tearing through his skin, tried to imagine it bayoneting through her own. She couldn't envision either, couldn't see herself as the hunter or the prey.

As Ana Lucia folded over into herself, Luis Rafael forced the knife into her hands alone, driving her hands to his gut, his chest, his neck as he plunged the blade into himself three quick times.

There, the monster flooded her body. Each stab brought excitement, as though she was being electroshocked back to life.

Blood spurted out from his chest first, wetting Ana Lucia's shoulders as he sunk to the floor. His face slid down her knees before he hit the kitchen floor.

Looking down at his gutted body, she could not scream. She saw his heart pumping blood up and out of his open chest like a gurgling drain. His fingers vibrated, as if he was willing himself to pull the protruding knife from his neck. All of this she saw but couldn't scream. She was too excited to scream. Though his blood covered her face like cherry tears, there was no sadness, no fear. With his blood soaking through her clothes to her skin, there was only excitement.

His squirming, dying body was his final punishment and first gift to her.

She ran out of the kitchen and back to where Maria Teresa lay in the middle of the floor like an abandoned puppet. She couldn't help the woman. She needed something from her though.

With bloody fingers, Ana Lucia tore through the drawers and the closet, in a manic search. It was inside a floral vase she found what she was looking for.

She found her identity.

There lay her passport, the one Maria Teresa had confiscated the first day Ana Lucia arrived. She would need it to prove to the police that she was a person, that she actually existed. More accurately, she needed it to prove her existence to herself, that this life wasn't but a dream.

She went next for her boots, the only pair of shoes they loaned her. Shoelaces untied, she ran out the front door and down the stairwell, leaving for the neighbors an erratic configuration of bloody handprints. Out of the apartment building, she ran into the late spring afternoon.

The sunshine met her with the smile of her mother.

She stood in place on the sidewalk, stunned to paralysis by the sound of children playing in the playground across the street. They squealed, they yelped, they bleated. They cried bloody murder, all in jest. Their euphoria infected the air. It changed her bleary eyes to a spinning kaleidoscope.

Crystals and fairies, seawater and fishing boats, white horses and green woods.

It was then that Ana Lucia knew what must be done.

Run.

Like the children on the playground, run.

Like her father never did, run.

Like the criminal she'd been made, run.

Ana Lucia came to from her stupor and with a single resolve to leave it all behind, took off down the sidewalk, running into the spring sunlight.

For freedom, she ran and ran and ran until she could run no more.

She can run no more.

A

This is me
You know now
All you can't un-know
You see now
All you can't un-see

This is me
You know all I know:
That there can be
Martyrdom without Redemption
Sensitivity without Love
Death Without Retribution

But none of that matters now
I am only me

This is me

So quiet you are in front of me,
I only wonder will there be now:
You without Me?

19.

BOBBY FEELS EVERY word Ana Lucia speaks at the bottom of his spine as they stand still by that pond in Parque de El Capricho.

He looks at her standing with her hands folded together like a school teacher. She is standing beside a voluminous cedar tree, the hair of her long black wig tossed back over her shoulders by the cool night wind.

The black evening is calm, unflustered by her story. It occurs to Bobby that God and nature have already borne witness to all the past holds—why should they be disrupted by any of it?

"I know these stories aren't what you wanted to hear," she says.

He can only nod.

"You can leave now if you want."

He nods again, though he doesn't mean to.

"I'll leave."

"You already did," Bobby says, fiercely afraid of her absence. "It didn't fix anything, Ana Lucia."

Her eyes go alight at the sound of his voice.

"After all those years you spent in that horrible closet, you must've figured it out, Ana Lu—solitude makes you tough, but only love makes you strong."

She looks away, running her hands up and down her bare arms.

What words can he say to warm her? What words can he say at all? How can he use funeral rhetoric when he knows nothing of death? Quoting the likes of Bobby McFerrin would be pure foolishness, an insult to the sacredness of her pain. He really just wants to say that he doesn't see her as a murderer. He wants to say there are no wrong stories a woman can tell the right man. Mostly, he wants to tell her how brave she is and has been since she was that ten-year-old crouching in the car after the police killed her parents.

Bobby realizes there are no right words for times like this, only wrong ones.

"Are you okay?" he says. "I mean, I know you're not. I just—I hope you don't hold anything against yourself for what happened. It wasn't your fault. None of it."

He feels himself gaining steam but stops. He is taking her moment. Right now, she is everything.

"I know it's not my fault," she says. "I've always known that. But I do blame myself for one thing."

"Ana Lucia, you can't—"

"I never thought to run away. I can't forgive myself that I was waiting for them to die to get my freedom. I could have run away in the middle of the night. I could have never returned when they sent me out for groceries. I could have done it, but I didn't and now there's something so wrong with me that I don't know how to fix it. When I think of that, I know I'm to blame."

"That's not right," Bobby says. "It's not true and it's not right. Look, I can't make you believe that not a single bit of this is your fault, but—"

In unison with a loud nightingale, Ana Lucia's sudden sharp cry crosscuts his words. Through her entire recounting of her past, she has not cried. But now she sobs, holding her forearm over her eyes, tears dripping over the sides.

Bobby wishes he were as old and wise and formidable as the tree she leans against. He knows he isn't, but when she looks up at him with the face of a woman much older than himself, he takes a step forward, opening his arms in faith, hoping her grand pain can fit into his little life.

She rubs her face against his chest as he holds her. He feels her tears through his T-shirt like the first warm drops of summer rain.

Bobby feels tears steeping over the rims of his own eyes. It isn't pity he feels for her. It's love. Real, real love. Objective love. He loves her as an object of glory, strong as an ox after battle.

"You don't have to cry," she says, looking up at him. "It's over now. Besides that, I know something that I didn't know before. Suffering—suffering is the most fertile ground. You never know what will grow of it. For me—I could hardly draw stick figures before all of

The Little Saints

this happened. When I made my first paycheck, I bought the paint and canvasses. I don't know why. I didn't know what to do with them, but my hands did. They know what to do, even when I don't know how to do anything but cry. The suffering has made an artist out of me, I guess. Now you see no gift is free of charge." She stops. "I'm not pretending to be something I'm not. I know my tragedies. I'm not running from them. No one knows what happened, not even the police. No one knew I even existed. I didn't exist here until two-and-a-half years ago." She hesitates. "When I left and I heard the children playing, I knew that I was going to be okay. Happy children are the voices that say nothing matters except that you're alive."

Bobby wipes his tears with the back of his hand, steadying his mind. There is something that should be said, but he's not sure how it should be said.

Ana Lucia apparently knows it.

"I know that something in me is out of control," she says. "But what can I do, Bobby? I don't know who I'll be if I lose more control. I only know what I am right now. I'm okay right now. And with you, none of it really matters. With you, I step outside of myself. I step into this other place and I feel safe. The place is called love, I think. I step inside love when I'm with you. I'm *in* love with you, Bobby."

Bobby breathes for the first time since she went away. He has found a teammate in her. They are searching for the same thing—for a way to make love work.

"What can I do?" he says quietly. "What can I do for you?"

"Live with it," she replies. "Live with *me*. That's what I'm learning to do."

"Are you?"

"I don't have another choice." She loosens herself from his arms. "You do though. I don't know if that thing that happened in your rehearsal room or what happened when I made you leave—I don't know when those things will happen again. I don't have control over that. I'm afraid of the monster in me, but I have to live with that. You don't." Her eyes glisten like holy water. "I really wish you would though."

"I, um, I probably—" he stops to consider his words. "Ana Lucia, I probably can't—"

"Can't?"

"—probably can't fight off your demons. It'd be a lie to say I could. I don't want to lie to you."

"Okay." She nods quickly, feigning reasonable understanding.

Bobby smiles, tickled by his sweet girl. "But I guess none of that matters so much because I'm gonna be here with you. Inside of this safe place you called love. I'm *in* love with you too, Ana Lu. But you already know that, don't you?"

Ana Lucia grins so bright, her youth is restored like polished brass. Face-to-face, they stand in this densely spun cocoon called love. Now, a firefly has entered the cocoon, sharing its jubilant light.

"Love is light, isn't it? I'm ready to see every bit of you, everything that's left to see."

She nods, her eyes falling from him.

"Look, I'm not—" he lowers his voice "—I'm not talking about sex or anything. I just want you, everything you are, all the time. You say you're scared of the monster in you. I'm not afraid of monsters, Ana Lu." Happiness bubbles up inside of him until he almost laughs with joy. "I swear, I've never been so stoked to know somebody in my life."

"I've never been so excited to be known."

He reaches for her, but she holds him off by the wrists.

"I want to show you something," she says. "I've wanted to show you this for a long time. Will you sit for me?"

Bobby sits, obedient, feverish for her leading. She stands in front of him, her shift dress shivering, her copper legs gleaming. He wants to reach for her but waits his turn.

She steps out of her Adidas, setting them aside neatly. Standing still, she takes a breath in preparation, looking around to make sure they are all alone.

Her feet begin to move methodically in a motion that makes her hips roll like a belly dancer. She turns slowly, giving him sight of her pretty, pretty bottom as it moves high and low, round and round just for him. It is a tribal dance she does, a seduction of the hips. Delicious hips. He can't help but wonder if this is how the virgins once prepared for their wedding nights.

Ana Lucia needs no beat; her body is music. The swing-and-freeze of her pelvis concentrates his attention on what is beneath that part of her dress. He swallows, salivating for this feast of the eyes.

Her gaze has gone off to the sky, even off to the land from which this dance came. Undoubtedly, her homeland. Bobby is reminded of the little girl standing between her parents in that old picture he found—the girl who must have watched and imitated her mother doing this dance a million times. This is who that little girl has grown up to be.

She is the most erotic thing he has ever seen.

His own body won't allow him another second without touching her body. He stands up, reaching for the pretty round bottom that has been calling to him with every swing of her hips. Holding and squeezing her there—right *there*—he kisses her with a mouth inflamed and swollen with hunger. She follows the pace of his lips, the pattern of his mouth brushing over hers again and again in perfect time. He presses her against his body with a passion that almost mimics violence, as though he could push his whole body inside of hers or perhaps pull her whole body inside of his.

"I want you now, Ana Lucia," Bobby whispers. "I'll be good to you. I swear it."

Ana Lucia snakes his shirt between her fingers, staring at her hand, as though commanding her fingers with her eyes. She lifts her face so that their noses touch. He inhales her warm, gently flowing breath.

"Say yes," he pants. "I don't want to take it from you. I want you to give it to me. I just need to know you're really ready because when we start, I'm not sure I can stop." Quickly, he adds, "But I will. Just tell me if you want me to stop."

The night takes another breath, an almost imperceptible wind swirling over them.

"I'm ready," she says.

"Are you sure?"

"Yes."

He takes a controlled breath. "Let's go home now."

She shakes her head, backs herself from him. Her eyes to his, she reaches for the first button of her dress, undoing it with shaky fingers. With all the restraint in the universe, Bobby keeps his eyes to hers, not pulling them away even as her hands travel down each button. The dress falls off of her like snake skin. After her panties fall, Bobby doesn't waste the effort of restraint as she goes through the calm, systematic removal of her bra. The long hair of her wig falling over her breasts, she is an image of the Lady Godiva.

Bobby knows it is his turn now. He starts with his shirt, then his pants. He hesitates before pulling down his underwear, fearing with all her softness, she'll be scared away by his hardness.

He can only think to say, "I love you," before he shows himself to her.

He kneels, smiling that she can't keep her eyes away from what he was afraid would terrify her. She kneels in front of him, her knees sinking into the grass. The cherry blossom petals lie around them like wedding rice.

Bobby reaches for her, cupping the back of her head and kissing her until she submits to his lowering her to the ground, on top of her dress. He gently removes the wig, letting free her damp curls. He smiles—oh, his silly girl with her silly disguise.

Not yet inside her, Bobby looks down at little trembling Ana Lucia beneath him and touches the tip of her nose with his in anticipation of the sough of her sea and the thrill of night swimming.

There is nothing he can say now with his mouth that his body can't say better, but he will allow this one line:

"You're so brave, baby. *So* brave, my brave, brave girl."

A

Lying beneath you,

the whole world has stopped

The eye of the universe has zeroed in

on me:

The one who has shed her baby skin,

Now clothed in you

Don't it all seem paradox?

In lightspeed travel from rare to ripe,

I am shameless as a child, unveiled

A body never felt so legitimate.

"Tell me what it feels like," you say in a quiet voice that almost pleads. Strands of your hair fall over my forehead as you slide in and out of me.

"It feels like...like the sun rose in me."

Blood creeps into your face, forming rosy blotches on your cheeks, as you work out your final act upon me. When you wipe the sweat from your forehead and collapse beside me onto green leaves, I think:

"I am so grateful. How can there be no one to thank? How can there be no God?"

To be sure, you've shown me: some form of God-heaven-the-angels-all-of-that...

B

Did you know?

The nerves under your skin—

they are like bomb wires.

I, adventurous

I probe, I push, I partake, I percuss

Until...explosion!

Humans made dynamite

But God made you, Ana Lu

Could there be a joy more violent

than discovering a you like You?

El Verano

صيف

L'été

Samhradh

Kiangazi

Summer

20.

ANA LUCIA AND BOBBY FINISH *Moby Dick* at the end of July. The ending is too ambiguous for Bobby's taste. Maybe even too morose. Everyone dies except Ishmael? That seems almost unacceptable to Bobby.

All Ana Lucia can respond with is the truth: these things happens.

Still, she realizes Bobby's Rockwellesque life has programmed him to fear the truth. In his world, the relentless appearance of death is nearly indecent.

So, he decides their next book will be a much shorter one with a happier ending. A book that even reminds him a little bit of *Moby Dick*.

"From inside the fish Jonah prayed to the Lord his God," Bobby reads. He leans forward in his chair. "He said: In my distress I called to the Lord, and he answered me. From deep in the realm of the dead I called for help, and you listened to my cry."

Ana Lucia looks down at her slick knees, mountains jutting up from the bathwater in the clawfoot tub. She is having a bubble bath as Bobby reads to her about Jonah and the whale. It is both her first time reading from the Bible and her first time having a bubble bath. She has decided the Bible is a good thing; some form of God might be real, even if only in their happy little apartment. Bobby said a bubble bath was a luxury in life nobody should deny himself. He doesn't like taking them much anymore, but when he was a kid, it was a treat his mother let him have every Sunday evening.

Maybe not the best treat in the world, Ana Lucia thinks. The bubbles are like dishwashing suds. After all the dishes she washed during her adolescent slave labor, she should hate the bubbles, except they do a good job covering up the tub's cracked porcelain.

Ana Lucia withholds any complaint about the bath. She and Bobby have lived together in peace for two months now. With her help, he has written a new song every night in the living room.

He probes to get inside her head, prodding gently as though at a beehive. There is a tacit understanding that their union hasn't cured her. Still, she allows him to borrow from her pain. She draws the pictures that inspire his songs, psalms detailing the kind of despair and human desecration he's never known. The pain has already been exposed; should it not be put to good use? Further, she uses him for his memories just as well, asking him more than once how he learned about the moon landing, what Tang tastes like, what all there was to do and see at a drive-in. She re-lives his life with him, finding some healing in her imputed past, the part of her life lost to the black hole of that closet. For so long, the lost part was the only part that mattered.

So now there are meaningful songs, bubble baths, and full kitchen cabinets. Bobby has not talked to his mother since revealing that he is married, but Dom brought over a piece of mail from her with a check.

Cutting her hand through a swirl of bubbles, Ana Lucia is able to consider what kind of sandwich she will make the two of them after this bath. Noticing the way the sunlight from the bathroom window glints off Bobby's bare chest, she finds no shame banking on him as a meal closer than the sandwich. She focuses in on the constellation of freckles on his shoulder, wanting desperately to reach out and touch the stars.

Bobby reads on, unaware of her appetite. "What I have vowed I will make good. I will say, 'Salvation comes from the Lord.' And the LORD commanded the fish, and it vomited Jonah onto dry land."

"Bobby," Ana Lucia says.

He looks from his leather-bound Bible to her. "Yeah?"

"I need your consejo."

"My what?" He raises his eyebrows, clearly perceiving some naughtiness in the word.

"Consejo is advice."

"Oh. Okay. What is it?"

"It's about Skylark."

"The girl from your acting class?"

"Yes." Ana Lucia pours a handful of bubbles over her knee. "She's been a worse distraction to me than normal. She talks every time I have a performance in the class, she talks the entire time. She bumps me with her shoulder every day. She pulled my hair yesterday and called it an accident. It's a drug."

"A drug? A drag, you mean?"

"Yes, a drag."

"Maybe she's jealous. Some girls get jealous of beautiful girls." He re-opens his Bible. "Why don't you tell her to screw off or something?"

"To screw off?" she says, testing out the new phrase.

"Yep."

"I can't say that."

"Why not?"

"Because I hardly know what it means."

He laughs.

"But, if you want to, you could come to my class and say something like that for me."

"No, I can't."

"Why not?"

He flips through the pages of the Bible, searching for where they left off. "Let's see—"

"Why not?" she says, sitting up straighter in the bath.

"Why not what?"

"Why can't you come to my class and tell her to—what was it?— *screw off?*"

"Oh. Well, it's basically cuz I don't want to. I've had enough trouble here to last me a lifetime. Otherwise, me and the other made men would rush the room and take her out Corleone style. I've never seen *The Godfather,* by the way. Maybe we could watch it on the projector, get you some good ideas or something." He grins and begins reading again. "Then the word of the LORD came to Jonah a second time: Arise! Go to the great city of Nineveh and proclaim the message that I will give you."

"Bobby?"

He looks up once more. "Ana Lucia Carter?"

"I have something to say."

"Yeah?"

She stands, coming slowly alive from the water like the Loch Ness. His own eyes come alive, though they appear sleepy as they slide down her body. Mounting his lap, she soaks his jeans, her body as slippery as Jonah's big fish.

"What do you call the spider?" she says.

"What spider? You saw a spider?"

"No. I just want to know the name in English for the spider with the long legs. The very famous one."

"Daddy long legs, you mean?"

"*Papi* long legs," she murmurs as she takes measure of his long legs, confounded again by how a man so often meek could grow to his size.

"I like that name," he says back. He holds her soapy hips. "Call me that every day, will you?"

She lays his hand on her breast, as if to say "I will."

His eyes blink, at loss.

"Are you okay?" she asks.

"I'm okay, thanks," He laughs at his awkward formality. "You dizzy me, is all. Your body is—it's like the best song. You know, like, when familiarity meets novelty. I could put your song on repeat forever, Little Lu."

Bobby touches her throat, bringing his mouth to hers and pressing both of his lips over her bottom lip—tasting it, nibbling it, savoring it—until her legs hook around him and the whole earth vibrates.

In the same moment, a clanking sound comes from the front door.

"Did you hear that?" he says, tearing his gaze from Ana Lucia to the open bathroom door.

"Hear what?" she asks absently, her mind in a whir.

"Someone's at the door."

"I didn't—"

He stands, wrapping a towel around her. "Somebody's messing with the door. I'm going to see what's going on."

"No—"

"Don't worry."

He heads out of the bathroom, feigning bravery with square shoulders, but walking entirely too fast to have had any real acquaintance with danger.

From the bathroom door, Ana Lucia resigns herself to watching him in all his immaculate ignorance walk bravely down the hall to the front door. There, he is met by a white-haired, pint-sized woman who has freely entered, dragging in her suitcase.

The woman startles at the sight of Bobby. In blind defense, she retrieves a pocket knife from her purse, swiping at Bobby's shoulder.

"Quien eres? Por que estás aqui!" the woman yells, swinging the knife across his bicep.

"Ah, shit!" Bobby howls in pain, attempting to patch his wound with his hand. Wine-red blood dribbles down to the floor from the cracks between his fingers.

It is the sight of his blood that restores Ana Lucia from her soft evanescence.

Binding her towel tight around her, she raises her voice, running down the hall to insert herself between the woman and Bobby.

In Spanish she cries out, "Ms. Peña, please stop! Don't hurt him. He's my husband."

That Bobby is still partly stranger to Ana Lucia is evidenced by the fact that his silent stare doesn't speak anything intelligible to her. Even her grandfather's muted looks told her something. Bobby's silence, on the other hand, removes him entirely from her, returns him to the foreign boy he was that first night in La Buena Vida. Then, he was a foreign world orbiting around her, drawing closer and closer to her light. Now, he is more like an unknown star in the distance, flickering in and out as she longs for him to simply put his arm around her while they sit side-by-side on the mattress in their room.

Their room—the room Señora Peña has subleased to her for the past two years. Maria Peña, a woman of sixty-three, is the sole caretaker of her mother in Andalucía and thus makes frequent extended visits to her. When Señora Peña put out the ad for someone to occupy her second bedroom so as to care for the apartment during her frequent absences, she made it clear that she was not looking for a roommate. The apartment was hers and hers alone, she told Ana Lucia after she'd answered the ad. Ana Lucia's job would simply be to look after the place in exchange for deeply discounted rent. It gave Ana Lucia a chance to pay for everything needed to sort out her legal standing as a citizen after her grandparents died.

"You should've told me all of this before," Bobby says as they listen to Señora Peña unpacking her suitcase in the room next door. He glances over at the white-bandaged wound on his arm.

"Would it have changed anything?" Ana Lucia responds quietly.

"I don't know. Maybe."

His voice doesn't give away anger, though if he knew what Ana Lucia knew, he'd be rejoicing. Had he truly known Señora Peña—despiser of all things American—he would have known what a miracle it was that she has decided to allow the two of them to occupy the room, even if she won't apologize for slicing Bobby's arm.

"Where would we live if we didn't live here?" Ana Lucia asks.

"I don't know. But I guess that's not the point."

She stares at him quietly. There is an irritated tremor in the frost-white rim of his pursed lips. A vexed breath quivers his nostrils. He is evidently making a discipline of swallowing down ugly words for her. Ever since she revealed her story to him, his kindness has become so reliable, she feels guilty for it. In this way, she realizes they are both living out love in fear—for her, fear that she will exhaust his love sooner than he can give it all; for him, fear that anything but pliancy will drive her to another moment of madness. She wonders how long love can eat the bread of fear before it spews both of them out.

"It's okay," he says with a yielding sigh. "Don't worry. If she lets us live here, we'll stay here until we get our own place. Don't worry."

"She shouldn't be here long. She never stays long."

What Ana Lucia doesn't seem to realize is that two weeks is a long time under the microscope.

Fourteen days and despite all of Bobby's efforts to faze himself out of Señora Peña's conscious world by keeping away from the apartment eighteen hours a day, he can't evade the taped notes she leaves around the house. Notes in Spanish about cleaning the tub after every use, not arriving after one in the morning, not storing more than five of their own items in the refrigerator at a time.

She tries having a talk with him. In the muddled Spanish of Andalucía, no less. He stands quietly in front of her until she is finally quiet. They hold eye contact until she goes on her way.

Her sensitivity to sound has made it impossible for Bobby to sleep the whole night next to Ana Lucia. It'd be too much not to touch her, turn her toward him, and thus conduct their midnight human orchestra.

He sometimes makes an effort to bring to mind Ana Lucia's violin cries and his own cello panting as he sits outside of the apartment unit smoking a cigarette in the stairwell at three in the morning. Indeed, he's taken up the bad habit again. Ana Lucia will have to understand; there's no other remedy to willfully ignoring the demands of his libido.

Of course, he hides the smoking habit from Ana Lucia and feels at least superficially justified in doing so. Wasn't the secret she kept about Señora Peña much bigger?

Good thing he can't get near enough to her for her to smell the tobacco on him.

Smoking is his replacement pleasure, and it's a pretty grand pleasure at that, for he can indulge in it whenever he wishes. He normally has a smoke or two with Dom after rehearsal, but this afternoon he shares a single cigarette with Betty, passing it back and forth with sibling charity as they walk.

The Little Saints

"I think you should see a doctor about the hand," she says as they turn onto Calle de la Cabeza. The sun is perched creamy yellow on the horizon.

"Yeah, I know." He holds his hand out, staring at the quiver that has returned since his first meeting with Señora Peña. "It doesn't do it all the time."

"Curious. Well, anyway, I wasn't sure if I'd tell you this, but I suppose your head can't get any bigger. Your songwriting has become a work of art. As I see it, your talent belongs in a museum. I knew you just had to dig inside yourself a bit. You really touch on human pain now. It's quite inspiring." Betty quietly loops her arm through his. "Listen, Young, I'd also like to make a comment about how you treated that brunette from yesterday. Your manner isn't functional for how a future superstar treats his fans."

Betty is referring to an interaction with a British girl from their show last night. At least, a Brit he'd perceived to be a girl until he noticed the bobbing Adam's apple and the chest flat as an ironing board. The boy had invited Bobby to his house. Bobby had pretended not to speak English. For the first time, he'd felt so out of sorts, he wasn't sure he belonged anywhere outside of Avon.

"You've got to be more inviting to your fans," Betty says. "You're working on a reputation here."

"I wasn't mean to her—I mean, *him*," he says. Betty responds with a click of disapproval, to which he insists, "I wasn't. Besides, I didn't know it'd be that big of a deal."

"You do quite well at not knowing, don't ya? At the very least, you should've made the lad think he had some chance. The idea that they've actually got a chance is what keeps them coming back to the next show."

"And all this time I thought it was the music."

"Not until your songs are on the radio." She smokes down the rest of their cigarette and tosses it away. "Listen and learn, Young. I'm aware that you're just a teenager—"

"I'll be twenty at the end of December. How old are you?"

"Being so young, I suppose you don't know much about Berry Gordy."

"I know him."

"He managed Motown, you see. He was able to take his artists to heights they'd never imagined. But those artists had to sign over their careers to him. Are you willing to do that, Young?"

He is caught off guard by the sobriety of her question, even delighted by it. "I think I am."

She playfully spanks his cheek. "Then, call me *Betty* Gordy. I'm going to whip you into shape, young sir. We'll give you career wings the classic way. You'll be an artist who not only knows how to perform but is a personality off-stage. Either that or you'll need to start crafting a verse-chorus-verse-chorus-kill-me-now pop tune, send it to a record company, and hope for a verse-chorus-verse-chorus-kill-me-now insanely famous pop artist to come across it and sell you to the masses. It's your choice."

Bobby pats his pocket in search for another cigarette. He pulls out one and offers it to Betty for the first drag.

She receives it with a sweet glance. "Thank you, Young."

"Don't you wonder what my real last name is?"

"I suppose you would've told me if you wanted me to know."

He realizes now that he wants her to know. At the same time, he fears for her to know, as it seems there may be no end to her knowing him. And though she is the kind of woman he could only imagine having sex with on a bed of stones—so different from Ana Lucia and her need for damp leaves against her back—he sees the benefit of diversity.

Or maybe it's none of that. Maybe it's really just Señora Peña and the physical distance it has created between him and Ana Lucia.

He will withhold his name from Betty. It's a business too risky for the moment.

As she passes the cigarette back to him, he doesn't restrain himself from knowing her.

"Betty—that's like your real name?"

"It is."

"It is?"

"Yes, it is." There is a pleasant wink in her smile.

For the first time, he likes her. It's as though a little red bird has perched on his shoulder, taking rest there.

"I'm supposed to meet up with Kyle and Dom," Bobby says as they turn onto Calle de Embajadores. "I gotta split now."

The Little Saints

Standing at the corner, she buries her hands into her jeans and draws out two pills. Swallowing them dry, she wastes no time answering the question that he wants to ask. "It's called Desoxyn, Young. Totally legal. It'll give me the extra twelve hours of wake time I need to get through the next show and after-party I've got tonight. Anyway, you and I should talk with seriousness more often. I like it. Besides, I've got to catch you before stardom takes you from me. It will happen soon. I'm sure of it. The question is, where will you fly away to first?" She opens her arms to him. "Well, I must crack on now. Gimme hug. Take care of that arm. Maybe it'll stop the quiver in your hand."

He hugs her, for the first time lingering. Afterward, he rests on his heels, hands in pocket, watching her as she walks off. For a moment, he wishes he could be the little brother who tags along with her on whatever evening plans she has that are so fun she'd pop pills to stay awake for them.

He makes his way back to the apartment to change clothes before meeting Dom at the bar. Tagged on the refrigerator, there is a note from Señora Peña.

From what he can gather, it is a goodbye note, a note reminding Ana Lucia that her flight to Andalucía is this afternoon and reminding her that she and Bobby must care for her home with even more care than they would their own.

Bobby is so happy for the note, he sticks it on his forehead, laughing out loud. Who knew he'd be saved so soon? God bless America...and Spain.

His prison sentence has ended. He reaches inside his pocket for another cigarette. He will have a victory smoke.

Ana Lucia takes time to review today's acting class and excuse herself once again for withholding the truth of her living situation from Bobby. She does this on her 11:30 bus ride home from La Buena Vida.

Sometimes it is better to keep secrets than willingly end one's own happiness, isn't it? That's why she never told Bobby about Señora Peña. Maybe it wouldn't have ended their happiness, but it would have slowed it down and why do that? They are together; now is the time for full speed ahead.

Full speed ahead to forfeiting the past. Full speed ahead in acting. Full speed ahead in love.

Now life can be embraced as truth rather than tolerated as fact.

Ana Lucia takes the stairwell up to her apartment unit two-by-two, animated again about the prospect of life.

As though life is responding to her bliss when, she is confronted by a blooming cloud of smoke when she opens the front door to the apartment. Flames lick the wood floor, creating rings of fire which caper around the room.

Ana Lucia's thoughts mingle with the smoke; she cannot lay a solid hold to a single one of them.

It is Bobby who gives frame to her thoughts.

"What the—" he says. "What happened?"

He stands at her side. His footsteps up the stairs were apparently crowded out by the thoughts in her head.

"It's fire," she hears herself say.

"How did it start? Didn't anyone smell the smoke before it got like this?"

What to say? The downstairs neighbors are never home. The adjacent apartment is vacant.

"Have you called the firemen?"

"I just arrived," she replies, numb.

"We gotta knock on somebody's door. You gotta talk to them. My Spanish isn't gonna work like yours."

"Bobby, I need..."

Evidently alarmed by how the fire transfixes her gaze, he hunches down to tip her chin up and meet her eyes. "What do you need? What's wrong? Is something happening to you on the inside?"

"I'm okay." She hesitates. "I have to go in."

"What? Why?'

"My parents."

"What?"

Her eyes search for a path through fire, one that will lead to her room. "I have one drawing of my parents. I can't let that drawing burn. I don't know if I can repeat it."

"You can't go in there, Ana Lu. You might not make it out."

"I have to go in."

Bobby steps back. It's clear to Ana Lucia that he is meditating, deliberating, deciding—choosing what kind of man he will be, whether a man at all.

Solemnly bringing his eyes back down to hers, he says, "I'll get it. Don't worry."

If not for the fact that Bobby is still deathly afraid of any law enforcement, he and Ana Lucia would have waited for the fire department to arrive so that they could have at least treated his blistered hand. Instead, when Bobby emerged from the apartment, teetering and battling for breath, his scorched hand holding the photograph, he said that they had to go immediately.

Now, as they walk in the dark toward his old apartment, Ana Lucia sees his eyes are wet from physical pain. She holds tightly the picture of her parents in one hand and tries reaching for his bubbling hand with the other to examine it.

He pulls his hand back. Caught off guard by his own coarseness, he says, "I'm sorry. Forgive me. Just-just don't touch it. Please."

Ana Lucia looks down despondent at the picture of her parents.

At Bobby's old apartment, Dom opens the door quickly. His hair is wet, shiny as icicles.

"Hey, what's up?"

Bobby holds his hand up limp like a rag.

"What the fuck happened?" Dom says, his eyes darting to Ana Lucia as he ushers them in and begins rummaging through the drawers in the adjacent kitchen.

She shrinks, stepping backward so that her back touches the front door. From there, she watches the boys in the kitchen. Dom pulls out a tiny First Aid kit.

"Fire at Ana Lucia's apartment," Bobby manages to say as Dom begins tending to his wound with an antibiotic wipe. "Geez, that hurts like a bit—"

"It's not gonna feel good, dude."

"Yeah. I know. I just—"

"What's all the fuss?" comes another voice. A terrifically Irish one.

Ana Lucia's mouth falls open at the sight of Skylark entering the kitchen in a long T-shirt and nothing else. From where she stands, Skylark cannot see her.

"What on Earth happened to you?" she says, pulling Bobby's hand from Dom.

"I burned it. I was trying to get something from a fire and the fire jumped up. I don't know." He looks up with her with trust, as though she is Mother Hen and he her duckling. Ana Lucia is instantly sick at heart, sicker than when he first snatched his hand from her.

She pulls him over to the sink, placing his hand under a stream of water. "It's still burning on the inside. It's like a steak still sizzling off the grill. You have to douse the burning. Might take a quarter of an hour to stop the burning."

She continues to hold Bobby's hand up under the water, her braless breasts touching his side through her thin T-shirt. Dom is at her left. Their words drop in volume. They are a secret society. Ana Lucia stands alone, unable to configure the scene and how Skylark fits into it. Perhaps Dom brought her home as a lover. That must be it.

"It's only a second-degree burn," says Skylark loud enough for Ana Lucia to hear.

"How do you know?"

"It ain't rocket science, Young. A third-degree burn would have you on your knees."

He sighs. His tears are gone. It's at that point, he remembers his other life. "Ana Lucia, where are you?"

The Little Saints

Ana Lucia steps into the kitchen slowly, dipping a cold toe into even colder water.

If Skylark is surprised by her presence, she hides it well.

She offers only a smile. "Hello, Ana Lucia. I'm Betty Warner, Naïve's manager. It's nice to meet you. Welcome to my home."

In the late evening, Ana Lucia glances over at Bobby as he lies on the floor, loosely holding his bandaged hand over his mouth. Like her, he is baffled by the notion that in all this time, they never put together that Skylark was Betty. With all Bobby's complaints about Naïve's wild manager and Ana Lucia's grievances with her rowdy hector, they hadn't guessed it.

Despite the discovery, Bobby told Dom that he and Ana Lucia would need to stay in the apartment for an undetermined number of days. He wasn't asking for his old bedroom back, just the living room. And they'd pay if they had to. Dom wouldn't hear of any shit like that, he said. He wouldn't accept a dime. Ana Lucia immediately tried remembering how much a dime was worth.

Dom offered his clothes for both Bobby and Ana Lucia to sleep in. A blue Dodgers T-shirt and black shorts for Ana Lucia. A pair of gray sweats for Bobby.

In Dom's oversized clothes, she has no need for the white sheet Dom gave them.

Curled up on the living room floor beside Bobby, she watches him as he takes to fiddling with the sheet.

"What a life. What a la-la-la-life," he croons at the ceiling.

She pulls Dom's T-shirt over her mouth. "Are you angry with me?"

"What?" He lowers the T-shirt back down from her mouth. "What did you say?"

"I said, don't be angry with me."

"Angry with you for what?"

"Your hand."

He holds up his hand limply in front of both their eyes. "You mean this ol' thing. Ah, don't sweat it. I was thinking about selling it to science one day anyway." He smothers her laughter with a kiss.

"We'll find another place. We just gotta figure out how we're going to keep Señora Peña from putting a hit out on us."

He intends to be funny, but Ana Lucia can't find the humor in the thought of Señora Peña finding her apartment a box of charcoal. She'll only know it by seeing it, as Ana Lucia has no number by which to reach her.

"Does it still hurt a lot—your hand?" Ana Lucia asks.

"Like a bitch. Forgive my French."

"French?" she asks, confused.

He half-smiles. "Nothing, nevermind. I was just saying it still hurts, is all."

"Even with the medicine Dominic gave you?"

He nods.

She asks the only thing she can think to with the picture of her parents lying on her right side. "Do you want to call your mother and father?"

"I don't know."

"What can I do for you?"

"Nothing, really. I'm a little thirsty, I guess."

"You want to me to get something from the kitchen?"

He touches his bandaged hand. "If you don't mind."

Ana Lucia tiptoes across the room, using the light of the moon streaming from the window as her guide. She stops, bending over to roll up her socks.

While she is still leaning, Bobby says, "Wait. Don't move."

She obeys, her body keeping the shape of a seven. She looks over at him. He has pulled himself to sitting position, gazing at her

"That," he says, his eyes following the shape of her body and resting at the curve of her bottom. "That shape—that's the most beautiful thing I've ever seen in my life. Swear that on everything I own."

She smiles, slowly erecting herself.

Bobby is medallion-faced as she approaches him. She lowers herself onto his lap. He kisses her slowly, then stops, distracted.

"I have to pee." He says, kissing her forehead and rising to his feet. "Don't fall asleep before I get back."

The Little Saints

"Leave her alone," Bobby says. These are his first words upon entering Betty's room.

Betty sits up on the bed in the dark bedroom, the gray light of the moon framing her. She is an owl, wide-eyed, a cunning Romani spirit, even at one in the morning.

"You must have started this conversation without me?" Betty replies. "I've not the slightest idea what you're talking about."

"I'm talking about Ana Lucia. You used the name Skylark in the acting class, which I should have known you were in, since you thought I was signing up for it. You're being a jerk to Ana Lucia. She's been telling me about it, and I didn't realize it was you, but now that I know, it's gonna stop."

"What a big man you are now. So much like my dear Carlos. But you should know by now that I'm exhausted with those kinds of lads. Get out of my room if you've got nothing more to say."

Bobby stands hunched, crippled by her confidence.

"Fine. Stay there if it suits ya," she says. She glances at her cuticles, unflappable.

He meets her audacity with feigned fortitude, stepping to her bedside. "Look, Betty—"

"Stuff it, will you." She sits up on her knees, nearly touching him with her own aroused breasts. "You don't have a say on anything that happens in the class. Besides that, I never knew you to be so controlling. Won't be good for your marriage."

"Why are you like this?" he says, stepping back, though the invisible red bird from the other day stays perched on his shoulder. He wills down his excitement "I don't want to play this stupid game with you. Just leave Ana Lucia alone."

"If I don't?"

"Why don't you try it out and see."

"Threatening me?"

"Absolutely."

Betty slides back down to her bottom, grinning. "Why, thank you, Young. I suppose you've never threatened a lass before, so that would make me a special case. I quite like the thought of being special to you." She bites her bottom lip. "As you wish. I'll leave yer wan in there alone."

Bobby flutters his eyes, incredulous. "That's it?"

"Unless you want more." Her eyes flash.

Betty has the lion's share of power in their relationship—probably always has—but if she knew the kind of demands she makes on his curiosity, she'd take full advantage.

"I don't want more. I don't want anything from you, Betty," he says, deciding at that moment there will always be a curfew on their interactions. "I'm going to bed."

"To floor, you mean?"

He hates that he can't hold back a laugh. "Leave her alone. Just remember that and you'll be fine."

"I will."

"Okay."

"Okay." She raises her brows, as if to ask when he will go.

He turns to the door, more unsteady than when he first entered it.

21.

WHEN SKYLARK—that is, *Betty*—gives up harassing Ana Lucia during class, Ana Lucia knows it is because of Bobby. This bothers her more than the bullying. Without an enemy, acting class loses some of its excitement. Further, knowing that Betty will forfeit her own guilty pleasure for Bobby suggests she shares a true alliance with him.

Ana Lucia sees it for the first time when the three of them have breakfast one morning in the kitchen.

Having started her morning off in romantic play with Bobby, Ana Lucia feels like being a goody-good wife, preparing a bowl of cereal for him. Betty follows up, pouring milk in the bowl as he holds it, glancing daringly at Ana Lucia.

Bobby notices none of it.

Ana Lucia pours him orange juice from the one centimeter left in the carton.

"Best not drink that," Betty says to Bobby. "Citrus wreaks havoc on the singing voice. You've got two shows tonight, a stór?"

"A stór?" Bobby says.

"It's an Irish term of endearment. It means, 'my treasure.'"

"Irish is a language?"

"Gaelic," Ana Lucia interrupts. "The language is called Gaelic."

Betty looks at Ana Lucia, an eyebrow lifted. "Oh, really? How long you been speaking it?"

Ana Lucia looks to Bobby. He chastises Betty with his eyes, his mouth harder than she's ever seen it.

Betty responds with a smile. "I'm sorry for being impolite to you, Ana Lucia. Please forgive me, love. It's just that I have something important to tell Bobby." She turns to him. "It's good news for you and the band. Naïve has officially been invited to L'Olympia in Paris for a showcase of up-and-coming punk bands." She takes Bobby's spoon, scooping up a bite of his cereal. "Don't look so confused. It's Paris's finest. The Cure and Black Sabbath both have performed there. I suggest you get prepared for it. Who knows what may happen?"

She finishes with a smirk. In light of the wondrous look on Bobby's face, Betty has won this round.

The push and pull between Ana Lucia and Betty continues throughout the week. Though Betty's audacity ostensibly makes her winner most days, Ana Lucia knows she is the ultimate winner by night.

Bobby swears making love to her takes away the pain from his hand. He can't fully stretch it yet and his guitar playing is limited to short strokes, but why sweat it, so long as he can look forward to having her by the end of the night? He finds pleasure in the pain as he hoists his upper body above hers to support the crest- and-fall rhythm of his lower half. Hemmed in between his two shaking but strong arms, Ana Lucia discovers a pleasure so thick, she can no longer see the ominous Skylark flying above them.

They try their best to be quiet at night, but the apartment is alive all day. Dom's pink light is on most nights. When he and Ana Lucia do bump into each other, Dom only gives a polite nod, one that makes Ana Lucia believe that he's as embarrassed around her as she is around him.

Bobby's cousin Kyle has nothing to offer her but an eyeroll every time he sees her. She once overheard him tell Bobby that it wasn't his fault that Bobby had been so stupid to get married and burn his fucking hand and damn near ruin their chances of playing the kind of show that would get them a record deal any time soon. His point: he wasn't obliged to be kind to Ana Lucia, so Bobby could kick rocks. That was that.

The following week after rehearsal, Bobby comes to see Ana Lucia at La Vida.

He orders a cherry pop, knowing full well they don't serve it. She places a Sprite in front of his place at the bar table.

"This is a mighty tall glass," he says. "I'm not sure I can afford it all."

The Little Saints

"Maybe you can let me have a taste, and I'll give it to you at discount."

"Ah, well, now that's the gee-nee-yus I've come to love," he says, pinching her cheek.

She reaches over the counter to take a sip from his glass. He watches her before bringing his mouth to hers, drinking the Sprite from her tongue.

He turns back to reading aloud the book of poetry he has brought for her. He is on a poem by Edgar Allen Poe:

In a kingdom by the sea,
That a maiden there lived whom you may know
By the name of ANNABEL LEE;
And this maiden she lived with no other thought
Than to love and be loved by me."

As she listens, drying a glass at the bar sink, she catches an unexpected sight out of the corner of her eye.

"Bobby, you have to go," she says, reaching over the bar counter and closing his book.

"Why?"

"I don't want you to—"

Señora Peña approaches swiftly. Her face is vicious, her eyes turned down, her mouth tight and trembling.

Señora Peña speaks to her in rapid Spanish, so that Bobby cannot catch a word of it. Ana Lucia tries to quell her with her most penitent expression, as the woman won't afford her a single word. Anger forms tears in the old lady's filmy eyes. Her voice gives out. Bobby politely takes hold of Señora Peña's arms. She wrenches him off.

Ana Lucia opens her mouth to speak, hoping her tongue will find words that her brain cannot. Señora Peña refuses it, smacking Ana Lucia across the face before spitting on her.

She storms out.

The two stare at each other in quiet incredulity.

Bobby reaches for Ana Lucia as she comes around from the bar counter.

"It's okay," she says, pushing past him. "It's okay."

He follows her to the bathroom where she rinses her face. "Tell me the truth."

"I can't right now." In the mirror, she catches the angry flitter of her left eye.

He tenderly dries her face with a paper towel. "She said something about the fire?"

"So bright, aren't we?"

"What did she say, Ana Lu?"

She stares at his clueless face in the mirror. "She found out how it started."

He shakes his head, putting on a confused smile. "How did it start?"

Ana Lucia holds down a huff, though she can't prevent the stiffening of her lips. "An abandoned cigarette."

True anger doesn't take into account rights. Maybe Bobby feels that she has no right to keep silence with him for more than a week. He forgave her the Señora Peña secret in minutes—nothing could cripple his desire for her. Is there no mercy for secretly taking back up cigarettes and nearly burning an apartment down?

There isn't. Not yet. She hasn't heard a word from Señora Peña, but surely consequences are to come.

Bitterness, no matter its sundry justifications, comes with its own consequences. Betty takes advantage of the palpable strain between them, adding a syrupy quality to her voice when she addresses Bobby while making her saltiness to Ana Lucia known with narrow eyes.

Saturday morning, Ana stands alone in the kitchen, in search of a clean dish for a bowl of cereal.

Betty enters in beside her, snatching the clean bowl from her hand and pouring her own bowl of cereal.

Her chewing is horse-like. "What do you think the chances are that you'll be going to Paris with us for the show?"

An insistent fire burning in her bones, Ana Lucia takes the bowl from Betty's hand, dumping her cornflakes into the sink.

Betty laughs, turned on. "Good for you, darlin.' But even the blind can see that you don't stand a chance of making it there. Especially not the way you're acting."

Ana Lucia looks to her left where Dom has entered. He is searching through the cabinets, shaking cereal boxes for anything that will make a full bowl.

"I wonder what will happen in Paris when you're not there," Betty continues. "So far from home, what a man will do is beyond knowing."

"Buzz off, Betty," Dom says with the same casualness of his gait. He shakes the last cereal box and tosses it in the trash. He pours himself a cup of coffee.

Betty lifts a curious eyebrow at him.

"Can't you find something else to do?" he says, giving a quick stir to his coffee and tossing his spoon into the pile of dishes with a monstrous clank.

He wields an odd power with his directness. In the same way no one dares ask about his pink-light adventures, it seems Betty won't question his assumed authority. She turns quietly, exiting the kitchen.

Ana Lucia understands well Bobby's affinity to him. The command of his presence is compelling.

For the next few minutes, the two of them move around quietly in the kitchen, having tacitly agreed to clean it together. They put up brown dishes, refill the mother duck cookie jar, wipe down cabinets. At the inadvertent touch of his arm against hers when they simultaneously hang up dish rags on the oven handle, Ana Lucia grows warm.

His touch is sunshine.

As though he knows virtue has left him, he stops to look at her. "You're not talking to Bobby right now?"

She nods, unable to hold her own under his gaze. She reaches for a rag to dry a dish.

"Well, you know, you probably should," he says. "He feels really bad about the fire. Plus, his hand—it hurts real bad. There are, like, real tears in his eyes every time we play now."

She nods again.

He grabs his lukewarm coffee from the counter. "Okay, well, forgive him." He raises his cup to her. "Have a good day."

22.

DOM IS THE next to get arrested, which would have been more of a pain to Bobby if not for the fact that Ana Lucia is talking to him again and he can stand the last sharp pains in his hand, even manage the quiver in his left. Further, he's come to a conclusion about the Señora Peña situation: it has no choice but to be okay. Señora Peña has likely come to realize, as he and Ana Lucia have, that bringing them to justice will be a futile endeavor. They are penniless and penitent. He hates the thought of being slick enough to slip out of danger this way. He swears he'll find a way to pay her back double-fold—no, *triple*-fold—when he makes it big.

For now, he must deal with Dom's trouble, which is made more troublesome by the fact that Carlos stands guard when he enters the police station.

This end of jail is far better than the one he's known. There is a man at a desk. A water fountain. A radio.

And Carlos.

Carlos gives him a haughty once-over. "You."

Purse-lipped, feigning fearlessness, Bobby replies, "Me."

"You still here? No legal."

"I'm still here."

"Betty still live with you?"

"She does."

"She happy?"

"I don't know." Bobby tosses his hair back. Carlos is no threat, just a victim of killer love jones. "Where's Dominic Russo?"

"Es in the cell."

"Why's he here?"

"Hmmm. How do I explain you?" He picks up a Spanish-English dictionary from the desk and browses through it. "Your friend arrested for *lewd* acts."

"You mean, like, sex?"

"Sex. In open." He winks. "*Chueca* sex."

Bobby shakes his head. "So, what's gonna happen?"

"You send her home, I send him home."

"Send who—" Bobby closes his eyes. "You'll only let him out if I send Betty back to you?"

Carlos grins. "So, you *not* a potato?"

"I can't make her do it. I don't own her. You don't own her either, man. That's all she wants you to see."

"What you say have no sense to me."

"Can we do something else? I-I have money."

"You think I—" Carlos grabs the dictionary from his desk once more, licking his index finger to help guide him through the pages. "You think I accept bree-bes?"

"What?"

"Bree-bes. Like you make offer to me for what you want. No legal."

"Bribes?"

"Yes. You think I accept *bribes?*"

"I'm sure you do." Bobby pulls out his wallet. "So, how much do you want this time?"

On the walk home, Bobby considers that he could make a joke about how losing three-quarters of his money will set him back at least a month from finding an apartment for him and Ana Lucia.

It probably wouldn't make a good joke. It'll only make his best friend feel guiltier than he already does.

"Lewd acts in public, dude?" he could say. "The pink light's not enough? You have to get at your girls on the street too? Taking a line from Betty?"

He can't say that either. It'll embarrass the both of them.

Dom is the first to speak. "I'm gonna pay you back."

"Don't worry about it, dude. Really."

"Did Carlos tell you what happened?"

"No, not really."

He nods and takes out the handkerchief he normally carries. He's been using it an awful lot. Bobby guesses that combined with the cough he's had for the past week, it's probably bronchitis. He once had bronchitis. Once had it so bad, he—

"I guess you're hungry?" Dom says. He walks with a spring, adding a bounce to his curls.

"Yeah," Bobby replies. "You wanna go to—"

"Yeah." Dom pauses. "Well, you need to get Ana, right?"

Bobby blinks, at first bewildered, then excited. "Right."

Maybe wishes do come true. His best friend has accepted his best girl as a permanent fixture in their lives.

The restaurant where they eat is Thai, red-lighted with paintings of Bankok on the walls and American music playing overhead.

They sit around a round red table, admiring the meals the waitress has just brought. Dom is a polite eater. Ana Lucia looks at him with what seems to be admiration.

Ana Lucia's earrings cast light shadows on her cheeks. She looks healthy. Healthy in her soul. Bobby wonders if it is love that keeps a person so healthy.

Ana Lucia stares at Dom. "You don't eat the meat either?"

Dom looks up from his rice, astonished. "I'm sorry, what?"

"She's asking if you're vegan," Bobby says.

He wipes his mouth, composed again. "Yeah, I am. Bobby C and me stopped eating meat freshman year. Best thing we ever did."

"What made you do it?" she asks.

Bobby's eyes move between the two of them. He reaches for the lonely, shriveled cigarette in his pocket and begins twirling it between his fingers. He relishes the feel of rolling paper between his fingers.

"I don't know why we started the vegan thing. Sometimes, I think I was just trying to give my mom a hard time with the food she cooked. Bobby was probably trying to do his usual John Lennon thing."

Bobby smiles demurely.

"Honestly, though, I think we were just trying to figure out some way to change the world from Avon or something. Started with saving the animals or whatever."

Ana Lucia is nodding the way Bobby's mother does, with the solicitude of a trained doctor.

It spurs Dom on. "It's weird. You're reminding me of something I haven't thought about in—*good grief*—in forever." He chews his steamed broccoli with an emerging smile, eyes aglow. He takes a sip of his water. "Bobby and me used to have this thing where we'd check the obituaries at night, just to see if there was some hero-type in Avon. It was mostly Bobby's idea. Think he was just trying to prove to himself it could be done, that rising from white-collar purgatory wasn't impossible. He's always wanted to be some kind of saint, which probably in itself makes him a saint." He looks over at Bobby twirling the cigarette. "A *cigarette* saint, but you know..."

Bobby glances at Ana Lucia penitently. "Just holding it. I'm not gonna smoke it. I swear."

Playful, she takes the cigarette from him and puts it between her own lips. The opening riff of "Dancing Barefoot" begins.

The night is perfect.

Bobby feels his spirit open wide. "So me and Dom had this plan of how we were gonna get world peace. We figured it all started with food. You are what you eat, right? All the money we got from selling records, we were gonna do this whole charity thing where we'd give away a ton of vegetarian food. We'd give it to poor people and just like, everybody. We figured it out: if you eat peaceful, you become peaceful. No flesh has to die for anybody to live. End war with food."

Dom grins at Bobby. "What do you mean by we *were* gonna do it?"

Bobby looks at Ana, happy. "Guess we *are* gonna do it. One day."

"So, Ana, what are you gonna be when you grow up?" Dom asks.

Ana Lucia holds out Bobby's cigarette as though posing for a Chesterfield advertisement. "I've got plenty of years before that happens. Maybe I'll be like you two working-class heroes of Avon."

Dom laughs. Laughs like the boy he probably was when his brother Francis was still alive. It's not a big laugh, but it's more immediate than his normal laughter.

Bobby revels in this great feat. He's given Dom the gift of Ana Lucia.

The waitress brings them their separate checks soon after.

"I'm paying," says Dom. He hands the checks to Ana Lucia. "Total it up for me, will you?"

Ana Lucia's expression changes. "Bobby can do it."

Dom pulls out his wallet. "Feminist?"

"What?"

"You don't take orders from guys? Like, a woman without a man is like a fish without a bicycle?"

"I don't underst—"

Dom takes the check slips from her hands. "No worries. I got it." He smiles at her. "I got it."

Entering the apartment after dinner, Dominic takes hold of Ana Lucia's arm as Bobby trots down the hall to the bathroom.

"What school did you graduate from?" he inquires.

"What?"

"I'm just wondering what secondary school lets you through without knowing addition or multiplication." His voice lowers. "Must be super hard being a waitress when you don't know math. You must be pretty brilliant to get through it."

He releases her arm. Her gaze falls oblique. For all her knowledge of literature, Bobby likely assumed she became proficient in math on her own as well. Dom apparently brings no assumptions. Smart boy.

"I'm pretty good at math," he says. "When I get back home, I'm going to be majoring in mathematical studies at U.C. Berkeley. The pink light won't be on most Thursday and Sunday nights around nine if you ever, you know, get the itch to improve your math skills." He releases her arm. "Just think about it. No pressure."

23.

THE FOLLOWING EVENING after acting class, Ana Lucia walks through the front door of the apartment with Betty at her side. When they reach the coat closet, Betty seizes her arm and pulls her inside the dark space.

"You're fat," Betty says.

The darkness of the closet brings back a familiar hell. Ana Lucia's breathing shrinks with the closing of the closet door.

"Not unreasonably fat, but fatter nonetheless," Betty carries on. "They say after a lass gets married, she soon forgets the golden rule: the same thing it took to get her man is the same thing it takes to keep him. Before you know it, she's put on an extra ten pounds or so. In your case, though, only your cheeks and breasts seem to be swelling."

Ana Lucia is paralyzed, stuck to a wall as though held by honey, as memories wheel around her like bees.

"You're pregnant, aren't you?"

Gun shots in the closet. Piss and feces. Vomit. Glops of menstrual blood. Jackets smelling of moth balls that graze the top of her head.

"You haven't had a period in two months. See, the time when you've had a period, you've rolled your little sanitary towels up nice and neat and place them in the rubbish bin by the toilet. Always so origami-like. I haven't seen that in two months. I reckon I miss those little art pieces."

That old man and his breath so sour from liquor. Or maybe from blood. He speaks blood. Surely, he drinks blood too.

"So, what are you going to do now, huh? What's it going to be for you? In case you're interested, I've had my own experience with this, and though it's not technically legal here, I know quite a few abortionists who can take care of this in under an hour. I meself got a hanger that'll take care of it in ten minutes."

The books will no longer save her.

"Come out now, little girl. You can come out now."

"What's it going to be, Ana Lu?" Betty urges.

Red is the color of roses and rage and riots. It is the color of the filter over her vision as she grips Betty's throat. Ana Lucia's nails, her *claws*, burrow into her pale skin.

Betty at first smiles, as though her insolence will thwart Ana Lucia's madness. She doesn't understand the degree of Ana Lucia's mania until she reaches for her locked wrists and cannot move them. Betty kicks, then reaches behind herself to turn the doorknob so that they fall out of the closet. Still, she fails to pull Ana Lucia's hands from her throat as Ana Lucia falls on top of her and begins pounding her head against the floor.

Red is the filter over Ana Lucia's vision until she hears a cool blue voice.

"No, no, no, Ana," Dom says. His arms are locked around her waist, pulling her off of Betty. "No, no. Be cool."

Ana Lucia can't be sure how long he's been there trying to get her off of Betty. Time had lost its stronghold on her. Only now does it return.

She watches as Betty scurries to her feet, holding her neck. She spits and sputters, "You're a lunatic. A fecking lunatic."

"Goodbye, Betty." Dom's voice is neutral. "If you don't need a doctor or something, just go."

"I'm not going anywhere, you son of a bitch. This little fecker tried to murder me."

"Okay, got it." His word holds the value of a shrug.

Goliath is defeated, her pride shattered in the face of apathy. Betty blows out a weak dragon's breath—her showmanship will allow for nothing less—before she walks down the hall to her room and slams the door.

Dom cups Ana Lucia's shoulder, bending down to look her in the eyes. "Look at me. Look at me, girl. You there?"

She nods, now grounded from her brimming hallucination, having landed back in reality with the gentle fall of an autumn leaf.

"It's okay," Dom says. "You're okay. I've got you. I'm not going to let Betty do anything. Okay?"

Dom straightens himself and pulls her into his arms, letting her face rest against his chest. His heartbeat is soft against her ear.

"Can you..." she begins.

"Can I what?"

"Can you not tell Bobby about this."

"I'm sorry, about what?"

He smiles, and she knows he's worthy of trust. A man who doesn't ask questions usually is.

This sensation Bobby has—he can't tell if it is jealousy. He's never been well-acquainted with that emotion.

Ana Lucia and Dom are spending private time together. He only knows it because first, Betty told him that she heard their voices mingled in Dom's room one night. She refused to tell him how she got the bands of blue and brown on her neck—Bobby assumed it was another Carlos fight—but she didn't hesitate in painting a picture of what was probably going on with Dom and Ana Lucia. Now, Bobby sees it for himself after returning home from the fruit market. Unseen, he stands beside Dom's cracked bedroom door, peering in at the two of them.

Dom sits on the edge of the bed, leaning forward as he prepares a joint. Ana Lucia sits on a fold-up chair beside him, a pencil and notepad in her lap.

Dom slips the pencil from her hand and scribbles on her notepad. "You gotta carry the three. You won't get the right answer if you don't."

"Okay."

Engrossed with the crucifix hanging from his neck, Ana Lucia takes it between her fingers.

Bobby winces for fear that she will use the chain to draw him closer to her. He swallows, hoping to control his frenzied heartbeat.

"Why do you wear this?" she asks.

"It's a crucifix. *Crucifijo* in Spanish. What, you never been to church, Ana?"

She shakes her head.

"Oh. Well, that's alright."

Ana Lucia releases the cross, staring back at her notepad.

Bobby lets out a quiet breath, relieved.

"Why is he like that?" she says.

"Why is who like what?"

"Why is he fixed to the cross?"

"Jesus, you mean?" Dom blows out smoke from his fresh joint. "Cause he had to die for our sins and all that. It's a long story, but I guess it just means that God would die for us—that's how much He loves us. Cuz, you know, human beings live shit lives most of the time. Most of us just bring shit into the world and blame it on the fact that we gotta exist somehow. Human nature, I guess."

"That's the..." She searches for the word. Eluded, she meets Dom's eyes. "That's faith for you?"

Bobby leans against the wall. Jealousy has begun to fade. In place of it, curiosity burns bright.

"I guess. Faith is a weird thing. It's like believing I could be loved despite my shit life." Smoke flows from his nostrils as he contemplates. He coughs. "Faith is believing you can be loved for nothing. Isn't that what you have with Bobby? You love him, but you can't explain why, right? Even if you added up all his good points, you couldn't make it equal love. There's no equation for love, no reason or logic for it. To know that is faith."

Ana Lucia is quiet. Her eyes dart toward the door. Bobby steps back silently, hoping his shadow cannot be seen. Even so, he looks on at their exchange.

Dom again takes her pencil to write, then hands it back to her. She writes silently.

Dom, disconcerted by her quiet, says, "I know I don't deserve it, but I know Jesus is living with me right here in this heart. It shouldn't be like this, but it is what it is. I'm true to myself—perverted, fucked up, sensitive. God's true to himself—loving, compassionate, patient. It'll all work out between the two of us in then end."

Ana Lucia's elbows are on her notepad, her face held up by her hands. She is his pupil. Bobby is too for the moment.

Dom continues. "He's with you too, in case you were wondering. Just give it time—you'll feel it on the inside. But you gotta get comfortable with the truth that God's first language is silence. Trust me. I still haven't gotten an answer to why my brother Fran had to die the way he did. But I know He's still right here with me, even when I'm in so much pain I can't fucking breathe." He brings his joint up to his eyes, seeming to be confounded by it, then despising it. "I know Bobby's obsessed with Lennon, but Lennon got it wrong once, you know. God isn't a concept by which we measure pain. Our pain is a concept by which most of us measure the existence of God. But why should God's existence depend on whether or not we feel pain?"

Bobby knows Ana Lucia well enough to know she will say nothing. She is good at letting a man meditate in silence, to stew in his own juices until he comes to a proper solution. It's what he loves about her. Dom will likely love it with the same passion. There are too many things to count that could be loved about Ana Lucia. Dom is a rare genius of art and science; his eye for Ana Lucia's brand of beauty is eagle-sharp.

New-found jealousy hits Bobby once more. His throat closes.

"Well," Dom says, again breaking the discomfort of their silence, "why don't we call it a night before Bobby gets back from the market."

Acting classes have ended. Work continues. Life with Bobby has become steadier with time. She wakes to him, works side-by-side with Khadijah, studies in secret with Dom, and lies down again with Bobby, sharing the minutiae of the day: customers and fans.

She loves most their predictable hours and times. Steady conventions and schedules were a relic of a childhood swiftly lost. Bobby is childhood. Strange how being with him touches her past and somehow expresses a future that feels like forever.

She only fears he will grow bored with the structure of domestic life. The child in him is still apparent to her. His are still little, ravenous hands reaching for higher heights. His vision of being a rock 'n roll Gandhi is yet so precious to him. And that she will be a cinema Mother Theresa is a dream he has created for her. She thanks him for it; he has not stolen her chance to dream but incited her to finally put her imagination to good use. She has decided that one day soon, she will try out for a theater company.

Nevertheless, the third week of September brings news so crippling, Ana Lucia needs the sapphire calm of Dom's presence.

She sits beside him on the bed. The sun being so vicious these last days of summer, he is shirtless. She hardly takes notice, except that he has a summer cold, a slight fever she can see in his reddened eyes.

"You know this stuff though," Dom says, reviewing the half-hearted multiplication she's done. He looks up from the notepad. "You got most of this stuff wrong. What's got your mind?"

"Nothing."

"You know, you have the right to not answer me, but you really shouldn't lie to me. It kills trust. Plus, I wouldn't lie to you."

She looks at him. He is the embodiment of sincerity. He and Bobby have the same eyes.

"I think I would have killed her that day if you didn't stop me," Ana Lucia says.

"Killed Betty, you mean? Ah, don't worry. I'd have buried the body for you."

She tries to smile. "Plus, she's right."

"Right about what?"

"She said I was pregnant."

"Oh."

Ana Lucia knows Dom has fully understood her, but there is no hysteria to be found with him. It seems he swallows in life—the good and the bad—as if it all comes from the same cup.

"You haven't told Bobby? If you did, I guess he would've told me."

"No, I haven't told him."

"Are you okay?"

"I'm okay," she replies.

"Are you going to tell him soon?"

"I don't know. I don't want to talk about it."

Silence follows. Truth be told, she wanted to test the pregnancy confession on Dom, to make sure the words wouldn't kill her if she finally said them out loud. Ana Lucia pushes back her hair. It springs back to her face.

"You're never here," she says suddenly. "Where do you go?"

"All kinds of places. This city is alive." He reviews the next page of math she has done. "Hey, look there, you got all of these rights. If you can multiply three-digits by three-digits, you got this multiplication shit down-pat."

"Where do you go?"

He sighs, half-smiling. "Little Ana Einstein, so passionately curious."

"Why do you skip my question?"

"Because I don't want to lie to you."

He begins to cough, his body wracked with mucus until he is folded over. Ana Lucia sets her hand down on his back, soothing him. His skin is boiling, though her hand is a cure to his cough.

Still leaning over, he looks up at her. "We're basically friends now, right? I don't lie to my friends. It's not good church."

"But you hide from your friends?"

He thinks. "The way I've stayed alright since my brother Fran's death is by not letting thoughts about him linger. I got a method for that. I keep my mind filled with new experiences, so I don't focus on the old ones."

"You just want to have fun?"

Dom falls backward on the bed, his feet still planted on the floor. He sets his hands behind his back, his chest wide open, as though physically offering his heart for her to see.

"Sometimes it's like the more pain you're in, the more pleasure you run after," he says. "Because you need it, Ana Lucia." He reaches over to touch her thigh kindly. "It's okay to use pleasure to help you forget."

Though they have silently agreed to leave the pregnancy announcement in some corner of nonexistence, it is clear that he refers to the new life growing inside her.

"I don't think I can forget certain things," she says, pushing back a persistent curl from her face. "Certain things will be with me always."

"Yeah, but you gotta find a way to keep the storm from wrecking you. You know, Bobby's mom is a therapist. Maybe if you guys— maybe you can meet her one day. She'll fix you up good."

Ana Lucia catches his eyes. "Did she fix you?"

"No. I think she wanted to, but we were too close for her to work any of her magic on me. I just don't want to see you go down. Hey, look, you ever heard of an asymptote before?"

"No."

He reaches for the notepad on her lap and holds it above his face, drawing on it. "Yeah. When we get a little farther with the math, we'll get into it, but here look, this is it." He hands the notepad to her, pointing to the lines he's drawn as he explains. "The idea is that this line here will always be approaching that line there, but it will never touch it. That'll go on into infinity."

"Okay."

"I used to think that was how it was going to be with me and happiness—that I'd always be approaching it but never touching it because of this big, tragic thing that happened to Fran. I thought the pain was always going to cancel out the pleasure in my life. But, see, now, I know that's not true. I know that if I just do the things that give me a thrill—whatever they are, for however long they last—I can intersect the line of happiness." He stabs the line on the paper with his pencil. "I know it seems like chaos, but the pursuit of pleasure is a discipline for me."

Ana Lucia's curl falls again in front of her eyes. She pushes it away, annoyed this time. Dominic pulls out the elastic from his own hair, unfurling his curls. He sits up, tenderly brushing her hair back into a ponytail with his hands. She feels the irregular heat of his skin as his arms encircle her and his fingers work through her hair. His cloud of heat makes her tremble, even brings mysterious tears to her eyes.

"I'm not hedonistic." He twists the last knot of her ponytail. "Or maybe I am. But I'm free now."

"Free from what?"

"Free from the fear of wasting my youth on vanity. But I've figured out that youth *is* vanity or whatever. It took me a long time, but I also figured out I'm not meant to be a saint. I do what makes me happy for however long it makes me happy. It's the solution right now, so I take it."

A knock on the door startles them both. Dom stands up carefully, patting her leg to bid her silent.

He opens the door, angling himself in front of it to block the visitor's view. "Pink light's on."

"I know." Kyle speaks on the other side of the door.

"Well, what do you want, man?"

"Who you got in there?"

"What do you want?"

Kyle's voice falls out of hearing range. Only his tone is discernible. He is explaining something exciting. Ana Lucia stares with interest at Dom's back.

Finally, Dom says, "I'll be out in a few to handle it. I just need a few, alright?"

"Fine."

Dom closes the door, walking back to her and sitting down. He writes on the notepad and hands it to her. "So try this one."

She begins the equation. "How did you hurt yourself?"

"What do you mean?"

"Your back," Ana Lucia says. "You have scars on your back."

"I do?" He shakes his head. "Oh, yeah, those. They're nothing."

"They look like you've been hit. Like a slave."

"I haven't." He takes her notebook, checking her math again, too casual for all that is between them. "I guess soon you're gonna know everything about me, right? I was short at the beginning of junior high. Summer before seventh grade, I was in pain all the fucking time."

"Emotional pain? Francis?"

"Physical pain. It's like I was hurting from the skin down to the bone. There were days I couldn't do anything. Like, I couldn't even ride my bike sometimes, it was so bad. Then, it just sorta stopped, a little bit after summer break ended. By that time, I'd grown from five feet something to almost the height I am now. Six-three or something like that. The marks on my back came from that. I guess it was my skin stretching so fast. That was the pain I was feeling."

Ana Lucia stares at him, awe-stricken. A thought—the right and only solution to her problem—pools at the bottom of her stomach like bitter medicine.

She will have to give Bobby the news of his impending fatherhood tonight. It will hurt her to the core, beheading the little child inside of Bobby who still hopes for a life of responsibilities that he alone chooses. It will be a pain she has never known—taking a life that has yet to be fully lived.

If nothing else, Dom has proven through his adolescent aches, growth rarely come without affliction.

And sometimes the only solution to pain is pain.

A

"I love you"
Is all you can say
When I tell you the news

You kiss my forehead
You thank me
Tell me:
"Don't you worry 'bout a thing"
Are you quoting Stevie Wonder?
Yes, yes,
You are.
You stand.
You pace—

Clickity-click-clack

—Till you see me
Seeing you

Obliged, you smile

Obliged,
"I love you"
Is all you can say

This, I suppose,
Is all a Connecticut kid knows to do

24.

"ARREBATO" MEANS RAPTURE in English. Fitting. There are enough up-close shots of heroin needles sinking into arms and coke being snorted up pinched noses in the film to warrant the title.

Bobby sits with Dom and Betty in the back room of an art house, watching the screening of Iván Zulueta's new art house film. The other attendees are so white and smile so unnaturally, they remind Bobby of prowling vampires. Some of them recognize him from the stage. He tries smiling. They all talk too fast for him to listen or care.

He wouldn't have come to watch this if it weren't for his need for a diversion of non-stop light and sound. In hindsight, this movie wasn't the best choice.

Whatever the case, being here is something to do at ten in the evening as he waits for Ana Lucia to get off work so he can walk her home.

When the movie ends, he stands with Betty and Dom in a dark corner of the room beside an empty statue stand. Bobby balls his hand to quiet its motor tremble. In his right, he holds a plastic cup of brown liquor some random girl handed him.

Dom pulls out his handkerchief, coughing profusely into it. The kid's clearly got the flu but refuses to do anything about it. Bobby's been tending to him for the past two days.

Betty vacillates between the brilliance of the movie and their upcoming trip to Paris.

To Bobby, she says, "You act like you didn't like the film?"

'I didn't say that. I don't know. It was too heavy for me, I guess."

She scoffs. "What a prude. This is the revolution. If you can get past the taboo of drugs and fucking, you can do anything. Nothing will be impossible for you."

He shakes his head. The word revolution has lost all meaning to him in his present crisis.

The crisis of responsibility.

In this crisis, he no longer has an idea of what he *could* do for the world but a clear vision of what he *must* do in his world.

Betty looks past Bobby but speaks plainly. "It's possible to conceive a youngin' while you're still a youngin'. Besides, you'll be twenty soon, won't you?"

Bobby's eye flutter. How could she know?

"You been layin' with her without a rubber," she goes on. "I don't know what you were expecting. Not only was it possible, it was inevitable."

Bobby sets down his full cup of beer on the statue stand. "I'll see you later."

"Don't be so sensitive, Young."

"Don't tell me how to be, Betty. And my name's not Young. You ready, Dom?"

"I'm staying," Dom says.

"Here? Dude, you're sick. You need to go home and rest or something."

He shakes his head, distant. "I'm going to see who I can see."

"Leave him be, will ya?" Betty inserts. "Just because your life is over doesn't mean Dom's has to be too."

Bobby sucks in his chest in so a big fat "fuck you" won't come out as easy as his next breath. He angles his shoulder to move past her, but before he can walk away, Dom sways and wavers. In a blink, he collapses to the floor, limp as a sack of potatoes.

In the emergency room, Ana Lucia is all Bobby wants. Yet, when she arrives, she doesn't say it'll be okay; she doesn't have that kind of faith. But she is there, and that's her promise: she will always be there. Betty has fled.

When the doctor that has taken Dominic meets them in the waiting room, he begins speaking to Bobby, not realizing that Ana Lucia will have to interpret for him.

When the doctor finishes, Ana Lucia turns to Bobby. "He says that Dominic's awake now. He was having breathing trouble."

"Was it from the flu?"

"I don't know."

Bobby frowns. She's lying. *Why?* "You don't know?"

Ana Lucia looks away.

The doctor's eyes are on her. He has clearly lost all respect for Bobby and his non-Spanish-speaking self.

"We can see Dom now. That's what he said."

Still perplexed, Bobby shakes his head as he follows Ana Lucia into the hospital room. Dom sits on the edge of the bed, buckling his blue jeans. Shirtless, his body is as white as the bed sheets from which he rises. His hairless flesh gives Bobby's stomach a jump.

"What are you doing?" Bobby says.

"Getting ready to check out."

"What are you talking about? You need to stay here."

He grabs his shirt from the chair beside the bed. "It's just the flu."

"Okay, but you gotta wait for the doctor to say you can leave." Bobby steps toward him. "Come on, man, don't make me have to—"

"Stay, Dom," says Ana Lucia, afterward quieting Dom's rebuttal with the raising of her eyes to his. "Please stay. For me."

As though arrested to still-life, Bobby takes in the static image of them. There has been a lightning flash between the pair. The lightning emanates from Ana and strikes Dom, briefly disabling his stubborn will. He stands in place, contemplating her wish. Bobby is baffled by her power over him.

But at last, the still-life goes live action. Dom wiggles his head through the opening of his T-shirt. "I'm sorry, Ana, I can't stay here. I'll pay for a cab for the three of us."

Over the next week, Bobby worries for Dom's frequent absence from the apartment. He arrives late for two rehearsals, offering no excuse, keeping his gaze latent as he saunters in. Three nights Bobby has waited up for him with Ana Lucia's sleeping head resting against his chest. He wonders if Dom's ongoing illness and absences are a little diversion dropped down to him from heaven. He doesn't have the strength to worry about the coming baby. He has only the vigor for second-long contemplations on how they ended up here in such a short period of time.

Bobby is momentarily raptured in one of these contemplations as he sits beside Ana Lucia on the high speaker in the rehearsal room, waiting for Dom. Kyle has already bailed—he wasn't willing to wait more than thirty minutes for the kid this time.

"Are you hungry?" Bobby asks, shrugging himself free of a rising thought of Dom's whereabouts. "I don't know if Dom's going to show up. I can get you something. You must be hungry. Let me get you something, okay?"

"I'm not hungry."

"Are you sick?"

"No."

"What can I do for you? Are you tired?"

"There's nothing to do," she says. "Will you put your hands in my hair?"

"Yeah, yeah. Anything you want."

He starts at the nape of her neck, coiling his finger through a soft, shorter curl. With his other hand, he massages his way up to her temples, pressing her face against his chest.

She lets out a silky sigh, seemingly in bliss. "I want to ask you something."

"Okay."

"What if I die?"

His hand falls back down to the base of her head. "You're not going to die."

"Everybody dies."

He hops down from the speaker, moving to the amplifier to plug in his guitar. "I don't want you to talk like this, okay?"

She nods, obedient only for a beat. "Some people have more of an opportunity to die sooner than other people. Sometimes I wonder if death has floated around me until it finally hits the—" she stops to motion with her hand, as though she is holding something between her fingers that she would propel. "How do you say this? The target. The thing on the center of a circle."

"Bullseye."

"Yes. I wonder if death has been floating around me waiting to hit the bullseye. Maybe I'm the bullseye."

"Please, baby, stop, okay?"

"If I die, then you'll have a baby all by yourself."

His hand shakes as he pushes his guitar cord into the amp.

Ana Lucia slides down the speaker until her feet touch the floor. She meets him where he is still kneeling by the amp. She looks down at him, sucking on her bottom lip.

"It would really be a pity because you don't want this baby," she says.

"I didn't say that."

"You didn't have to."

He thinks that she will let go of his gaze, that she will be destroyed by his resignation, by his inability to protest her words. But she doesn't shrink back, for where he is a coward, she is a paladin. He is the one who drops her gaze, closing his eyes as they fill with tears. Where being seen by her once filled him up, it hollows him out to the nothing-man he really is. If he had the strength, he'd flee from her in shame.

He feels her easy hand brushing his hair from his face so that neither his shame nor his tears he can hide.

His eyes flutter open at the sound of the door opening. It's Dom.

Bobby stands, running his hand beneath his nose to clear away tears. "You're here."

"Yep," Dom replies. He settles himself immediately behind the drum set.

"Where've you been?"

"Church."

"What?"

"Church. You good with that?"

"Yeah, man." Bobby coughs away his tears. "Whatever you want to do, it's fine."

Dom twirls his drumstick between his finger and pushes his wild hair behind his ear. "Coolie. Let's get ready for Paris, folks."

25.

ANA LUCIA DOES her math alone until sunset. She sits in Dom's room, staring at his pink lava lamp.

Dom is not here. The fact that he has something much worse than the flu might explain that. Maybe he has gone back to the doctor.

She too should see a doctor. She is pregnant. A good mother would see about her child.

But Ana Lucia's mother is dead. How unfair it is that Ana Lucia should become a mother when her own had been stolen from her so early on.

She can still submit to the idea that God may exist. But who He is to be so cruel—it makes her wonder whether it is He or herself who is not loveable.

"Ana Lucia."

The light comes on.

"Yes?" She is nervous. Bobby has never seen her in Dom's room before.

"Hey," he says.

"Hey."

To her surprise, he continues, "I feel sorry for you."

"What?"

He stands in place. "I'm just saying that I feel sorry for you, that you're not me."

She shakes her head. "I don't understand what you're saying."

"I know you don't. I feel sorry that you don't get to see you through my eyes. You'll never know how good it is to look at something that magical. You're where it's at, Ana Lu—that's the only thing I know for sure."

She jumps up from the bed, rushing to press her face against his chest. His heartbeat is dance music, so opposite to Dom's.

"I can't wait to be with you in Paris," he says. She can hear his voice in his chest as the rumbling of a speaker. "I never thought about being with you there in that city. But now that I think about it, I know I really want it."

His doublespeak is plain. Perhaps he doesn't mean it yet, but he has said it and it suffices the moment.

He pulls her back to look into her face. "So, guess what? Dom wants me to meet him at church."

"Church?"

"That's where he's been going. Can't believe he's been going to evening Mass all these days."

Ana Lucia purses her lips. She can believe it.

"Come with me, will you?"

She nods. "Okay."

It's a wonder to Ana Lucia how precise cinematic presentations of Catholic churches are to real-life. The ceiling of the church she and Bobby enter is umbrella-shaped, its walls concave, making the church an exquisite merry-go-round of crosses, flowers, and paintings of Jesus and the Queen. Dominic sits on the stairs of the altar, a row of lit votive candles in front of him. The candles produce an ominous shadow of him on the ivory wall behind the altar.

As they approach, Ana Lucia can hear his labored breathing. He is preciously startled when Bobby touches his back. He soon recovers, inviting them to take a seat on either side of him.

"You alright?" Bobby whispers.

"Good." He runs his hands down his arms. In one hand, he holds a rosary. "Just cold."

"What's up, man. You wanna pray a rosary or something?" Bobby's asks, smiling as soft as the flames. "We haven't done that since confirmation."

"No. I just want to say something to you. Both of you, I guess." His breath comes out filtered, as though he is freezing to the bone. "Fran was wrong, you know."

Bobby pushes Dom's hair back from his face, a gesture Ana Lucia would have found peculiar if she didn't know so intimately both boys' tenderness. "Wrong about what?"

"About the thing he told me back in the shed when I was eleven, how he said that doing whatever the hell you wanted would make you happy?" He looks up at the painting of Jesus on the wall. "Forgive my French."

Ana Lucia can't help smiling, realizing now the meaning of French.

"Well, Fran was wrong about that. Jumping from pleasure to pleasure won't make you happy. Doesn't matter how many drugs you do. Doesn't matter how many women or, you know, *men* or whatever you sleep with."

Ana Lucia looks over at Bobby. His face hasn't changed, so appropriately naïve. He didn't understand what Chueca sex referred to before and still doesn't. She won't bother waking him.

"The pursuit of pleasure is just a lifestyle, not a life," Dominic says. "It doesn't take much courage to do whatever the hell you want. Audacity? Sure. But courage? Not really. I've been thinking, people can only feel really good about life if they—" his eyes glint, like a shaft of light over a polished blade "—if they lived it with bravery. Like, you did the things you were supposed to do even if it scared the shit out of you to do them. Because doing what's right—well, dude it's just good church." He chuckles at how well the phrase fits.

"Is that what the priest talked about tonight?" Bobby whispers.

"There was no homily. These are just my thoughts. They might be God's thoughts. I don't know." He turns his face completely toward Bobby. "Jumping from pleasure to pleasure won't make you happy, dude. Commitment is the thing. Committing to one thing and sticking with it. You never really do that. You wanted to play drums first, remember? But you saw a guitar in the store window and you had to have it. You told your mom you'd pay her back for it with your paper route money. I guess you never did that. After graduation, you told your dad you were going to spend the summer with him, just for some father-son time. But you changed your mind. You said New York was calling you. You felt it in your bones, remember? Until you didn't. Then, you had to have Madrid. It was the right thing. You were almost ready to leave until you met Ana."

Bobby looks down, so fragile from shame Ana Lucia could cry.

"I'm not trying to embarrass you, Bobby C," Dom says. "I was just thinking about all this stuff here last night. The thoughts were, like, divine or something." He laughs a little but is only able to sustain his laughter a second before another fit of coughing erupts. Recovered, he says, "Courage is the key, dude. And courage happens when commitment beats desire." He turns now to Ana Lucia. "I'm glad you're both here because it makes sense. You guys made a commitment. Like, a real commitment. Love's a one-way ticket; you guys can't go back now."

Bobby and Ana Lucia say nothing at what seems to be his concluding remark. The chiming of the church bells announces that it is nine o'clock.

"I want to go home now," Dom says.

He presses his hands against the marble step to stand. He is thrust back down by the locomotive heaving that travels through him. A torrent of blood pushes its way up his throat and out of his mouth.

He looks at them, calm but helpless with blood-stained teeth.

"Dom!" Bobby cries.

Ana Lucia holds up her shirt to his mouth to catch the current of blood flowing from his mouth. "Dominic."

She can't catch the stream of blood as his heaving continues. His drops of blood sully the white marble floor, as though flowing from the large hanging statue of the crucified Jesus above their heads.

Bobby pushes Dom's blood-tipped hair from his face. "Don't worry, Dom. You're gonna be alright. I'll go find the priest. I'll find a phone."

Ana Lucia stands. "Let me. I can speak Spanish better."

"It's okay, it's okay," Dom tries, smearing the blood across his cheek as he attempts wiping it from his mouth.

"Hurry!"

Ana Lucia runs down the long aisle out of the sanctuary. She yells for a priest to no response. By chance, she reaches a door that leads to a courtyard where a man walks the grass in prayer.

"*Ayúdame!*" she cries, pushing through the door to the outside where the man paces.

He responds with an accent unfamiliar. "Que pasó, hija?"

She tries English. "My friend is in the church. He needs help."

"What kind of help?" the man replies, his English more in tune than his Spanish.

"Only—just come!"

The priest follows her, his black vestments flying like a flag beside him.

When they reach the sanctuary, Ana Lucia stops at its entrance.

Bobby meets her eyes with the force a dagger. He holds Dominic limp in his arms. His tears fall onto his Dominic's face, mixing with his blood. He rocks him with the brisk edginess of a mother rocking her distraught child to sleep.

Ana Lucia can only look behind the altar at the picture of the woman in agony holding a dead Jesus in her tender arms.

El Otoño

خريف

L'automne
Fómhar
Majira ya majani kupukutika

Autumn

26.

ONLY AN HOUR HAS passed since Ana Lucia and Bobby left the hospital without Dominic, but the house is already stunned by his absence, the rooms dim and coarse-grained---a classic horror film to weary eyes.

Bobby puts an album on the turntable. A Blind Faith song plays. Back in their days in the rehearsal room, Bobby sang along breezily about not being able to find his way back home

Now, he sits at the old table in the kitchen, having set the telephone in the center of it. Ana Lucia sits beside him, intermittently looking at the phantom-figured blood stain Dom left on her shirt. The dusty kitchen lamp casts an orange light at the crown of his head. He holds his hand over Ana Lucia's stomach.

"Mom," he says, holding the receiver at the crook of his neck.

Ana Lucia leans over, holding her face against the phone to hear his mother.

"Bobby." Her voice is deeper than Ana Lucia's mother's had been. "What's—"

"Dominic is dead."

"What?"

"Dominic died this evening."

His mother waits, measured and motherly.

"Honey, are you sure?"

"Yes."

"Bobby, how did he die?"

A tear slips down his cheek. "I don't know. He's been really sick. I thought it was just the flu or something. I don't know. The doctor said it was some kind of pneumonia."

Ana Lucia writes the full name on the back of a receipt that sits on the counter. It is the likely cause tonight's doctor gave them after

Dom was pronounced dead—the same ailment the doctor told her in the hospital when Dominic first fainted. It's the name she hid from Bobby.

Bobby looks at the little paper, then pushes it away.

"Pneumocystis pneumonia," he says. "He couldn't—he couldn't breathe."

"Sweetheart—"

A rush of red takes over Bobby's whole face. He collapses into himself crying.

His mother's own crying can be heard, static-laden.

"Can you please come home, Bobby? Please."

Bobby continues to cry, his face nestled into his elbow.

"Mrs. Russo sends both of her sons abroad alive and well and receives them both back in caskets. I can't do it. I can't lose my only son, Bobby. I *can't*."

He sniffles, clearing away his snot with his palm. "I know."

"Bring your wife if you want. I don't give a damn. I just need you to come back here." Her voice breaks. "I just need to touch and feel my son."

Bobby only responds with a cry that matches hers. Ana Lucia's own tears fall. To hear mother and son sharing a cry so sacred, she grieves not only Dom but the absence of her own mother. She wishes that Bobby would agree to just go home and to take her with him, so that his mother can be hers as well.

He doesn't agree. Instead:

"Can you tell Mrs. Russo to call me please?"

Bobby insists on sleeping in Dom's room indefinitely. Ana Lucia lies beside him, unable to adjust to the ivory-cold of his skin. For him, death has brought nothing but coldness. For her, it brought first coldness, then the warmth of the sunny afternoon she'd walked into with children playing at the playground, gay and squealing.

In grieving for Dominic, she understands that the tie that brought the two of them together in the first place was their intimate relationship with grief during their youth.

A week after Dominic's passing, Ana Lucia kneels down beside Bobby in the bedroom. He sits in the patch of light on the floor that streams in from the window.

"It's okay," she says, touching his hair with unassuming fingertips. It is feather-soft. "Maybe it isn't okay. But it will be. I think it will."

She tries not to be presumptuous of how he will foster his pain over time. For now, he is dry and brittle earth, where he had once been soft and fertile land, absorbing everything around him with fascination. He hasn't cried once since they began sleeping in Dom's room.

"Sometimes," she continues, pressing a tiny slip of paper into his hand. "Sometimes pain is the only solution. Suffering is the fertile ground, remember? The mining is as important as the diamond, Bobby."

It's okay if he doesn't hear her. He will eventually come to the same conclusion.

"I love you," she says.

"Love you too," he murmurs.

Ana Lucia turns over in her mind the fact that he had been waiting for something like this—something which would make his life a tragedy, from which he could draw inspiration for songs all on his own. He was looking to grow but not to mature.

If he'd wanted to know, she could have told him the truth: nothing really makes you an adult except death. Though Bobby can't see it right now, their close-up acquaintance with pain will bring them closer together.

Or maybe it won't. Ana Lucia has no way of telling. For now, it's best to leave it alone.

The next day when she arrives home from La Buena Vida in the evening, she doesn't go to the bedroom to check on Bobby. Better to let him be. Instead, she heads to the bathroom for quiet time alone.

Inside she finds Bobby leaning over the tub, Betty kneeling down beside him, rinsing his hair.

His blonde hair. Vanilla blonde hair.

He looks up at Ana Lucia. "It's for Paris," he says.

Betty peers up at her with a grin. Ana Lucia is sick from head to gut.

Sitting on Dom's bed, Ana Lucia looks up at Bobby as he stands at the entrance of the bedroom minutes later, his shoulder hugging the doorframe. His hair color accents the icy quality he's already assumed. His eyes, still framed by chocolate brows, are so forlorn, he appears almost bored with his beauty.

"Your hair is blonde."

"I know," he says, stepping closer. He picks up a Patti Smith record from Dom's dresser and stares at it. "I hope you don't hate it. I hope—I hope you're still attracted to me or whatever."

"I am."

He kisses her, his lips cool but sweet and lingering. "I just needed to do it. For me, you know?"

"I know," she says. "Listen, I need something too, Bobby."

"Yeah?" He sighs, taking a seat beside her on the bed. "I have to make sure everything is right for sending Dom's body back before we go to do the show in Paris. I don't know. My mom said Mrs. Russo needs the help, so I gotta do it."

"I'm sorry."

"It's alright. It's nothing."

Ana Lucia measures out a sufficient silence before saying again, "Bobby, I need something."

He places an unlit cigarette in his mouth and squeezes her knee. The cigarette is one left behind in the pack beneath Dom's pillow. "Anything you want. What's up, baby?"

Ana Lucia slides the cigarette out from between his lips. "I need you to tell Betty that she can't go to Paris."

"What? Why?"

She quietly sets the cigarette down behind them.

"I need her there, Ana Lu," he says. "She does everything for us, like all the rubbing elbows and stuff."

Ana Lucia's breath hitches. She will excuse him. In his grief, perhaps Bobby couldn't tell how the word *need* would slice her gut, deflate her like an old tire.

"You have Kyle," she says.

"Ana Lucia, please, just don't do this right now." He brings his eyes to hers, contrite. "I love you."

The phrase—sincere, childlike as it had ever been—doesn't bring back her breath. The word *need* has glued her feet to the ground.

"I don't want her to go with us."

"I'm sorry." He lays his hand delicately against her stomach. "I don't want to upset you."

"What happens if I say that you have to choose her or me to go with you?"

Pink spreads over his cheeks and down his neck. He slips his hair behind his ear. "Can you—can we just not do this? Not now."

"I have to do this." Ana Lucia stands.

"I can't believe you're like this." He remains sitting, shaking his head. He laughs to himself—at best irritated, at worst in agony.

"I don't trust this," she says. That is to say, she doesn't trust Betty with his vulnerability, the vulnerability that is somehow more evident with his baby-blonde hair. "I don't trust this situation."

"That's a problem of your own making, baby."

"Don't call me baby." She is surprised by how quickly his affected apathy skins away her sympathy.

"I don't need this. Not now."

He stands to head for the door. Ana Lucia places herself stubbornly in front of him.

"Please move," he says.

"No."

"Please."

Bobby moves to the door. She blocks his exit.

"I'm asking you to please move. I've never asked you for anything, ever." He grabs the door handle roughly. "Just move."

"I don't ask you either—for nothing."

"Move, Ana!"

"I said no. For once, I say no. You listen." She can hardly believe how quickly her English decays in light of her anger. In all the years of abuse, had she never been this angry before? Should it be love, not hate, that brings forth the worst in her?

"What do you want from me, Ana Lucia?"

"I want you to forget about Paris. I want you stay here, so you can heal."

He shakes his head. "Being here's not gonna heal anything. I need to go. I need to be on that stage. It's the one thing I've got to give. It's the one thing I know I was born for."

"It'll be the one thing you die for," she says, her mouth quivering. "You haven't learned anything from what happened to my parents and grandparents? They tried to save the whole world, and they died. They're dead. And they left me here. Alone. Are you going to do that too? I think you look out of the wrong end of the telescope. Life is not about fixing the world. It's about *you*, Bobby, fixing *you*. Don't you understand yet, you stupid, blind Catholic boy? The command is not love *humanity*; the command is love your *neighbor* as yourself. That's what you told me. Yourself and your neighbor are right here, Bobby. Everything you need to face is right here, not in Paris, not in the great big world. But doing that is too hard for you, isn't it? That's why you go from place to place, idea to idea, isn't it?"

He laughs, doleful. "You don't know me at all. And I guess I don't know you either. Maybe you needed someone more like Dom, somebody who knows how to hold his pain as good as he holds his liquor. Maybe that's why you were spending all that time with him before he died—because you need someone like him. Well, that's not me. I'm not *that* guy. I'm sorry, Ana Lucia, sorry I can't be that guy. But I'm not gonna let you guilt me out of the one thing I have left."

His words are a knock-out punch.

Breathless, Ana Lucia says, "The one thing you have left?"

"Just please, move out of my way."

She stands still, her mouth set.

Bobby turns around, erratically searching for something. He grabs Dom's old pair of boots from the floor and throws them at the wall. He reaches next for the glass hash pipe, shattering it against the vinyl floor. Every breakable item he can find, he snatches up with fury, slapping them at the wall, onto the floor, through the air as a complement to each of his words. "Can't you just *listen* to me? Please. For once. I just want to leave. I can't be stuck here like this. It'll break every bone in my whole fucking body to fit into this box you're trying to put me in. I can't do this anymore."

The cry in his voice douses Ana Lucia's fire. Yet, before she can reach for him, she is thrusted from the door as it opens suddenly.

Betty pushes her way inside. She inserts herself between Ana Lucia and Bobby. "Let him go."

"Get out." The tremble in Ana Lucia's voice has started from her fingertips.

"Do you really want to do this?" Her height over Ana Lucia is her threat.

Bobby wedges himself between them. He addresses Betty first. "If you touch her, I swear on my life, Betty, I'll fuck you up so bad, you'll wish you stayed with Carlos." He turns back his attention to Ana Lucia in front of the door. "Move out of the way, Ana Lucia. Dammit, just move!"

"I said no, Bobby."

"Are you his warden now?" says Betty.

Bobby uses Ana Lucia's paralysis at Betty's audacity to maneuver his way out of the bedroom. He heads to the front door, Ana Lucia and Betty tagging behind him.

"Where are you going?" Betty probes.

"I'll be ready tomorrow for Paris," he replies. "I'll see you at the train station."

Having kept his eyes forcefully away from Ana Lucia, his meaning is clear. She is no longer invited to Paris.

A

The worst part:

Not that you choose Music
Over me
Not that you put Paris
Before me
Not that you take her
Instead of me

The worst part:
You place your Grief
Above me

How will Love ever compete with Grief?

B

The worst part:

When all I wanted

Is to land at my knees,

Bury my face in your womb.

Hold you for dear life

I didn't know the way

Grief has

Taken me to the sea

And there, drowned what's left

—Of me—

Made a corpse

To lie among Seaweed

Grief has

Turned Love to Ugly.

And at last,

Made my Insides

A familiar Monster

27.

ON THE TRAIN ride to Paris, Betty insists on narrating every city they pass through. She's taken this route at least seven times with Carlos.

The first city is Ávila. Bobby pays no attention to her commentary on this one. Besides, he can hardly see the scenery which slurs and smears against the window as the conductor moves the high-speed train down the track.

Bobby looks down into his lap. The shake in his hand is gone. Gone for good, he knows instinctually. It was an apparent foreshadowing of what was to come with Dominic.

On his lap, there is the tiny slip of paper Ana Lucia had handed him two days ago. It is a pencil-drawn portrait of Dominic. It is an exquisite testament of Dom, if for nothing else than the eyes. The eyes are living.

He looks around himself, alternating between pursing his lips and chewing them, savoring the bitterness of the words that were on his lips last night.

Kyle sleeps in the seat across from him with his mouth open. The first thing Kyle remarked when seeing his blonde hair was, "You look like a chick. A hot chick, but a chick."

Next to Kyle is a kid named Felipe, Naïve's temporary drummer. He has long, shiny hair and a glassy forehead that looks as though his skin has been buffed and waxed. Bobby sort of hates that the kid is only seventeen and is better skilled than Dom.

Passing through the green city of Irun in Basque country, Betty begins a lesson on Basque people who have their own language, a language that they alone speak. Most still refuse to learn Spanish in favor of their own language.

This takes Bobby back to Dominic, how in his head, he still holds conversations with him that he alone can understand. They are exchanges without words, much like the ones they'd had when Dom was alive. He tries to work out how Dom could have passed away but not perished.

He starts to believe for a moment that he's actually losing his mind. He supposes sleep will cure it.

Or drugs. He now understands a junkie's yearning for oblivion, to overcome the impossibility of dissipation—

Hendaye in the southwest of France is a sea city. Once Betty and Carlos had stopped at a restaurant there to have mediocre tilapia.

—Dissipation is one of many impossibilities. Before, impossibilities excited Bobby for the prospect of a miracle; now, he refuses to fertilize something in him that will no longer grow. Death destroys hope. Having experienced his own cub's share of disappointments, Bobby was sure he'd had at least a peek at the darkness. Now, he sees there are shades of black. Death is the blackest of blacks, the black that is truly an absence, as it takes away sight altogether.

I didn't see you, Ana Lucia. I saw death, and I was telling it to move out of my fucking way. And it wouldn't. It won't.

Resting his head against the train window, Bobby considers that hope and faith are just a setup for disaster. Not that he'd ever had faith that Dom *wouldn't* die. How does one center hope around something unimagined?

It'd just never occurred to him that Dom *would* die. Maybe in the general sense that all men die, but Dominic wasn't *all* men. He was *a* man...and barely that at twenty years old.

Had he died at thirteen, would it have made a difference? Had he not been born at all, what would it have changed? Twenty years out of, say, a hundred-year life-span would round down to zero, to nothing, to never having existed at all.

Bobby knows some form of insanity has taken root in him when he wonders if Dom ever really existed at all.

In a sleepy voice, Betty announces that they are at the Gare Saint Lazare rail point. Bobby sees the sign for it and thinks it sounds nothing like how it is spelled.

It bothers Bobby that pneumocystis pneumonia are two words he can spell better than pronounce but that will be printed on his brain for life. And if at his ten-year reunion someone asks what ended it all for Dominic Russo, he won't be sure that he's pronouncing the first word of the disease right. It won't matter though. The Great Thief wouldn't have been stopped by a thousand fluorescent lights shining upon him.

Dom will live among all the men who will die without a name, just like his brother Fran. Except Francis died in Vietnam and that made him a hero. Maybe among the endless rows of military tombstones, an anonymous child will drop a yellow rose over Fran's in honor of all unsung war heroes.

Tears finally spring to Bobby's eyes when he realizes that a day will come when he will say the name Dominic Marek Russo and a breeze won't even rustle the leaves.

His own crying pulls up the image of Ana Lucia's tear-streaked face from just beneath the surface of his thoughts. Was she crying the way she had when her grandfather abused her? He abused her the way a man is most apt to: with a burn of ice rather than fire. He'd frozen her out, went hiding in his little igloo to avoid a hard discussion. He thinks how often men are turned to monsters when anger compensates grief. Surely, this was the cause of her grandfather's madness.

And to think—Bobby had thought he was a man because he knew how to take care of a girl emotionally. In years past, he'd even been dumb enough to believe that sex made a man. He'd soon found sex only proved man is an animal like any other preying animal. More recently, he'd refined his theory to believe that finally reaching the threshold between sex and love-making freed him from the levity of childhood.

Now, he knows none of that makes a man. Death is the marker of adulthood. Goodness and mercy have followed Bobby all the days of his life until the day he cupped the back of Dom's head and learned that a dead man's eyes don't instantly close the way they do in the movies. Now that death has happened in his life—now that the door has opened—he realizes it can happen again. Worst of all, he will look at the future with a jaundiced eye, without the mercy of illusion.

Then there is life, which at times seems as scary as death and highly less predictable. There is a baby, whose life seems to predict his own death.

I don't want to hurt you, Ana Lu. I'd rather die than hurt you. If I am something, you will feel like nothing. I can't allow that. But when you are everything, I must be nothing. I don't know how to be nothing yet.

Hurting you feels like I smacked myself in the face with a metal shovel. The pain of hurting you is so deep, it's like searching for the end of a horizon. I don't know if I'll ever reach the end of this pain.

Bobby knocks his head against the train window. Ingratitude is a disease, a cancer that spreads to every limb of one's life so that dissatisfaction becomes the final end of every pursuit.

Even love.

He knows a man can get used to affection but what happens after? It hasn't happened yet, but is it inevitable? Will love turn into a matter of caregiving. The baby will need to be taken care of. Ana Lucia is still sick within herself. Will it get worse, until she no longer needs constant *affection* but rather, twenty-four hour *care?*

"Welcome to Paris. The city of love."

Bobby turns to see Betty grinning at him. Kyle and the drummer Felipe are standing. Bobby looks out the window. They are inside the rail station. The first passengers have stepped onto the platform.

The four of them scarcely have time to check into their hotel rooms before they must prepare for this evening's show.

From the outside, the venue is a very regular building. On the inside, it is larger than any place they have performed. A small balcony juts out over the doorway. To the left of the entrance, a broad stage extends out from the front wall. The stage stands as tall as Bobby's waist. Large multi-colored lights hang above it.

The show starts at eight. There is a lineup of five other acts, half of them French. The French kids are golden people. Not blonde but golden. Golden skin, golden eyes.

Bobby doesn't admire their beauty, for he is dead, dead to the sight of them.

When Naïve's time comes to perform, Bobby doesn't try speaking over the crowd. He counts off and begins playing. Hard and loud at first. The performance goes on as a showcase of the colors he can create with his voice. Sometimes he sings with a screech, red and wild, neon with staccato. Other times with a mumble, cold and blue, a silver flute. No matter what the tone, the crowd hangs onto every inflection, the way Ana Lucia hangs onto the back of his shirt with every embrace.

Still, he's dead, dead to praise.

His voice rings more mystic, as if waving with one hand for his love to come nigh. It is raspier from the deep-throated cries he'd let out in the cheap hotel room he stayed in last night when he fled from Ana Lucia.

Though it is clear the crowd is enamored of him, he is dead to the dream. All he wants is the past, not the present nor the future.

So, success is the product of agony?

Well, fuck success. Fuck it all.

Bobby is back at the hotel by one in the morning. He opens his room to find Betty sitting on his bed.

He isn't surprised. He takes a seat at the round table that sits in front of the bed. He will ignore her until she leaves.

Betty takes a seat across from him at the table, bringing with her the eight-track player sitting on the nightstand. "A Day in the Life" is playing. A street light beams through the window behind the bed, irradiating her face.

As though in a silent movie, she quietly pulls out of her purse her drug baggies and holds each up for him to see. She carefully puts together two joints filled with white powder. She lights one and hands it to him.

He smokes the heroin, pretending it's a cigarette for conscience sake. He listens to the song on the player.

This is his first time being high, and he slides into it without ceremony. He is happy in his flesh, but the knowledge that unhappiness lurks around the corner keeps his high from floating to the Exosphere.

Fuck it. Fuck the drugs.

"Are you hungry?" she says.

He shakes his head. What a fool he and his mother had been taking that tuna casserole to Mrs. Anderson next door after her husband died. So stupid—that tradition of bringing food to comfort those in mourning when there is rarely an appetite left for the bereft. The only thing worth bringing is the dead back to life. Who can do that?

Betty leans across the table with an addict's lethargy. "I never even thanked you for what you did for me, getting me away from Carlos. I want to thank you for that. You're my hero, you know that?"

"You thanked me already. A ton of times. I'm not a hero, Betty."

"Oh, but you have always wanted to be a hero, haven't ya?" She smiles lazily. "I think you have a calling to hero-hood. It's a simple call—to just live through *this*. Not to be John Lennon and save the whole fecking world with your songs but just to survive your little life. You've been spending all your time thinking you were born to *become* something when you were born to simply *be*. Your time will be better spent now accepting your crosses, not reaching for the ones that don't exist for you. The death of Dominic is your cross. Now, put on your big boy johns and carry it. I did it. You can do it too, you little fucker."

She laughs, then begins to weep, her mascara running down her high cheeks. He touches her shoulder. He knows she's remembering the death of her family. He's almost embarrassed by her plain show of grief.

"Are you okay?" he says dumbly. He slips the bag of powder from between her fingers. "Let's just—we should put away this shit. We're both pretty fucked up now. You might really hurt yourself."

"I don't want to die," she weeps.

"I know. You just don't want to live anymore. I get it."

"No, that's not it, you blind lamb. I want to *live* again. That's what I want. That's all I've ever wanted. And you seemed so full of life, Young. I wanted that. I *want* that. That's why I want you."

Bobby shakes his head. "I can't do this with you, Betty."

She falls silent, but begins to keep time with the wagging of her foot against his shin under the table. She holds a Gioconda gaze.

"Do you love me yet, Young?" she says after he takes the last puff of his joint. "Do you love me for saying what I've said, at least."

"Listen, I'm not—"

"Not what?"

"I need rest. Can you just go now? Please, just go."

Her eyes slide to the bed across the room. "If you're tired, let's go to bed."

Bobby pushes back his chair, detaching her foot from his shin. "I'm sorry if this hurts you, but I need to be one hundred percent clear. The love you're looking for—I don't have that kind of love to give you. I love Ana Lucia. I *love* her. It's not some kind of joke. It's not because I feel like I have to. It's just a fact of life. Have you ever been loved before, Betty? Like, really *loved*."

"A fact of life?" She rises from the chair, placing herself on the top of the table, her legs spread theatrically like a painted lady of the Old West.

He is hostile to his own desire but can't fight off the trembling in his thighs. "What do you want from me, Betty?"

"It's always been the same." She burrows her face laggardly into his neck. "I don't want to possess you. I just want to have you." Bobby feels her tears falling on his neck. "I'm hurting too. My life almost killed me, Young. Everybody I ever loved died in one day. That's why I can tell you that what you're going through isn't the hellfire. It's the refinin' fires of purgatory. Purgatory is the beginning of paradise."

She begins to cry out loud again, her whole face sunken into his neck. He is crying now too, though not for the loss of Dom. He's crying because he doesn't know how he won't ruin his life with Ana Lucia this evening.

He doesn't want love. He wants brutal sex, someone to beat down into the bed, to exorcise his demons out upon.

Betty takes him by the collar, buries her face deeper and deeper into his neck. She kisses him there with the kind of bravado that lets him know this is her show. She wants to show him how good she is at this.

He resigns to it, just wanting to finally get it over and on with it. Death has made him a man. Now, sex will make him a boy again. It will take death away for some minutes.

Make it go away, Betty. Make it go away.

The evening after Bobby leaves, Ana Lucia finds herself bleeding. She immediately pays Khadijah a visit.

They sit outside on her balcony, side-by-side in the plastic chairs that look out at the black dome of the red-brick prison in the distance. It is Carabanchel prison, the prison her grandfather helped to build as one of Franco's political prisoners. It's a prison built by its own prisoners. The times Ana Lucia has sat out here with Khadijah staring at one of the largest prisons in all Europe, she has been able to forgive her grandfather, even if only for a single heartbeat.

Ana Lucia sighs, looking out at the aging summer and the ball of fire in the sky that is dying earlier and earlier. It's shortly after eight and the sun is beginning to make its descent, withdrawing its warmth.

She misses Bobby.

Ana Lucia crosses her legs to alleviate some of the familiar discomfort of being wet. She sighs again.

Khadjah looks over at her. "Don't be sad. It wasn't a miscarriage. You were never pregnant."

Ana Lucia looks at her friend.

"You told me you were pregnant, and to be honest with you, I didn't believe it," she says. "I've seen my mother pregnant five times. It has a look, has a smell. You never had it."

Ana Lucia wonders what smell she could mean. "I think I was pregnant though. But I bled today."

"It was likely an irregular menstrual, habibi. You say you didn't start your first menstrual cycle until you were sixteen. You're only nineteen now. Your body is probably still adjusting to the cycles. It happens." She pushes an errant curl behind Ana Lucia's ear. "Be thankful, it happens. It will be good news you can give to your husband when he returns. It will be a gift that will make him feel as guilty as he should for leaving you here and going to Paris."

"I can't do that."

"Make him feel guilty? Of course, you can."

Ana Lucia shakes her head. "He was adjusting to the idea of becoming a father, I think. He was becoming happy with it."

"Of course." Khadijah can't help her sardonic smile.

Ana Lucia understands Khadi's disbelief. Ana Lucia has known skepticism the majority of her life. But now that possibility of God and faith are rising inside of her like a misty moon, she has less attraction to sarcastic incredulity. One experience—one moment having felt the way Bobby runs his fingers over her stomach now as though appreciating fine silk—and Khadijah would know for certain that Bobby is falling in love with the supposed child, the child whose existence might shatter all of his dreams. In this way, what Dom proposed is true—faith is knowing that love exists without reasonable explanation.

Ana Lucia pockets the notion, as she once pocketed her grandfather's change, and keeps it for herself. It's nothing she can sufficiently explain to anyone, let alone Khadi Incredulity.

She will say one thing:

"His best friend is dead. Telling him that there's no baby will be like taking another life from him. He can't handle that right now."

"I guess you know him better than I do. So, the question is, how long will you wait to tell him?"

Ana Lucia thinks. "We'll see."

Bobby gains courage from the spider spinning its web beneath the windowsill in the living room of the apartment. He's three times brushed away the web with a swing of his broom. The spider's humility is only matched by its tenacity as it reworks and re-weaves its original design. Bobby won't kill the spider nor ruin his web again. He will show the little creature mercy.

Blessed are the merciful, for they will be shown mercy.

It's evening, Monday. Kyle and Betty have retired to their rooms after the train ride home. Neither spoke to him on the journey home. Kyle was destroyed from a weekend of debauchery. Betty didn't bother talking to him after he refused to talk to her.

Dom was there on the train beside him too, not as quiet as the other two. He was speaking out loud Bobby's conscience. In the living room, he stands beside Bobby as a silent ghost, no longer the Aaron to Bobby's Moses. Bobby realizes now he will not have anyone to supply for him the words he must say to Ana Lucia or the courage to say them. Except the spider, who upon second glance, has disappeared.

As Bobby stoops down to search for the spider, he hears the front door open.

Ana Lucia enters the living room, stopping at the entrance, watching him like a child awaiting the punishment of her parent. Her work shirt is untucked from her pants.

He realizes now he had forgotten the message of her beauty. Baby hairs donning the edges of her forehead, adorably disheveled curls, glassy irises swimming in milky whites, puffed lips agape, anticipating—her beauty's message is uncorrupted innocence. Even her life's tragedies haven't injured it.

Now, here he is preparing to lay his guilt over her innocence. He's almost tempted to hold back his confession.

"Are you okay?" she says to him, stepping forward to look down at him as he still kneels in hopes for the return of the persistent spider.

Bobby shakes his head.

"What happened?" she asks.

He stands. "I did the worst thing I could've done."

Bobby watches the erratic rise of her shoulders with the sudden snag in her breathing. Her chest falls slowly. The vibration of their hearts walloping in their chests—it's a wonder the whole house can't hear it.

"I did one of the worst things I could have done," he says again, quiet.

"You killed somebody?"

"I killed something." He falters a moment. He stands. "I think I killed something."

Their eyes meet. It's too late to retreat.

"What did you kill, Bobby?"

He massages his canine tooth with his tongue. He might faint.

"Say it," she says. "You have to say it. Because if I have to say it, then..."

...then she will be both the victim and her own assailant. And he will have found shelter in the tornado he created. And when that tornado carries her off, there will be no hope of her return.

"I made a mistake with a girl."

"Who did you make a mistake with, Bobby?"

"With her. With Betty."

His confession darkens the cloud overhead. If there had been an audience, they would have all jetted off like squirrels. Bobby is now aware how alone they are in this moment. All alone in the storm.

Neither of them can take shelter under the storm cloud, but Bobby is stupid enough to try.

"I didn't have sex with her." He holds his palm over his mouth briefly. "It-it came really close. But I couldn't do it. I couldn't do that to you."

"How close?"

"What do you mean?"

"How close did it come?"

He stares at her baby hairs. He wants to kiss her forehead.

Looking at the gerbera daisy eyes, he knows what she wants. She doesn't want a play-by-play account of how he'd let Betty print her lipstick mark on him as she undressed and bowed down before him. She doesn't want to know that to keep her from reaching into his pants, he had to clutch her shoulders until he left scarlet fingerprints on her skin. Ana Lucia isn't looking for an explanation of how many places Betty got to touch him before he decided he wouldn't be dead forever and that he had to stop this ugly self-pity. He refused to undress her, refused to touch her, refused to have sex with her, refused letting her have any kind of sex with him, though with tears she had begged him to. After being refused the sex she felt she had earned, Betty refused to leave his room. So he left, spending the rest of the night walking the streets.

The truth is, there's no way that Ana Lucia wants to really know all of this. What she wants is for him to hurt her with the account. Because she knows how much hurting her will hurt him. She knows.

What can he do but accept her punishment?

"Do you want to know everything?" he says quietly.

She removes her gaze from him. She has removed herself from him. His chin trembles, an avalanche. Tears tumble down his face, one after the other.

Her face is dry. "Once, in the kitchen, Betty told me it was going to happen. I didn't believe her." She looks at him with contempt, as though she might spit on him. "Did she touch you where I touch you?"

For the first time, he sees her innocence corrupted by a vengeance so sour it pinches the edges of her mouth.

"I stopped it. I did, I swear to—" He stops.

"What do you want me to say, Bobby?"

"I just want—" he sniffles. "Just let me show you I love you more than this. I love you. I really—" he breathes. "—*really* love you, Ana Lucia."

"Well, I guess that's the difference between you and me, Bobby. I don't have your faith. I don't believe in things I can't see."

The next time he sees a spider, Bobby is tempted to squash him with his bare hand. He doesn't. Dom is whispering to him, insisting to him that the lives of little creatures are ones to be spared. Dom tells him that once upon a time the Viet Cong had seen his brother as nothing more than an insect.

Besides that, Bobby C, you can't blame the spider because he's been given a chance to build his house again and you're still trying to figure out what to do with your own shambles.

It's prime time to write a song, isn't it? All the greats write songs about how they battered the love that had once nourished them. You can tell the story about how Ana would rather sleep on the living room floor again than risk waking up back-pressed-to-back with you in the bed. There must be some lyric you can come up with about how she angles herself to keep from touching you when you pass by and how she leaves the food you cook untouched. Talk about your fear that she is quietly planning a way to escape you and take your baby with her. It hurts like a bitch, doesn't it?

This isn't the end of your troubles, is it? I mean, you've called your mother twice and haven't been able to reach her. That must make you feel even more like the bastard you were in Paris. Plus, you don't get the chance to enjoy that Betty has told you about an important contact she made—a record exec who caught your show in Paris. Who will you share the good news with?

Not me. I'm gone, remember?

But if you're looking for someone to confess to, there's always a priest. No more biding your time, Bobby C. You never know how much of it you have left.

Trust me.

True enough, it is Dom's voice that has led him here.

Bobby sits before the lattice of the confessional. The priest inside speaks English. He's Irish, his accent cleaner than Betty's.

Bobby goes through the form. Two months since his last confession. Venial sins first. He saves the big one for last, though he follows it with a chaser. His best friend died. He was out of his mind with grief.

After he finishes, Bobby waits for absolution. Instead, the priest asks, "Do you understand your duties as a husband?"

"I think I do." He coughs quietly, wrings his hands. "I know I have to take care of her. It's not just that I have to; I want to." The anonymity of the confessional gives flight and fidelity to his words. "I don't think I ever felt so high in my life like when I feel like I can keep her safe. It's like a—I mean, I know this sounds dumb—but it's like a *privilege*. Something like that."

"So you feel you've done a proper job keeping her safe?"

"I know I messed up, Father."

"Yes, but will you answer my question?"

"I try, Father. I really try." He hesitates. "We're gonna have a baby. And I—I didn't want the baby. I do now though. I mean, there are times when I still don't. But I know that it's my responsibility, and sometimes I guess I'm even *stoked* about it. I—" He stops. "I'm not perfect, but I'm trying. I swear to God, I'm trying."

The priest is silent. Bobby wonders if he is weighing whether to chastise him for swearing in the church.

"W-what is it? Please tell me, Father."

The priest's voice is quaking, robust. "There's no person your wife needs protecting from more than you. There's no person who can hurt her more than you can, because there's no one who can love you the way she does. Now, you've got to put away this softness of yours."

Bobby's indignation brings a shudder to his jaw. He knows he deserves the punishment, but he can't help shielding himself from the lash. "I'm not upset because I'm soft. Sometimes guys need to, like, cry. If they don't, they just get to be these brainwashed stones. They don't care about anything but proving themselves. I don't want to be like that. I don't want to fight wars. I don't believe in war. I believe in peace. That's all I want. That's why I came here. That's why I confessed."

"What wars will you fight to keep your peace?" the priest returns. "Your softness is not determined by the number of tears you cry. There are plenty soft men who win wars without shedding a tear. Yet, they are men who cannot properly love their wives. They're simply men unwilling to do what is hard for the sake of what is right. They bend to every difficult situation. They flee when times are tough, as you did after your friend died. Their life's pursuit is pleasure. When pleasure disappears, so do they—sometimes physically, sometimes emotionally. That's what happened to you in Paris. Perhaps you shouldn't have ever gone. Your wife didn't want it."

"I don't get it. You're saying I'm soft?"

"You can best judge that."

Bobby holds his breath, as though physically pressing down his resentment. He speaks gently. "I don't understand, Father. I know I was wrong, but does that mean...does that mean that's it for my life? That's it for my—for my calling?"

"Your calling?"

Bobby hesitates. How can he explain a vocation of rock 'n roll? "I know I was born to do what I went to Paris to do. I was born to make songs. It feels like God made me to make a statement in this world, to change things, you know? But it seems like you're telling me that to do what's right with Ana Lucia, I have to give all of that up."

"If in your mind that's what doing what is right means, then the answer is yes. Oh, what damage is rent to the soul which refuses suffering for the good of another."

The rebel in Bobby rises faster than he can contain him. "What if I'm not ready to give up everything?"

"Then, you're not ready. But you must remember, love doesn't come   at   half-price."

To be certain, Ana Lucia was prepared to apologize to Bobby for burying him under the weight of her jealousy the evening before Paris.

When he came home confessing his transgression with Betty, empathy took flight. In its place, the pursuit of karma. She was surprised by the power of vengeance.

Anger is a deep-set stone in her chest cavity—she can hardly breathe because of it—because he has stolen her feather-weight ignorance.

After work, she decides that church is what she needs. Good, good church. Confession—getting the weight off of her chest.

In English, she asks an English-looking lady for an English-speaking priest, as though it is something that can simply be ordered. She sees all Spanish priests as hypocritical pawns of the Franco Regime.

The lady does speak English and there is an English priest. Well, not an English priest. An Irish one.

She asks for a confession, again ordering one like she is at a restaurant. The priest takes her to a confessional booth. She wonders what the point of anonymity is since he has already seen her face.

He doesn't seem to mind it. "In the name of the Father and of the Son and of the Holy Spirit.

"I want to confess the sin of my husband," she says.

He chuckles in a stereotypically Irish way, light and higher-pitched than his speaking voice. When she doesn't join him in laughter, he is quiet, clearly confused.

"I've never been to confession. I don't know the rules of this. I'm not Catholic in the strict sense."

"In the strict sense? What other sense is there, dear?"

"Bobby is Catholic."

"Bobby?"

"He's my husband, the one I'm making the confession for. He was--" She scans her brain for an English word she'd never thought she'd use. "He was the infidel."

"An infidel? Your husband?"

"Yes. He didn't have sex with another woman, but he let her touch him." Her English again declines as anger ascends. "Not his whole body, but—do you understand what I want to say?"

"He was unfaithful to you in some way. Then, mustn't your husband make the confession?"

"He probably has already. He's religious. But I'm the one who needs help. That's why I'm here. I want to be free of his infidelity. Free in my heart."

"You want to forgive him, yes? So, you are confessing to the sin of unforgiveness."

Her breath slips away. "Me? I've done nothing wrong."

"Perhaps you have done one thing," the priest says. "You have allowed your mind to gain ascendency over your heart, dear. You want to forgive, but your mind tells you that you shouldn't, that a sin so big requires retribution. Love doesn't bow down to such logic. Love prefers mercy to justice, you see. And so God is love."

And so God is Love? Ergo, God is not Karma? If this is true, the scales may always be unbalanced between two people in love.

"What if I'm not ready to forgive him?"

"Then, you're not ready. If not now, maybe you never will be."

On the bus ride home, Ana Lucia decides to remember who she is. To not hold Bobby's treason against him is a simple act of the will, as the priest put it before she left the confessional. She decides to remember the part of herself who has let every offense since her grandparents' death slip through her hands like water.

She will take the gift of imagination her reading has given her and create a Jane Austen other-world for them, one where she is Anne Elliot and he Frederick Wentworth.

Still, she will wait to tell him she isn't pregnant. It's a tie that binds them right now. She fears what might happen at the cutting of that cord. Freedom may become so attractive that he can't hold himself back from another woman. Besides that, she would only be supposedly a little over two months pregnant; her pregnancy wouldn't necessarily be showing by now, would it?

Ana Lucia relaxes in her omission, convincing herself she is doing this for Bobby. He wouldn't be able to live with himself if he used his freedom as an excuse for vice.

When she enters the apartment, he is standing alone in the bedroom, skimming through *Moby Dick*, as though willing a different end to the story. She knows the look on his face when he glances over at her, startled. He was having a conversation with Dominic in his head and is embarrassed by it, as though she can actually see the thoughts in his head.

She wastes no time submitting her heart to her eye. Rosy-cheeked and shiny-haired, he is still as *pretty* as he'd been the first night he'd walked her home from La Vida. He is still the golden thread woven into her dark mosaic.

"I forgive you," she says.

He sets the novel down slowly on the dresser. "What? You do?"

Gratitude brings a sparkle to his eye. He is on the edge of a smile but doesn't chance it, possibly in fear of grabbing too avidly for a gift she could take back.

She moves toward him. She places her hand on his Adam's apple, waiting to feel the vibration. "I forgive you. Now, forgive me for whispering 'que te folle un pez' just now when I first saw you. I hadn't forgiven you completely yet."

"No clue what that phrase means."

"It's a Spanish curse. If I told you what it means, you'd never look at fish the same." She lays her hand flatter against his Adam's apple.

"You know, you're really a bad influence, Ana Loo Taboo," he says, the words more baritone than usual to give her an extra kick in her fingertips. "Now dance with me, will ya?"

He explodes into a fit of daffiness, lacing his fingers between hers and twirling her in circles. He skips her over to the record player, puts on a single, and dances her around and around to Lennon's "Instant Karma," setting his hand on her lower back to guide her. Beaming, he yells the lyrics like a stadium anthem, as they all shine on, like the moon and the stars and the sun.

Had Ana Lucia known forgiveness would bring him back to *this* life, she would have done it sooner.

As the music quiets, he follows the shape of her left ear with his index finger. "Unreal. You're unreal, Baby Lu. Listen, I want to take you away."

"Take me away?"

"Let's leave Madrid for a couple days or something."

"To where?"

"To—" he picks the book up from the dresser, tossing it from hand to hand. "—to the sea."

28.

—ON TO THE SEA, where there is no ambient light, and the glassy eyes of the stars can watch over them.

There is a thought which passes by Bobby like a monster locomotive. The stars are many light years away, distant, so distant that their light does not reach the earth for millions of light years. Those stars will be like God to him right now, looking out over him but not close enough for His light to be seen yet.

Dom was the one who taught him about the stars—Dom who he still talks to all day but whose body will be transported back to the United States tomorrow. All of the Spanish bureaucracy has hindered progress, whatever progress could be made with a dead body in waiting.

In three days, he and Ana Lucia will set out by car to Cadiz, to stay in a hotel beside La Caleta beach. This Thursday morning he has decided to leave the house early to purchase the airplane tickets.

Before he can reach the front door, Betty catches him in the kitchen. The room is still, save the blast of morning sunshine that spills onto the parquet floor.

She speaks to him over the cup of coffee at her lips. "Are you okay?"

He observes her makeup-less face.

"Fine," he replies, tucking his hair behind his ears and looking away.

"Withhold your wrath from me, will ya? I don't regret the other night."

"I know you don't."

"I needed you, even if you wouldn't let me have you."

The Little Saints

He says nothing.

"I have news for you, Young. The man from Paris—his name was Jerry Black. He's a Yank, you know?"

"I didn't know."

"Of course you didn't. You only have care for the music, don't you? Jerry Black wants to have a serious talk with ye lads about your destiny in music. Wants Naïve to go back to the States to have a real talk. He'd also like to see you perform there in your natural habitat. The truth is, he wants to begin something official with you. He's already back in New York hisself."

A smile meets Bobby's lips. He can feel his own forehead beam, a ray of light shining from his inside.

Betty sets her mug on the counter. "Young, Madrid is not the place to be if you're trying to make something of yourself. I've always known that but wanted to keep you here for me own selfish reasons. But I've exhausted that." She holds her breath for a beat. "And I realize that I do love Carlos. And even if I don't love Carlos, I belong to him, just the same that you belong to your music."

His cheeks glow. He's the warmest he has been since he knelt by the candles in the sanctuary before Dom split the veil.

"I booked a show for you this weekend," she continues. "Felipe's coming to play again for you. I hope it'll be your last show here. I hope you take advantage of what I'm doing here for you. I hope you'll go home. Connecticut's not so far from New York. The man even said he'll send for you and Kyle if that's what it takes. In what universe does that kind of luck strike a lad?"

Bobby is still smiling, shaking his head at loss for what fortune has followed tragedy.

"Just go," Betty says. "Take the money you have, get your plane ticket, and just go home Monday. Leave this life behind and begin anew. If I can do it, you can too." She takes a step toward him, taking the center of his shirt between her fingers. "She'll be okay. The baby will be okay, if she chooses to keep it. You won't get in trouble for making one decision to make yourself happy. And if yer wan in there really loved you, she'd understand that the life she can give you will never measure up to the lad that you are. Besides, there's no way—no way—that you'll be accepted as a package deal."

He tears her fingers from his shirt. "This conversation is done, Betty."

"I love you enough to let you go. To that point, I'll let my actions speak for themselves. You'll enjoy the fruits of my labor and I won't ask a thing from you. I won't ask to go with you. I won't ask any profit from the success of your band. The only thing that I ask is that you take advantage of the opportunity, that you just live your dream."

Bobby forces himself to look away, to shut the door on her words. Now, they are packed in a small closet that will come out as an avalanche if the door ever opens.

"I can't do a show on Saturday," he says quietly. "I won't be here."

"Where will you be?"

"Cadiz."

"With yer wan, I take it. How're you gettin' there?"

"Flying."

"Have you purchased the tickets?"

"Going to do that now."

"Rent a car. It'll be cheaper."

Ana Lucia knows little about cars but she recognizes the SEAT 600 when she sees it; Khadijah's father drives one.

Saturday morning, shortly after ten, Ana Lucia leaves wispy footprints in the snow frost as she walks outside the apartment to the curb. It is an abnormally cold October day.

Bobby stands by the banana yellow vehicle, a midget of a car, the headlights small and perfectly round like a child drawing of eyes. The tininess of the car scares Ana Lucia, but she will be strong. It's large enough for the two of them.

Bobby leans against the car, bundled in a peanut-colored car coat, its width swallowing him. Ana Lucia herself has decided to be as pretty as she can this morning. Despite being a product of an oft-apathetic counter culture, it is clear to her that Bobby's soul is warmed by pretty—dresses and jewels, headbands and soft hair. All of these she wears: a blue and green checkered baby doll dress, plastic-pearl earrings, a thick lime headband, the same color as the child-size mood ring she wears on her thin ring finger. She contends patiently with the cold, all for the boyish wonder in his eyes when he sees her.

"We're driving this to the airport?" she asks.

"Nope. We're driving this to Cadiz. It's only six -and-a-half hours away. It'll be a rad road trip, just you and me." He covers his mouth, yawning. He didn't come to bed last night for packing and a restlessness that kept him fiddling with his guitar to the early morning.

"Whose car is it?"

"It's ours for now," he says. "You look like Daphne."

"Daphne?"

"The foxy chick from *Scooby Doo.*" He smiles, taking her small brown suitcase from her hand and helping her into the seat.

The inside is not sleek but all its parts are thin—the green dashboard, the steering wheel, the clutch. The space upfront is so small Ana Lucia wonders how Bobby will fit his legs inside.

Taking his seat on the driver's side, his knees sit up awkwardly, like the Huang Shan Mountains she'd once seen in a China geography book. He pays it no mind though, reaching around her headrest to take hold of the seatbelt and buckling her in. She looks up at him with ardor. He looks back, natural, unimpressed by his own courtesy.

As Bobby starts the car, Ana Lucia touches the electronic device fastened to the dashboard.

"What is this?" she asks.

"It's an eight-track player. It didn't come with the car; I put it in last night. The music's in the back, right there."

Ana Lucia turns back to see a box of eight-track tapes. She reaches for them, shuffling through a catalogue of no less than fifty.

She chooses the one with the blurred picture of five brown-haired boys in front of a blue background. She doesn't know if Deep Purple is the name of the album or of the band. She places it in the player.

Bobby grins when the fast sputter of a guitar fills the car. He takes a quick glance at the map on the dashboard and pulls away from the curb. "So, about *Scooby Doo*. Scooby Doo is a dog. A German shepherd. No, wait, he's a Great Dane. Whatever. He's got four teenage friends, even though, they look like they're twenty-five or something. Anyway, there's Shaggy. He's the hippie one. You know what a hippie is, right?"

"Right," she replies, settling her head back against the headrest.

"Okay, so Shaggy's a hippie. Kyle used to say he was on heroin, but it's my contention that he was just vegan or vegetarian or something."

"Your *contention*?"

He grins. "Yep, my contention. Anyway, Velma's next..."

He goes on and on. There are a million things to think of, but with Bobby's husky, sleep-deprived voice as background music, Ana Lucia will only think of how much like a magazine model he looks as he drives, the wind twirling his stray hair like a yellow Easter ribbon as they drive down the interstate.

It's a cotton candy kind of late morning, with blue skies and white billowing clouds. They've left the light snow behind. Her eyes grow heavy as she watches his hand easily controlling the steering wheel and jolting the gear shift back and forth, side to side. She enjoys the luxury of feeling the heat of the sun without suffering the cold outside.

Soon, she is asleep but not asleep. She never loses awareness of his presence, though she must be in some realm of sleep, because when she feels his hand on her belly, the song on the player is *Jesus Children of America*. It is half past twelve.

Her head rests against the window. Outside she sees that they are winding around a mountain road, brown winter earth and bare trees on either side of the road. The sky has grown ashen, though remnants of blue remain behind them.

"Are you hungry?" he says.

She turns her eyes to him sleepily, nods a little.

"Okay, good, good. We'll get you guys fed and get some gas. We're running really low."

Bobby's casual use of "you guys" would have forced greater guilt inside of her if not for the abrupt manner he cuts the steering wheel to the right. Carefully, he pulls the car onto the shoulder of the road.

"What's happened?"

"Nothing." He chews on his lip, an almost mischievous grin veiling his frustration. "We ran out."

"Of what?"

"Gas." Bobby opens his car door. "Look, I can walk to the closest station and fill up a bottle and bring it back. The next exit is like a couple of miles away. It won't take super long, but I don't want to leave you here."

"Let's go."

She steps out of the car and stands next to Bobby, appreciating the grand expanse of brown, bare earth. He takes off his coat and holds it open for her. As she snuggles herself into the warmth he has left behind, he turns his back to her, bending his knees, a silent signal to her. She climbs onto his back, struggling to keep her short dress from flying up. She circles her arms around his neck as he clutches her thighs to keep her attached to him.

Resting her cheek against his head, she is lulled by the up and down buoy of his paced walk. A slight mist causes her hair to react, puffing it up in large waves that blow in front of her eyes.

"So, you ever heard of *The Jetsons*?" he says.

"I don't think so."

"Another killer show. It's futuristic. I remember I used to get the theme song stuck in my head whenever we had to do spelling tests at school." He starts to sing. "Meet George Jetson, his boy Elroy—"

"Bobby?"

"Yeah?" he says, innocent, earnest.

"What about Jerry Black?"

"What? Where did you hear that name?"

"From Skyl—from Betty. I heard her talking with Kyle about him. She must have told you. You never told me."

"I just found out," he replies, his hair brushing her cheek as he looks down solemnly at the ground. "Besides, there's nothing to tell really."

"It's really good news for you, isn't it? It's what you wanted. It's what you came here for."

"I guess." He lifts his head. "You're what I came here for."

She refrains from saying what they both must know to be true: he couldn't have come for something he didn't know existed.

Instead she assures him, following the shape of his ear with her finger. "I'm happy for you. I hope you know that."

In appreciation, he clutches her thighs tighter.

"So what happens next?" she inquires.

"I'd have to go to New York to meet with him and perform and a bunch of other stuff. I don't really know."

A bubble, silent and full, hangs over them.

She refuses not to prod it. "What happens with us?"

Bobby stumbles and stops, not for the question but for the object that lies at his feet. It is a dog. Dead. Its arms and legs are curled toward each other. Blood pours from his open mouth, the only sure sign that he is dead and not sleeping.

Though his feet almost touch the animal, Bobby doesn't step back from it.

Ana Lucia slides down his back, her feet hitting the frozen ground. She stares at the cold-smoke swirling from his nostrils. "Bobby?"

He sniffles. "I'm okay."

She looks up, watching a cloud pass like white smoke over gray.

When she brings her gaze back to Bobby, the whites of his eyes are decorated with red vessels; he's straining to keep the tears away.

"I loved him," he says.

"I know you did. He was easy to love."

He squats down beside the dog, as though he might touch it. "I loved him more than I ever loved anybody." He shakes his head. "Not more than you. It's just, he loved me more than anybody."

Again, he shakes his head, despaired. "Not more than you. Just, more than anybody I ever met before you."

"I know." As the clouds roll over the sky, trepidation creeps over her. There's lightning and thunder shut up in Bobby's rain cloud.

"I still love him."

"I know."

Now, he is on his knees, his head bent toward her stomach. "I wonder if I did this to him."

"Did what to him?"

His tears water the dirt and the dog's sandy fur. "God's final punishment is giving you exactly what you want, isn't it? I wanted it so badly."

"Wanted what?" She touches his hair with timid fingers.

"I wanted the pain. I wanted the experience to make me this great artist or something. Maybe God took him away because I wanted it so bad. And I knew it when I heard her scream. It's the way she screamed."

Ana Lucia holds his hair back from his face. "What scream, Bobby?"

"When Mrs. Russo called and I told her, her scream was like nothing I've ever heard in my life. It was like the screams from an inferno. She screamed the scream I wanted to, but I couldn't because I knew he'd still be alive if it wasn't for me." His tears overflow, his pink nostrils quiver. "There's a price for being ungrateful for what you have. Dom would have never ended up in Madrid if I hadn't gotten so restless in New York. Pneumonia would've never found Dom in New York, definitely not in Avon. Kids only die of war there, not disease." He covers the center of his face, pressing down on his nose. When he removes his hand from his face, he is in unadulterated misery, his skin scarlet and wet. "He was gonna be a math teacher if this thing didn't work out with the band. It's all he really wanted. He didn't even want a wife or kids or anything. I took the one little thing he wanted. I hate it. I hate it so much."

His back heaves. The storm is ready. The clouds are slack, prepared for the thunder, the lightning, and the rain. Yet, it all happens in a way that is far softer than Ana Lucia could have imagined. Bobby sobs, his shoulders vibrating with the soul of a tempest, not an earthquake. He buries his face into her stomach, embracing a waist too small for his long arms.

She sighs slowly. Relief. She can cradle him in his grief. It isn't too large. It isn't too tough. She is enough for him.

As a car passes by, she snakes her fingers through his hair, pulls it softly. "It's not your fault."

He sobs, burying his face deeper into her belly.

"Bobby." She clasps the sides of his face, detaching his face from her stomach and forcing his eyes to hers.

In this way, though she is not with child, she is a mother, having this boy look up at her with a blind assurance that the cure is in her words.

"It's not your fault, Bobby," she says. She realizes now she is not forming words; they are being formed in her. "No. No. No. That isn't how life works. That can't be how your God works. Everything has a cause but not everything has a blame. Even—even if you were ungrateful for what you had, Love wouldn't punish you in this way. Love prefers mercy to justice. Mercy to justice, baby. Mercy to justice."

This is the lullaby she sings to him as the hard rain begins to fall.

There's no sun, only rain when they return back to the car with a bottle of gas at dusk. Their clothes are thoroughly drenched after the walk. The clothes cling to their skin as they cling to each other, Ana Lucia's face resting against his chest and ribs as they come upon the car.

He only separates himself from her to put the gas in the tank. She goes off to stand by a short tree, several yards away. The headlights of a passing car shroud his vision briefly before his eyes rest on her from behind, his coat draped over her arm. The wet became too heavy as they walked, so she took it off. Now, she is like a store mannequin, her body visible through the little wet dress.

It's the sight of her breasts, which he can see from the sides hanging like ripe fruit, that causes him to put down the gas bottle and make his way toward her.

She can't know, he thinks as he walks, she can't know what gravity she produces, how she reduces him to instinct and desire by her simple being. She erases every bifurcation of extremes. She is wisdom and innocence, purity and eroticism, naivete and enlightenment, all wrapped up in a wet dress, mindlessly tapping her foot against the ground as she waits for him to fill up the tank.

The rain falls in strips like beaded door curtains as he takes long strides toward her.

She startles at his arm coiling around her waist but reclines into him when he gently squeezes the hinge of her jaws.

He brushes aside her hair, making room for his lips at the base of her head. The passion of his voice is dimmed by her skin as he begins burrowing his face into her neck. "Do you have any idea how much I want you?"

His hand still holding her face, he can feel the muscles in her face twitch as she bites down on her lip in time with his teeth sinking down gently into her neck. He almost laughs at the thought that they are both biting her.

"No, no," he says between tugging her skin between his teeth and lips. "There's no way you could know how much I want you. You can't know. Just let me show you, okay?"

As she submits under the urgency of his kisses, every touch gives the sensation of first and last. She turns around to take his mouth with the fervor of kissing him for the last time. His hands fall to her bottom, squeezing and pushing her further to him with the zeal of his very first time touching a woman. They move back toward the car, attached to each other, as if to say that they cannot let go, lest this be the last time they will ever know each other.

He speaks to her with a discreet anxiousness, as though a chance to make love to her for the first time has finally arrived. "Can I have you? Please." He kisses her again, his mouth wetter with cold rain drops. "Pretty please. *Por fi.*"

She answers by reaching for the handle of the passenger side door. He thinks better of it, pulling open the backseat door instead. She lets herself down inside, staring up at him.

Bobby looks up at the stars which have begun to emerge. They are the glass eyes he had hoped for, pretty enough to make a wish upon.

His thirst for her voids out fear of being seen on the roadside. He pulls off his shirt, letting it fall to the dirt.

The space inside is viciously small, but he makes room for himself, pressing his knees into the seat, while she lies in the space between them.

He realizes he needs a strategy to get the wet dress off of her in the tight space. Lightning and thunder have begun, adding terror to the experiment of car love. He wants her more.

Desire can accomplish anything. His tongue stays engaged with her, with every part of her, as he shimmies the dress up and off her. With Ana Lucia's guidance, he matches his part to hers in the darkness.

Inside, she is plush, warm—a fitted slipper for him. He closes his eyes to better the sensation of her but for only so long can he bare looking away from that pretty, pretty face.

Upon opening his eyes, he finds vivid fright has taken over her face, a fright so Hitchcock-worthy, he wonders if she is exploring some peculiar fantasy.

Before he can respond to it, his vision goes black. Only when his sight comes back does he realize Ana Lucia has stricken him in the eye with a tightly furled fist.

She delivers another blow to his chest, following it with quick jabs to his nose and forehead, as though she could smash him to pieces. She begins kicking, her legs machine-gun swift. The car quakes and shudders, in tune with the thunder outside.

"Hey, hey," Bobby yells, reaching for her wrists. 'What are you—"

Her face juts up and her teeth clamp down on his neck.

Startled tears burn his eyes, his skin trapped so solidly between her teeth, he is sure she will draw blood.

Bobby's horror soon staggers the pain. In seconds. his amenable lover has turned to rabid animal. Eyes blushed burgundy, sweat pouring heavy as the rain outside, the woman beneath him is a stranger, a squatter in Ana Lucia's body.

His disorientation dissolves. He makes the decision to deal with this person beneath him as he would a criminal, the thief who has taken his girl.

Bobby sobs as he pins her down to the seat with what feels like police brutality. His blood changes substance to electricity, burning every inch of his skin as he holds her down.

Unable to counter his strength, she does what only a captured animal can do. She screams—a furious fox call. Over and over and over, she cries out for freedom, her mouth opened wider than he's ever seen it.

"Please, Ana Lu, please," he yells, his words almost strangled by his own sobs. "I love you. I love you so much. Please be still. *Please*! I'm not gonna hurt you. It's me, Ana. It's me."

She screams louder as to avenge his power over her.

When Bobby begins to fear that both his eardrums and the windows will burst, her cries come to an abrupt stop.

Straightaway, the car is forest calm. Ominous.

Slowly, he releases her arms, holding his hand over his neck, where he teeth prints are now engraved. How silly the sudden calm makes him feel. Looking at himself naked and limp from the waist down, he recalls with hatred every second that led to this moment.

"I'm sorry," he says, scant aware of what he's saying. "Sorry. So sorry. I don't know what I am."

He takes her hands cautiously, lifting them to get her attention back. She refuses to meet his eyes.

Sunken, Bobby releases her hands. They remain rigid in the air, suspended the way they had been the first time in the rehearsal room.

"Ana Lucia," he says, pushing her sweaty hair back from her face. Her eyes remain static.

Bobby pulls himself from her, manic. He jerks his pants up and gathers her stunned body, mechanically moving her limbs so that he can move her.

Hot and queasy, he manages dressing her. He slides her out of the car, scooping her into his arms and opening the passenger door to place her in the front seat. In the moment, she is a plastic doll, her limbs having need to be moved manually to fit properly inside the car.

"Ana Lu," he whispers to her, buckling her in. "You can hear me, can't you? I know you can. I'm going to take care of you. Don't worry."

He closes the door, rushing to the driver's side. Bobby is moved by the faint sound of his own weeping. It must have been the space—the small, confined space—which brought back the sensation of the evil closet.

He starts the car, his leg trembling with the motor.

Ana Lucia jolts with the car. He hears a deliberate breath. Her eyes unlock.

Bobby turns the car off again. "Ana Lucia."

Her eyes flutter.

"We're going to find a hospital, okay? I'm going to take you to the hospital."

"No," she says.

"No?"

"Please, no." She stares out at the storm sky. "I need to go home."

On the drive back to Madrid, Bobby feels the episode calcify in his chest. It is there for good, a monolithic memory.

In the passenger side, Ana Lucia sporadically whimpers. She has been crying since the moment she had the courage to glance at him and saw the raisin-rimmed bite marks she left on his neck.

Back in Madrid, Bobby drives to La Fábrica, where they can be alone.

Ana Lucia tentatively laces her fingers through his as he leads her first to the bathroom where they can change into the extra set of clothes they have pulled from their luggage. On the walk, her hand feels so cold and wooden, so foreign, he is tempted to find some excuse to let it go.

Neither of them bothers turning on the light when they enter the rehearsal space. Instead, they feel their way to the large speaker, hopping onto it side-by-side.

Thoughts turn over in his head, though he's not sure they can be called thoughts since they are vacant of words. He simply feels. Embarrassment. Fear. Irritation.

And disbelief—at the throbbing in his neck, love's bite. It seems pain inflicted involuntarily plows through the flesh with the same rigor as an intentional cleaving, gouging the heart all the same.

Yet, amid his unsavory passions, there is a sudden revelation from an invisible world: Ana Lucia is his inheritance. She is fine china, a bequeathal in need of delicate care. The heaviness of this understanding makes his vision blurry.

After some time, Ana Lucia asks, "Are you okay?"

"I think I am."

"I want to talk."

"Okay."

"I want to talk about what happened," she says.

"Not about that, Ana Lu." He closes his eyes. "Anything but that right now."

Her pain at his response burns bright in the dark. "Can we talk about the baby then?"

He laughs spontaneously. The baby.

"We can talk about it later," she says, retreating.

"No, no. Let's talk about it now."

Fear flashes over her face like a light shadow. With whatever is left inside of him, he will take away the fear.

Resolve: a final emotion to add to word-deprived thoughts. He knows now for certain that love only requires one thing: everything.

He curls his pinkie finger around hers. "Let's name it Dominic. Or, who knows, maybe Dominique." He pauses. "I know it doesn't feel like it'll be okay right now, but one day—one day our kid is going to be the sound you hear at the playground." He pushes his hair back. "I want to tell you something you probably already know, okay? I don't know what I am. And I guess that's made me a coward because I've been putting off stepping into what I'm supposed to be. But see, cowards don't go to heaven."

She looks down in quiet confusion.

"That's what Saint Paul says. He talks about fornicators and liars and all the rest not getting into heaven either. Everybody talks about that stuff. But nobody ever talks about the fact that cowards don't go to heaven." Bobby taps the side of the speaker. "Cowards, cowards, cowards."

"What's a coward? I've forgotten. I knew before. Sometimes, I forget..."

He laughs softly, then sighs. "A coward is a guy who learns he's having a baby and the only thing he can think about is what it's going to do to his dreams. A coward is the kind of person who relies on the future to avoid the present. I guess a coward asks for experiences so he can write songs about them, but runs away as soon as they come." He laughs again—this time, at the number of tears he's able to produce in a single day. "I'm scared to death I'll let you down, that I'll never be as strong as you need me to be. Because you need a strong guy, Ana Lu."

"Does this mean you're leaving?"

"Good grief, no. No way. I'll never leave you. But maybe you'll want me to leave one day. Maybe I won't be enough for you."

She says nothing, closes her eyes, then spontaneously combusts:

"Bobby, I'm not pregnant."

Silence.

Bobby jumps down from the speaker to turn on the light. He has to see her face, has to see that this is real.

When he returns to her, he looks up at her face, knowing her confession is true. He goes back to turn off the light.

Hopping back onto the speaker, he allows the darkness and silence to swallow them. It seems to eat up every intelligible thought, only leaving him with one feeling.

Relief.

"I'm not mad," he says.

"I thought I was pregnant at first," she says.

"I'm okay."

"Then, I found out I wasn't, but I didn't want to tell you."

"I'm not angry," he says. "Don't worry, it's okay."

"Do you really understand what I did, Bobby? Can you really see it? I'm selfish for you. Selfish in the worst way a person can be selfish. I hate thinking that your life is more than our life. The thought that you'll grow bigger than me feels like—what is the word?— like a *betrayal*. I'm afraid that when you see how much more worthy the world is of saving than me, you'll choose it over me. I lost my father because he chose to love the world the way you want to. I miss him every minute, Bobby. I don't want to miss you."

Bobby looks down at his feet, crosses his ankles. "You know, my grandmother was sixteen when she married my grandpa. People used to do it at that age all the time. I guess the world seemed a lot smaller then. Everybody could be happy with whatever little piece of earth they got. But for me, it seems like my dreams get so big they block out the gifts right in front of me. Dreams that big probably aren't worth anything. It's probably all just the emperor's new clothes, you know?"

"How can you know that if you never live your dreams?"

"I don't know. Ana Lucia, just let me say this. I've figured it out. I finally figured out what I'm supposed to do. It aint about saving the whole world. It's about saving the people in your own world. If everybody did that, there'd be no such thing as heroes because we wouldn't need them. Do you understand what I'm saying?"

She nods, touches his face.

"Nothing's going to take me away from you. Not my dreams. Not music. Not charity. Not fame. Not money. Nothing. Not even—" his voice grows bolder—what an instant narcotic self-sacrificing heroism can be "—not even Jerry Black. I'm not gonna meet with him. I'm staying here. I'm gonna take care of you. We're going to get you help—like, *real* help—and everything's gonna just *be*. I'll be here for it all, for as long as you'll let me."

He breathes. He has told the truth as he knows it. He will be here. He can promise that. Whether it will all be okay or not is another matter. How can he know? He hasn't lived long enough to even know what being okay really means.

That thought alone brings him to laughter and tears again.

Bobby looks over at Ana Lucia. Tears fill her own eyes. He kisses her, both of their mouths wet with tears and saliva.

For him, it is a first kiss—a kiss free of every ambition except what is right in front of him.

Two days pass. Ana Lucia avoids blinking as much as possible to avert the nausea brought on by snapshot images of her teeth impressions on Bobby's neck. When she comes home from work the afternoon of the third day, she finds Bobby standing at the kitchen counter, the phone cradled in the crook of his neck. He holds a newspaper in his hand, squinting to read it.

In Spanish, he stammers to ask for the manager of the establishment he has called. Ana Lucia can't hear what is said on the other side, but when Bobby thanks the person, she knows the manager isn't available.

He places the receiver back on the hook.

"Bobby?"

Bobby looks up at her, startled. "Hey, you're here."

"You were talking on the phone?"

"Yeah, it was nobody, really. I was just calling a few places. I'm looking for a job. Maybe a cashier or something."

"Why?"

He scrunches his brows. "What do you mean?"

"Good afternoon. Anybody want a popsicle?"

Bobby and Ana Lucia turn their attention to Kyle who now stands by the refrigerator, the freezer door open. He is shirtless, small-torsoed and surprisingly tan for the winter. He holds a grape popsicle.

"Dude, it's like zero degrees outside," says Bobby, moving toward the hall. "I gotta take a break here for a second, Ana Lu. I'll be back."

Alone with Kyle, Ana Lucia tries to think of some way to excuse herself, but his gaze arrests her.

"Did you see it?" he says, stepping toward her.

"See what?"

"See this." He reaches for the breadbox on the counter beside her and lifts it. Underneath, there is a paper folded into a triangle. He hands it to her. "I found it yesterday. Thought you should see it. Might change your whole fucking life."

The Little Saints

October 15, 1980

Mom,

I'm sorry I haven't really written. I meant to. I really did. I hope you're okay.

Lately, I've been thinking about something you used to say.

"As the sapling is bent, so the tree grows." That's how the saying goes, right?

I'm starting to think you're right. I'm starting to think that maybe all of us are bent somehow. How far we're bent makes all the difference.

I guess Dom was so far bent from Fran's death, he could never recover. There was a limit to how high he could grow before he would be the tree that topples over.

And he did. Topple over, I mean.

I was never a bent tree. Thanks to you and Dad, life has been a straight course. I realize now that I'm more strait-laced than I ever wanted to think.

The last time we talked, you asked if I was happy. I guess you didn't ask that exactly. You asked if it makes me happy to break your heart. It doesn't.

I miss you. I really do. There's a part of me that really wants to come home, but my life is really complicated now. I love Ana Lucia more than I thought I could love anything. And now, we're going to have a baby. I'm sorry to tell you this way, but this is the only way I knew how to. I know you understand.

This isn't easy for me. Nothing is easy right now.

Dom's dead. I know that's the thing. But there's something else. I'm grieving the loss of the life I thought I was supposed to live. It hurts. But I guess one life has to die for another life to come into existence.

Honestly, I don't know if I can do this.

It's hard to let go. It's like letting go of Dom. He still lives in me and that makes me miss him even more. That old life of mine, the old dreams—they still live in me. They're like this dead weight inside of me. It hurts more than I can say.

You said before that I needed to awaken my courage. I'm trying, but I'm terrified. Part of me knows that the only way to really have what you want is to want what you have.

Please don't be angry with me. Be proud of me, if you can. For once in my life, I'm trying to see something through to the end. I really want to fulfill my obligation.

I love you, Mom.

I love the life you and Dad gave me in Avon. I should have told you that a long time ago.

Thank you for the copy of Moby Dick. It helped a lot.

Yours,

Bobby

29.

ANA LUCIA HAS never felt so married as she does now.

The cornerstones of marriage are purported to be commitment and sacrifice. Bobby has committed. Bobby has sacrificed.

True love cannot be driven. True love always takes the driver's side. It compels humans beyond where their own desires will take them.

A day after reading Bobby's letter, it compels Ana Lucia to pack her belongings when Bobby is at a job interview.

It compels her to stare at Bobby on the sidewalk outside of Khadijah's apartment when he arrives there at eight in the evening.

He hands her the goodbye note she left him on the dresser. "What's this?"

She says nothing.

"Ana Lu, this letter makes no sense to me. Can you just get your stuff so we can go home? We need to talk. I don't want to do this like this."

"It's already done," she says. "I saw the note you wrote your mother. It was the saddest thing I've read in my whole life. I've read a lot of things, Bobby."

He seems to lose the strength in his face, his mouth turning down, his cheeks drooping.

She wishes there was something he could say, but there is not. There is no parachute. They are in free fall. And if she is honest, they have been in free fall since the beginning. The fall has gained speed the closer to Earth they've gotten.

Even so, he will try to save them.

"I wrote that note for my mom. I wrote it before we left for Cadiz. I wrote it when I thought you were pregnant. It was before I realized the truth about what life really is."

"That note was the truth. I'm sorry you didn't feel you could give it to me." Ana Lucia runs the back of her hand under her leaking nose. "I'm really sorry."

"Are you...are you *leaving* me? Over a letter that I wrote when I was confused? Come on, Ana Lu, don't do this. *Please.*"

She nods, a child too timid to make her intentions known in words.

"I'm not gonna let you do this to us," he says, reaching for her arm. "Now, please just get your stuff and—"

"You're destined for the history books. I want to read about you some day. You don't need an obligation holding you back."

"Obligation?"

"I don't want to be an obligation," she says. "I want to be a dream."

He bows his head in recognition of the words he wrote in the letter and quietly returns, "You're more than an obligation to me. You're more, more than a dream to me. You don't get it? I don't need a dream. I need *you.* I *need* you."

He holds out his hand for hers. Ana Lucia stares at the hand—the wholesome hand that has held hers, fed her, put the handle on her tea cup. Now, it is the hand of temptation, the hand that will draw her away from the sacrifice of love if she takes it.

She knows no other way to resist the temptation than to run. She runs to the call box, buzzing Khadijah to let her back in.

She runs through the apartment building doors, runs up the stairwell to the Piaf's unit, runs back to Khadijah's bedroom when the door opens.

She runs and runs and runs.

A

Sometimes the cruelest acts are the kindest ones.

We know you would not have left me on your own.

For your bravery, we raise a glass of champagne

Should your bravery take refuge for a moment

Should your Catholic conscience fall mute

You will find

You have forfeited little Charlie's golden ticket.

Life offers no consolation prize for such losses

So I have chosen to take the loss in-kind

*Chosen to forego blowing out the candles on the life you wished
for*

For my bravery, I drink from the cup of bitterness

The chalice of your salvation

B

The salvation you give

Is my death

30.

DOM SAT WITH BOBBY the first time Ana Lucia left him.

Not even his ghost will sit with Bobby the second time. He puts The Delfonics' "Tell Me This Is a Dream" on repeat from morning till evening and remembers in tears Ana Lucia's comment that his soul is not completely punk. Death and abandonment have taken away what fight he had.

To hold himself together, Bobby drowns out the voices in his head that will tear him apart. They would say to him that he's dead without her. They would ask him what good a dream is without the one you love. They would also blame her for not telling him from the beginning who she was, for letting him fall in love with a girl he'd have to keep losing.

Bobby guesses it is his mother's voice that will glue him back together. It is the voice of one who does not believe in miracles. Without hope for miracles, Bobby feels a queer relief. He is no longer tossed here and there by waves of hope. Life without hope is a life of bald logic.

So, this will be the logical order: he will say his goodbyes and then be on his way.

He arrives at La Buena Vida at sunrise, a week after Ana Lucia left him. Ana Lucia is there working behind the bar. There is one patron sitting with coffee.

Bobby holds his guitar case in one hand and a tiny, fifteen-peso amp he just bought in the other. He sets both down when he reaches the counter where she prepares a café con leche.

"Hey, how are you?" he says, unpacking his Fender.

She says nothing, just stares at him bewildered.

"So, I'm going home in three hours," he says.

"Home?" The hand which holds her coffee cup trembles.

"Avon. Then, I'm headed to New York to meet with Jerry Black. Should be a lot of fun. Probably would've been nice if you could've come with me, but you can't have everything in this life, can you?"

He feels her eyes on him like a laser beam as he plugs the amp into the wall and the guitar into the amp. The guitar cord has enough length for him to move back and forth between her and the amp.

"I think it would've been nice for you to have seen Broadway or something, but maybe one day you will. Who knows?" He begins fiddling with the tuning knobs. "Anyway, I wrote this last night for you, and I just—" he strums once to check the sound "—I just wanted to perform it for you once, since we'll never be seeing each other again. It's not so good, but nothing really is without love."

He begins, unafraid.

Once upon a dream
I fancied a little girl
And that little girl
Fancied a boy named Me
She wore her pain like a cloak
While I wore my heart on my sleeve
Saying the one thing I had to believe
That I'd never be sorry

Ana Lucia's eyes are now intent on him, truly intrigued and scared, maybe even a little impressed by the country-blues turn he has taken.

In the days of everything
I loved that little girl
And sweet baby girl
Loved that ole boy named Me
When her secrets she gave up
Love's glory took me to my knees
First night loving baby on them wet leaves
I knew we'd never be sorry

Her mouth edges a smile. Tears fill her eyes.

The Little Saints

Bobby switches keys for the bridge, the first bridge he's ever written.

Should've known it'd come to be
This boy'd make mistakes bigger than his apology
Had to confess to Little Girl how weak I could be
Saying I got no excuse for my baby
Just a lifetime of sorry
And just like that, it came to be
That Little Girl forgave a dumb boy named Me

Bobby returns to the original key, his strumming softer. His eyes are hinged on her, unmovable.

Once upon a fantasy
Flying high in my dreams
I learned that a boy
Must travel the angry sea
Little Girl said breaking my heart's how it's gotta be
When a woman she became
A man she made out of me
For that, she gave no—"

He stops playing, waiting for her to finish the line.
Bobby plays the ending chord again. "For that she gave no..?"
He stops again, looking into her forlorn face, waiting for her to say the last line. He gives it one more try.
"For breaking my heart, she gave no—"
"Sorry," she says quietly, a single tear slipping down her cheek. "She gave no sorry."
Bobby nods. "She gave no apology. That's right, Little Girl."
He strums a couple bars more and ends with a slightly off-pitch solo, something he imagines Neil Young would have played.
At end, he looks her in the face, tries to forget that she is still Christmas morning to him, and says, "Take care of yourself, Ana Lucia."

From Madrid to Hartford is twelve hours, including one stop in
Dublin. He sleeps the whole time, even through the layover. It's a
blank sleep, dreamless, addictive.

So addictive that on the ride from Hartford to Avon with his
father, he doesn't even try to fight sleep after answering his father's
first question of why he dyed his hair blonde.

"Bobby, kiddo," his father says, waking him.

Bobby opens his eyes and there is the house. Large but not
offensive. White with a red door. Sixteen windows on the front. A
lovely American house.

His father redirects him by the shoulders when Bobby tries to
help with his own bags.

"Go in the house, kid. I've got this stuff."

Inside the house, it smells like cake. Bobby removes his jacket,
leaving on his wool scarf to keep hidden the yet ripe wound on his
neck. He heads to the kitchen to investigate. There, his mother stands
at the island counter with another shorter woman he hadn't expected
to see. He's never seen the woman without makeup. He can see the
veins which make her face look like it has literally cracked from grief.

"Bobby," his mother says, reaching up to hug him and touching
his hair. "You said it was blonde again, but I didn't know it'd be this
blonde."

"I know," Bobby says, pulling himself from her. "It was just, I
don't know."

"Bobby." The woman beside his mother holds out a bouquet of
carnations for him.

"Mrs. Russo," he says, though he doesn't touch the flowers.

Bobby can feel that she wants to hug him. He contemplates it a
second before taking a tentative step forward, offering himself as a
temporary Dominic. She hugs him, pressing her face against his chest.
Bobby strokes her hair.

"Thank you for coming back," she says.

"You're welcome," he says quietly.

When she pulls back from him, his shirt is wetted at the chest, as
though his own heart has shed tears.

"I wish you could have been here for the funeral," she says with a
sniffle. "He would have wanted you there."

Bobby can't help but think that Dom wouldn't have wanted him
there at his funeral; Dom would have wanted to still be alive.

But Bobby understands now that words are words no matter how inaccurate and sometimes people need them like food to get through the day.

"I know," he says. "I wish I were there too."

"Was he happy there in Madrid?"

His mother interjects. "Bobby probably needs a little time to settle in, Maria."

"Was he depressed?" Mrs. Russo presses.

"No," Bobby says, "I don't think he was."

She is quiet, waiting for more. Bobby for the first time appraises how much she looks like Dom. His mother had always said it before but with Dom's hair being curly and Mrs. Russo's straight, he'd never seen it.

For the resemblance, he wants more than anything to tell her the truth, as though giving the truth to Dominic himself. He thinks deeper on her question about Dom's happiness.

"I think he was most happy after he got sick," he says. "He was going to Mass all the time. I think maybe he knew what was gonna happen. I don't know. I don't think he wanted to die or anything, but he was somehow making himself ready."

A brightness comes to her eyes. It seems to Bobby that she might hug him again, but instead she hands him the flowers she has been holding, as to say welcome home.

"I'm tired now," he says. "Jet lag. I think I'll go to bed now. I'm glad you came, Mrs. Russo. Really glad."

He smiles softly at her, then wanders off to the staircase, knowing the third step will creak as it has since he was five years old.

He enters his bedroom to find it untouched, tidy as he'd left it, his blue bed still made, the baseball equipment and memorabilia he never wanted aligned perfectly on the cherrywood dresser. The room having been unlived in for almost a year is physically cold, though he is warmed by the beautiful island in the corner where the three guitars he left sitting in a semi-circle are waiting for him. He goes for the acoustic Ibanez, the most subtly beautiful of the bunch with its blonde wood. He is hardly three chords into "While My Guitar Gently Weeps" when the door opens.

"Tired, huh?" his mother says. She sits down on his bed. "Emotionally, I mean. I know this is very disconcerting, coming back so suddenly. With a little bit of time and perspective, you'll see how much you gained from your time there. I'm sure you've discovered so much about yourself."

She knows about Ana Lucia leaving—he told her when he announced that he'd be coming back—but she won't mention it; he'd made her promise never to speak of it. She pats the space beside her. He obliges her, putting his guitar down to sit behind her.

His mother pins his hair back from his eyes with her hands. "Your eyes are older. You've changed in a remarkable way. Trust me, when things settle, you'll see the insanity was for your benefit. In anti-psychiatry terms, madness need not be all breakdown; it may also be breakthrough."

He lies out on the bed beside her, letting his arm fall over his eyes. The tears have started.

"I hate this," he says.

"What do you hate, Bobby?"

"My whole life, really. You were always pushing me to find myself. That whole becoming a man thing—decide who you're gonna be—that whole thing screwed me up big time, you know. It would have been better if you'd just told me who I was, like every other parent does. Then, I could have stayed here and Dom wouldn't have died. I wouldn't have—" He stops. "I'm sorry, Mom. It's not your fault. I know that. I'm sorry."

She is quiet. He peeks under his arm through tears to see if she's still sitting beside him.

She takes a breath. "You know, the hardest thing in the world is being a mother. It's a million times harder than what I do for a living. We're expected to prepare our kids for a life whose course we know nothing about. I didn't—I *don't*—know how to do that. Going to New York and Spain was supposed to be a glorious discovery, Bobby. I wanted you to have that discovery. *You* wanted it, remember?"

She swallows. She's afraid of her own words. All his life, he's never seen his mother afraid of herself.

"You took your chances, Bobby," she says softly. "Only in youth can you be fearless enough to pull your life apart and see what happens. Youth allows you to believe that you'll have time put it all back together again. And you will." She pauses. "Despite everything, you have to know that growing up isn't supposed to be painless." She holds quiet a moment. "Bobby, I love you."

They hold each other's gaze, silent.

The Little Saints

Then it happens, the thing he had never expected to do in front of his mother ever again. He turns on his side, curls up, and sobs. He sobs for everything good and bad. Blood rushes to his face, heats his whole body. His mother lays her hand on his side to calm his shakes, slowing down the expanding of his ribs.

Then, she takes the greatest risk she ever has with him, lying on her side and pressing against him, wrapping her arms around him, fitting herself like a puzzle piece against him.

He meets her gamble, rolling over onto his back, allowing her head to fall onto his chest. He pets her hair, a touch of fine silk.

"Mom," he says, "do you remember how you told me about these psychological experiments with babies? Like, how they didn't give the babies any physical affection or attention or anything like that. And the babies all, like, died or whatever. "

Her body trembles with quiet laughter. "They didn't die, Bobby. Most of them were substantially delayed mentally and socially."

"Oh. Well, I just wanted to say that if I had to be a psychological experiment or whatever, I'm glad I wasn't that one. You're a good mom, the best I've ever had."

She kisses his cheek. It's a dry kiss. This year apart, she's hasn't forgotten how much he hates sloppy kisses.

He smiles, though he's not happy, not healed. He is proud. All the words he has spoken were for her benefit. For the time she is in his room, he can care for her and forget his own hollowness.

Forgetting is the cure for now.

31.

ANA LUCIA HAS taken on a second job to afford her new apartment in La Latina. It's furnished by the landlord with a single bed and a couch for the little living room. There had been one more decoration: a large image`
of Bobby's profile she couldn't keep her hands from painting on the wall. In tears, she painted over it the same day she drew it.

She sits on the couch in that living room in the dark. Three months have passed since Bobby left. She has refused to count the exact number of days and hours. Refused.

Forgetting is the cure.

There are plenty other memories to contend with. This Monday morning, she faces the only one worth remembering in her present distress:

Ana Lucia is ten years old. She is on a fishing boat with her father, lazing on the aquamarine sea. The springtime sun is planted low in the sky, the forest spread out like Middle-earth at the opposite shore from which they have rowed.

Javier casts his net for a third time this afternoon. Ana Lucia watches the water, waiting for some unsuspecting fish to tangle itself.

She dips a finger into the water. It is cool as peppermint.

When she looks up at her father, he has turned his attention from the water to the forest beckoning from the shore.

"Livingston is eternal spring," he says. "When I lived in Chicago, there was a proper winter. All the flowers and trees died for the season. You've never seen a bare tree. One day you will."

Little Ana Lucia looks at the dense throng of trees in the distance. She couldn't imagine it naked. The only winter she has seen is on what little television she's been allowed to watch.

Her father continues. "By May, all nature came back to life in Chicago. Just when you think nature has lost herself, you find she's only recycled herself."

Ana Lucia purses her mouth. She likes the word recycle, though she can't comprehend her father's words.

"Look what God has done, Lucita," her father says, his blue eyes briefly observing the canopy the clouds form above them.

Ana Lucia watches as the first fish tangles himself in the net. She looks up, trying her best to be impressed by her country, the only land she's ever known. She tries to love it anew, knowing that as her father says, what is loveliest is not always most loved.

Still, she is distracted. Her father has mentioned God. She can count the number of times her father has spoken of God. She has always known that he held some belief in a higher power, but he has never spoken about Him with such fervor.

"Daddy," she says, "I don't believe in God."

Her father raises his eyebrows at her. "When did you make that decision?"

"I never decided to believe."

He looks at her, almost grinning. As always, he is impressed by her. "Then how do you explain it? How do you explain everything around us? Did it come to exist on its own?"

She shrugs. "No one knows."

"No one knows? You say no one knows, Chiquita mia?" Her father breaks out into a smile so big, Ana Lucia hears phantom laughter in it. With strong arms, he pulls back up the net, nearly bursting with fishes. " *Vamos!*"

Together, they row back to shore. Ana Lucia is excited for the catch. It's for her mother, fresh fish for the restaurant.

Helping her father to bring the net onto dryland when they reach the shore, Ana Lucia stops. There's something she wants to ask.

"There is a God, Lucita," her father says, as usual knowing the answer before the question. "You should know it. There is a God. Look everywhere and you see it. How could the earth be a genius without a Greater Genius having created it?"

Ana Lucia watches him as he sorts through the fish, unsnarling each one with care.

"Nature is the most brilliant of all God's creation," he says. "Unlike humans, it doesn't know agony because it doesn't refuse the suffering of seasons. It bends to the changes time brings it. It must know that things will get better, that everything lost will return. Nothing in all creation is wasted."

None of it makes sense to her, yet she knows it to be true. A knowing that can't be unknown.

"I want you to remember this: when I'm dead and gone, you'll know that God never threw me away. He only recycled me in you, Chitquita mia. Nothing is wasted with God."

Ana Lucia—so young, so free—doesn't find a response necessary. She simply grins when she watches her mother approach in her rose and yellow gomesi dress.

"You've brought my fish at last," Katina says. "Let's go pack them away."

Ana Lucia watches her parents carry the steel bucket of fish. They walk and walk toward the horizon until she can see them no more. They are happy.

They are a memory that will never die.

Thinking back on the ten-year-old memory, Ana Lucia has come to the surest conclusion of her life: God is real. There is too much symmetry in her life for there to be no Designer. All these years she has not rejected God; like most everyone, she had rejected the God of her imagination but continued to wrestle with the idea of a God so simple, He became enigmatic.

The Lord gives; the Lord takes away. Perhaps it is simply a fact, not a testament to the lovability to God or man. Better, maybe it is a witness to the fact that Resurrection is the meaning of Life.

She and Bobby had read together that the Lord gave shade to Jonah in the unbearable heat, but He reserved the right to revoke the shade. It is a fact but not an end. An opportunity, not a loss.

And so if these tears are shed at the loss of love, they will also be dried in some marvelous way.

When and how are the only questions that elude her.

Four months to the day after leaving Madrid, Bobby is on the set of his first video shoot. Jerry Black says it will be reminiscent of Blondie's "Heart of Glass." Kyle has gone wild for it, talking to every cameraman, producer, and light person on set.

Today marks the first day Bobby hasn't awoken to Ana Lucia as his first thought. His first thought this morning was of what he would wear. His next thought was whether Ana Lucia would approve of it.

He wears the Truth T-shirt he first met her in. Maybe it will be a signal to her if she ever sees the video.

Nothing else has signaled to her, not even the letter he sent her at their old apartment the day after John Lennon died. Maybe if Betty was still there, she'd have mercy on him and somehow get it to Ana Lucia. He was hurting something awful and would have done anything to make contact with her. The letter was surely intercepted by a new tenant. He called Khadijah's apartment once. The Arab man from before answered. Bobby hung up. He listened to "Lucy in the Sky with Diamonds" the rest of that day.

Ana Lucia in the Sky with Diamonds....

Now, the polaroid of her from the rooftop restaurant is pinned to the inside of his shirt. The costume designer asked about the bulge, but he pretended not to hear her. The lady went on her way; Bobby was getting a reputation for being a little stubborn.

He is kind though, so kind that the little blonde girl beside him, a set assistant, doesn't mind bothering him.

She must be eighteen, but she looks up at him as though at twenty years old, he's an adult and she a child.

She hands him a small piece of paper. "I think you dropped this over by the door."

He receives from the girl the paper he'd scribbled on a few hours ago before his flight took off. It is his ritual list. As usual, it contains three points. Only this time, he will recycle the list for his next trip; the points won't change.

1. Be good here
2. Do good here
3. Find good here

The assistant stares at him as he folds the paper neatly and places it back in his jacket. "So, um, I didn't see a name on the paper. I kinda guessed it was yours. But, um, like, what's your real name? It's not Jimmee Young, is it?" she asks.

He laughs a little. "You don't want to know."

"Why wouldn't I want to know? Is it like Werner Pickle or something?"

He smiles. "No, it's nothing like that. If I tell you my real name, it'll just kill the illusion for you. You should hold on to illusion for as long as you can. For as long as life lets you."

"My real name is Bridget Stevens. Everybody calls me Terri though. It's, like, my middle name. I'm named after St. Teresa of Ávila."

Bobby smiles, despite the little stab of pain in his chest. "She was a good saint." He looks over at a workman trying out the smoke machine.

"I don't know that much about her, really."

"She was a mystic. She had a lot of really deep experiences with God. She was a doctor of the church, actually."

"Then, you're Catholic?" she says, excited like only an eighteen-year-old can be. "Like, a *real* Catholic. Like, you know stuff."

"A little stuff."

"So, if you won't tell me your real name, maybe you'll tell me your confirmation name."

"Casimir of Poland."

"Never heard of him," she says.

He gives a small wave to Jerry Black who has entered from the other side of the room. "Yeah, I know," he says to the girl. "Hardly anybody's heard of him." He looks down at her. Her eyes are a velvet brown, neutral, beautiful for their simplicity. "It's probably best that way. The little saints are the best ones. They don't need big lives, just little lives with a lotta love for the people in their little worlds. I'm starting to think that's all anybody ever needs."

She smiles wide at him. Maybe a little piece of her has fallen in love with him already. She probably doesn't yet know the difference between a man and his words. There really should be no difference, but men whose words match perfectly their character are perfect men. He's only heard of one Perfect Man.

He pats the girl's shoulder before he walks away. He knows he'll never love her. She, like most everyone else, is a passerby.

Bobby hasn't quite figured out if he is passing through life or if life is making a journey through him. Whatever the case, he's learning that all things are passing. For weeks he has wondered how seriously he can take life in light of this fact. To himself he can finally say:

However seriously you can take life knowing that all things existed before you and will exist after you—take it just that seriously.

Every generation has thought itself the savior generation, has believed their cause uncompromisable, has looked at the last generation with condescension for the way the world was left. Every generation has passed on and away, no matter how indispensable they considered themselves at the time.

This video shoot will pass on. His music career will even pass on. He will enjoy them all for as long as he can have them, then he too will pass on.

That doesn't mean there's no good worth doing. There is. But Bobby realizes now he doesn't have to reach far into his fantasies to do that good. A kind word here. A courtesy there. A smile at the cameraman. An "I love you" to his mom when she drops him off at the airport. A lighting of a candle for Dominic Marek Russo on the video set and a prayer for his pilgrim spirit on his journey to God—a wind to shake the leaves. They're all little treasures, and their sum is of greater worth than the aspirations of a future that can never really be known.

Watching Kyle chatting up a makeup artist in the corner, Bobby decides he is happy for the first time since Madrid. He'd once had a chance to sacrifice his dream to prove his love for the only girl he is sure he'll ever love. It hadn't work, it had passed like everything else. But he'd tried. He'd made a million mistakes—been utterly selfish and even *soft* at times—but in the end, he'd loved until it hurt. Loving Ana Lucia for the time he could is his heart's crowning achievement.

So, he is happy.

This happiness isn't an opiate. It's an abiding gratitude for the peace of the present moment. There's none of the former fixation on what is to come or what is left behind.

Bobby trusts this brand of happiness more than the other, for the fire of suffering has tested it, melted away what could not survive hardship, and left behind all that is necessary to make it through today. Today is all he has.

Today is all anybody ever had.

Four months, fifteen day, seventeen hours, twenty-three minutes since Bobby walked out of La Buena Vida.

A time came two weeks ago when Ana Lucia couldn't keep herself from adding the time up. She had to make some calculation of her pain just to get her mind off of it.

She realized that evening that she could not resolve the pain on her own.

Now, she is here to seek out professional help. She must recycle herself.

She arrives at the place with a single bag in her hand. The wedding picture the imam took of her and Bobby is in her back pocket.

The woman waits for her at the door entrance. Somewhere in the distance she can hear the sound of children playing. There must be a park nearby where they are playing.

It is March.

The woman's eyes are large, beautifully spaced apart, her hair graying, her cheeks sculpted as though hewn with a carver's knife. Ana Lucia now knows what the English authors meant by a "handsome woman."

"How are you, Ana Lucia?"

"I'm well."

"How long did it take to get here?"

"It's taken a long time. Too long." She looks the woman in the eyes. "But I'm glad to be here."

The woman smiles. Maybe she's charmed by Ana Lucia's accent. After all these years, she still maintains some hint of Garifuna mixed with Guatemalan.

"I won't be the one to counsel you. It wouldn't be the best idea, all things considered. Dr. Montoya—I've known her thirteen years—

she's better suited for this. She'll be here in an hour just to meet you for a half hour or so before dinner."

Dinner. She wonders what a handsome woman like this fixes for dinner.

The woman leads her to her little office upstairs. Ana Lucia takes a seat at the desk across from her. Her eyes fall instantly on the picture of her family.

Her son is thirteen or so in the picture but already taller than both his parents.

The lady notices Ana Lucia noticing the picture. "Bobby's father is picking him up from the airport now. He had another video shoot in New York."

"He must have been really excited about it."

"Not excited exactly. He's glad about it though. His dreams are coming true. He's getting the chance to see that hard work really pays off."

She wants to ask the lady—still technically her mother-in-law—if reaching those dreams has left any room for her.

"He's at peace," Mrs. Carter continues. "And I've always wanted peace for him. Ever since he was a little boy, he always seemed to be reaching for something. He's no longer reaching. He's learning to simply receive and take responsibility for what comes his way. It's interesting to see how he came to be this way. He could have been a Spartan warrior and killed two dozen slaves as an initiation into manhood. In a different time and place, he could have become a man by entering into the Massai warrior camp. But it's 1981 and we live in Connecticut—there's nothing so concrete as those initiations to make boys into men. The only way now to cross that sea is to meet one's own suffering with courage and stability. Bobby has done that. He is doing that. He's become a man."

Ana Lucia nods. She loves this woman already—the way she talks, the way she maintains eye contact, how she pushes her silk sheet of hair from her face the same way her son does.

"I want to be honest with you, Ana Lucia. When you first called and told me about everything last week, I wanted to hang up. I didn't want to open this part of Bobby's life now that he's found peace."

"I understand." She does understand. They have the one same interest.

"It was my husband, Bobby's father, who made me realize that Bobby doesn't just need peace. He deserves happiness. It took me some time to see it, but you're what makes him happy."

Ana Lucia puts a delicate hand over her chest, as though to keep her heart from flying away.

"I didn't tell him that you were coming. That was also his father's idea. Bobby's always liked surprises. I'm the one who wanted all of his life to be pre-determined. Surprises always seemed too risky to me."

Ana Lucia nods. "Do you think he still—"

"He does, Ana Lucia." She leans across the desk, touching Ana Lucia's hand. "He does. I only ask you one thing."

Ana Lucia feels her own eyebrows raise slightly. Her heartbeat sounds in her ears.

"These days of therapy may be the hardest days of your life. You may have to remember what you'd much rather forget. But for him—" she takes hold of Ana Lucia's hand "—for yourself, do whatever you can to be healthy."

Ana Lucia thinks she's nodding her head, but realizes she hasn't made any show of agreement at all when Mrs. Carter says, "Promise me, Ana Lucia."

"I promise."

It is a new vow, a vow that will surely sustain the first one she made to Bobby.

They hear the door open downstairs and feel the shaking of the floor when it closes. Mrs. Carter's office is close enough to the staircase that she can hear Bobby's breathing. She knows it's his breathing; she can hear the tenor of his voice in it.

Mrs. Carter stands. "Are you ready?"

Ana Lucia nods, standing. She thinks again on a truth she'd uncovered a week ago. The life she was living with Bobby before had not been a new life. It had been a conclusion of an old life. This life now, in his country—this is the new life. Where love once seemed the finished line, she realizes it is the beginning.

Bobby's mother ushers her toward the staircase.

There at the bottom, Bobby stands. He doesn't see her at first, busy attending to the suitcase he lugs in. Addled, he stops. He isn't looking at her. Not yet. It seems he has felt her presence on his skin like a first raindrop.

With moonstruck eyes, he looks up at her, his complexion awakened to gold, his suitcase dropping from his hands to the floor.

She smiles, gripping the banister with quivering hand.

He is still the wonder-boy who stood at the foot of the staircase that first night in her apartment building—the prince waiting at the foot of her tower.

At last, Ana Lucia has let down her drawbridge, the one that will lead to her new life. It is a surprise life, an unexpected afterlife. It is a life where the children's park is not far and the sound of their playing testifies to the Springtime.

It is a life of risk and opportunity.

It always has been.

It is a life of pain and play.

It is now.

It is her life, it is *their* life.

It always will be.

THE END

Author of *Arabella Park* and *Block 24,* Evan Tyler is a critically-acclaimed author who has captured a loyal following with her emotionally-charged works. She is also the founder of Epicet Media.

For more information, visit www.epicevantyler.com and follower Evan on Instagram: @epicetmedia

Made in the USA
Columbia, SC
12 February 2020